The Sporting House Killing

A Gilded Age Legal Thriller

G. Reading Powell

This book is dedicated to the trial lawyer,
that stalwart defender of the rule of law.

Chapter 1

Jasper wasn't so sure this was a good idea, but Cicero was already squeezing out the first-floor window.

"Let's go," Cicero said quiet-like after he hopped on down.

"Somebody's fixing to catch us," Jasper whispered out the window, then glanced back at the door. No light coming under the door from the hall.

"No, they're not." Cicero crossed his arms. "Everybody's in bed. Now come on."

Jasper heaved hisself up on the windowsill and listened. Still quiet. So he jumped out. Even with a crescent moon, it was dark as pitch. He waited for his eyes to get accustomed to the dark and followed Cicero up to the street corner.

This late on a Sunday night, Webster Street was deserted. On Fifth Street toward downtown, two lights bounced around, getting bigger and bigger—a hackney carriage with its sidelights burning.

Cicero stepped into the street. "Here comes one."

Jasper glanced back at Maggie Houston Hall, where they'd lived since starting college last fall. Cicero always complained it didn't have indoor plumbing like most newer buildings did. *It's 1894*, he'd say, *you'd think Baylor could do better*, like Waco was in ancient Babylon or something. Truth was, their outhouse was downright fancy. It was painted and even had paper sheets instead of corn cobs.

Professor Charlton and his wife lived in the dorm, but they always went to bed early. Jasper checked their window one more time. Sure enough, the lights was still out.

The hack horse trotted up, and Cicero hailed the driver. "We need a ride, mister."

"Aren't you boys out kinda late?" the hack driver said. "I'm headed home."

"No, sir. The matron told us it was just fine."

Jasper looked at his shoes, his hands in his pockets. She'd said no such thing. What was he getting them into?

"Would you take just one more fare for the day?" Cicero asked.

"All right, get in."

They settled in behind him.

"Where to?"

"Corner of Washington and First Street."

The hack driver twisted around and eyed them both. "How old you boys?"

"Twenty-one," Cicero said.

They ain't twenty-one.

The driver shook his head and turned the carriage around, and the horse trotted back up Fifth Street for downtown. They rattled across the railroad tracks on Jackson, then Mary Street.

Jasper leaned close to Cicero. "I ain't so sure we oughta do this."

Cicero poked him in the arm. "You said you were thirsty."

"I did, but I don't know where we can get no sody water this late on a Sunday night."

"We're not drinking soda water, you numbskull. We're drinking beer."

He wiped his palms on the legs of his pants. They should just get on back. "Well, we can't get no beer neither. You heard the preacher. All them saloons is closed today."

Cicero looked at him like he was about to let loose some important secret. "I know where we can get some."

"How you know that?"

"A senior told me."

"Who?"

"Pat Neff."

"I don't believe it," Jasper said, crossing his arms. "He don't drink beer."

Before long, the hack turned right on Washington Avenue and after several blocks passed a place with a beat-up ol' sign: the Red Front Saloon. A crowd of fellas tarried out front. Whether Preacher Jones said so or not, this saloon sure was open. Jasper hoped they wasn't going there. The hack kept on but slowed when the street went from gravel to dirt near the end of Washington, almost to the river.

The driver pulled over to the curb on the right. "That's two bits."

"Here, mister." Cicero handed him a quarter.

"Watch yourselves, boys."

"Yes, sir," Cicero said.

The hack rolled off and turned right onto First Street.

Jasper swallowed hard. "Why'd he say that?"

"He's just being sociable."

There was just enough moon to make out a steam barge chugging down the Brazos River toward the suspension bridge. The only folks out on the streets was them fellas back at the Red Front. Another hack clattered over the gravel toward the bridge over the creek.

Cicero took off lickety-split across Washington, heading for a two-story red-brick building. The windows on the first floor all had curtains, but they was cinched back, and bright light was pouring out from inside. The upstairs windows was dark. A man and a lady hunched close on the curb across the alley to the left of the building. They was likely smoking, judging by the two small orange lights flickering around them.

Jasper rushed ahead to catch up. "We ain't going inside, is we?"

"Of course we are."

Cicero stopped at the door. Piano music blared out through the door but then stopped. Wasn't nobody in sight through the front door window into the entrance hall.

"Why don't it have a name?" Jasper asked.

"It doesn't need a name."

"Just looks like a house to me." Jasper waited expectantly, but Cicero didn't do nothing. "You gonna knock?"

"I think we just go in." Cicero opened the door and stepped into the entrance hall. "Come on."

Jasper pushed in close behind him. Straight ahead, a staircase went to the upper story. The piano music had come from a room to the left, and all of the sudden a lady appeared in the entrance to that room. She was all decked out in a tight red corset and a frilly white petticoat. She had black hair pinned up on top of her head and a white flower stuck in it. A red ribbon was around her neck, and a gold locket hung down. Hung way down. Jasper couldn't help but stare. It sure was hot in there.

"See something you like, honey?" The lady flicked open a fan and fluttered it quick-like, blowing them dangling curls off her shoulder. She leaned up against the door frame and cocked her head.

It was awful hot.

"Welcome to my boarding house, gents. I'm Miss Jessie." She winked at Cicero. "Why don't you come in the parlor and get acquainted?"

"Yes, ma'am. We sure will," Cicero said, hurrying in.

So much for just going to get a drink.

Jasper stood in the entrance for a spell. The parlor was lit up and seemed pretty well-suited to getting acquainted. Everything was just so red, like the color of a prickly pear except brighter. Red sofa. Red pillows too. A mirror that went all the way to the floor. The lamps had red shades and dangling tassels. Red chairs was here and there. A big blue-and-red rug had designs all over it like flowers and such. A piano was up against one wall, but there wasn't no bar and there wasn't no beer.

He should probably go on into the parlor. "We was only wondering if we could get a cold drink, ma'am."

"Why, of course you can," Miss Jessie said, taking a seat. She leaned back, draped one arm over the chair back, and with the other hand drew her petticoat back to show off her legs. They was crossed and sure was long for a lady. Her stockings was trussed up north of her knees with black garters. "Big Joe, be a dear and go down to the Red Front and get some cold Busch beer for these fine gentlemen."

"Ma'am, do you mind if we get Lone Star beer?" Cicero asked. "I'm real partial to it."

"Joe, make that Lone Star. Get a dozen."

"Yes'm," he said, departing.

Jasper hadn't even noticed him appear behind them in the hallway.

Miss Jessie's cheeks was red as her sofa. Maybe she was hot too. She cocked her head again and smiled at Cicero from behind her fan. "And what's your name, handsome?"

"Cicero, ma'am. It's just Cicero."

"Well, Mr. Cicero, have a seat over there by Miss Sadie." She pointed to the sofa across the room. It was humpbacked like a camel he'd seen in a book and had fancy wood carving on both humps.

The lady on the sofa, Miss Sadie, was dressed in a gown that hung real low. It was sort of like the one Momma wore around the house in summertime, but it looked different on Miss Sadie. She smiled back at Cicero from the right-hand hump. She had a sweet face—was probably not any older than him or Cicero— and light hair in a topknot with a ribbon. Her lips was real red, but they was beet-red, not prickly-pear red.

"Have a seat right here," she said to Cicero, patting the cushion close beside her. She had a real soft way of talking, like a house cat purring.

"Good evening, Miss Sadie." Cicero sat at the far end of the sofa under the left-hand hump. He sure enough looked like he'd just seen one of them eight wonders of the world.

Jasper plopped into a chair that near swallowed him. He straightened back up and scooted to the edge, ready for when it was time to leave. When he grabbed hold of his knees, he noticed his trousers was hiked way up and showed some holes in his socks. He pulled his pants legs down, but they was too short. The mirror was directly across the room—dang, if his face wasn't beet-red too. He wiped it with his sleeve and swallowed hard. It sure was hot in there.

"And what's your name, honey?" Miss Jessie asked him soft-like.

It took about a year for his words to form up and file on out of his mouth. "Jasper, ma'am. It's just Jasper. I ain't got no other name, just Jasper."

"Is that right? How unusual." She turned to the other lady. "Sadie, isn't Mr. Jasper an unusually charming gentleman?"

"Yes, he sure is," Miss Sadie said, smiling now at him instead of Cicero.

"You've got a nice house here, ma'am," Cicero said. "Doesn't she, Jasper?"

"Yes, ma'am." Everybody looked at him. What else could he say? "It's red."

Dang, that was a fool thing to say, but that's what hopped out when he opened his mouth.

Sudden-like, somebody come down the stairs and they all turned to look. A man crossed the hall arm-in-arm with a lady. They disappeared again just as quick toward the front door. She giggled, then squealed like a piglet. The door opened and slammed shut.

That new lady come into the parlor then and eased onto a low sofa kind of thing with curves and a hump back on one end only. She was younger than Miss Jessie, probably a little older than Miss Sadie, but still couldn't be more than twenty. She had curly brown hair with a long curling strand dangling to one shoulder. Her gown hung across from her other shoulder. Momma never wore hers like that. This lady was like a Greek goddess he'd seen in books, and when she smiled—dang, she was pretty.

"Gentlemen, this is Miss Georgia," Jessie said.

"Good evening, ma'am," Cicero said, staring.

Jasper couldn't get any words formed at all.

Miss Georgia looked from Cicero to Jasper. "Are you gentlemen bankers?"

"Oh no, ma'am, we're in college," Cicero answered.

"Oh?" Miss Jessie asked. "Which one?"

"Baylor."

"How nice. Are you from Waco, Mr. Cicero?"

"No, ma'am. I'm from Washington County."

"I don't believe I've ever been there," she said.

"You don't sound like you're from around here."

"I moved here from St. Tammany."

He grinned big. "Oh. You know, I thought maybe you were French."

As Cicero talked on and on, something he was practiced at, Jasper took in the parlor closer. It was all new with clean, bright-colored flowery wallpaper and shiny wood edges. A big statue stood on a black stone slab next to him. It was solid gold, and it was a lady. One hand held up a lamp, which wasn't lit, and the other one dangled in the air like she'd just turned loose a butterfly. The plain truth about her: She was downright naked. On the wall to each side of the mirror was photographs of other ladies with their backs turned. They was naked too. It didn't much look like any saloon he'd ever seen, though he hadn't been in many at all, to be honest.

He wiped sweat from his forehead.

"Take off your coats and get comfortable," Miss Jessie said.

"Oh, we's fixing to leave after we has a drink, ma'am," he said, but Cicero pulled off his coat and tossed it on the sofa.

Big Joe returned with a small crate of beer bottles and put it on the end table. Cicero took one and guzzled it, wiping his mouth on his shirtsleeve. Jasper got one too but didn't open it.

"Gents, would you care to dance?" Miss Georgia asked.

Jasper was struck dumb, but Cicero wasn't. "I sure would, ma'am." He hopped up like a toad off a pad, then hoisted his beer and took a big swig.

"Just put a quarter in the piano," Miss Jessie said.

"Oh yes, ma'am, I will."

He dug deep in his pocket, found a coin, and put it in the coin slot. The piano roll commenced to spinning around, and them keys punched themselves like some invisible piano player was on that red stool. Land o' Goshen, that was really something.

Miss Georgia pulled Cicero to the center of the room, and they whirled around to the music. At first Cicero put his right hand gentle-like on her low back, but before long he pressed her real close.

Jasper glanced at Miss Sadie, who winked back. He quickly looked back at the dancers.

Miss Georgia whispered something in Cicero's ear. As they turned, Cicero got his beer from the table. He drunk a gulp and danced and laughed until the music stopped.

"Jasper, put a quarter in," he said, not letting loose of Miss Georgia.

He did. Two songs and another beer later, Cicero and Miss Georgia danced toward the hallway, and she grabbed his hand and led him along. He took the box of beer, and they went out the parlor and up them stairs.

They was gone sudden-like, and Jasper found hisself all alone with them other two ladies. The music stopped, and they looked at him like he was supposed to do something. He sure hoped they wasn't thinking he was going upstairs with Miss Sadie to get acquainted.

"Would you care to dance with Miss Sadie?"

He sat there, gripping his knees. There just wasn't no words.

"Jasper, darling, how about a dance?" Miss Sadie repeated.

He jumped to his feet. "I'm feeling a might peaked. I best get on back to the dorm."

"Oh, please don't rush off." She got up real quick and put her hand behind his neck.

He flinched. Without a word, he took off for the front door, but Big Joe stood in the doorway, arms crossed, and he remembered the beer. He reached into his pocket and grabbed all his coins. He shoved them at Joe without counting, dropping both his silver dollars on the floor, and bolted out the front door past a bald man coming in.

In the middle of the street, he paused for a deep breath. The air was easier outside. He looked back. A light was on in the room above the front door. He didn't know exactly how long it would take Cicero to finish getting acquainted with Miss Georgia, but he figured it couldn't be long. He'd wait outside.

There was a telephone pole across the street. He plopped down next to it on the curb. It was dark and still and quiet, nobody else out. A horse snuffled to his left. A hack was parked on his side of the street, no driver anywhere. The light upstairs in Miss Jessie's house went out. He tried to listen, but there wasn't nothing to hear.

His mind drifted back to that red parlor. For the first time, it occurred to him it'd had a smell—sweet, maybe, like when Momma dressed for a social, except this sweet smell was downright different. He could still smell it. And he could still see some things stuck in his mind. That preacher had talked about places like that. That must've been what give Cicero the idea, 'cause that's when he'd asked Jasper if he had any money.

Well fiddle-dee if he'd think about that no more. Jasper settled back against the pole, took a deep breath, and shuddered. He might be in a big city leaning against a telephone pole beside a fancy gravel street, but he still felt easier under the open night sky than inside that house. At that very minute, the moon was shining over his family's farm too. Everybody was long since sleeping. In fact, the roosters'd start up pretty soon. He pushed the red and the smell and the ladies out of his mind. Slow-like, his tensificity settled. He let his breath out again. After a spell, he dozed off.

No telling how much later, something woke him up. He shot straight up. It sounded like it was from the house. Was that a lady hollering?

"No, stop!" a lady screamed from the house. "Get out!"

The room upstairs was still dark. That was where the scream come from. He jumped up. The commotion scaryfied him, and he took off running up Washington.

He never looked back, just run as fast as he could, and got to the dorm before long. Out of breath, he crawled through the window and jumped into his bed, still in his Sunday-go-to-meeting clothes.

He shut his eyes tight.

"Lord, this is Jasper Cantrell of Fayette County, Texas. I sure hope you'll forgive me. I didn't mean to do no sinning, especially on a Sunday, and I'm awful sorry for it. But mostly, Lord, please make sure my friend ain't in no trouble. He's Cicero Sweet of Washington County, Texas. We's roommates at Baylor University in Waco, Texas, in America, and I'm sorry as I can be I run off and left him in a whorehouse. Amen."

Chapter 2

If there was a finer Monday to conduct the practice of law, Catfish couldn't imagine it. In fact, this was a superlative day to wrap up the last murder case he'd ever have to defend. Judge Goodrich had finally promised to stop appointing him to defend alleged killers. This afternoon, after pleading Willie Bond to manslaughter in the Nineteenth District Court and passing Noah Griffin's horse-stealing case in the Fifty-Fourth, it would be a very fine day for savoring a White Owl cigar by the soft glow of his reading lamp at home.

Across the work table in the center of the office, Harley flipped a page in a treatise on encumbrances. It was a fine day to watch his son slowly season into professional manhood, as he himself had done thirty years earlier; to study his face, to see there the precious similarities with two others, to remember when the four were together. Such a fine day for remembrance.

In the front room, young Miss Peach was finishing up the papers for filing. Catfish couldn't abide the incessant, mind-numbing clatter of her confounded typewriting contraption, but she and Harley had insisted on getting one. It was a fine day to escape the modern law office, too.

He stood, and every joint cried out in protest against disturbing the status quo ante. He never used the walking stick

Harley had given him. Canes were for peacocks and decrepit old men.

"I'm going next door."

Harley nodded and continued reading.

"Colonel Terry," he commanded the hound at his feet, "get."

The hound bounded past Miss Peach drumming away at the confounded clicking contraption.

Catfish passed in a more leisurely fashion. "Going next door."

"Yes, sir."

It was a fine spring day.

Mrs. Goodhue, with a garden of daisies shooting from her straw hat, advanced up the sidewalk carrying some parcels.

Wonder what bee was in her bonnet today?

"How do, ma'am."

She exhibited no mirth at the day. "Mr. Calloway."

He and the colonel headed for the Old Corner Drug. They took their usual spot at the soda fountain.

The soda jerk, a winsome young fella with sandy hair, freckles, and a white apron, appeared across the counter.

"Morning, Mr. Catfish. The usual?"

He winked. "Thanks, Jimmy."

It was a fine day for a soda water. The boy's whistling drifted along the counter. An electrified ceiling fan whopped overhead, but at least the breeze was fresh. Other customers hoorahed at each other across tables in the back. The front door stood open behind him, as usual in the spring. Outside, electric trolley cars rattled up and down Austin Avenue, sparks crackling from their wires when they turned onto Fourth Street. They honked at dawdling mule carts or carriages, and horses whinnied in protest.

Jimmy brought his soda bottle. He dropped his Stetson No. 1 on the counter. Could there be a finer day?

The colonel curled up at his feet. Sleeping here or sleeping there was all the same to him. His square head rested on his paws, his floppy ears splayed on the floor to each side as if he needed stabilizing against toppling over. Probably did.

It was a fine day to catch up on the Saturday newspaper. Catfish pinched his pince-nez spectacles onto his nose and began reading, by habit, back to front. Not much but advertisements on the last page.

On page seven, his eyes immediately arrested at an announcement placed by Thaddeus Schoolcraft. He skipped to page six. It was too fine a day to sully with a single thought about Thaddeus Schoolcraft.

He moved on to a six-handed euchre game hosted by the Fairchilds for Miss Berry and some other guests on page six. Nice folks. Page five, sarsaparilla and fig syrup advertising. Mind reader's pitch for unread minds on page four.

It wasn't until the front page that there was anything of particular note: *Sam's Red-Hot Shot; The Bombardment of Satan's Stronghold Continues.* Preacher Sam Jones was in town for several weeks of revivals at the Tabernacle, and he was sure to stir folks up over something—likely the saloons or the sporting houses. *Satan's Stronghold.* Catfish snorted. Some people just couldn't abide whores being whores.

It was a fine day if you weren't a sporting girl.

He spread the paper on the counter and curled the errant ends of his mustache back into place as he read: *Uncle Jones then delivered a few gentle remarks anent the collection. He said: "The hat will be passed. Let each lady and gentleman contribute something. The balance of you needn't give anything."*

He chuckled. That preacher had at least half a wit after all. He sipped his bottled soda.

Next came the sin of profanity: *"I think I have heard as much swearing among the men of this town as any town I was ever in. Old cussing colonel, old cussing judge, old cussing citizen. Young men cuss. I want to hold them up tonight and show what infernal scoundrels they are. Cussers from Cusserville."*

He laughed. "Cusserville must be over in Dammit County."

There was movement in the mirror across the counter as a young fella took a seat to his right around the corner of the fountain.

When he glanced over, the fella spoke. "Excuse me, sir, did you say something?"

"No no, sorry, just reading to myself," he answered with a grin. "Sometimes reader and audience forget themselves."

"Brann's my name," the man said, smiling back. He was about thirty years younger, with hair as dark as his own was white. He had a wry smile and an accent from somewhere east of the Mississippi. "William Cowper Brann." He extended his hand.

"How do. Name's Catfish Calloway." They shook. "Ever been to Cusserville?"

"No, I haven't." Brann gave him a puzzled expression.

"I was just reading about it in Sam Jones's sermon—you know, that evangelist from Georgia?"

"Indeed." Brann whirled his stool around to directly face Catfish. "In fact, I'm in your fair metropolis in part because of him. I'm reporting for a daily newspaper. He's appearing as a divine proxy, and that's news."

Catfish rocked back on his stool. "What'd you think of him?"

Brann pondered it for a split second, resting his right elbow on the bright metal counter. "He's a proverbial cornucopia of bombast, an idolater of idiomatic ignorance, and a man unafraid to speak his dull mind." He slapped the counter. "I find him entirely worthy of countervailing ink."

Jimmy appeared across the counter. "Can I get you something, mister?"

"Shoot him a Waco on me," Catfish said. "He's from out of town. And a Circle-A for the colonel."

"Yes, sir, Mr. Catfish," Jimmy replied. "In a jiff."

"The colonel?" Brann asked.

"Meet my hound dog, Colonel Terry." He bent over and scratched his hound's floppy ear. One eye arched up in gratitude. "He mostly goes by 'Colonel.'"

Brann touched a hand to his brow. "I salute you, Colonel. What are you having?"

"He's partial to ginger ale."

Jimmy brought a glass for Brann and a bowl for the colonel.

Brann examined the darker liquid in his own glass. "So mine's not ginger ale?"

"No, it's the specialty of the house." Catfish showed the name on his bottle, DR. PEPPER'S PHOS-FERRATE. He thumbed over his shoulder. "Concocted across the street."

Brann shook the ice-filled glass and took a sip—"Fruity, very refreshing"—and then a longer draw. "Now, back to Preacher Jones. What is your learned opinion concerning his favorite subject, the ubiquity of sinfulness and selfishness here on the banks of the Brazos?"

"Couldn't make much of a living here without it."

Brann's eyes widened in surprise. "Are you a man of the cloth too?"

He laughed. "No, sir. Not by a far stretch. I'm a lawyer."

"Ah, so we have something in common."

"What's that?"

"We both make a living off sin and greed." He took another drink. "I find vice exceedingly more stimulating than virtue."

"Sinners hereabouts do too. What paper you work for?"

"The *San Antonio Express*, but I also write essays for a journal."

"What's it called?"

"*The Texas Iconoclast*."

"Haven't read it."

Brann looked disappointed. "*Was* called that, actually. I sold it just last month to Will Porter in Austin. Do you know of William Sydney Porter, by chance?"

"Can't say as I do."

"At any rate, I fully intend to buy it back someday. I'm not sure he's genuinely committed to the métier."

"But you are?"

He bowed his head. "Irreverently and proudly."

Catfish raised his Dr. Pepper. "Well, sir, here's to your success."

"To sin, greed, and jural elocution."

"And editorial eloquence."

They clinked and drank.

A fine day to meet an interesting fella, even if he was a reporter.

"I'm most intrigued, Mr. Calloway—"

"Catfish."

"I'm most intrigued, Catfish, by your fair municipality's official sanction of sin."

He smiled. "You mean the Reservation?"

Brann nodded. "Indeed I do. I'm not sure I know of any other city in the land that explicitly legalizes the oldest profession by official ordinance."

"I think there's one other place somewhere east of the Mississippi."
Brann took a drink. "Where is your den of iniquity situated?"

Catfish waved over the counter to the north. "Couple of blocks thataway. Mostly other side of Barron's Creek. Sodom's over there"—he gestured again—"between Second and Third Streets, but Gomorrah's this side of the creek right down on Washington Avenue, spitting distance from City Hall."

"That's convenient. Maybe your mayor spies on them from there."

"Maybe." He finished off his drink and slid the bottle across to Jimmy with a wink.

Brann's eyebrows narrowed. "Does the city do anything more than just permit them to operate?"

"Yes, sir. About five years ago they started to license 'em, inspect 'em for the clap, and watch 'em like a hawk. In fact, if you wanted to pick one out by name, they even got sort of a directory at the city secretary's office. They call it the bawdy house register. Every madam and every sporting girl listed by name—least, the names they give."

Brann looked thoughtful, then shook his head. "Why would a bastion of Baptists like Waco condone open vice?"

"Well, it's not like making it illegal puts an end to it, is it?" he asked with a chuckle. "The powers that be in City Hall decided we'd collect fees from licensing and inspecting instead of court fines. Not much different in the end, except fellas around here get less clap."

Brann smirked. "So City Hall went into the skin trade. Fascinating. But perhaps members of the bar prefer that vice remain illegal?"

"Don't matter much to lawyers. Sporting girls still get in trouble with the law one way or other. They attract drunk farm boys and cowboys like flies to a bull's ass. And the coppers sometimes pick up girls who go outside the Reservation."

"It sounds like a prison without walls."

"Well, sir, they can leave the Reservation, maybe go to a store, but they gotta stay in their hacks or they might just get hauled to the calaboose for vagrancy."

Brann looked skeptical. "How do they shop if they can't even get out of the carriage?"

"The shopkeepers don't mind taking goods out to the street as long as the girls don't come in and mix with decent folks. Money's money, isn't it?"

"Indeed—but as a matter of fact, Preacher Jones took on the city for its part in the skin trade in last night's sermon." Brann pulled out a copybook and flipped some pages. "Listen to this: 'You can hang a few anarchists in Chicago every few years and think you have killed out anarchy, but if you have a law on the books you don't enforce, you've got anarchy right here in Waco, Texas.' He gave your mayor hell. Let's see"—he skimmed through his notes—"here it is. 'I wouldn't be the mayor of Waco the way the town is run now. If the devil were mayor and the imps of hell were aldermen, they wouldn't make any change. They'd be just fine with all them painted women in the Reservation, every single one shamelessly naked, sweaty with the execrable lust of he-ing and she-ing.'" He looked up. "And your mayor and some of his alderman were right there with him on the stage."

Catfish snorted. "They got an earful."

"Oh, here's a good part: 'If you can block off a place, call it a Reservation, and license licentiousness, why don't you reserve a few blocks where a man can commit murder and go unpunished?'"

Catfish shook his head. "This is a town of only twenty-seven thousand folks, but we've got about thirty-five churches, almost fifty saloons, and over sixty sporting houses. It's the only place in the state where City Hall blesses all of 'em. You lob a firebrand evangelist into that tinder, and sparks'll fly. Maybe even a blazing fire."

"A conflagration in Satan's Stronghold."

A fine day for Satan.

There was a flash of movement in the mirror as a Western Union messenger boy on a bicycle rattled over the threshold. The colonel's head popped up. The boy dropped his bicycle on its side and rushed up to Catfish.

"Mr. Catfish, telegram for you." The boy was breathless. "Miss Peach said you were here."

"Thanks, Billy." He tipped him, and the boy left.

Catfish popped his pince-nez spectacles back onto his nose and unfolded the telegram: CATFISH. NEED HELP. SON CICERO DISAPPEARED. SENDING ROOMMATE YOUR OFFICE. HENRY SWEET.

It had been such a fine day.

Chapter 3

Jasper was downright scaryfied. He'd finally had to tell Professor Charlton that Cicero hadn't come back, but he hadn't said any more than that. He told the professor he didn't know where Cicero was at that very minute, and that was true. But even that stirred up a hornet's nest. Before long, a deputy sheriff showed up at the dorm, but Jasper didn't tell him much neither.

He was worried about Cicero mostly, but he was scared for his own self too. If anybody found out he'd went to a whorehouse to drink beer, they'd boot him straight out of Baylor before he could spit. His family would be shamed. Them folks at his church back home in Fayette County had put offerings in the plate just so he could go off to college. His parents didn't ask them to. Folks just did it on their own because it was the neighborly thing to do, like helping with a barn raising. Momma and Daddy found out about it that Sunday morning at the same time he did, when the preacher announced it from the pulpit. Momma cried. Money was hard to come by for sharecroppers, especially those days.

Momma worried about him all the time, even when he was back home. She said "Watch for snakes" when he took off for the woods more times than Papa said grace. When he left home for college, his first time being away from home, they both give him a talking-to about city things to be wary of. Beer was one. And Momma said, "Don't let some girl talk you into doing something you shouldn't be doing." Reckon he'd figured out now what she was talking about. If she heard about all this trouble he'd gotten into in the city, she'd be disappointed in him. Daddy too. In fact, he'd be awful sore.

Once the deputy left, Jasper had breathed easier, but then Professor Charlton told him they had to go downtown to some lawyer office. He just knew they was on to him. He ain't never been in no lawyer office. In fact, he didn't recollect ever even laying eyes on a lawyer before. As far as he knowed, there wasn't none in Flatonia, but they probably had two or three over in the county seat. He wondered if they wore wigs like that lawyer Buzfuz in the book he'd read in English class. He hoped they wouldn't talk as much as the folks in that book.

The office was next door to the Old Corner Drug. A gold-painted sign on the front door said CALLOWAY & CALLOWAY, ATTORNEYS. Professor Charlton said they was father and son. He followed the professor into a front room, where a nice lady was working on one of them letter-typing machines he'd seen at Baylor. It rattled like rain on a tin chicken shed. She took them into a bigger room that was longer than it was wide, with a high ceiling and fans dangling from long shafts. They was humming and going round and round, but it was still awful warm in there. Jasper felt like he had before his first class at Baylor, waiting for the professor in a classroom full of boys and girls he didn't know and was too shy to meet.

The lady asked him and Professor Charlton to have a seat at a long table in the middle of the room. Other tables was around the room, stacked with books and papers and such. Against the left wall, right in the middle of the room, was a big ol' rolltop desk like the postmaster had back home, with papers sticking out of pigeonholes and a stack of papers with blue wrappers and red ribbons. Heavy-looking books was stacked on the top. Another desk was across the room on the opposite wall. Electric lights was hanging from the ceiling. Maybe someday his family could get an electric light for the house. It would sure help Momma with her mending at night after supper, but for now they couldn't even afford enough oil for the lamp. They made do with candles.

They waited not more than ten minutes before a man arrived, and then another one not long after. They was both tall. The older one seemed to run things. Lawyers, they said, but he expected that, of course. They was Mr. Calloway and Mr. Calloway, and they wasn't wearing no wigs. It was yet to see if they was big talkers.

The older one was the kind of fella that makes you look twice. He didn't need no wig 'cause he had a bushel of white hair of his own. He had a white mustache that curled up at both ends. Daddy would call his face ruddy. But it was them eyes that grabbed hold of you and wouldn't let go. They was real blue, like Grandma's sapphire pin Momma wore sometimes. His wearing clothes was different too, the kind of long black coat that none of the city fellas wore anymore and a silver fob hanging from a watch chain on his vest. Lawyers in Texas looked more like preachers than that Buzfuz lawyer in the book.

The other lawyer, Mr. Harley Calloway, wasn't exactly no yearling. He was a younger version of Mr. Catfish Calloway, with the same face but without the wrinkles. His eyes wasn't blue, and he didn't have no mustache. His suit of clothes was more like other city fellas wore these days.

"Tell us what happened to Cicero," the older one said, leaning forward across the big table.

"Well, he didn't come back last night."

"Where'd he go?"

Jasper crossed his fingers under the table just in case. "He went out."

"Out where?"

"Don't know exactly." He tightened down on his fingers.

The older lawyer glanced at the younger one and got real quiet. Seemed like he was just thinking. At that moment, he was the scariest old coot Jasper'd ever eyeballed. Then he asked some more questions, dead serious like a preacher, but Jasper still didn't give him much information. Every now and then the lawyer'd pick up some spectacles, pinch 'em onto the tip of his nose, and write something down. When he looked up over the top of them specs, it was like his questions might punch right through a brick wall. Them blue eyes just wouldn't let loose. But he didn't get nothing out of Jasper. It wasn't this fella's business if Cicero was still getting acquainted with that lady at the whorehouse, and Jasper wasn't about to tattle.

Finally, the man stopped firing off questions like a six-gun, leaned back in his chair, and looked over at Professor Charlton. "Professor, I know you have other responsibilities. If you want to head on back, we can take it from here."

"I do need to get back to campus," Professor Charlton said. "Jasper, Mr. Calloway and his son are here to find Cicero. Please do what you can to help them, and they'll bring you back to the dormitory later."

"Yes, sir."

What was this lawyer fixing to do?

After Professor Charlton left, the younger lawyer got up and went over to his desk, where he sat and read a book. The older lawyer took off his coat. He was packing some kind of artillery under his shoulder. He took that rig off and hung it up on a hook by the door with his coat. For some reason, he turned the flame down on the table lamp. Then he settled back into a chair on Jasper's side of the table, propping his feet up on the table like he was fixing to take a nap.

I'll be. He was wearing boots.

The lawyer ran his fingers through his hair, leaving it flopping down like a horse's forelock. Made him look younger somehow. Then dang if he didn't grin like Daddy, and everything just got different.

"Colonel!"

Jasper hadn't even noticed the dog, who must've been sleeping by the front door. He padded over and stood by Mr. Calloway, who reached down and rubbed the two big ol' floppy ears.

"Got a dog?" Mr. Calloway asked him.

"Yes, sir," Jasper said. "His name's Lightning."

"How'd he get that name?"

"He's afraid of it and hides under the front porch."

"The colonel doesn't cotton to it, either," he said, leaning way over and letting the hound dog lick his face. "Where's home?"

"Fayette County. Near Flatonia."

"I know it, sure. Been there. Good farm country. Your daddy a cotton farmer?"

"Yes, sir."

"Mine too," he said with a big smile. It was like he was remembering some good days back home. "How about a soda water?"

"Sure."

"Miss Peach," he said to the lady in the front room, "would you be so kind as to go next door and fetch some Dr. Pepper's soda for my friend?"

She appeared in the doorway between the two rooms. "I'd be happy to."

"And get that bowl of Circle-A for the colonel."

One furry eyebrow arched up at the sound of his name.

"I don't think he finished the one I got him earlier."

"Yes, sir," she said with a wink at Jasper.

Miss Peach was young and she was a looker, but she was real different from them girls in the whorehouse. She had red hair all bundled up on top of her head and the sweetest smile he'd ever seen. Of course, she was a full-growed woman, but she couldn't be all that much older than him. He was eighteen, so she was maybe twenty-one. He watched her walk out the door and head for the drugstore. She had a real skinny waist and wore a pretty blue dress that dragged the floor except when she lifted it up a little, and the sleeves of her white blouse was all puffed out. But she was real businesslike too. She had a stiff stand-up collar with a black bow tie just showing at the front.

"Miss Peach is my stenographer."

"Yes, sir. She's nice."

Mr. Calloway dropped his feet back to the floor and scooted his chair a little closer. He bent over, rested his forearms on his knees, and gave him the blue eyes. "Son, Baylor doesn't really have to know every doggone thing about last night. I don't see any reason it's a bit of their business. But I gotta know it all if I'm gonna help Cicero. His daddy's an old friend of mine. He wired me today and asked me to find him."

"Yes, sir."

"So please," he said, friendly-like, "do you know where Cicero went to last night?"

"Yes, sir."

Mr. Harley closed the book, whirled his swivel chair around, and eased it up to the table across from Mr. Calloway.

"Tell Harley and me what you know, son."

"Well, we was at the revival with that banty preacher."

"Sam Jones? At the Tabernacle?"

"Yes, sir."

"What happened there?"

"Well, I was downright edgy. It took that preacher three syllables just to say 'Jesus.' He wasn't even halfway from hellfire to brimstone before me and Cicero was ready to give religion a rest for a while."

"Did you go somewhere after that?"

"Back to the dorm."

"Did you leave again?" Mr. Harley asked.

Mr. Calloway sat up. "Did *Cicero* leave?"

"Yes, sir. I think so."

"Where'd he go?"

"To Washington Street."

"Where on Washington Street?"

"Almost to the river."

Mr. Calloway glanced over at his son. "Did he go in a hack?"

"Yes, sir."

"Do you know who the hack driver was?"

"No, sir."

"Where'd Cicero go when he left the hack?"

"He went—well, I reckon he went to a brick house across the street."

"Was that brick house on the side of Washington closest to City Hall or the other?"

"The other."

"Whose house was it?"

"It was, I reckon . . . . it belonged to a lady name of Miss Jessie."

"Miss Jessie who?"

"I don't know no other name."

Mr. Calloway looked at Mr. Harley again. "See if you can find Miss Jessie's place and learn what you can."

"Right." Mr. Harley got his hat and left.

Miss Peach come back with a sody water. Jasper took a big gulp and then wiped his mouth on his coat sleeve. She put the bowl of ginger ale in the corner, and the dog lapped it up.

"Miss Peach," Mr. Calloway said, "get on that talking-phone you coaxed me into buying."

"The telephone?" she said, real irritated-like.

Mr. Calloway rolled his eyes at Jasper and spoke like she wasn't in the room. "She says everybody's gonna have one someday. Got my doubts." He winked.

"They got one at the dorm too," Jasper said.

"It's 1894, Mr. Calloway," Miss Peach said, plain botheration all over her face.

"And it'll be 1895 if you don't get on with it," he said without even looking her way. "Ring up the police office and see if they've run across Cicero down in the Reservation."

"Yes, sir."

Mr. Calloway smiled like Daddy did on Sundays. Maybe he wouldn't tell nobody at Baylor after all. He pulled a cigar out of a White Owl box on the table, bit the end off, and spit it into a brass spittoon by his desk.

Smoke puffed out from the cigar, and Jasper coughed. He didn't care much for smoke. The fan picked it up and blew it around the room, and pretty soon the whole place stunk. He coughed again, and Mr. Calloway quit puffing on it. Jasper turned his face aside to try to avoid the last of it. Leaning there against the wall by the desk was a cavalry saber. He looked for the dent in the scabbard and sure enough, there it was, just like Grandpa's.

"Was Cicero in any trouble last time you saw him?"

"No, sir. He was happy as a lark."

"I thought he might be."

"Mr. Calloway," Miss Peach said. "All the police officers are at the courthouse for an inquest."

He faced her sudden-like. "An inquest? Into what?"

"A killing."

Jasper started shaking. *God, please not Cicero.* Then he just cried. He couldn't help it. Miss Peach come over and sat beside him. She put her arm around him and held him tight. Jasper wiped his eyes with his sleeve. Dang it, he was too old to be crying.

"It's all right, Jasper," she said soft-like. "The operator didn't know who it was. It's probably somebody else."

But maybe that lady hollered 'cause Cicero was hurt. Jasper worked up his courage. "Mr. Calloway, I've gotta tell you something else. I need to tell you real bad."

"What is it?"

"I ain't sure at all, but maybe a lady screamed inside Miss Jessie's."

Miss Peach gasped. "Why didn't you—"

Mr. Calloway touched her sleeve.

"Tell us what happened," Mr. Calloway said, real calm-like.

Jasper took a deep breath. "I was outside waiting on Cicero— I need to tell you, sir, Miss Jessie's is a whorehouse—and he was inside getting acquainted with one of them ladies."

"What happened then?"

Tarnation, but he began crying again. "I just run—I'm so sorry, I truly am. I reckon I was scaryfied. I can't think of no other reason I done it. I been praying no grief come to Cicero, but he got hisself killed."

"Jasper, I'm sure he's just fine," Mr. Calloway said, real kind-like. "I want to find out what happened first, and we'll talk some more later. I'm going to the courthouse right now. Miss Peach will get you back to your dormitory. Don't worry about Cicero, son."

He got up and strapped on his artillery and put his coat over it. He turned back to Jasper and smiled. "And you won't get in any trouble yourself. I'm your lawyer from now on, and I ain't never had a client kicked out of any school anywhere for any reason. Whatever a client says to me ain't for nobody else's ears but mine."

Did he need a lawyer? He'd left all his spending money at the whorehouse. "I ain't got no money left, sir."

"You won't owe me a thing."

"Yes, sir. Thank you. I'm obliged."

Mr. Calloway tossed a calling card on the table in front of him and hurried out.

WILLIAM "CATFISH" CALLOWAY

CALLOWAY & CALLOWAY

ATTORNEYS-AT-LAW

109 N. FOURTH STREET

WACO, TEXAS

AUDI ALTERAM PARTEM

"That's Latin, ain't it?" Jasper asked Miss Peach.

"Yes, it is."

"What's it mean?"

"'Hear the other side.'"

Chapter 4

Harley was only in his fourth year of practicing law with Papa, but everybody in every courthouse knew Catfish Calloway. "Oh, you're Catfish's boy" was something he'd gotten used to. His name gave him immediate credibility with every judge he appeared before, whether his legal positions merited the trust or not. On those occasions where they didn't, the judge's face often told him "I expected better from Catfish's boy."

He helped try some of Calloway & Calloway's bigger cases. Papa called it riding shotgun, but Harley didn't mind because that's how he learned. He tried a few smaller cases on his own, but Papa relied on him more for his knowledge of the law, especially the law of evidence and procedure. For that, lack of experience didn't matter. Harley argued all the law points in their cases.

It was investigative work Papa'd sent him on this time. At Miss Jessie's bawdy house, no one answered the door, so he decided to check the sheriff's office for reports of Cicero. Then he ran into Papa, who said there was an inquest into a killing. He didn't know who'd been killed yet, but he was worried it might be Cicero.

A deputy said the inquest was in the first-floor courtroom of the McLennan County Court, so they headed there together.

Justice of the Peace Gallagher was questioning a witness from the bench when they entered.

He paused the interrogation. "Catfish, you and Harley know anything about this killing?"

"No, Judge, just here to watch," Papa answered.

"All right, have a seat."

They took the right front bench in the spectator gallery. The woman in the witness chair was handsome though not quite pretty, probably in her late twenties. She was neatly dressed in a waist jacket and high-necked blouse with a large black bow. Her black hair lay curled and pinned beneath a straw boater. A slight accent gave her a certain elegance. The court reporter busily took down her testimony.

Judge Gallagher, who also served as the acting coroner for McLennan County, had empaneled a coroner's jury of six men. He usually gathered them from the town square in such situations; in murder cases, he wanted his inquest jury to see the body and couldn't wait for the sheriff to issue summonses. They listened from the jury box. The bailiff and several police officers, keystone hats in hand, also listened. Police Sergeant Quinn stood, arms crossed, in front of the judge's bench next to a cot with a body laid out, covered head to foot with a blanket.

"Sorry for the interruption, Miss Rose," Judge Gallagher said. "After you heard that gunshot, what did you do?"

"I got my pistol and waited at the bottom of the stairs."

"Was anyone else with you?"

"Yes, my assistant, Big Joe, and one of my other boarders, Miss Sadie."

Maybe her accent was French or Cajun.

The judge took notes. "How many whores you got?"

"I had five boarders until this happened."

Papa leaned over to Harley. "Must be Miss Jessie."

"Where were the others?" the judge asked.

"Elsewhere."

The jurors appeared intent on the witness. The scratching of the court reporter's pen on his pad and the humming of ceiling fans were the only noises in the room. Occasionally, on the street outside the open windows, a horse neighed or a trolley car clattered past.

"What'd you do?"

"We went upstairs to her room. We listened outside the door but didn't hear anything."

She seemed quite at ease in front of a judge and jury. Most witnesses directed their answers to the one questioning them, as in a conversation. Miss Jessie seemed to understand her testimony was as much for the jury as the judge. It probably wasn't her first time in a courtroom.

"I knocked and called out her name," she said, "but there was no answer."

"What'd you do then?"

"We went inside."

"What'd you find?"

"Miss Georgia was lying across the bed with blood all over her and the sheets."

"What did she look like?"

"Her eyes were wide open." She turned from the judge to the jury. "She had a look of ineffable terror on her face."

Papa made a barely audible grumbling sound. Harley had studied his father many times and thought he knew all his courtroom habits and practices, but grumbling was something new. He probably felt frustrated that he couldn't cross-examine this witness, like a horse he couldn't ride, or a gun he couldn't shoot, or a whiskey he couldn't sip. Papa had made his reputation cross-examining prosecution witnesses. Careful observation of the witness was the key; he picked up every nuance, every subtle facial expression. Then, in his boyishly charming way, he would steal the stage from the witness. Harley had practiced the art of observation himself, but stage-stealing was another matter.

Harley settled back in his chair.

Judge Gallagher paused to finish writing something. "Step down, Miss Rose, and go over there to that cot. I'll ask the officer to pull the blanket back just a bit for you."

The jurors all sat upright and craned their necks to see. Quinn pulled the blanket back just enough to reveal the face to the witness while blocking the view from the gallery. Papa leaned to see around him, but Harley couldn't see a thing.

Miss Jessie looked at the face and began to sniffle. She dabbed her eyes with a handkerchief.

"Do you know that woman?" the judge asked.

"Yes, Judge, that's Miss Georgia."

"Miss Georgia who?"

"Georgia Virginia Gamble."

The judge wrote something, then looked up. "How old was she?"

"I don't know, perhaps nineteen."

"Was she a whore in your bawdy house?"

"Yes, she was one of my boarders."

"All right, ma'am, take your seat again, please."

She returned to her chair, still sniffling softly.

"Did you—"

A train whistle shrieked a loud blast, and the rumbling of the train made it impossible to hear what the judge was saying. The building vibrated slightly. The Cotton Belt switch track ran just a block away.

"Sorry for the interruption," the judge called over the noise. After the train had passed, he continued. "Did you see any weapons in the room?"

"Yes. On the floor at the foot of the bed, there was a derringer."

"The bailiff will show you a pistol, ma'am."

The deputy sheriff picked up a small pistol from the court reporter's desk, held it by the tip of the handle, and showed it to her. The jurors watched intently.

"Is that it?" the judge asked.

"Yes, sir. That's the one I saw."

"Does it appear to you to be a Remington Model Ninety-Five derringer?"

She shrugged. "I suppose."

"How about that dried blood on the barrel?" The judge peered at her over his spectacles. "You know how it got there?"

The deputy held the derringer up for her to see.

"I presume when she was shot."

The deputy took it to the jury box as she answered, walking it past them. Each juror leaned forward to examine the bloodstain on the right side of the short barrel.

"Do you know who owns the derringer?"

"Yes, sir. It's Miss Georgia's. She keeps it in her room for protection against unruly men."

To Harley's utter surprise, Papa jumped to his feet. "Pardon me for interrupting, Your Honor—amicus curiae here—but maybe you were wondering where she kept her derringer?"

Everyone turned to see who the curious spectator was. Harley covered his eyes with one hand.

"I sure was, Catfish," the judge answered, "but I don't need no curry-eye help."

"Sorry, Your Honor," Papa said, sheepishly retreating to his seat.

Sometimes Papa did things Harley'd never dream of doing himself. He cut a glance at his father, hoping to remind him they weren't making an official appearance here. They didn't even have a client yet, although he had the distinct impression Papa believed otherwise.

"Where'd she keep it, ma'am?" the judge asked, glaring at Papa.

"On a nightstand right next to her bed. She kept it in the drawer."

Papa started to get up again, but before Harley could grab his sleeve, Judge Gallagher extended his hand in a stopping motion. "Was it on the same side of the bed she was laying on?"

"Yes."

"What else did you find in her room?"

"Just the usual things you might find in a lady's bedroom."

"Was anything on the nightstand?"

"I believe there was a box of Ozmanlis pills and a hairbrush."

Harley had never heard of an Ozmanlis pill. Papa's expression didn't change.

"Did you see anyone else in the room?"

"A gentleman passed out drunk on the floor."

Harley glanced at Papa, who kept the witness in his sights.

"How do you know he was drunk?"

"I saw him drinking in my parlor, and he was already tipsy when he went upstairs with Miss Georgia. He took a box of beers with him, and we found all the bottles scattered around the room, empty."

"Where was he laying exactly?"

"On the floor at the foot of the bed."

"Where was he in relation to the gun?"

"It was about two or three feet from him."

"Describe the gentleman for us."

"He was in his late teens or early twenties. He had wavy black hair. He was unclothed."

"Completely naked?"

She dabbed her eye. "Yes."

"To your knowledge, was he Miss Georgia's customer?"

"Yes."

"Do you know his name?"

"It was Mr. Cicero."

***

After the inquest, Papa tried to talk with Miss Jessie but she hurried off, escorted by a large man who wouldn't let him near her. Papa stopped to see the girl's body. Sergeant Quinn, who was still stationed by the body, arms crossed, allowed them to look.

Harley hadn't seen many shooting victims. She was so young and pretty. Miss Jessie had been right; she looked scared. Papa pulled the cover down to inspect the wound. Right in the heart. He asked if he could turn her over to see the exit wound, but Sergeant Quinn said there was none.

"Look at the whore, Mildred," a lady said from behind them outside the bar rail.

Word must have spread quickly, and now a small stream of townspeople were crowding in to see the body. It was that way with any killing, but a dead prostitute stirred even more curiosity. There were some boys, of course, but the women escorted them right back out of the courtroom. Over and over, the word "whore" popped out of the low gabble of the crowd while they leaned across the rail straining to see, pointing and whispering among themselves. Sergeant Quinn didn't let the gawkers inside the bar rail.

Whatever her sins, she didn't deserve this. Harley was ready to leave.

Quinn spoke to Papa. "You involved with this one?"

"Maybe. Don't know yet. Got the boy in the calaboose?"

"We do."

To Harley's relief, they departed for the county jail, which was just behind the courthouse in a two-story red brick building with limestone quoins, the same second-empire style as the courthouse. Harley was interested in architecture and much admired the public buildings designed by one of Papa's friends, Waco architect Wesley Dodson.

Deputy Whaley allowed them to meet with Cicero away from his cell. The boy was handcuffed, but the jailer shut the door and left them alone with him around an old, beat-up table. Papa had sent for Miss Peach, and she joined them.

Cicero Sweet was tall and lanky, with wavy black hair and a pleasant disposition. Miss Peach would probably consider him quite handsome. He seemed polite and not the murdering type. He acted like a scared boy trying hard not to show his fear.

"Your father and I go way back," Papa said.

Cicero laid his hands on the edge of the table, but then gripped it tightly. "Yes, sir."

"He wired me this morning, asked me to help you. He probably can't get here himself till tomorrow."

"Yes, sir."

"I'll wire him as soon as we leave here and let him know we made contact." Papa gestured to Harley. "This is my son and law partner, Harley, and this is Miss Peach, our stenographer." She pulled a notepad and pen from her bag. "She'll be taking down what you say today, so we'll have it later to remember exactly what you told us."

"Yes, sir."

Papa could turn from gregarious to sober in the blink of an eye. He leaned forward, resting his elbows on the table and folding his hands under his chin. He spoke with a calm confidence. "Cicero, you're in mighty serious trouble."

"Yes, sir, so it appears."

"Tell us about it."

"I don't have much to tell. I don't know anything about a murder."

Papa nodded his head as if he was carefully considering that answer. "Can you explain to me how you got yourself in that bothersome circumstance?"

"No, sir." Cicero shrugged. "I can't really do that."

Harley's head popped up from his notebook. Didn't he understand how serious this was? How damning the circumstances?

"Why not?" he asked.

"I don't remember anything."

Harley wrinkled his nose. "You don't remember going to the bawdy house?"

"Yes, sir. I recollect going there, but it's real hard to recall exactly what happened once we got inside."

"Why's that?" Papa asked matter-of-factly.

"I must've drunk way too much, Mr. Calloway. I've had a bad head all day, and I just don't remember much about last night. I've tried, but it just doesn't come back to me."

Papa seemed to be studying Cicero's forehead. There was a bad bruise above his left eye, and Harley leaned forward to see. "How'd you get that knot on your head?"

"I don't rightly remember that, either."

His hands were still on the table edge, but no longer so tense.

"Let's go about it this way," Papa said. "Tell us everything you do remember about last night."

"Yes, sir. Me and Jasper went to hear the preaching at the Tabernacle. I remember that because it was way too long. He went over pretty near all the sins. We decided to get something to drink after we got back to our room and took a hack down to Washington Street. I'd heard about a place you could get beer even on a Sunday."

Harley tilted his head. "Did you know it was a bawdy house?"

Cicero nodded. "As a matter of fact, I believe I did."

Papa spoke in a tone Harley'd heard many times when he was a boy. "Now son, did you go there for the beer or for the girls?"

"Well, the honest truth is probably both. That preacher got my curiosity up."

"Tell us what happened when you got there."

"All I really remember is we had some beer and did some dancing."

"Who'd you dance with?"

"A real pretty girl. I don't recollect her name."

"Miss Georgia?"

"That's it. Anyways, I remember dancing with her."

"Who else was there?"

"There were two other girls. And maybe a man too, but I don't remember him very well. And my roommate, Jasper, of course."

"Who was the other man?" Harley asked.

"He worked there, I think. I don't know his name."

"Did you go upstairs with Miss Georgia?"

"I must have, but I don't remember anything about that."

"Do you remember getting in the bed with her?"

"Shucks, you'd think I'd recollect something big like that, but I sure don't."

Harley leaned back and watched Papa. He ran his hands through his hair, resting his elbows back on the table. He swept his hand across from cheek to cheek as if something wet were on his whiskers and then propped his chin on the palm of his left hand. His head cocked left. He stared at the boy, his eyes becoming bluer somehow. Harley knew what all that meant: After due consideration of the facts, Catfish Calloway had serious worries.

"They found you passed out plumb naked on the floor of a sporting girl's room with a derringer an arm's length away and the girl shot dead on the bed, and you say you can't remember how all that came to be?"

"No, sir."

Papa stared at him and shook his head. "Boy, if you don't recall pretty quick, you're gonna find yourself in prison for the rest of your life."

Chapter 5

The Houston & Texas Central Railroad train came rumbling along the river toward the passenger depot on the east side of the river, shrieking like a banshee as it pulled into the terminal. A dozen or so people, Catfish and Harley included, waited on the platform. The colonel dozed by their bench.

Catfish smiled to himself. The whistle reminded him of the first time he'd ever met Henry Sweet. They'd been young men then—boys, really. At the beginning of the war, they'd embarked on a journey from New Orleans to Nashville along with a thousand other farm boys in their newly formed regiment. Most had never stepped outside their own counties. In those days, before war robbed them of youthful innocence, train rides were an adventure. The sound of the guns was still far away.

There were endless good-natured tricks perpetrated by those rowdy young Texans, and that blasted Henry Sweet had been at the bottom of more than a few of them, but Sergeant Miller always blamed Catfish. One time in Mississippi, they stopped to water the train and Henry spotted a scrawny calf grazing near the track. They were always hungry, even that early in the war, and Henry got the idea he'd requisition that beast. Privates didn't have that authority, of course; not even sergeants could requisition livestock from civilians for food. But Henry reasoned they needed horses because they hadn't been issued their mounts yet—and the army did requisition horses. Henry talked Catfish into helping him sneak the bellowing calf on board the train. Henry strapped his saddle on it to make it legal, and Catfish mounted up and prodded the poor, terrified beast down the aisle of the passenger car, to the hoots and hollers of their friends.

Just as the ruckus was at its loudest, Sergeant Miller appeared through the door at the end of the car. "God damn it, Calloway, you stupid-ass clodhopper."

But Henry told the sergeant that Catfish's family back in Washington County all rode cows. The furious sergeant had dragged Catfish off the hapless beast, and the calf had gone flying off the slowly rolling train.

Over thirty years later, Catfish could still see the sergeant's red face, and he laughed out loud.

"Papa, what's funny?"

Catfish sat up. "Nothing. Not a thing funny."

The locomotive dragged its string of passenger cars, hissing and chugging, to a slow rolling stop. Steam shot out from the locomotive.

Henry was the first passenger off. Catfish broke into a big grin, waving wildly, then jumped off the platform bench and hurried toward him. The colonel hopped up too. Henry tossed his head in greeting. He limped slightly from the war and used a cane. He carried a carpet bag in the other hand. Like Cicero, he had thick, wavy hair, but his had gone gray long ago.

Catfish stopped short of his old friend, stood at attention in the center of the platform, and saluted. Henry shook his head and kept walking with a grin.

They embraced like kin.

"Catfish, you old silver fox, it's been a long time."

"Too long."

They'd made a point of getting together often right after the war, riding a hundred miles to meet at a convenient stagecoach inn and eat and drink and smoke cigars into the morning. They remembered comrades and retold stories of good times and bad. There are no such friends as comrades-in-arms, and those who hadn't gone through a war couldn't understand. But as Catfish and Henry began new lives, their visits grew fewer and the years between them greater, eventually becoming decades. Reconnecting was never hard, though, because the bond forged by shared peril held fast.

It had been almost ten years since they'd last been together. Now they were both in their sixties. Henry couldn't really be as old as he looked; Catfish mostly just felt old inside. There were some advantages to age, to be sure, starting with the obvious one: A long life was preferable to a short one by a country mile. But of the things most satisfying about old age, chief among them was old friends. A long life made lifelong friendships, and Henry Sweet, God bless him, was such a friend.

"And this must be Houston," Henry said, facing Harley.

Catfish glanced away. He should have written him about Houston long ago.

Harley smiled easily. "No, sir, Houston was my brother. I'm Harley."

They shook hands.

"Happy to meet you, Harley. Your father wrote me about you. You're practicing together, aren't you?"

"Yes, sir." He took Henry's bag.

Harley had always been perceptive, Catfish thought approvingly. He put his arm around his dear friend and led him through the terminal.

"Come with us. I know you want to see your own boy as soon as you can."

"I do."

They loaded his bag onto the surrey and headed for the county jail, down Bridge Street directly for the bridge across the Brazos to west Waco. Harley took the reins while he and Henry sat in the back talking. The colonel nestled beside Catfish.

"How's Cicero holding up?" Henry asked.

Catfish squeezed Henry's arm. "As well as anybody could in the county jail. He hasn't been charged with anything yet. While you visit with him, Harley and I'll see about posting bond. The judge wasn't in when we were there before."

"I'm good for whatever amount is needed." Henry locked eyes with him. "He didn't shoot the girl, did he?"

"I don't believe he did, but the state will have a strong case if they charge him."

"Any eyewitnesses?"

"That's their weakness."

"I see." Henry pondered that a moment. "How's he feeling?"

"They're treating him fine. He's a confident boy, but I know he's worried. Problem is, he can't remember much about that night."

Catfish leaned close to Harley's ear. "Pull over when we get halfway across."

Harley nodded.

The horse clopped onto the suspension bridge, rattling the timber deck and making it hard to talk. The long wire rope cables of the bridge hung from one tower, dipped gracefully toward the center point, and sloped up again to the opposite tower. This was a busy thoroughfare, with carriages, pedestrians, and beasts going both ways. Young Toby Topper was doffing his tattered old top hat to folks as he rode his bicycle.

When they reached the middle of the bridge, Harley pulled

over to the side. Thirty feet below, the Brazos ran high from recent rains.

Catfish pointed across the river, up Washington Avenue. "You see that two-story brick building on the right side of the street?"

Henry strained to follow his direction. "I do. Is that where it happened?"

"Yes, sir. That's Miss Jessie's sporting house." He tapped Harley on the back. "Let's go."

"And did Cicero actually know it was a whorehouse when he went there?" Henry asked.

"He did. He admits it. He remembers dancing with a girl—the one that got killed—but he can't remember anything else. He said he was drinking beer."

"Will his roommate back him up?"

Catfish nodded. "But Jasper took off when Cicero went upstairs with the girl. He fell asleep outside and was woken by screaming from the building. He turned tail and ran all the way back to the dorm. Miss Jessie called the police, and they found Cicero passed out at the foot of her bed. He was stark naked, and a derringer was in arm's reach."

"He doesn't own a derringer."

"It was the girl's."

Henry shook his head. "It does look bad."

"They might not prosecute him at all. Some folks feel like things just happen in the Reservation. There's some feeling that sporting girls know what they're getting into when they enter the trade."

"And Cicero's not a killer."

"Of course not."

Henry turned to him. "If he's charged, you'll represent him, won't you?"

He well understood Henry's concern, but his friend had had no way of understanding his reluctance. "I'll see to it he gets the best defense possible."

"But you'll defend him yourself, right?"

He made a show of waving at Toby Topper as they caught up and passed him again. "We'll see what happens. But I promise you I'll make sure he's in good hands."

A strong hand came down on his knee.

"No, Catfish. I don't trust anybody but you. Promise me."

He patted his friend's hand. "Let's just wait and see what happens. It may never get to that."

Henry didn't look satisfied, but Catfish changed the subject anyway. "I got you a room at the McLelland Hotel right above our office. We'll take you to see Cicero, and when you're done we can go to the hotel."

Henry smiled grimly. "I'm grateful you're here for us."

"I know. You'd do the same if it was Harley."

"Of course." Henry squeezed his arm. "I feel bad that I haven't seen you since Martha's funeral. I'm sorry I'm a little out of touch. Does Houston live here too?"

He shook his head and abruptly leaned forward, looking ahead, so that Henry couldn't see his face. They should worry about Henry's son, not his own. Thankfully, they pulled up at the jail moments later. Back to more immediate matters for now.

***

"I didn't do it, Father," Cicero said. "I swear I didn't."

"I believe you, son," Henry said, extending his hand across the table to grasp Cicero's. "But it sure looks bad the way you were found."

"I know, and honest to God, I don't remember how I got

there or how she got dead." A tear rolled down his cheek, and he wiped it away with his sleeve. He gazed at his father with absolute fear in his eyes.

Catfish knew that look. He glanced away.

"Don't worry." Henry spoke to Cicero, but the words seemed directed at him, as if he were pleading with his old friend. "You have the best lawyer in the state."

"I'm not worried," Cicero mumbled, staring at the table. "Thank you, Mr. Calloway."

Catfish flashed a quick smile. "I won't let anything happen to you. You can count on that."

He pushed his chair back and rose. Maybe they wouldn't charge the boy. Maybe defending him wouldn't even be necessary.

Pray God it's not.

***

Harley walked with Papa back up Austin Avenue from the courthouse toward their office.

The clerk had just told them the judge wasn't going to grant bail, said the judge wouldn't even consider it. That was a surprise. Papa assured him a wire to Mr. Sweet's bank would confirm his ability to post the bond, but the clerk said that didn't matter. Harley didn't understand why.

On the way back to the office, they ran into Bootblack Ben under the awning in front of Sam Kee's restaurant. He shined shoes on the town square, and Papa always stopped to talk to him.

"How do, Mr. Moon."

"Sure is good to see you, Cap'n Calloway, Mr. Harley." He gave Colonel Terry a vigorous ear rub. "Y'all be needing a shine today?"

"Sorry, we're in a rush now. I'll try to get back by tomorrow." Papa started to walk off but turned back instead. "Tell Mrs. Moon I really cotton to that sweet tater pie of hers. I hope she got her crop in."

"Cap'n, you done told me that three times," Ben said.

"Well, sir," Papa said with a wink, "you can tell her three more times if it gets me another pie next fall."

Ben broke into a big, toothless grin. "Sure enough, I'll tell her."

Papa took off up Austin Avenue. Harley followed one step behind. He knew better than to talk about the case until Papa said something first. Papa liked to chew on things before discussing them.

They were both lost in thought when the *ding-ding* of the trolley rang out behind them, and the colonel growled. Harley hadn't noticed the trolley or even that they were walking up the middle of the track. They stepped out of the way, and it clickety-clacked past. The overhead electric wires sparked and crackled as the trolley changed lines turning onto Fourth Street.

"Thanks, Catfish," the conductor shouted on the way by.

They stepped onto the sidewalk in front of the drugstore, and Papa pulled out a cigar. He looked above the Old Corner Drug at the clock protruding between two owls in the cigar sign on the corner of the McLelland building. It was about to strike noon.

"This one confounds me," he said finally.

"How's that?"

"That boy ain't a murderer, but he does look like a boy who might get drunk and do something he later regretted."

"I agree with that. He's young and probably can't hold his beer very well."

"On the other hand, for the life of me, I can't understand

how a boy could be so drunk he passes out right after shooting a girl in the chest with a derringer. If he was that drunk, how'd he hit her? 'Course he might've pressed it right up against her, but I didn't see any powder burns on her body, did you?"

Harley shook his head.

Papa leaned against the telephone pole, puffing on the cigar. "A barrel that short emits a prodigious flash. So he's sober enough to hit her in the heart at some distance, but too drunk to remember it. And how'd he get her gun? Doesn't make sense to me."

"Do you think he's lying about not remembering?"

"I don't." Papa shook his head and headed down the sidewalk toward the office. "No boy of Henry Sweet would be a liar. And besides, the madam testified he was passed out, which supports his story."

"Maybe he got knocked out somehow."

"Maybe. That must have been a pretty hard blow to his head to leave a knot like that. That may account for his memory loss."

"That's what I was thinking." Just before they got to the office door, he stopped and touched Papa's elbow. "Can I ask you a question?"

"Sure."

"If he gets indicted, are you going to represent him?"

"Why wouldn't I?" Papa went inside without waiting for an answer.

Papa knew why. He shouldn't have to hear it from Harley.

Chapter 6

The bar of the McLelland Hotel was the busiest place on the busiest street in Waco. It was Friday afternoon, and folks looked worn out from the week. Catfish was ready for a good stiff drink as he greeted the other regulars and kept an eye peeled for William Brann to enter.

The hotel was right above the Old Corner Drug and his own law office at the corner of Fourth and Austin Avenue. It had been brimming with guests all week because of the two big conventions in town, and as both wound down, the conventioneers were reconvening at hotels, restaurants, and bars across the city. Waco was busting at the seams with veterans, drummers, and pilgrims following Brother Sam Jones as well as the usual visitors there to take the artesian waters. Some found healing in the waters of the Natatorium, while others discovered it in the hymn-filled air of the Tabernacle. Whatever the attraction, hotel proprietor Joe Knapp looked exceedingly pleased.

The bar was packed. It was mostly businessmen, chattering like church women in small bunches under clouds of cigar smoke. Catfish didn't need to listen in to know that the talk was of cotton deals, cattle deals, and real estate deals. There were railroad men and liquor drummers. The saddle maker and the general manager of the trolley line were locked tight in conversation. Wealthy lumber merchant and banker William Cameron presided over a long table near the front—money talk, judging by the presence of the bank presidents: Mr. McLendon of Citizens Bank, Mr. Watt of Provident National Bank, Mr. Seley of Waco State Bank, and Mr. Rotan of First National Bank. Whatever their talk, bar manager Smith looked pleased when he checked on them.

Catfish's vantage point was a big round table in the back corner. All the regular bar patrons knew that table had a permanent claim laid to it most Fridays. The seven men there swapped stories and argued politics over cigars, liquor, and cold ginger ale.

Catfish's guest arrived by four thirty.

"Let me introduce you to our muster, Mr. Brann," Judge Warwick Jenkins said. "You know Catfish Calloway, of course, and his son, Harley. The next gentleman is Wesley Dodson, who's an architect."

"Most of the places I work at in this state are his creation," Catfish added.

"An exaggeration," Dodson said modestly. He and Catfish were about the same age and were longtime friends.

The judge pointed to the next man. "This is Bob Lazenby. He's got the Artesian Manufacturing & Bottling Company. And to his right is Sterling DeGroote. He's a wool gatherer."

DeGroote grinned in response. "He means I'm a manager at the Slayden-Kirksey Woolen Mill."

"To your left is Professor Jeremiah Perkins, who supplies most of the intellectual firepower of this group. And I'm Warwick Jenkins."

Catfish tapped cigar ashes into a spittoon. "He's my old law partner's brother and now judge of the county court."

"An esteemed conclave you have, gentlemen," Brann said.

Catfish put a hand on Brann's shoulder. "He's an editor, boys. Met him at the Corner Drug the other day. He specializes in exposing transgressions of the human race, so he's a natural for us."

"You'll notice," Judge Jenkins said, "there are no other newspapermen here, and that's intentional. We prefer honest fellowship, but Catfish assures me you're the exceptional editor."

"Indeed, Your Honor, I make my living by honest diatribe alone."

"Bravo," Lazenby interjected. "Diatribe is the weapon of choice in this group."

The conversation, enlivened by braying diatribe and counter-diatribe, ranged from cotton prices to bimetallism, tariffs to unemployment, and William Jennings Bryan to the simmering revolt in Cuba before finally taking a local turn.

"What brings you to Waco?" Professor Perkins asked Brann. The professor was a younger man than the rest, and he had the same midwestern accent as Brann.

"Your fair metropolis is the venue for several interesting gatherings this week."

"So you're covering the Texas Veterans Association?"

Brann nodded. "I've also attended some sessions of the Travelers Protective Association. Conveniently for me, both happened to meet down the street at City Hall."

"I was at the veterans' meeting too," Lazenby said. "I'm sorry the rest of you missed it. When General McCulloch asked the San Jacinto veterans to stand, I don't think I've ever heard such cheering."

"You're correct about that." Brann leaned back in his chair and spoke as though they'd gathered just to hear his thoughts.

Seemed used to taking the floor. "There were twelve of them, and they were revered by the convention like apostles incarnate. All were bent with age and had frosty white hair. Though I'm a relative latecomer to Texas, I'm a student of that battle—your glorious Yorktown, I believe—as well as the general course of your struggle for independence. I felt myself honored to be in their presence. It would not have been different had Washington and Lafayette appeared by magic."

"I was at the TPA meeting," the judge said. "Gentlemen, Mr. Brann was elected an honorary member."

"I felt honored until they also voted thanks to Sam Jones for his sermon," Brann replied with a wry smile.

Catfish laughed. "Maybe association with him will get you past Saint Peter someday."

"It would surely be short-lived. He would easily arouse the angels against me, and Saint Peter would have no choice but to swing the gate the other way." Brann lit a cigar and turned serious. "By the way, Catfish, your client featured in Jones' rant in the ladies-only sermon the other night."

He'd been afraid of that. The last thing they needed was a fire-eating preacher riling folks up against Cicero before the grand jury convened. "What'd he say?"

"Of course he crowed about his murder prophecy at the men-only service the night before. But you'll be happy to know he placed most of the responsibility at the feet of the local officials who licensed the bordello."

"I understand some of the alderman's wives were there and felt his heat a little too closely," Lazenby added.

Brann slapped the table with delight. "By God, one lady did scamper out of the Tabernacle in a huff. He'd just issued his heavenly edict for the wives to fetch their husbands back from

Gomorrah before it's too late. He proclaimed the imps—that's what he called the aldermen—had blood on their hands. It wasn't a very Christian thing to say."

"He's gotten people stirred up about it," Lazenby said.

"I confess ignorance," Dodson said. "What happened?"

Lazenby leaned forward. "A college boy murdered a whore in the Reservation."

Harley shifted in his chair. "Now wait a minute, Bob, that's not what happened."

Catfish jumped in. "Hold your fire, boys. Harley and I can't talk about it. We might be involved if they charge him."

"Do you think they will?" DeGroote asked, with surprise on his face. "I just assumed they'd let it go since she was a whore."

Lazenby shook his head. "They'll prosecute. Just to prove Preacher Jones wrong, if for no other reason."

"I personally know Cicero Sweet," Professor Perkins said, "and I don't think he did it. He's a fine lad."

Lazenby laughed derisively. "Well, maybe he is when he's in the Baylor Chapel, but I hear they arrested him in the whore's room with his drawers down and a gun in his hand."

"That's not right," Harley said, but Catfish put a hand on his arm.

"Let it be, fellas," he said.

Thankfully, the conversation moved back to politics, as it always did, and the gathering broke up a short time later.

Catfish and Harley walked out with DeGroote.

"Catfish, I need to tell you something," DeGroote said when they got out on the sidewalk.

"About what?"

He waited for two people to pass, then lowered his voice. "Your client."

"You mean Cicero Sweet?"

DeGroote had a pained expression. "I hesitate to mention it, but I feel as though there's something you should know. You best speak about it with my son, Peter. He's on a trip now but will return soon."

"Tell us," Catfish said. "What is it?"

"Wait to hear the whole story from Peter." He hurried down the sidewalk.

"What could it be?" Harley asked.

Catfish stared at the departing DeGroote, then took a breath and expelled it. "More to Cicero than meets the eye."

Chapter 7

It was the following Monday, April twenty-third, a week after the killing. Catfish had been in his office drawing up a will for Old Man Calhoun when Miss Peach came in and told him that Mr. Simon Shaughnessy, known by his friends and associates as Cooter, had called and wanted Catfish to come to his office— immediately. Catfish obligingly put away his papers and headed down the street.

Shaughnessy was a cotton factor and one of the wealthiest men in town. An elected city alderman and one of the Democratic Party leaders in the county, he was a big man not only in politics but also in physical size—weighed about two hundred and fifty pounds, although he stood no more than five and a half feet in boots. He had pendulous jowls and sagging tow sacks under his black eyes. Not the kind of fella you'd go fishing with.

Shaughnessy's office was on the top floor of the Provident Building. Dark oak paneling covered the walls, and fancy crystal light fixtures dangled from the ceiling in the reception area as well as his private office. The man's desk was as big as he was. Catfish felt like David sitting across from Goliath. The old boy'd doubtless given that effect a great deal of forethought, because the desk was perfectly clear except for a miniature cotton bale.

After an exchange of pleasantries, Shaughnessy quickly got to business. His jowls jiggled as he spoke in a forceful, throaty voice. "Mr. Calloway, I want to visit with you about one of your clients."

"Which one?"

"It's come to my attention you've been employed to represent a murderer. Mr. DeGroote tells me you're a family friend of the murderer, I believe."

"No, sir," Catfish answered, making a show of surprise. "I haven't been hired to represent any murderers lately."

Shaughnessy pushed on, undeterred. "Your client is a hot-blooded young man by the name of Sweet. Misnamed and misbred, it appears."

The man knew nothing of the Sweets. "I do know a young man named Sweet, but that boy is in fact well named. May I ask how you're interested?"

"Yes, sir. I'll tell you." Shaughnessy shifted forward in his swivel chair, which squeaked and groaned under the pressure, and cocked his head to one side. His black eyes stared all the way through Catfish. "I'll tell you plain and simple. He murdered a whore. Your client has broken the law, and we can't tolerate lawlessness in our city."

Catfish shrugged. "Well, sir, truth is he didn't murder her. You must be mistaken."

Shaughnessy charged on. "They caught him virtually in the act. I've spoken with several gentlemen of substance, and it's our desire that this unfortunate matter be resolved swiftly and surely, for the good of the city." He pulled a box from his drawer. "Cigar?"

"Kind of you, but no thanks."

Shaughnessy took one for himself, sliced off the end, and

flicked it into a spittoon at his feet. He lit up and blew a cloud of smoke. "What we require of you is simple: Plead your client guilty to first-degree murder, and I'll see to it he gets out of prison long before he's an old man."

For the first time he flashed a smile, but it disappeared like the smoke.

This fella was used to getting his way.

"Mr. Shaughnessy, that's mighty thoughtful of you, but I don't believe we can do that."

"And why not, sir?"

"Because as I've said already, he's not guilty."

Shaughnessy, now hunched over slightly, stared at him and took another draw on his black-as-night cigar. He rocked back, the chair creaking again under his weight, and blew smoke at the ceiling. He stabbed the earthy Figurado directly at Catfish. "I'm not sure you quite understand what I am saying to you, sir. If you plead him guilty, he will get prison time." He flicked ash into the spittoon. "I could only put it plainer if I said he would not be sentenced to death."

"Oh, I understood exactly what you're saying." Catfish stared straight back at the black eyes. "My answer's the same."

Shaughnessy considered the answer without expression. "Perhaps you know the grand jury meets tomorrow afternoon. You say you understand my position, but I'm not sure it's really quite clear to you, so I'll be blunt. If you don't agree to my terms, young Sweet will be prosecuted to the fullest and made an example of. We won't tolerate lawlessness in the Reservation. There'll be no mercy, and he'll hang—hang, sir. Hang by the neck until he's dead."

What itch was he scratching? Or whose back? Catfish glared back. "Appears to me it's you who's having trouble understanding. Cicero Sweet has no interest at all in pleading guilty to anything, much less first-degree murder. He's innocent. Didn't shoot her."

"Your reputation is not that of a fool, Mr. Calloway."

Catfish grinned. "Well, sir, that's awful nice to hear. My momma'd be proud. Thank you very much. Is there anything else you want?"

"You, sir, are impertinent. I might add that your own prospects for future legal work in this town are now in serious jeopardy. I have many friends. So I advise you to think again about my proposal."

"Good day."

***

The next afternoon, the courtroom doors were shut with a deputy posted outside to prevent any eavesdropping. That meant one thing: The grand jury was indeed in session. Others had gathered in the waiting area outside the district courtroom too, waiting to hear what indictments they would return. Harley spotted a reporter among them, but Papa ignored him.

The young man got up from the opposite bench and came over to them. His hat was pitched to one side in a jaunty fashion, and he wore a striped vest with a heavy gold watch chain draped in a rakish way.

"You gents are lawyers, aren't you?" He didn't sound as if he was local.

"Yes, sir. Most days," Papa said. "What can I do for you?"

"Do you mind if we talk?"

"About what?"

"The bawdy house murder. I hear the grand jury is in there meeting about it."

"Do tell," Papa answered with apparent lack of interest. "And you're who?"

"Babcock Brown, *Dallas Daily Times-Herald*, at your service," he said with a grin.

"How do, mister," Papa said with a forced smile.

That look, Harley knew from experience, meant *conversation's over.* Papa took the Monday edition of the *Evening News* from his lap and popped it opened in front of his face.

The reporter appeared surprised. "Does this mean you're refusing to talk?"

"Not refusing," Papa said from behind the paper. "Just not talking."

The doors opened, and a couple of dozen men with serious expressions hurriedly departed and disappeared down the stairs. One of them was an alderman—not Shaughnessy, thankfully.

Harley peered through the open doors. Another gentleman lingered inside, speaking with the county attorney. He looked familiar. He had a horseshoe mustache and a black bowler and carried a blackthorn cane. As he turned toward the door, Harley realized he did indeed know this man. He looked older than he remembered, but then again it had been eight years.

To his surprise, the man came out and stopped right in front of them. He nudged Papa's newspaper down with his cane and cracked a wry smile. "Well, well, I haven't seen you in quite some time, Mr. Calloway."

Papa's eyebrows shot up. He neither spoke nor moved.

"Funny we should meet here of all places."

Papa didn't react.

"I heard you didn't go to court anymore."

Harley shifted in his seat. Papa wasn't afraid to go to court.

Papa's eyes narrowed.

"Well," the man said after a moment of silence, "I heard you might have an interest in one of the cases we took up today. I can't talk about grand jury business, of course, but you might want to check the true bills."

Papa didn't blink.

The man huffed and began descending the stairs, his cane clicking the cast iron steps every other one. He stopped on the landing and looked back. "I'm surprised you're still defending murder cases. I didn't think you could bear to watch another client . . . hang."

He thumped his way down the rest of the stairs.

Papa stared at the newspaper, but he wasn't reading.

"Thaddeus Schoolcraft," Harley murmured near Papa's shoulder after the man was gone. "The railroad detective, right?"

Papa gave a tight nod.

The county attorney was the last man out of the court chamber. Harley had seen Tom Blair in action in the courtroom several times and had a number of cases against him, though none had gone to trial. He was a formidable adversary. A pony-built man in his late forties, the popular Blair, known by everyone as Captain Blair, had served as the county's chief prosecutor off and on for years. In one trial, Blair had supposedly gotten into an argument with the opposing lawyer, leading to a fistfight across the counsel table. Judge Gerald had adjourned until they finished pummeling one another, and then the trial had proceeded as before. Papa deeply respected Blair's ability.

"Howdy, Catfish," Blair said in a friendly way. "Good to see you too, Harley. How's working for the old man?"

"Good afternoon, Captain. Papa's like an overseer sometimes, but he hasn't administered any lashes yet."

Blair winked at Papa. "Grand jury just returned some true bills. You might be interested in one of them."

Papa's eyes widened. "Who?"

"Let's see here," Blair said, examining the document as if he didn't remember the name, though the ink on the foreman's signature was likely still wet. For an experienced politician, he wasn't a very convincing actor. "Name's Cicero Sweet."

Harley suppressed his reaction. The indictment wasn't surprising but what was the charge?

"Cicero Sweet indicted, is that so?" Papa said.

"You have a minute?" Blair asked.

"Sure."

Harley and Catfish followed Blair back into the courtroom, and Papa shut the door on the reporters. The prosecutor slouched in a chair at the bar table and propped his feet on another chair.

Papa leaned against the jury rail. "What you got?"

Blair passed the document to Papa. "Here's the indictment."

Harley peered over his father's shoulder.

In the name and by the authority of the State of Texas: Be it remembered that on the sixteenth day of April 1894, the defendant, CICERO SWEET, in the City of Waco and the County of McLennan, did then and there, willfully and with malice aforethought, murder GEORGIA VIRGINIA GAMBLE, a single woman of this county, against the peace and dignity of the State of Texas.

Papa straightened.

Harley wasn't exactly surprised the indictment charged first-degree murder. It was common to indict on the most serious possible offense and then try the case on a lesser included offense like second-degree murder or even manslaughter. He'd expected this.

"Rumor is you're defending," Blair said.

"Yes, sir. Boy's father is a friend. When's the arraignment?"

"Thursday."

"How about agreeing to bail?"

"Can't do it," he said, shaking his head. "The judge won't have it."

"He got a soft spot for sporting girls?"

"He just doesn't like citizens getting shot."

"First-degree's pretty hard, Tom. Cicero's just a boy."

Blair's expression grew serious. "It's a death penalty case, Catfish."

Harley was stunned, but Papa didn't react, except for the slightest tightening of his jaw.

"Would you consider probation for a guilty plea?" Harley blurted.

Papa's glance said he shouldn't have opened his mouth.

Harley leaned back against the jury rail.

Papa deliberately turned the indictment to the second page. Only the foreman's signature and the date appeared there.

"No probation," Blair said, shaking his head. "I don't think I could convince the judge to approve it. People want the maximum punishment to send a message. That preacher's gotten under everybody's skin. I might push for a deal, but only if the boy goes to Huntsville for a long time."

Papa lifted his chin. "No, sir. No prison time. No probation. Plea will be not guilty. When you gonna set it for trial?"

"Next term. It'll be the first setting on the July docket." Blair swung his feet to the floor. "Look, my friend, you've got a hard one."

"Why's that?"

"Don't play dumb with me. I know you already know this. The boy was caught naked and passed out in the bawdy house with a derringer at his fingertips and a dead whore on the bed."

Papa smiled faintly. "Well now, Tom, you know things aren't always the way they look."

"Maybe not always, but they are this time."

"Why's that?"

"I've got witnesses."

"Who?" Harley asked.

"Eyewitnesses?" Papa added.

"Next best thing. Three people right under the bedroom when it happened. They heard the gunshot and found your boy there by the dead whore minutes later."

Papa huffed. "You gonna build a case on the testimony of sporting girls?"

"Why not?" Blair smiled, but then turned serious again. "But that's not all we have, anyway."

Harley folded his arms and forced himself to look down.

"What else?" Papa calmly asked.

Blair's eyes narrowed. "The boy confessed."

Chapter 8

How did Papa appear so calm at hearing their client confessed? Harley unclenched his fists.

"So he confessed, did he?" Papa said. "Well, I'll be. That's news to me, and I talked to him myself. Who'd he confess to?"

"You know I'm not going to show my cards before trial," Blair said with a grin. He got up and headed for the door. "I'll be seeing you."

Papa took a chair.

Harley met his eyes. "Do you think Cicero really confessed?"

"He's puffing." Papa swatted the air as if the news were a bothersome horsefly. "If he really had a confession, he'd be willing to tell me the name of his witness just to scare me. He's thinking about the next election. It's time to show folks how tough he is. He's campaigning as much against Preacher Jones as his actual opponent. Yes, sir, Tom's champing at the bit to try this one, whether he's got a case or not. He's counting on a jury convicting Cicero just 'cause of the circumstances."

Harley sat on the corner of the state's table. "Those circumstances look pretty damning to me." How could it have been any clearer? They were alone in the room. The gun lay beside him. She was shot dead. Why would Blair say he'd confessed if he didn't have a witness that he did? This was one to plead out, not try. Get the best deal they could. "You don't still think he's innocent, do you?"

"I do, for a fact."

Harley tilted his head. There must be something he was missing. "Why are you so sure?"

"No son of Henry Sweet would do something like that. They're not that kind. I'll be damned if I'll let Henry's boy get punished just so the politicians can answer Sam Jones in the election."

That was all? Harley's head dipped to his chest. "All right. What do we do?"

"Since he can't remember anything, the only way to defend Cicero is to find the real killer and prove it in court."

Harley stood. Maybe he was wrong. Papa had defended murder cases as long as Harley had been alive. "Tell me what to do."

"I want to know everybody who was at the sporting house that night—or might've been. Who had a motive to kill her? I want to find out everything I can about all of 'em. Mainly Miss Jessie. She's the star witness, and she was hiding something at the inquest."

"What?"

"Don't know exactly. Just a feeling I got. Let's make a call on her."

Harley smiled. "During daylight hours, I hope."

His father grinned back. "But first, you go talk to Jasper again and see if he remembers anything else. Press him for details."

"Right. What about Peter DeGroote?"

"Yes, sir. Forgot about him. Go see Peter after you talk to Jasper, and then we'll scout out the sporting house together."

"Right."

Papa steepled his hands on the table, lost in thought as Harley jotted some notes.

"I overheard you and Mr. Sweet talking in the back of the surrey the other day," Harley observed mildly, without looking up from his notepad. "I got the feeling you weren't sure you'd defend Cicero yourself."

"That was before he got indicted."

He snuck a peek at his father. "Did you know Thaddeus Schoolcraft was on the grand jury?"

"No."

He waited for his father to say more about the railroad detective, but he didn't. Why couldn't they talk about this? He tucked the notepad into his jacket. "Are you sure you ought to try Cicero's case?"

"Of course. Why not?"

"It's just . . ." He struggled to maintain a neutral expression. "If Mr. Sweet is such a good friend, maybe you should get somebody else to handle it."

"Why's that, Harley?"

"I don't know, maybe you're too close to it. And besides, you haven't tried a murder case since—"

"I know the last murder case I tried." Papa's eyes darted away. "And as far as referring the case to somebody else, there's nobody else I'd trust to do it right."

"Why? There's other good law—"

"I promised Henry I'd give it my personal attention."

"Mr. Sweet would understand. I think Mr. Sleeper would do a fine job." Harley took a breath. He hadn't tried a felony himself yet, but he knew he was ready. "Or me, Papa. I could try it."

Papa leaned forward, resting his arms on his knees, and looked up with the wisp of a smile and a blue-eyed gleam that was now just for him. "I know you could, but it's my responsibility and mine alone. You'll ride shotgun for me." He glanced at his satchel, and his voice cracked. "Henry saved my life once. I owe him."

Harley had never heard this before. It must have been in the war. But if Papa felt that way, why had he seemed so reluctant to defend Cicero when Mr. Sweet first asked?

Papa sat up. "Why don't you go on back to the office, and I'll be along directly."

"Yes, sir." Maybe Harley was wrong. They'd see.

***

After Harley had gone, Catfish remained in his old seat at the defense table. So many times he'd risen to announce *Catfish Calloway for the defense.* He rocked back in the creaking swivel chair.

The saddle-leather satchel resting on the table in front of him was old and worn now. How many times had he heaved that bag onto the bar table? It was big enough to tote Judge Clark's *Criminal Laws of Texas* and still have room for a case reporter and the White Owl cigar box he used as his trial box. His sons had given him that satchel for Christmas some years back. With their mother's help, they'd arranged for Tom Padgett to make it using his old cavalry tack. The gold lettering on the outside of the flap, CATFISH CALLOWAY, was chipped and faded. Tom had sewn a brass Texas star button onto the flap beneath his name.

Catfish loved the feel and smell of that old bag, and it always made him think of his sons. And his pals from the war. *Martha, you always accused me of being sentimental. Guess you were right.*

He wiped away the dampness in his eyes and unbuckled the bag.

He opened the trial box and dug through the things he used in court, pens and pencils and such, until he found the spent minié ball. It was mostly misshapen but still cylindrical at the base. He rolled the old bullet in his hand. It was tarnished with the passage of so many years, but his memory of that day in Kentucky was not.

I won't let you down, Henry.

Pasted on the underside of the cigar box lid was a sheet of paper with the Latin inscription *Audi Alteram Partem.* He put it there to remind him of his calling: Hear the other side. Did he still have it in him to make a murder jury hear the other side? He hadn't the last time, when it had mattered most. That had been eight years ago now, but that memory was untarnished too.

He propped his elbows on the bar table—the same table—and cradled his head in his hands. Before him, the witness stand—the same witness stand—was fifteen feet away, now vacant. To his left, twelve empty chairs. The judge's bench loomed silently to his right. He stared at the witness stand, letting the memories wash over him. He drew a deep breath of polished wood and saddle-leather from his satchel. His eyes lost focus. The familiar witness stand blurred before him. He blinked, but it got blurrier. A man appeared there, his face indistinct, staring back. Catfish shut his eyes, but the man remained. His mind formed a question for the man, but no words came out of his mouth—no answer from this witness. Another question formed but failed, and still no answer.

Why wouldn't the words come? Why couldn't he make him admit the lie?

Catfish lowered his head like a bull, glaring at the witness. The man raised his blackthorn cane to nudge up the brim of his bowler hat, revealing a hideous grin framed by a horseshoe mustache. The man laughed, and the laughter spread to twelve new faces, all indistinct, in the jury box.

Gentlemen of the jury, why can't you hear the other side?

To Catfish's right, on the bench, a black-robed figure joined in.

Why were they all laughing? Why did his words fail him?

He felt a presence beside him and swung around to see. In the client's chair sat another man, his face indistinct yet so familiar, younger than the others. He wasn't laughing: *I don't want to die.*

Then all went quiet. His client vanished. The laughing stopped too.

Catfish turned back. The man with the mustache and bowler had gone, as had the twelve jurors and the judge. He closed his damp eyes but couldn't shut out what he knew was there—the scaffold. A body swung there, turning in a gentle breeze.

Before the face could turn toward him, he forced his eyes open and jumped from his chair. He dropped the minié ball into the cigar box, stuffed it into the satchel, and escaped the courtroom.

On the front steps of the courthouse, he drew in deep drafts of fresh air. His faithful companion was waiting there patiently.

"Let's go, Colonel. Time to save a boy's life."

And a father's broken heart.

Chapter 9

Harley lashed the carriage horse toward the DeGroote home. What was it that Peter DeGroote knew about Cicero Sweet? Mr. DeGroote left the impression it was something bad. Maybe it would knock some sense into Papa. It was already so clear from the circumstances—they should persuade Captain Blair to accept a guilty plea in exchange for prison time.

Harley was no longer fresh out of the new law school at the University of Texas. There was still much to learn from Papa, but he could do more than carry his father's brief case to court. He hadn't pressed before now because the time never seemed right. They'd been through hard times together, Mama dying while he was in Baylor and then losing his big brother during the law school years. Harley had come home still unmarried, and he and Papa had found healing in hard work.

Papa was a rock. He'd endured the same losses, but he never let it get him down. On the other hand, Papa still wouldn't turn over the reins on important cases. Didn't he trust his own son? Harley was ready to be beyond the struggles of the past and get on with his career.

Meanwhile, Waco was boldly flexing its muscle as a commercial center nestled along the river. There were twenty-one thermal artesian wells as well as four colleges and universities.

The Chisholm Trail might no longer cross the Brazos on the Roebling-built suspension bridge, but five railroads now ran through Waco. Talk was that three more would extend their lines through town by the next year. There was still money to be made trading in cotton and cattle, but investment also poured into the woolen mill, the two electric street car lines, the bottling businesses, and the gas and electric companies. Bankers and homebuilders prospered with them. Clients needed lawyers to help them secure that prosperity. This city on the frontier between industrial audacity and wild west grit had its own brand of pluck, and it was time for Harley to be a part of it.

He couldn't just wait for it to happen. The good times wouldn't last forever. The year 1893 had been a bad one most other places. The collapse of the wheat market had devastated the heartland of America. A credit crisis and high unemployment ravaged the entire country, and labor unrest plagued the industrial cities back east. Ordinary people had lost their homes to foreclosure. Stock prices had plummeted. Three railroads had failed, and hundreds of banks closed. Maybe hard times elsewhere were what brought desperate women to the Reservation.

After four years of riding shotgun for Papa in court, it was Harley's time to take the reins.

He turned onto Sterling DeGroote's street in Provident Heights, a new suburb on the northwest edge of town. Mr. DeGroote had moved to Waco from New York following his friend Samuel Colcord, a New York developer whose ambition was to turn this suburb into an aristocratic neighborhood. Already it was really something. The homes were like smaller versions of the mansions built by captains of industry and commerce back east.

Sterling DeGroote appeared to have bold ambition too.

Harley tried not to crane his neck like a rube as the DeGrootes greeted him in the foyer. He'd never visited a house with its own indoor ten-pin bowling alley, though he'd read about places like the Breakers and George Vanderbilt's new home in North Carolina. He wasn't so sure Mark Twain was right that the extravagance of the captains of industry was just gilding over the hardship of the ordinary people who made them rich.

They settled into velvet-upholstered chairs in the parlor.

"So, Peter, do you live in the dormitory?" Harley asked.

"No, sir. I still live here—until I graduate," he said, with a smile toward his father. "It's a long way from school, but the Hobson rail line really helps. And sometimes when I'm late, Father lets me use the buggy. It's fast."

Peter DeGroote was a handsome young man, probably about twenty or twenty-one, with a fresh, dimpled face and a winning smile. He was smartly dressed in a serge coat and white duck trousers.

"Your father said there's something you know about Cicero Sweet we need to hear about," Harley said.

Peter sat back in his chair and crossed his legs. "Yes, sir. I know him."

"How?"

"I'm a senior. Baylor has a literary society, and last semester I debated against him. He's a freshman."

"When was this exactly?"

"Probably late November."

"What happened?"

Peter leaned forward, uncrossing his legs. "It was actually after the debate. I beat him—at least according to the judges—and a young lady-friend of mine who'd come to watch brought a picnic lunch to share afterward. We went across Fifth Street to Waco

Creek and spread a blanket on the bank under a cottonwood."

Someone else to track down. Harley recorded the story in his copybook as fast as he could. "Who was she?"

"Chloe Malone. Anyway, we were just down there enjoying the day, and Cicero came up from campus. He had a Lone Star and was drinking it in big gulps. I couldn't believe he had beer on campus. I warned him he'd best hide it before somebody saw him, but he just ignored me. I think he was upset about losing. I got the feeling that he thought he was a better talker than he really was, maybe because of his name. He started mouthing to me and bothering Chloe, and I asked him to leave us alone, but he didn't. He sat down, uninvited."

Peter shifted uncomfortably in his seat. "Chloe didn't like it, and I asked him to leave again. He finished his beer, threw the bottle in the creek, then pulled another one out of his coat. So I got up and just stood over him and told him to leave."

"How'd he react to that?"

"He stood up, too, and got up in my face and cussed at me." He held up his hand to demonstrate how close it was. "He had a foul mouth, and I could tell it upset Chloe. I told her we'd better leave, but then Cicero pushed me down. Well, one thing led to another, and pretty soon we were swinging at each other. He knocked me into the creek, and then he bothered Chloe while I was getting out."

Just like he suspected—Cicero was no saint. "What did he do?"

"He tried to take her hand."

"What happened then?"

"I jumped on him and we rolled around, scuffling. Chloe tried to stop us, and finally Cicero must've just gotten tired of it. He said he'd had enough of unsociable people, and he just walked off."

Peter glanced at his father.

Papa needed to hear this. "Were you hurt?"

"No, sir, not really. Just a little sore."

"Did you report him?"

"No, sir. I figured he'd just get over it, and so I just let it be."

"Have you had any trouble with him since?"

"I haven't run into him much."

Mr. DeGroote had been sitting back and listening up to that point. "I advised him to avoid the boy. He appeared to be a troublemaker to me."

"Yes, sir." Harley nodded. Perfectly consistent with his conduct in the whorehouse. "Peter, have you heard anything else of him? Any other trouble he's been in?"

"Just that he can't handle his beer and gets into fights."

Worse and worse. "Who told you that?"

"I'm not sure. Just some of my friends." He glanced at his father again.

"Have you ever heard anything about him going to the Reservation?"

"No, sir."

Harley stopped writing to refill his pen with ink. A full report to Papa would bring him around. "Does Chloe live in the women's dormitory?"

"No, sir. She doesn't actually go to school here. Her family was in town visiting friends and taking the waters. I met her at the Natatorium. She lives on the east coast somewhere, maybe South Carolina."

"Do you have her address?"

Mr. DeGroote nodded and left the room. He returned with her family's address.

Ink seeped through the joint in Harley's fountain pen. He

screwed it tighter and wiped his fingers with his handkerchief. "Have you seen her since that day?"

"Yes, sir. Once or twice, but not after they went back home."

"Thank you, Peter, you've been very helpful."

"I'm sorry to get involved in this," Mr. DeGroote said, "but your father is my friend, and I thought he should know. Maybe the county attorney will let Cicero plead guilty to something less than murder."

Papa would have to reconsider once he heard what Peter had to say. It was a side of Cicero he hadn't seen. Did Mr. Sweet know?

"Yes, sir. We appreciate your friendship."

Harley packed his copybook and pen into his briefcase. Papa's friendship with Mr. Sweet had gotten them into this fix, but a true friend wouldn't expect him to win an impossible case. Papa would see.

Chapter 10

He met Harley on the street corner across from Miss Jessie's two-story brick sporting house. Catfish puffed on a cigar, with the colonel at his feet, while a string of wagons rolled past on First Street from the suspension bridge. He waved at the teamsters as if he knew them. As he told Harley often, today's passerby could be tomorrow's juror.

Harley had been busy on the case, and Catfish wanted to hear his report before they met Miss Jessie. Harley arrived with a look that said he'd pinned down all the answers. He revealed his conversation with the DeGrootes in professional detail, consulting his notes. But Peter DeGroote's story about Cicero didn't ring true. It was out of character.

"I expect he's exaggerating what happened," Catfish said. "Likely they just bowed up to each other like boys do in front of a pretty girl."

Harley kicked a rock on the sidewalk. "Peter was sincere. I'm sure it happened like he said."

"Peter's not gonna run tell Blair about it, is he?"

"No, sir."

Catfish crossed his arms. "Well then, let's not worry about problems we don't have yet."

"I got the girl's address. I could send her a wire."

Catfish let out a sigh. They didn't have time for any wild goose chases. "Got more important things for you to do. She won't be here just to testify anyway."

Harley stared off toward the bridge.

A surrey came rattling along through the gravel pavement on First Street. A teenage boy had the reins, and a gray-haired grandmother and two young girls sat in the back. They were darling, dressed in frilly skirts and flowery bonnets. Martha had always wanted a girl. When they spotted Colonel Terry, they broke into giggles and waved as if he were a long-lost friend. The colonel's head popped up, but he stayed sphinxlike on the street edge. Good dog.

"How do, ladies," he called. "Beautiful day for a ride."

Their surrey turned the corner, the girls watching the colonel over the back seat, giggling all the way.

Catfish turned back to Harley. "What'd Jasper have to say?"

Harley took a deep breath and slowly let it out as he flipped through his copybook. "Jasper said a fellow came downstairs with Miss Georgia and then left. All he could say was he looked pretty young and Georgia liked him."

"No physical description other than that?"

"No, sir."

"All right, there's a man to find. What else did Jasper say?"

"Another man came in just as he went out, older and bald."

"Dress?"

"He didn't remember."

"Did he say anything?"

"No, sir."

Catfish wagged his head and grinned. "Sunday night's a busy one for Miss Jessie."

"One last thing," Harley said. "Jasper remembers a hack

parked across the street, but he didn't see a driver anywhere."

Now there was something. Catfish studied the place where the hack must have been. "If it was a hack, the driver might have gone into the Red Front for a drink while his passenger visited either Miss Jessie's or Miss Ella's."

"Or he might have gone in himself."

"True. Or it could've been somebody's personal rig—maybe not a hack at all." He pulled out his Waltham, inserted the key, and wound it. Then he glanced at the clock tower on City Hall, opened the watch case, and adjusted the minute hand. "Let's be sure to run that hack to ground along with the hack driver who took the boys to the Reservation."

"Already done that, Papa."

Catfish smiled. *That's my boy.* "What'd you learn?"

"I found the driver who took the boys, but not the other. He works for City Transfer. He remembers picking the boys up near Houston Hall and bringing them here. He dropped them off over there on the sidewalk." Harley pointed to the southwest corner of First and Washington, directly across the street from Miss Jessie's sporting house. "The last he saw of them as he turned this corner, Cicero was taking off across the street for the house."

"What time was that?"

Harley checked his copybook. "He didn't remember exactly, but he said it had to have been around eleven because that's usually when he goes home."

"Did he remember the boys saying anything?"

"Not much. They talked about getting a beer. Cicero was pretty anxious to get there, and Jasper wasn't. That's consistent with what Jasper told me."

"Was anybody else out on the street?"

"He remembered some fellows down at the Red Front."

Catfish stepped into the street. "All right. Let's go see Miss Jessie's for ourselves. Colonel, get!"

Miss Jessie's sporting house was the only brick building on that side of Washington. The rest were mostly one-story wooden frame houses, although a big two-story frame house sat across the alley from Miss Jessie's—Miss Ella's sporting house, Harley had learned from Sergeant Quinn. The Red Front Saloon was just beyond that. The alley paralleled the river on the east and Barron's Creek on the west. There were probably twelve to fifteen run-down frame sporting houses on that alley. The sporting girls probably got less comely and the prices got lower the further down you went.

A drunk lay sprawled in the alley. Otherwise, only mangy curs had ventured out. A messenger boy on a bicycle sped by, causing the colonel to growl, before turning down the alley and almost running over the drunk.

"Colonel's leery of contraptions," he said, scratching the dog's ear.

Harley elbowed him. "He must get that from his master."

There was neither a sidewalk nor a porch in front of Miss Jessie's. They stopped in the street while Catfish examined the building from the foundation all the way up to the top of the metal cornice.

"Harley, look up there." He pointed to the pole next to the building. "Any of those electricity wires?"

"The top one is. The one on the bottom is a telephone line."

"So she has a talking-phone?"

"It looks that way."

He glanced across the alley. "And Miss Ella's got one too."

He went to the corner of the house where he could view the other sporting houses down the alley. "The others don't. How many folks in Waco you reckon got talking-phones these days?"

"I don't know, maybe one in fifty residences. Half the businesses at most."

Catfish slapped the telephone pole as he passed. Five hundred folks jabbering on those wires. The modern world was a wondrous thing. "How much ours cost us?"

"Oh, maybe several dollars a month."

A luxury for those who could afford it. "So consider this. Miss Jessie Rose's got a two-story brick place with a fancy cornice in a neighborhood of falling-down frame houses. She's got electricity. She's got a talking-phone. I don't see an outhouse, so I expect she's got indoor plumbing. And all that right here on a nice piece of Washington Avenue real estate, only a hop, skip, and jump from all the fellas working downtown and on the river."

"True." Harley looked a bit mystified. "What's the point?"

Catfish swiped his mustache with one hand. His son needed to learn that facts had to come before conclusions. Doing it the other way around would get a client convicted. "Don't have one yet. But it's particularly interesting, isn't it?"

He moved closer to the building. The bricks around the window framing were charred black on every window. "Huh."

Inside, a flicker of movement whisked by in the split between the closed drapes.

Somebody was home.

Catfish drew back from the window. "Look to you like there's been a fire?"

"It does," Harley answered. "You know, I think I remember some building here burning up in a fire last year, maybe the year before."

The front door opened and a man stepped out. Big, burly

fella dressed in a plaid shirt, sleeves rolled up to the elbows. Curly brown hair. One drooping eyelid. No smile. He was the same fella who'd been with Miss Jessie in court.

He cut his eyes between Catfish and Harley. "Can I help you gentlemans?"

"How do, mister." Catfish extended his right hand. "Name's Catfish Calloway, and this is my son, Harley. We were admiring the architecture."

"Yes, sir," he said, crossing his arms. Not moving.

"This your house?" Catfish continued.

"I work here."

"Is it Miss Jessie's house, by any chance?"

Stock still. "What of it?"

"I was wondering if we might have a word with her?"

"She's busy right this very minute."

Catfish smiled. "Mind if we wait inside?"

"Miss Jessie don't allow no dogs."

"Set!"

Colonel plopped on the edge of the street, eyes on Catfish.

The man nodded for them to follow and led them into the parlor. Nobody else was there.

"You can be waiting in here."

"Thanks. And your name is?"

"Joe."

"Joe Riley, by any chance?"

"No." He disappeared down the hallway.

"Who's Joe Riley?" Harley asked.

"Nobody I know."

The place reeked of sweet perfume, like somebody had emptied a bottle somewhere. Catfish had expected the place to be gaudy, but it wasn't—with the exception, perhaps, of the art.

There were more photographs of naked women than you could shake a stick at. But for them and the gilt statue and the perfume, this might have been the parlor of a banker's house.

There was a framed certificate on the wall. He put on his pince-nez and read aloud. "'Know ye that whereas Miss Jessie Rose, on the first day of April 1894, paid to the city secretary the sum of fifteen dollars and seventy-five cents, being the license imposed on a bawdy house, and otherwise complied with the regulations of the city ordinances in this behalf, therefore, the said Jessie Rose is hereby authorized and empowered to operate a bawdy house of five rooms for the term of three months, from the first day of April 1894. Signed William C. Cooper, secretary of the city of Waco.'"

He drew back for a look at the walls and trim. "This room's been painted not too long ago, and the molding's new."

"May I help you gents?"

Miss Jessie glided into the room with a different bearing than she'd displayed at the courthouse. She was more casual in her dress today. As a matter of fact, there was considerably more of Miss Jessie than of her dress.

"How do, ma'am," he replied. "I'm Catfish Calloway and this is my son, Harley."

"I'm pleased to make your acquaintances. Have a seat. Would you care for some amusement?" She lit on a chair and winked.

"Well, that's awful kind of you to offer us your hospitality, but we're here on business," he answered, as though she'd offered a cup of tea.

She eyed him closely. "I remember you from the inquest. Are you a new deputy?"

"Oh no, ma'am, nobody so important." He handed her his calling card.

"What's your business here?"

"Would you mind answering a few questions about the killing? And maybe let us take a gander where it happened?"

She glanced at the card and tossed it on the table. "Whose *partem* are you representing?"

"We're defending the boy accused of the killing."

"The murderer?"

"Well, folks say he's a murderer. Do I understand correctly you're one of those?"

She raised her eyebrows. "He shot her in her bed."

"You have any differences with Miss Georgia?"

"No."

"How about this house? Own it yourself?"

She pressed something on the table next to her chair and stood up. Big Joe appeared in the hallway almost instantly. Catfish's question must've touched a nerve.

"I said all I have to say in court," she said with a forced smile. "Unless you gents are interested in something else, I have important matters to attend."

So that was that. With the interview so abruptly ended, they walked up Washington past Miss Ella's. A girl sat in a rocking chair on the front porch, painting her nails, and waved at them as they passed by.

"Pay me a visit, gents?" she shouted.

"How do, miss. Not today, thanks."

"Your loss," she yelled. "I like your dog."

Catfish glanced at his son. "Friendly folks in this neighborhood, Harley."

Harley fussed with his tie, eyes straight ahead. "I'm not sure what we learned today that helps us."

"Main thing, Miss Jessie's hiding something. Not sure what.

She runs a pretty highbrow sporting house and seems well educated. Did you say she came from New Orleans?"

"That's what Quinn told me."

"Got a touch of Creole in her accent."

Harley snapped back into business mode. "I know a deputy in New Orleans. I could wire him and see if he knows her."

Now he was thinking. "See if she's been arrested. And if she was a high-class sporting girl there."

"Right."

Something, or somebody, was missing from this picture. "Maybe we should talk to the other girl instead of the madam. What's her name? Sally? Sar—"

"Sadie. But I don't think Miss Jessie—or her man Joe—is about to let us near her."

"They're not, for sure, and it's not likely she'll leave the Reservation. But I got an idea I'm chewing on. I think Miss Peach can help us with Sadie. I want you to head over to the *Evening News* office and see if you can find any reports about a fire at Miss Jessie's. Probably not important, but I'd like to know anyway."

"Right. But how does any of that help Cicero?"

"Well, there's your query, isn't it?" That missing somebody might just be the killer. "We need to ask Cicero about a few things. That supposed confession, for one. But let's also ask both Cicero and Jasper about these two other men there that night. Maybe between them they'll remember something else they haven't told us. Get Jasper to meet us at the jail in the morning."

Harley stopped on the sidewalk outside their office. "And we ask Cicero about the fight with Peter, right?"

Catfish shrugged. "Sure, that too."

Killers got other folks to lie for them. Folks who needed them. They had to find out who Miss Jessie Rose was protecting.

Chapter 11

Jasper went to the jailhouse early so he could visit with Cicero private-like before them lawyers got there. He was feeling real queasy. The place stunk of piss and puke, and the air was stock still. Drunks, likely hauled in the night before, snored loud from cots against the back wall of the cell. Down at the end, somebody was rattling the bars and jabbering about Abe Lincoln spying on him, and he wanted Marse Robert to come bail him out. Somehow, the fat ol' deputy slept through all of this in a chair by the cell block door.

Jasper knelt outside the bars, and Cicero come over and sat cross-legged on the other side. Inside the cell, a plate of un-eat food drew about a hundred flies. It buzzed like a feedlot. Cicero sure looked poorly, like he nary slept in a month, though he been there just a few days. He didn't really shave yet, but a weed patch of hairs sprouted from his chin anyways. His eyes was red around the edges.

Cicero leaned over and grabbed the bars with both hands. "Jasper, I sure do appreciate you coming to visit. I've been hard up for friends in here."

"How're they treating you?"

"Tolerable. They haven't got me pounding any rocks yet." He smiled.

Jasper decided he'd get right down to what he wanted to know. It was bothering him bad and had been ever since that night. "Tell me what happened in that whorehouse."

Cicero cut a glance at the prisoner in the next cell and lowered his voice. "I don't know. One minute I was dancing with Miss Georgia—you saw that—and the next minute some copper was dragging me from her room."

"Was Miss Georgia dead?"

"I don't remember seeing her. My head was real hazy. God's truth, I don't remember anything."

Jasper rubbed the back of his neck. "Well, somehow that girl got herself shot dead, and they's saying you done it."

"I know," Cicero said, smashing his face against the bars, "but I didn't kill her. I didn't even have a gun. You know that."

"I do, but somebody must've shot her."

"Well, it wasn't me." He leaned back. "That's all there is to it."

"How you know if you can't remember nothing?"

"You know I'm no killer, Jasper. Why would I go and shoot a whore?"

That was a good question. He couldn't figure it out neither. "I don't know. But she's shot dead, and you was there. Folks is saying they's gonna hang you."

"They don't go and hang anybody who didn't do anything wrong." He started shaking the bars like he'd shake them loose. "I'm telling you, somebody else killed her."

"Who? How's Mr. Calloway supposed to prove that if you can't remember nothing?" This was getting exasperating.

Cicero got real quiet-like and let loose of the bars. He lowered his voice a hair above a whisper. "It would help me if you'd tell the judge I didn't shoot the whore."

Jasper shook his head. "I can't do that. I didn't see what happened."

"Well, you believe me, don't you?"

"Sure."

"Then you've got to say it."

Jasper looked away. He felt real helpless-like, because he wanted more than anything to help his friend but didn't know how to go about it. "I can't tell a judge something's true if I don't know it for a fact my own self. That'd be lying."

Cicero's eyes wetted up. "I'm telling you the truth. I didn't kill her. If it's the truth, then you can't be lying if you say it too."

"I ain't sure. Why don't you just say it to the judge your own self?"

"The lawyer says I can't. He says I've got to have a witness swear to it."

"I reckon Mr. Calloway will find you one then."

Cicero wiped a tear away with his sleeve. "Aren't you my friend?"

"Of course I am."

"Well if you are, you'll lend me a hand on this. You know I'd help you if you were in here instead of me."

"I know you would, and I want to help you out. I want to do that more than anything in the whole world. It's just—I'm not sure about swearing on a Bible something I don't know's true."

"If you don't witness about the truth for me, Jasper, they're going to hang me just like those people are saying." Cicero gripped the bars so hard his knuckles turned white as cotton. "You don't want that on your conscience, do you?"

"No, I sure don't." He rubbed his sweaty palms along his pants legs. "I'll have to talk to Mr. Calloway."

"Just tell him you know what happened and can testify for me. That's all you need to say to him."

"I already done told them I didn't see nothing."

Cicero looked like he'd just figured out the answer to a schoolmarm's question. "Tell him it just came back to you. You know, you just thought real hard about it, and in a flash you remembered."

That didn't sit much better with him. "I'll talk to him."

The sleeping deputy jumped up as the door to the cell block clanged open and Deputy Whaley come in.

"Lawyers are here." Deputy Whalen nodded at Jasper. "They want to see you first. Follow me."

Jasper got up, but not before a last whisper from his pal.

"Remember what you promised, Jasper."

When he entered the other room and took one look at them law people, he knew what he had to do. He'd already been worried like the dickens, and then Cicero gone and asked him to make up a story. He could just hear the preacher back home: *Thou shalt not bear false witness against thy neighbor.* So he sat down across the table from Mr. Calloway, Mr. Harley, and Miss Peach, and he done it. He told them what Cicero had said. Right or wrong, he done it.

"Cicero's scared, and that's understandable," Mr. Calloway said. "He knows he didn't kill that girl, but he's frustrated he doesn't know what to do about it. Nothing to worry about. He's not doing anything wrong."

"I been fretting over what happened all night long ever since then. I don't know whether I'm awake and thinking or asleep and dreaming. It's just heavy on my heart."

"I know," Mr. Calloway said.

"It's like one of them nightmares I has sometimes. It's like seeing Momma and Daddy's house on fire with everybody trapped inside, but for some cause I don't know, I can't move a muscle to put the fire out. I keep hoping I'll just wake up, but it don't happen."

"I've felt the same way, son. But the judge is gonna tell you that you can only swear to what you know for a fact because you saw it with your own eyes. If you didn't see it, you can't swear to it."

"That's what I was thinking."

Mr. Calloway ran his fingers through his hair, and it flopped over his face. "There's one thing maybe you can do to help him."

"What?"

"I haven't decided on this yet, but it's something we might do."

"Yes, sir?"

"I can call you as a character witness. You can stand up for your friend by doing that, and it won't peeve the judge."

Maybe he could help after all. "What would I be saying if I was a character?"

"That you know Cicero's got a good reputation as a lawful and peaceful person, not the kind of fella who'd kill somebody."

"Why, I can do that for sure, Mr. Calloway." He nodded at Mr. Harley too. "I can swear to that 'cause I know it's true."

"The thing is," Mr. Harley said, "if you've ever heard anything bad about him at all, even just back fence talk or gossip, the law allows the prosecutor to bring it out and make Cicero look bad."

Jasper shook his head hard. "I ain't never heard nobody talking bad about Cicero Sweet. Everybody likes him."

"Good, good." Mr. Harley had a kind smile, just like his daddy. "That'll help him. You can do your part for him that way."

Mr. Calloway had the deputy bring Cicero in without his

father. He said Mr. Sweet's presence might affect Cicero's answers. Miss Peach prepared to take notes as Cicero settled next to Jasper.

"Boys," Mr. Calloway began, "got some more questions for you. I thought maybe if the two of you were together, you'd remember something you didn't think of before."

"What do you want to know, sir?" Cicero asked.

"First thing—another fella was there when you arrived. Came down the stairs with Miss Georgia and left. What'd he look like?"

Jasper looked at Cicero.

"I didn't really see his face," Cicero said.

"Me neither," Jasper added.

"Hair color? Clothes? Anything about his voice? Did he say something you remember?"

"Nope."

"No, sir."

"All right." Mr. Calloway lit up a cigar.

Jasper coughed, but maybe smoke would choke out the jail stench.

Mr. Calloway eyed Jasper, then Cicero. "Jasper passed another fella coming out, older and bald. Cicero, you ever see him? Maybe in a hallway or the parlor?"

"I never saw him."

He turned to Jasper. "Say anything to you as he passed?"

Jasper tried to picture the man, but he passed him in a hurry to get out. "No, sir. He looked my way, but—" Hang on, there was something, wasn't there? He looked up. "I think maybe he winked at me. It was odd-like."

Mr. Calloway glanced at Mr. Harley and back at Jasper. "Winked at you?"

"Yes, sir."

"Did he smile when he winked?" Mr. Harley asked.

"No, sir. Just winked."

"That's peculiar," Mr. Calloway said.

He and Mr. Harley exchanged looks again. It was hard to stay calm when these men were talking between themselves with no words.

"Here's what I want you to do for me, Jasper," Mr. Calloway said. "Waco's not that big a place, and this fella probably lives somewhere within a mile or so of where we are right now. I want you to keep an eye peeled for him everywhere you go, especially on the trolleys and on the sidewalks. Can you do that?"

That was easy. Relief washed down the back of his neck. "Yes, sir, I sure can."

"Good. Let me move on to some other things. Either of you see any bad blood between Miss Georgia and the other girls?"

"No, sir. Not as I can recollect," Cicero replied. "What exactly have you got in mind?"

"Miss Georgia get along with Miss Sadie?"

"She sure did," Cicero said. "You could tell they were friends."

Jasper nodded in agreement. They'd been real nice ladies.

"How about Miss Jessie? Miss Georgia worked for her. Look like they were on good terms?"

"Yes, sir," Cicero answered, "from what I could see."

"I didn't see no bad blood," Jasper agreed.

Mr. Calloway said to Cicero, "Jasper told us he saw a hack parked on the street outside Miss Jessie's. You see it?"

"No, sir. I don't remember seeing a hack at all."

Mr. Harley raised a hand from his papers. "I have a question." He glanced through his book and then addressed Cicero. "Do you know Peter DeGroote?"

"I sure do. He's a little older but goes to Baylor too."

"Did you ever get in a fight with him?"

"No, sir, not as I recall."

"Maybe after a debate? He and a girl were having a picnic?"

Cicero's eyes got bigger, and he nodded. "I do remember debating him. He whipped me good. And I remember seeing him and a girl afterward."

"Did you get in an argument with him?" Mr. Harley asked.

"No, sir, I didn't. We're friends."

Mr. Harley glanced at Mr. Calloway, who didn't look back.

"Cicero, you don't remember anything that happened upstairs, and Jasper wasn't there," Mr. Calloway said, leaning back and shaking his head. "We're gonna have a hard time putting on any kind of case for you."

"Yes, sir. I wish there was something I could say."

Mr. Calloway stood up and paced around the small room. He went to the door and told the deputy they were almost done. Then he leaned back against the wall.

"One thing we can do is call some character witnesses. I've already mentioned this to Jasper."

"What's a character witness?" Cicero asked.

Mr. Harley explained it was somebody familiar with Cicero's reputation—what people said about him. "In a case like this, we can call a witness to say you've got a good reputation in town as a peaceful person, not someone who's violent by nature."

"Well, I sure have a good reputation, sir," Cicero said. "Just ask anybody."

"We'd call somebody knows you well," Mr. Calloway said. "Maybe respected folks at Baylor. You think of anybody there who'd stand up for your character?"

"I expect my professors would. They all like me. Professor Perkins sure would."

"That's good. The state gets to cross-examine the character witness to show he hasn't heard everything folks are saying about you—hearing only the good and not the bad, if you follow me."

This thing was going to work out after all. Jasper spoke up with confidence. "I get what you're saying, sir, but there isn't any bad. Cicero's a stand-up fella."

But Mr. Harley kept pressing Cicero. "So for example, Captain Blair would be permitted under the law to ask the character witness if he'd heard anything at all, and he could bring up specific things he thought had happened. The law calls them prior bad acts, like fights or brawls you've been in."

He peered at Cicero. "So let's say we put up President Burleson, and he says you have a fine reputation about town as a peaceful man. Captain Blair could then ask him, 'President Burleson, have you heard Cicero Sweet got in a fight with one of his classmates?'"

"I haven't ever done that," Cicero protested.

"Just an example of what could happen," Mr. Calloway said. "Harley's not saying you did."

Cicero nodded.

Mr. Calloway looked stern. "So what we need to know, Cicero—and I ask you to search your memory and be sure about it—is there any violence in your past of any kind?"

"No, sir. Never."

"Never got in any shoving spats while you've been at Baylor?"

"No, sir. Not a one."

"Are you sure?" Mr. Harley asked.

Cicero exchanged a puzzled look with Jasper. "I'm damn sure. Don't you believe me?"

"We do," Mr. Calloway replied, "but we have to be careful about this. If there's something bad, it wouldn't be admissible in evidence unless we call a character witness to support you. But then it'd come into evidence to impeach your character witness."

Cicero shook his head like a bull in a hay barn. "There isn't anything like that. Honest."

"All right, then," Mr. Calloway said. "Harley, why don't you talk to Professor Perkins and see if he'll testify for us?"

"Right."

"Cicero, one last thing."

"Yes, sir."

"The county attorney told me you confessed guilt to somebody."

Cicero shoved his chair back from the table. "That's a lie! I did no such thing."

"You know why somebody'd make up such a thing?"

"No, sir. Who is it claims I did that?"

"He wouldn't tell me."

Cicero folded his arms. "Well, sir, he's not being honest with you then. God's truth."

"Papa," Mr. Harley asked, "do you plan to call Cicero to the witness stand?"

Mr. Calloway looked back and forth between the two boys at the table, considering. "That's a hard question. I'm glad you mentioned it. I'm not so sure we'd gain much, since Cicero can't remember anything. Might just be putting him up for Blair to punch at."

"I can say I didn't do it," Cicero said to Mr. Calloway. He turned to Mr. Harley. "Because I didn't."

"Not if you don't really remember what happened upstairs," Mr. Calloway said.

"I could say it anyway. And Jasper could back me up." He looked at Jasper like he should jump in and help.

Jasper slouched and looked away.

"No, son, I won't have you commit perjury."

The deputy appeared at the door and took Cicero back to his cell. The lawyers pushed their chairs back from the table. Jasper looked questioningly at Mr. Calloway.

"Thank you, son, you've been real helpful here today," Mr. Calloway said. He turned to Miss Peach. "Now then. Didn't you tell me you took a drama class at Baylor?"

"Well, actually, it was elocution. But I did perform several public recitals." She looked puzzled. "Why?"

"Elocution, huh?" He grinned. "I expect that's close enough."

"For what?"

"A performance, Miss Peach. It's time for a little performance."

Chapter 12

After their jail visit, Miss Peach returned to the office with Mr. Harley to close up. It was dark when they finished, and he suggested it would be better if she didn't ride her bicycle home. She boarded with Mr. and Mrs. Sparks at Tenth and Columbus, too far to walk. He offered her a ride.

She turned over her thoughts about her assignment for tomorrow as she sat in the carriage waiting for Harley to unhitch the horse from the post. Most of her job was clerical, but sometimes Mr. Calloway entrusted her with more important tasks—a "performance," as he called it this time. It was more like spying, really, and actually quite thrilling. If Mother knew she was doing such things, she would've insisted that Father drag her back to Eulogy and lock her in her bedroom.

Mr. Calloway had asked her to find out everything she could about Miss Jessie's operation and the bald man, in particular. He told her to go to Miss Jessie's under a guise. He'd suggested a perfume peddler, but that was silly. Men had no idea at all. She'd already devised a ruse and played it out in her mind several times.

She examined the address Harley had written down on the back of his calling card: the corner of Washington and First Street. Not far at all. She would ride her new Victor Flyer there— perfect. No need for Harley to drive her. They'd seen him before, anyway, and he'd be recognized. This way, they'd think she'd ridden the department store delivery bicycle.

Harley climbed in and took the reins. "Walk on!"

The carriage lurched forward.

She flipped the calling card over before putting it away. "'*Audi alteram partem.*' He wants me to go hear what the other side has to say."

"He's all about hearing the other side of things."

Mr. Calloway also kept that old Latin expression on top of his office desk. She'd never considered why. "He's written it everywhere."

"Literally carved it in stone."

She waited for him to explain that, but he didn't. "Why's it so important to him?"

"It's a long story."

"I'd like to hear it. We've some distance to go."

He glanced at her and nodded. "You've probably already noticed this, but most of our clients in criminal cases are guilty. They're generally not the kind of people you'd be proud to know. It's the nature of the criminal law practice. I think he likes to remind himself why he does it so he can keep going when it gets hard. Most people just don't understand it."

She'd felt funny herself about helping some of their clients. "What do you mean?"

"It goes back to when I was in college. A man named Roberto Nuñez killed an elderly man in broad daylight on the town square with twenty or so people watching. He got drunk on tequila and started shooting up town. An old gentleman was just coming out of a barber shop and took a bullet in the chest. It was a pretty clear case, and nobody would defend Nuñez. Townspeople were angry about such a senseless killing and threatened to just string him up."

Harley lashed the horse. "The judge asked several lawyers, but none would touch it, so Papa sent the judge a note and said he'd do it. When I asked him why, he said no accused man in this country should go without a lawyer."

They came to Washington Street, and he clucked at the horse. They turned onto Washington, and she expected him to put the horse into a trot since it would be a long, straight stretch of road. He didn't. After a moment, he continued speaking.

"Word got out that Papa was representing Nuñez, and some of his friends turned on him. I was sitting with him on the front porch when a neighbor came over and yelled 'How could you defend a murderer?' Papa just looked at him calmly. 'I'm defending you, Clarence,' he said, and the man said he didn't know what Papa was talking about." Harley glanced at her and shrugged. "I didn't either, frankly. Papa said, 'I'm defending your wife and your grandchildren.' Clarence looked at him as if he were crazy. 'I ain't got no grandchildren.' Papa, calm as ever, just said, 'But you will someday, and I'm doing this for them.' The man said Papa was crazy and stormed off, angrier than before. Papa said that man never did understand, nor did most people in town, to be honest—me included, for a long time."

She shifted on the seat to face him more directly. "What happened?"

"They tried him, and he got convicted. Everybody, including Papa, expected that. He was guilty. But Papa appealed the conviction."

"Why? If the man was obviously guilty?"

"Papa said it was his job to defend Nuñez, not to judge him. He didn't think the trial had been fair. I'll never forget it—he said every man deserves a fair trial, especially a guilty man. When

I asked him why, he said it was because if the state could get away with convicting a guilty man unfairly, they could do it to an innocent man too."

He turned to her. "I finally understood then what he meant about representing Clarence's unborn grandchildren."

She squeezed his arm gently. She understood too. Her face warmed. It was as if they defended not the criminal but the entire community—no, the very principle of fairness itself.

Harley clucked and tugged the reins. "Haw!"

They turned right on Ninth Street. Night had settled all around this neighborhood. Only the clopping of their horse broke the peace.

"How did the appeal come out?"

"Papa won. The court ordered a new trial. They said the trial had been conducted unfairly, so the state tried him again. It was in the summer and I was out of class, so I watched. Townspeople were there in droves. Some of them called Papa names. They were packed into the courtroom, and they were angry, both at Nuñez and at Papa."

His voice cracked. "I watched him at the counsel table as the trial began. The judge asked for counsel's appearances on the record. When his turn came, Papa stood up straight as an arrow. People hissed at him from the gallery, but he didn't pay any attention. He looked the judge in the eye and said in a voice more powerful than I'd ever heard, 'Catfish Calloway for the defense.' It sent a chill down my spine, and I knew right then I wanted to be a lawyer just like Papa."

He wiped his cheek with the back of his hand.

Like father, like son. She smiled to herself. "And the verdict?"

"Convicted again, of course. And Papa appealed again. He argued the jury charge was erroneous, and the court of appeals agreed and ordered another trial."

"So they tried him a third time?"

"No. Within a week, somebody found Nuñez hanging by the neck in his cell block."

She gasped. He pulled the reins and came to a stop in front of the Sparks house. "Whoa!"

"Was it suicide?" she asked.

"That's what the sheriff's deputies said." He took in a deep breath, then shrugged and smiled. "Well, you didn't really ask me about all that, but that's where the Latin motto comes from. I graduated from Baylor not long after that case and went off to the new law school in Austin. Baylor had closed its own law school, where Papa had gone, thinking the state didn't need two law schools. Then after I graduated, I returned to Waco and went into practice with Papa. On my first day in my first law office, I found a box of calling cards on my desk." He gestured at the card she held. "They had my name and '*audi alteram partem.*'"

She alighted from the carriage and watched him pull away. Mr. Calloway had a way of making Harley and her both feel as though they were doing something important. Tomorrow she'd do her part.

They wouldn't let him down.

Chapter 13

Sadie had invited Miss Peach right into the parlor once she'd explained that she was there from the department store, Goldstein-Migel. So far, so good. Miss Peach sat on the edge of a sofa trying not to touch it. There was red velvet upholstery everywhere, just as Harley had described. The entire room was uncommonly tacky. He'd warned her about the art but not the overwhelming perfume. She pushed through her nausea.

Though it was early afternoon, Sadie was attired in a sheer linen nightgown draped low across her bosom. It was like a sign in the window announcing she was open for business. She wore her light brown hair up, a few stray strands escaping an otherwise tight knot. Just a little younger than Miss Peach, she was actually quite attractive despite an abundance of face paint. Her lips were so very, very red.

"I love your lip coloring, Miss Sadie. What shade is it?"

"Red."

"Of course."

"What can I do for you, honey?" A negligible coarseness in Sadie's manner popped out when she spoke, but on the whole she seemed quite pleasant.

Miss Peach made to open her bag. "A gentleman came into my department and expressed a desire to purchase an evening gown for you. I believe he's an admirer of yours."

"Pshaw, I ain't got no such admirer. You're in the wrong place."

"You *are* Miss Sadie Wiggins, aren't you?"

"That's me."

"And this *is* Miss Jessie's Boarding House?"

"Last time I noticed." She shrugged her bare shoulders.

"Then I'm at the right place. Since I'm here to do a fitting, perhaps we might do it more privately in your bedchamber?" She glanced out the doorway into the entrance hall.

"Wait a minute," Sadie said. "A fitting? A fitting for what?"

"I'm so sorry I wasn't clear. This gentleman is purchasing an evening gown for you, and I'm here to measure you for it."

"No, you're not!" Sadie said, her face showing utter surprise.

"Once I have your measurements, I'll come back with two or three gowns I think might serve you well. Shall we go to your chamber?"

Sadie seemed hesitant. "Who is this gent?"

Miss Peach fumbled through her handbag. "It's in here somewhere . . . Well, bless me, I must have misplaced it. I had a note which bears his name and address."

"I don't know no gent who'd buy me a gown, lady. I still think you're at the wrong house."

"No, I'm sure it's for you. I spoke with him myself. He mentioned you specifically. I don't recall his name, but he was an older gentleman, quite bald."

Sadie snickered. "So's half my customers."

"He told me he hadn't been able to visit you in about two weeks. He said something about a friend of yours dying the night he was here, and he wanted to visit you again when things settled down. He said you were upset about your friend, and he wanted to give you a gift to make you feel better."

"You mean when Georgia . . ."

"That's it, I recall now he mentioned the name Georgia."

"Let me check." Sadie went to a ledger book on a table in the parlor and flipped through it. "Oh, was it Winky-Blinky?"

"Excuse me? Winky-Blinky?"

"Well, his name's supposed to be Bill. At least that's what he calls himself when he makes an appointment." She pointed to the ledger. "We just call him Winky-Blinky."

Miss Peach put a hand over her mouth. "Why?"

"That's what he does. His right eye blinks and blinks and blinks, like he's got something in it." She laughed. "Then it stops blinking, and his left eye winks one time. It's an affliction is what it is. He does that over and over if you talk to him much, so I don't talk. I shut my eyes when we're getting acquainted"—she laughed again—"'cause I don't want to watch all that winking and blinking up close. But anyway, that's what we call him."

This had to be the same bald man that Jasper said winked at him. This was great progress.

Sadie came back and sat down next to Miss Peach. "So Winky-Blinky's buying me a gown. Ain't that something?"

Miss Peach couldn't tell whether the look on Sadie's face was delight or disgust, so she smiled anyway. "I believe him to be quite fond of you, miss. Let's see, I think he said he's in real estate, isn't he?"

"Real estate? Not that I know of. He's a drummer of some kind. Don't know what he sells—never pays cash here anyway. Miss Jessie just writes him down in her book. But like I said, I didn't encourage much talking."

"A salesman? Maybe so. Shall we go to your room now?"

They went down a hallway to Miss Sadie's bedroom.

Thankfully, neither Miss Jessie nor anyone else were around.

Miss Peach kept up the small talk as she measured Sadie. "You're a very nice person, Sadie, and I'm so pleased to make your acquaintance."

"Well, you know how I make my wages, don't you?"

"One has to work, right? I'm sure it's thrilling to do what you do."

Sadie's face showed it wasn't. "You think I like this life?"

"If you don't enjoy it, why do you do it?"

She laughed. "You ever hungry, lady?"

The only way she would gain Sadie's confidence was by playing along. "Sometimes."

"What do you do?"

"Well, I have a meal." She stretched a cloth tape measure around Sadie's waist.

"How you get food?"

"I buy it."

"So you got money to buy food?"

She wrote down a measurement and then looked up at Sadie. "I see what you're getting at. But why don't you just do something else?"

Sadie laughed even louder. "Listen, when *you* get hungry, you work. You go to that fancy department store and sell dresses and such to other fine ladies." She tossed her hand in the air. "You sell your clothes to whoever wants them. But for me, I sell the only thing I got people will pay money for."

Miss Peach made a show of concern. But it was genuine. "Don't you have family?"

"Not much of one," Sadie said with a snicker.

"What do you mean?"

"My daddy died when I was young, and Momma married a

goddamned good-for-nothing. He beat me, and he took me whenever he got tired of Momma. He had boys from some other damn woman, and they was mean and trashy, and they took me too."

"Oh, my. How old were you?"

"Thirteen."

"I'm so sorry." She truly was. "What'd you do?"

"I just went along with it till I couldn't no more, and then I run off one night."

"I had no idea. How long have you been with Miss Jessie?"

"A year."

She was startled by a knock at the door and a husky male voice. "Miss Sadie?"

"Come on in," Sadie said.

The door opened just enough for Big Joe to lean in. "You got a gentleman waiting on you." He eyed Miss Peach.

"Tell him I'll be there in a minute."

"Yes'm."

Joe didn't leave. The door creaked as he pushed a little further into the room. He loomed over the women with his thick chest and powerful arms. He smelled bad. One eyelid drooped, but the other eye crept slowly up and down the length of Miss Peach.

"You a whore?"

"Oh no," she stammered. "I'm from Sanger Brothers."

"I thought you said Goldstein's," Sadie said.

"I just started at Goldstein-Migel. I'd been at Sanger's before that." She craned up to address Big Joe and managed a smile. "I'm fitting Miss Sadie for a gown."

He grunted andleft.

Oh, my.

"Don't mind him," Sadie said. "Joe's all right as long as you don't cross him."

"He seems nice enough." She collected herself and glanced around the room. Though the whole sorry business was squalid, Sadie's room was quite clean and not unpleasant. Some things weren't that different from her own. Sadie had an ivory-handled mirror and brush on her table. "It seems like a very nice place to be."

"Nice?" Sadie shrugged. "It pays. That's all I care about."

"I haven't ever been inside a . . . boarding house before. To be honest with you," she added sheepishly, "I wasn't expecting something like this. It's very elegant."

Never mind the art, the red velvet upholstery, the perfume, and the brute.

"Better than most. No fleas, not many rats, no holes in the roof, and you don't have to squat in a shit-stinking outhouse. I worked in worse."

"Miss Jessie must be well-to-do."

"Well, the owner is, anyway."

Miss Peach's foot began to tap. "She isn't the owner?"

"Oh no, she's just the madam."

"Who's the owner, then?" She hoped Sadie wouldn't be scared off by more direct questions.

"Some rich gent owns it. I don't ever see him, just hear her talk about him to Joe. She calls him the boss." She straightened up her nightgown. "Anyway, you about done measuring on me? I got a paying customer."

***

Catfish lit up a White Owl and propped his feet on the law office table, eager for their reports. "Miss Peach, what'd you find out?"

Her big brown eyes fluttered. "I'm a better stenographer than spy."

She could even employ modesty deftly. Rose Greenhow couldn't hold a candle to Miss Peach.

"Did they discover you?" Harley asked.

"No, no, nothing like that. But I'm not sure I learned anything important. Miss Jessie was out, and Big Joe made only a brief appearance. I met with Sadie. An unfortunate girl. She's led a hard life. I don't think she had anything to do with Georgia's death, but she might know more than I was able to find out from her."

Catfish blew a smoke ring at the ceiling fan and watched it disperse above him. "What'd you find out about the bald fella?"

"Sadie calls him Winky-Blinky, but his real name is Bill. She didn't know his family name. They call him that because he winks and blinks his eyes all the time—you remember Jasper said the bald man winked?"

Catfish nodded. Wouldn't be hard to find a winker.

"Sadie said he's a drummer but didn't tell me what he peddles. She said he never pays cash for a visit. Miss Jessie just records it in a ledger."

Sporting on credit wasn't the usual course of business. Bill probably wasn't his real name. "Harley, maybe somebody over at the TPA knows him. Why don't you ask around at Post H and see if anybody knows a bald drummer named Bill who's got an eye twitch?"

"Right." Harley made a note.

"What's the TPA?" Miss Peach asked.

Catfish tapped his cigar over the spittoon. "Travelers Protective Association. Sort of a cross between a fraternal order and a trade association for traveling salesmen. Big outfit all over the country."

"They had a convention here the week of the murder," Harley added.

"Sadie and I talked about him and about Georgia's death," Miss Peach said. "She didn't act like he had anything to do with it. I think she would've spoken differently if she feared he was the killer."

"Maybe." Catfish tilted his head. "On the other hand, if he's somebody important and he did have something to do with the killing, she'd likely keep it to herself."

"Even if he's not the killer," Harley added, "he might know something or have seen something."

Catfish was anxious to hear what they learned about the madam. She was the key to the case. "Let's talk about Miss Jessie."

Harley pulled some papers from his case. "Let me jump in here a minute." He unfolded one, which appeared to be a telegram. "I heard back from my friend in Orleans Parish. He didn't know of any whores named Jessie Rose."

"Well, that's a big place. Maybe she used a different name there." Catfish turned to Miss Peach. "Sadie tell you anything about the madam?"

She nodded. "Like you suspected, Miss Jessie doesn't own the house. A man does, but Sadie didn't know his name, or at least she didn't tell me. She told me the owner is well-to-do and Miss Jessie calls him 'Boss.' He clearly wasn't Winky-Blinky, though."

Catfish sat up. A rich owner made sense. He smelled a killer. "He's more than just a landlord if Jessie calls him 'Boss.' And that explains how she's able to afford the house after only a year in town."

Harley looked puzzled. "How do you know she's only been here a year?"

"Made a call at the city secretary's office this morning. The bawdy house register shows she was a prostitute last year and a madam this year. She wasn't in the 1892 city directory or bawdy house register at all, so if she was here then, she wasn't set up yet. Somehow in one year she went from a working girl to running her own house—and a fancy one at that." He eyed them both. "Some rich fella's backing her."

"Why are you so interested in who owns the house?" Harley asked.

"Miss Jessie's hiding something, but she didn't kill Georgia herself."

"Why do you say that?" Miss Peach asked.

"Doesn't make sense Jessie'd kill one of her own girls. For running the place, she probably gets a cut of the total take, makes as much money off her girls as she does herself. And besides, if she did kill Georgia for some reason—or if Big Joe did, or Miss Sadie—they'd probably just dump her body in the river and let somebody find it downriver, far away from the sporting house. Leaving her there and calling the police wouldn't make sense."

He rose and paced around the worktable. Killers lied, but just as often they got their underlings to lie for them. She was protecting the money man, and poor Cicero was how she was doing it. There wasn't any other explanation. Find the boss, find the killer. But if he wasn't Winky-Blinky, who?

He stopped pacing. "Anything else, Miss Peach?"

"No, sir. That's all. Sorry I couldn't find out more."

"Thanks, darlin', good work." Needed to give her a raise in pay. He turned to Harley. "I expect we should track down who actually owns that building."

Harley smiled and reached for another paper from his case. "I might already know who he is."

That's my boy. "Who?"

"I found an article in the *Evening News* back in March of last year, and I copied it." Harley read it to his father. "'The three-story brick building in the Reservation, occupied by Josie Bennett, was destroyed by fire between the hours of two and three o'clock this morning. The framework of the building is a total loss, but the walls remain standing. It was the property of W. R. Orman—'"

Catfish tensed. Orman?

"—and was insured for $5,000 in the following companies: North British, $3,000; Dockery & Co. Agency. $2,000, Phoenix of London; J. H. Sturgis & Co. Agency. The insurance on the building covered the loss. The insurance on the furniture will not cover the loss. Most of the inmates of the establishment were out of the building at the time the fire broke out.'"

Some things didn't make sense. "The sporting girls were gone at three in the morning?"

"That's what the article said."

"That building was three stories, but Jessie's is only two," Catfish said. "Why do you think it's the same one?"

"I drove through the Reservation after I left the paper. There's only one other brick house, and it's on Second Street across the creek. It's a two-story too, but it doesn't look as though it was burned in a fire. I figure they cut Jessie's place down to a two-story after the fire. Some of the top-story walls might have crumbled from lack of support."

"Probably right." He couldn't hold it back any longer. "And the rest of the article makes sense too."

"What do you mean?" Harley asked.

"W. R. Orman is Bud Orman." Harley apparently didn't recognize the name. "Never heard of him?"

Harley seemed uncertain.

"He's in real estate, and he owns most of those run-down

sporting houses on the alley near Miss Jessie's. I've even heard it called Orman's Alley. I'd forgotten all about him until now."

He scratched his head, knocking his locks over his forehead, and looked from Harley to Miss Peach. He smiled. "And then there's one more thing."

"What's that?" Harley asked.

"Bud Orman's a convicted murderer."

Chapter 14

Harley settled at his desk facing the colonel and Papa, who were together on the floor, an empty bowl nearby. Papa had a cigar hanging from his mouth, and a trail of smoke drifted up until the fan caught it. Miss Peach's typewriter rattled away through the open door between the reception area and their inner office.

Harley spread his notes out before him. "You were right about Bud Orman. I did some checking in the county records, and he was convicted not only once but twice."

William R. Orman, known around town as Bud, was a tinsmith by trade but had engaged in a number of different enterprises over his many years in Waco: gambler, saloonkeeper, land trader. He'd owned the Kentucky Saloon on Second Street at the time he was involved in the murder; since then, he'd operated in the skin trade, owning a number of bawdy houses between Washington Avenue and Barron's Creek.

"Do you know him personally?" Harley asked.

"Met him once, and followed his trials in the newspaper, of course. Scrawny little fella, maybe about forty or fifty. Likable enough on the surface, but if you scratch him a little, you find a cheat. Scratch deeper, you find a liar. Go all the way to bone, you find a skunk."

Papa raised his head to blow smoke upward, then went back to watching the hound dog enjoy a good belly rub. That was Papa's way—to chew on facts until they were well digested. Colonel Terry and a White Owl both seemed to aid his catabolism.

"Remind me about the murder," he added.

Harley glanced back at the news article. "It was in '85. He shot a hack driver named Bud Houghston."

"Oh yes, Bud Houghston." Then Papa snickered. "Probably needed killing anyway."

Houghston had claimed Orman was spreading a lie about him sleeping with a colored madam named Annie Brown, so Houghston told people Orman's mother and sister prostituted themselves to colored men. This little feud went on for a day or two until Orman shot him in broad daylight while he was driving his hack down the street. The state tried Orman the first time and the jury found him guilty, but the court of appeals reversed it. They tried him again, and the second jury found him guilty. That got reversed too. The third time around, the jury acquitted him.

"If I recall," Papa said, "George Clark represented him in that case. No wonder he won on appeal."

Harley nodded. "Judge Clark was one of his lawyers on the appeal, but maybe you forgot. It was Captain Blair who defended him in the first trial."

"No, really? Tom Blair . . . Isn't that something?" Papa had a big grin. "I bet our county attorney won't appreciate the irony if his old client turns up being involved in this murder too."

"Herring and Kelley were also in the first two trials. He hired every lawyer in sight. They did a good job. They convinced that third jury he wasn't guilty."

"The jurors probably heard the judges in Austin didn't think Orman was guilty. That's cockeyed, isn't it? First time I've ever heard Austin folks utter a kind word for anybody in Waco, and it's Bud Orman, of all people." Papa paused in thought. "He have any other trouble with the law?"

"One other criminal case. It was against his brother, who apparently didn't care for the woman Bud married. This was his second marriage in '89. The brother—his name is Richard—hit the woman with a brick, and Bud filed assault charges against him."

"Assault with a deadly brick, huh?" Papa grinned and reached for the colonel's floppy ears. "Colonel, that's a disagreeable family, and you ought to be thankful you're not theirs."

Colonel Terry arched one eye open but quickly closed it again.

Harley flipped through his notes for another case. "And there's a few civil cases he filed. You'll be interested in this one."

"Tell me."

"He sued two whores."

"For what?"

"For rent money." Harley shrugged and grinned. "On the bawdy house Miss Jessie runs now."

"No?" Papa's eyes widened. "You telling the truth? He sued Miss Jessie?"

"Not her."

Papa looked confused.

"Let me back up a little. A couple of years ago, he built that house and rented it to a whore named Josie Bennett."

"Josie? You think the paper got it wrong and it was actually Jessie?"

"No, it was Josie for sure. She turned madam, but then for some reason sold her lease to another madam named Ada Davenport. In March of last year the place burned, as the

116

newspaper article said. The same day as the fire, Josie sued Ada for the loss of her furniture. The madams had some insurance on the furniture but not enough. Orman's security in the lease was the furniture, which burned up of course. They couldn't pay Bud the rent they owed, and he didn't have the furniture to foreclose on. So he sued them. Ada had moved on to Fort Worth by then. This lawsuit is still pending in county court."

"So Miss Ada moved on to Fort Worth …"

Harley nodded.

"What became of Miss Josie?"

"According to the city directory, she's now boarding in a place just around the corner from the house, on First Street."

"It's peculiar, Colonel." Papa scratched the dog's head before turning back to Harley. "You might pay her a call and see what she knows about Miss Jessie and Bud Orman."

Another visit to a bawdy house. He could still smell the perfume from the first. "Right—oh, and daylight, Papa?"

"Daylight, son."

"Yes, sir."

The colonel let out a moan about that time. Papa rubbed the hound's head vigorously with both hands, eyed something on his chin, and pulled the colonel's jowls back to inspect him more closely.

"Look at that," he said. "He's got some gray hair."

Harley laughed. "Are you surprised? He's been with you too long."

"May be."

Papa went back to thinking and scratching. Harley sighed. He was ready to go see Miss Josie, but Papa hadn't moved.

"What'd you find in the deed records?" Papa asked eventually.

"Huh?"

"Does Orman have a mortgage on Miss Jessie's furniture?"

He had no idea what his father was talking about. "I didn't look in the deed records."

"Why not?"

"You told me to look for Orman's criminal records. I went another step and looked at the civil court records too. But you didn't ask me to look at any deed records, Papa."

He knew the look Papa gave him in reply. It meant *if it was me, I would have thought to check the deed records next.*

On the first case he'd ever helped Papa with, he'd interviewed an eyewitness at his father's suggestion. When he reported back, Papa asked if he'd talked to the woman's aunt's housekeeper. Harley didn't even know she had an aunt, much less why he would want to speak with her, and it was beyond his wildest contemplation the aunt might have a housekeeper or she might be somehow important. She turned out to be the witness who broke the case wide open.

That was the first time he'd seen that look.

"Orman got burned by fire once," Papa said. "You can bet your bottom dollar that if he required Josie to give him a lien on her furniture, he did the same thing with Jessie—but this time, he would've required her to get enough insurance on it."

"Right. But how will that help us?"

"Colonel, what do you think?" The colonel opened both eyes and looked lovingly at his master. "You figure it's better to know more or know less when we're defending a murder case?"

The colonel's long sigh was likely all the explanation Harley would get.

"I'll look at the deed records as soon as I finish talking to Josie Bennett," he said.

"Have you run down that bald drummer yet?"

Harley skimmed his copybook. "My friend in Post H says just about every drummer here for the TPA convention was bald. He didn't know of any who had an eye twitch."

"So Bud Orman's our best bet at this point. After you talk to Josie, we'll pay a social call on him."

"Right."

"Not likely Bud Orman is Winky-Blinky, but we better make sure. Let's get Jasper to go with us when we visit Bud."

"Yes, sir. What do you think Orman has to do with Miss Georgia's killing?"

"There's your query, isn't it? The way I see it, a man who'd shoot a hack driver in daylight over an insult wouldn't bat an eye at killing a sporting girl in the dark."

That seemed reasonable, except nobody had said Orman was there that night, and Papa had always told him not to jump to conclusions. Especially the ones that were too obvious.

Chapter 15

Harley watched the pedestrians on the suspension bridge while he waited for Miss Josie Bennett to answer his knock. As a boy, he'd loved to sit by the road and watch the cattle cross that bridge, packed shoulder to shoulder, heading north on the Chisholm Trail. The ground rumbled like thunder, and they threw up a cloud of choking dust. There might be a thousand head at a single crossing. But it was the cowboys he really admired. They rode as though they were born to the saddle, bringing a stray steer back to the herd with just a whistle and a crack of the quirt. They never seemed bothered by any troubles.

He and Houston used to pretend they were on a cattle drive. Papa had a couple of saddles they'd sling over sawhorses, and they'd ride them all the way from the Rio Grande to Abilene. Houston was the trail boss, and Harley rode drag. Their hound dog, Mulberry—the colonel's sire—served as lead steer, though he didn't care for their rawhide quirts. Houston would tie a long stick crossway on the dog's head, which made a perfect longhorn until he finally shook it loose. They were usually into Kansas by then, anyway. Those were the best days ever. Harley told his parents he wanted to be a real cowboy someday, and Papa'd just smiled.

Now there were two railroad bridges over the Brazos just five hundred feet downriver from the suspension bridge, and no more cattle drives. Harley had admired the trains when they first came, but they never dislodged the cowboys and cattle drives from his imagination. Papa always said he didn't much care for what the world had become in modern times. Maybe he was right.

The door behind him squeaked open, scattering his memories. A woman in her thirties stood in the doorway.

"Miss Josie Bennett?" he asked.

"Afternoon, honey. Would you like to come in?"

"Sure, if you have time."

"I have time for you." It seemed like a half-hearted attempt at being coy.

Miss Josie's place was a far cry from Miss Jessie's. It looked as if she was the only working girl there, and the place was more than a little run-down. If this room was her parlor, it was about half the size of Jessie's. No nude statues, no nude photos, no wallpaper, no velvet love seats. Only a half drunk whiskey bottle on the table. Like Miss Jessie's, the place smelled of perfume, but the perfume was heavier and smelled cheaper. Josie looked cheap, too.

She eased up to him just inside the front door and ran her fingers through his hair. "It'll be three bucks for an hour."

"Well, no ma'am," he said, backing away.

"All right, mister, two bucks. But no slapping, no hitting, no French stuff, and it's over sharp after an hour no matter what."

He cleared his throat. He had no interest in whatever she was talking about. "I'll sure pay you two bucks, but I won't take an hour of your time."

She gave him a worn-out smile. "You might be surprised, honey." She turned toward an open door, through which a dilapidated bed was just visible. "Come on back."

"Oh . . . ma'am . . . oh, wait just a minute." He couldn't help but stammer. "We don't need to go back there. I just want to talk."

She stopped and faced him. "Talk, huh? Dirty talk is still two bucks."

He put his hands up. "Not dirty talk. I just want information." He handed the money over. "Here."

She pulled up her gown as if she was about to remove it. "You want me to take this off while we talk?"

She just didn't understand. "No, no, that's not necessary. Let's just sit and talk."

"Suit yourself. It's your two bucks." She plopped on a stuffed chair with the upholstery worn off the arms.

He pulled a chair from a beat-up old table. Something scampered across the floor from under the table.

"Nice day, ain't it?" she said.

"It sure is." He felt an overwhelming urge to get straight to the point and get out of there as soon as he could. "What I wanted to talk with you about is that house you used to have around the corner."

"The place that burned?"

"Yes."

"You from the insurance company?"

He pressed his lips together and shook his head. "I represent a young man accused of killing a girl in that house."

"You're a lawyer?"

"Yes, ma'am."

She shook her head. "You don't look much like one. All the lawyers I ever seen is old and fat."

"Yes, ma'am. There's quite a few like that."

She got up and went to the table to retrieve the whiskey

bottle. "I heard about that killing." She took a swig directly from the bottle and extended it to him, but he declined. She fell back into the chair and took another drink. "That killing don't matter much to me, but I hope your client hangs."

"Well, we don't believe he did it."

"Sure, that's what they say most every time. I seen a killer or two."

"Yes, ma'am." The rat crawled on top of an old sofa behind her. It darted across and then hopped onto the cushion. "Well, anyway, do you know Miss Jessie Rose?"

She laughed as if that were the funniest thing she'd ever heard. It was the first time she'd displayed any spirit.

Maybe he was getting somewhere.

"Does that mean you do or you don't know her?"

"Oh, I know that thieving, lying, goddamned French bitch-whore." She slammed down another drink of whiskey. "I sure do."

"So you don't much care for her?"

She smirked. "How'd you know?"

"Can you tell me why?"

"'Cause I just don't," she said, her rancor building.

"I see. What can you tell me about her?"

"She's a thieving, lying, goddamned French bitch-whore."

He nodded.

"Oh, and one more thing I can tell you," she said and took another swig. "I don't like her much."

"I think I understand. How about Miss Georgia Gamble? You know her?"

She wiped her mouth with her arm, then belched. "Met her, that's all. Nice girl who didn't deserve what happened to her."

"Can you tell me anything about her?"

She belched again. "Nope."

"How about a girl named Sadie?"

"I know six whores named Sadie."

"This one works for Miss Jessie."

"Don't know her."

"Do you happen to know a man who works for Jessie called Big Joe?"

She looked surprised. "Big Joe still working there? Well, ain't that something."

"So you know him?"

She nodded and smiled. "He worked for me when I ran that house. Big Joe's a good man."

"What's his last name?"

"Joe."

"I see."

She crossed her arms. "I'll say this, mister. If a customer shot a whore in a house Big Joe worked at, that customer wouldn't be alive today."

"Why's that?"

"Big Joe takes care of the girls. I'm surprised he didn't kill your boy."

"My client was passed out drunk. We think another man was there, though, and he was the one who did it."

"Did you find his dead body floating in the creek?"

"No."

Josie nodded and guzzled the whiskey. It splashed onto her face and neck. She absentmindedly dabbed at her amber-stained gown. "Then there wasn't no other man."

"I see. Let me ask you about something else." The stench of cheap whiskey was beginning to overpower the other odors. He felt queasy. "You leased that house from Bud Orman, didn't you?"

Her expression changed. "What's that got to do with the murder?"

"I'm not sure it does. We think Bud Orman might be involved somehow."

"It wouldn't surprise me none," she laughed.

"Yes, ma'am. Why's that?"

"That goddamned son of a bitch was always mad at the whores because they didn't turn more."

"He was mad at the whores? You mean, when you were there?"

She screwed up her face. "He's always mad at his whores because they don't work hard enough to suit him."

"If Orman shot her, and Big Joe was—"

"Big Joe works for the boss man."

"So Big Joe wouldn't protect the whores from Orman?"

"I told you Bud's a goddamned son of a bitch."

"Sounds as though you don't care much for him."

"You're a smart fellow, ain't you?" Her sarcasm intensified with every slug of whiskey.

"What can you tell me about him?"

She set the whiskey down. "All right, I think you've about got your two bucks' worth. I don't need no more trouble from Bud Orman. Nice to see you, honey." She headed to the front door and opened it for him. "Come back for a frolic sometime when you're feeling more frisky."

"But—"

She shoved him out and slammed the door.

Orman had a powerful effect on people. Was Papa right about him?

Chapter 16

Jasper wasn't sure exactly what it was Mr. Calloway wanted to know, but he'd arrived at the law office as requested. Miss Peach said her boss was out but would be back soon, so he stepped outside to wait. Fresh air always suited him better, even on a warm day. He found a spot in the shade on the street corner by the alley, settled down on the curb, and propped his back against a light pole, sipping a bottle of sody water.

The Garland Opera House was on the other side of Fourth Street and across the alley from it was the Artesian Bottling Company. There wasn't no opera going on, but there was plenty of sody water loaded onto a wagon with a sign in big letters: DR. PEPPER'S PHOS-FERRATES. IDEAL NERVE & BRAIN TONIC. His nerves was right fine, but maybe that sody he was drinking would perk up his brain a little for his geometry test.

A wagon hauling seed rolled by with a couple of farmhands perched on top of the bags, joking and carrying on about something real humorous. They reminded him of home, which he missed sorely. The city was awful crowded, and things here was downright different. It was like a place where you could step out of your own time and into the next one to see what was up ahead. Electric lights made good sense, and indoor plumbing at the main school building had sure been nice back in the winter.

Telephones might be a fine idea too, though he ain't yet had occasion to use one. Ice cream and sody water was positive improvements for the progress of mankind, but there was times like right at that very moment when he didn't much care for the big city.

Life back home on the farm might be a string of endless chores, but the daily routine was something you could count on, along with Momma's meals. He didn't mind chopping wood, really. Or plowing. Picking cotton in the summer was work—made your hands raw and your back sore—but there was always fishing to look forward to. At least he'd be home for harvest in the summer by the time the cicadas started singing. No better napping than in the shade of the front porch after picking cotton all day, when the cicadas would sing a body to sleep. He'd wake up to the smell of Momma's supper afterward.

An old cowboy come along on a fine-looking mare, ambling down Fourth Street in no apparent hurry, hunched over the saddle horn like he'd had a hard ride into town. He was whistling a mournful tune—sounded like "Lorena," maybe. Grandpa whistled that too. Pretty soon, the trolley come clanking along in the cowboy's tracks. Or maybe he was on theirs. The trolley conductor honked his horn and the cowboy eased his horse off the tracks, still whistling, never looking up.

A hack come rolling up Fourth and turned in front of Jasper into the alley. The passenger in the back seat, a woman in a fancy wide-brimmed hat with flowers and bows, turned her head and looked straight at him as the hack passed.

Land o' Goshen, it was Miss Jessie!

She made no expression, didn't say howdy neither, and then the hack was on down the alley. It stopped under a big iron walking bridge that crossed over the alley from the second story of one building to another across the way. Nobody got out. Pretty soon, a man come out of the building to the right and went up to the carriage. He went back inside, and it wasn't long before another man come out. This one sure looked like that bald fella from the whorehouse. He carried a big square box to the hack and handed it to Miss Jessie. The man went back inside, and the hack rolled on off.

Jasper jumped up and ran back to Mr. Calloway's office.

"Miss Peach, I'm sorry to be a bother," he called through the open door, "but I just seen that bald man."

"Which bald man, Jasper?" she asked with a beautiful smile.

"The one I seen going into Miss Jessie's on the night all that business with Cicero happened."

"Are you sure?"

"Looked just like him. I'll admit a fair distance betwixt us, but bald sticks out."

She headed for the door. "Show me where he is."

He led her down the alley until they stood just under the overhead passageway and pointed to the alley door. "I think he come out of there."

She stepped back to the edge of the alley and looked to her right, counting doors with her finger. "One, two, three, four. It must be Sanger Brothers."

"Who's they?"

"The big dry goods store. The storefront's on Austin Avenue." She took off down the alley. "Follow me, Jasper."

"Yes, ma'am."

She led him around the corner and onto Austin Avenue, then slowed to a stroll. They passed a bookstore and a small grocery before she stopped in front of a window display. The sign painted on the window said in big gold letters SANGER BROTHERS and under that DRY GOODS, CLOTHING, SHOES, MILLINERY, LADIES SUITS AND WRAPS, FANCY GOODS. There was a dry goods store back in Flatonia, too, where he went with Momma once a month to stock up on things they needed, but that one didn't have nothing like this store. In the Sanger window, a statue of a woman stood all dressed up in a fancy dress with a big floppy hat covered in flowers. She looked downright real. Some other women's clothes, all fancy, hung on racks.

"I don't want that man to leave before Mr. Calloway or Mr. Harley gets back," Miss Peach said. "We're going inside to find him. I want you to point him out when you see him."

"Yes, ma'am."

He followed her inside. He ain't never seen so many clothes and shoes and such. They walked through a long, narrow room with shelves on both walls. The shelves had stacks of boxes, must've been hundreds. In front of the shelves was high-back bench seats and stools. A few ladies sat there while men put shoes on their feet. Open boxes was on the floor all around 'em. There was enough shoes in that room for every woman in Fayette County to have three pair. Momma wouldn't believe her eyes.

"Jasper, look at the men, not the shoes," Miss Peach said under her breath.

None of 'em was bald. Miss Peach led the way through a door into another big room. Long wooden counters had boxes stacked on top. A sign said HOSIERY, whatever that was. Men and ladies walked around, helping folks doing their shopping. He looked at all them men, but the bald fella wasn't nowhere. They checked all the first-floor rooms, but no bald man.

She led the way to an elevator. "Let's go to the second floor."

"I ain't never been in no elevator, ma'am. I always just take the stairs."

She went in anyway, and he followed.

"Good afternoon," she said to the elevator operator. "Two, please."

"Yes, ma'am."

"Should I hold on to something?" Jasper asked.

She smiled. "No, it's an easy ride."

The elevator arrived after a spell. The operator pulled the door open and said through her nose, "Second floor, millinery department."

Ladies was trying on hats in there. Then he spotted the man.

"That's him!" He nodded toward a bald man wearing a gray suit and bow tie. He was talking to a lady looking at a hat.

"Are you sure?"

"Yes, ma'am, that's him."

"Wait here," she whispered, "and don't be obvious watching us."

"Yes, ma'am." He started whistling Yankee Doodle, so he wouldn't be obvious.

She walked slow-like toward the man, pausing every few feet to look at a hat. She stopped and picked one up. She put it on her head and adjusted it two or three times. Then she walked over to a mirror on the counter near the bald man, who was still with the other customer. She tugged it lower on one side and turned her head different ways while looking in the mirror. It either fit or it don't. Maybe she was just stalling.

The other customer thanked the bald fella and left with her new hat. The bald man spotted Miss Peach and went up to her.

Jasper eased closer so he could hear. He stopped whistling but was careful not to stare.

"May I help you, miss?"

"Oh my, yes, you certainly can." She touched the brim of the hat and tried that smile of hers on him.

"That's a lovely Milan straw," the man said. "I think the velvet ribbon and hyacinths really make the hat. Were you looking for an evening hat?"

"Mm-hmm."

"You look very nice in it."

"Do you think so?" She batted her eyes.

"I do indeed. It goes well with your lovely red hair."

"It's ginger." She showed him that sweet smile again. "I prefer a hat that shows it off but doesn't overbear it, if you know what I mean."

"Of course, ma'am. That one looks just the thing."

She turned this way and that, looking back over her shoulder at the mirror. "A handsome man like you would certainly know."

He colored red, then winked. "Well, I have served a number of fine ladies."

"It's for the soiree at Mayor McCulloch's on Saturday. Do you honestly think it's pretty on me?"

"Any hat would be pretty on you, but this one fills the bill nicely."

She shrugged her shoulders like she didn't know what she thought. "I'm just not sure. I'd like to bring my husband in to give his opinion."

She was married? Dang. Jasper shuffled his feet and tried to look like he belonged there.

"Would you hold it for me? I don't want any other ladies to snatch it up."

"Of course, ma'am."

"May I ask for you by name, sir?"

He commenced to winking at her again. "Certainly. I'm Buford Lowe, at your service." He bowed his head.

"Oh, Mr. Lowe, you've been so very helpful. I'll be back as soon as my husband can get here."

She'd tricked him good about that hat, but Jasper sure didn't know she was a married lady. He sighed and followed her out.

***

Miss Peach led Harley and Jasper through the first floor to the elevator and up to millinery. She spotted the bald man, offered her arm to Harley, and headed toward him.

The dreadful man saw her and waved. His face twitched: three blinks, one wink. He'd be jerking from ear to ear quite soon. She suppressed a smile.

"Mr. Lowe, I'd like you to meet Mr. Harley Calloway," Miss Peach said.

"Pleased to meet you, Mr. Calloway," Lowe said. "You have a charming wife."

Harley didn't smile. "Truth be told, she's not really my wife. She's my stenographer."

Lowe hesitated, then broke into a knowing smile. "Oh, I see. You have a different . . . interest . . . in this young lady's appearance?"

He deserved what was coming.

Harley crossed his arms. "Actually, my interest is you."

"Oh," he replied, his eyes widening. "In what way, sir?"

"I was wondering if you could recommend a good bawdy house? Maybe Miss Jessie's?"

Lowe's mouth flopped open, and his eyes blinked and winked uncontrollably. "I, ah . . . ." He spoke in a quieter voice. "I don't know any bawdy houses, sir." He looked around the store, still blinking and winking.

"Oh, really?" Harley replied in a normal tone, causing Lowe

to put a finger to his lips. Harley didn't lower his voice. "Miss Sadie in particular spoke very highly of you."

"I . . . I, ah, don't know any Miss Sadie," Lowe whispered.

"She gave me your name as a reference, Mr. Lowe. You said your first name is Buford, right?"

"Yes," he croaked. He was about to burst.

"She even said you worked in the millinery department at Sanger Brothers. I believe you have sold hats to Miss Jessie Rose herself?"

The man froze, speechless, both eyes blinking wildly, and then scurried off down the aisle. He glanced over his shoulder and nearly ran out the back door. It was all she could do to stifle a laugh.

Harley raised an eyebrow at her. "Papa would quote Proverbs about now, wouldn't he?"

She answered with a smile. "I do believe we just saw the wicked flee."

"When no man pursueth."

Chapter 17

"So Winky-Blinky's been right around the corner from us all along?" Catfish asked, still standing just inside the door as they crowded around to give him the report.

"It looks that way," Harley replied.

He took off his coat and hung it on the hook by the door, then peered at Jasper. "Sure that's him?"

"Yes, sir. I'm real sure." Jasper seemed excited. "You wanted me to keep an eye peeled for him, and so I watched him good."

"He has an eye twitch just as Sadie described," Miss Peach added.

As he passed behind her, Catfish noticed she'd drawn daisies on her notepad—dozens of them, all in rows, each perfectly the same as all the others.

Sweet girl. She was young, all right, but she had a pretty good sense of people, and he'd come to rely on her for much more than just taking notes and banging away on the confounded typewriting machine.

"You think he's a killer?" he asked her.

"That man a killer? Not at all." She drew another daisy, then shuddered. "He's more oily than scary. After Mr. Harley confronted him, he was very nervous."

"I agree," Harley said. "He's not the kind of fellow to strong-arm anybody."

Catfish paced around the room in circles. Not that kind, huh? But Lowe must be the right one—he'd run off like a scalded dog when Harley asked him about the sporting house. He was hiding something. The guilty do flee when no man pursued, even guilty men who didn't look the part. Maybe he had some kind of connection with Bud Orman. And even if he wasn't the killer, maybe he'd seen Orman there.

"Is Lowe in the city directory?"

"Yes, sir," Harley answered. "He lives on Mary Street."

"Good, let's pay him a call at home. I expect he's not too keen on folks knowing about his visits to Miss Jessie's. That's probably why he skedaddled."

"Right."

Catfish checked his pocket watch, then settled into his swivel chair and lit a cigar. They'd visit him after finishing with Jasper.

The colonel had been standing dutifully by the door, ready to leave every time his master paced toward the door. He ambled over and collapsed with a groan under Catfish's dangling hand.

"Jasper, let's go back to Miss Jessie a minute. You said her carriage passed right in front of you. Did she see you?"

"Yes, sir. She turned toward me and just looked me right in the eye, then went on about her business."

"Anybody with her?"

"Just a hack driver."

"Did you know him?"

"No, sir. Didn't pay him much mind."

"Wasn't the same hack you saw the night of the killing, was it?"

"Oh no, sir. That one was red, and I'm pretty sure it didn't have but one seat."

He yanked the cigar from his mouth. A one-seat hack?

Couldn't have been for hire—must have been a personal carriage, maybe even the killer's buggy.

He gave Jasper a paper and pencil to sketch it. The boy drew a buggy with one horse, one seat with a spindle-back, and no top. Didn't see many like that around. Should be able to find it.

He curled the tip of his mustache. "What'd the horse look like?"

"Tall roan, maybe sixteen, sixteen two. Didn't have no markings."

Catfish leaned forward, arms on his knees. "When the salesman handed over that box to Miss Jessie, what else did you see?"

"Nothing."

"Did she give him anything?"

"No, sir."

"She didn't pay him?"

"No, sir."

"That's peculiar." But it was consistent with Sadie's story.

"Maybe she bought it on credit," Miss Peach suggested.

"Or she could have paid before when she selected the item," Harley said.

Catfish leaned back. "Not likely. Sporting girls don't go inside stores. I'm inclined to agree with Miss Peach that she bought it on credit. Likely a hat. Maybe picked it out of a catalog?" He turned to her. "They have a mail order business?"

"Yes, sir."

Lowe was a customer of Miss Jessie's, and she was a customer of his. Catfish whirled his chair around and tapped cigar ashes into a tray on his desk. "There's another possibility to consider."

"What's that?" Harley asked.

He puffed on his White Owl. "Maybe he barters goods for sport."

"Surely not." Harley shrugged. "Why wouldn't he just pay Miss Jessie rather than pay the store? People would ask why he's buying things."

"I'm not thinking he pays the store."

"He steals from his own employer?" Miss Peach asked.

"He's in a perfect position to. Nobody would question him." He put out his cigar. "Yes, sir, that's what's happening—he's doing in-kind trade with the sporting girls. Maybe Bud Orman arranged it." He got up and paced toward the door. How could they confirm Lowe's arrangement with Jessie? He looked at Miss Peach. "How about you going to Sanger Brothers to check your account balance?"

She looked puzzled. "I don't have one."

"No, but maybe Miss Jessie does. If she does, that would explain why she didn't pay him. If she doesn't, my theory might be right. It's likely nobody but Winky-Blinky has seen her face to face." He laughed at the thought. "Say, could she call in on that talking-phone to order something? Like a mail order?"

"She could." Miss Peach looked uncomfortable. She blotted the ink on her pen and rested it on her notepad. "So what I hear you suggesting is that I go into Sanger's pretending to be Miss Jessie?"

"You're our only female thespian."

"What do I do if she does have an account there?"

He reached into his pocket, pulled out his money clip, and peeled off a ten-dollar treasury note. "Make a payment—and here's my wager that she doesn't have an account. But after you get back, whether she's got a credit line or not, call up Miss Jessie on that talking-phone and tell her you're from Sanger Brothers and want to see if she's happy with her recent purchase."

"It's a telephone," she said with a smirk.

"What?"

"It's not a talking-phone. It's just a telephone." She groaned. "A telephone's only purpose is to talk."

"Exactly. You can't send a telegram through those wires, can you?"

"Of course not."

"So it's a phone just for talking, not telegraphing."

She stood up. "Mr. Calloway, I'm your stenographer, not your witness, so I would appreciate it if you don't cross-examine me." She placed her hands on her hips and aimed a glare right between his eyes. Mighty bold for such a slip of a girl.

"I'm sorry, Miss Peach," he said as innocently as he could. The poor girl complained all the time that he cross-examined her. "I was just explaining what I meant. But whatever you call it, I want you to go check your balance before you start talking on it."

"Yes, sir." She went into the front room but popped her head back through the doorway before she left. "You know, you're not paying me enough to be a spy."

"Go on, now." He flicked his hand at her. "Scat."

The colonel got up expectantly but settled back after she left alone.

"Mr. Calloway," Jasper said, "do you mind if we have some private talk?"

Catfish wheeled his chair to face Jasper. "Of course. Harley, why don't you go to the livery and get the surrey? We'll drop off Jasper at Baylor on the way to see Buford Lowe."

"Right," Harley said. He departed, leaving them alone.

"What's on your mind?" Catfish asked.

He let out a long breath. "Folks at Baylor been asking me what I know about Cicero."

Catfish softened his tone. "What've you told 'em?"

"Mostly that I don't know what he was doing at that whorehouse, which is mostly right. It don't set well with me not telling what I do know."

"Who's been asking?"

"Professor Perkins, for one."

"Don't worry about him." Perkins was a friend and wouldn't do anything to hurt Jasper. "He already knows what happened, and he's not gonna get you in trouble. Who else been asking?"

"Professor Charlton. Him and his wife lives in our dorm. He was the one I first-off told about Cicero not coming back that night. He's asked me some more questions, and I don't feel right lying to him."

Catfish didn't really know Charlton. "It sounds to me as though you haven't actually lied, just held back part of the truth."

"Yes, sir."

"That's not really lying."

"It sure feels like it is." He stared at the floor, then looked back up with worry written all over his face. "Mr. Calloway, to be real honest, I'm scaryfied they's gonna find out I gone to a whorehouse and had a beer, and then they'll boot me out of school. That'd shame my mother and father, and I can't abide that. All our neighbors pitched in to pay my tuition."

Catfish locked eyes with Jasper. Houston'd had that same look. He'd been older, of course, but the look was the same. Eight years later and the fear, the plea for help were still so vivid.

Damned if he'd let anything happen to Jasper. Not this time.

He clicked twice at the colonel, who came over and plopped down between them. Jasper leaned over and rubbed his floppy ear.

"Well," Catfish began, "first thing is, you didn't know you

were going to a sporting house, did you?"

"I thought we was going to get a drink."

"And you didn't even touch a sporting girl, did you?"

"No, sir. But one touched me, right before I got out of there."

He smiled. "That doesn't count as being with a girl. And as for the beer, I thought you said you didn't even open it."

"No, sir. I didn't, but I knowed we was going there to drink beer."

"That doesn't count as drinking. As far as I can tell, son, you didn't actually do anything wrong. Just thinking about sinning's not wrong—otherwise, lots of good folks'd be sinners."

"Preacher Jones don't agree on that."

Catfish swatted the air. "Preacher Jones isn't from around here."

"It sounds right the way you say it, but folks at Baylor is real strict about things like that. They give us this student handbook, and it says we's supposed to act Christian all the time."

"Jasper, as I told you before, I'm your lawyer too. You gotta trust me."

"Yes, sir."

Miss Peach breezed back in the front door and clicked across the floor straight to Catfish.

"Mr. Calloway," she said, handing him the ten-dollar bill, "there's no account at Sanger Brothers for a Jessie Rose or a Rose by any other name."

He smiled. "Good work. Call up Miss Jessie right now and see how she reacts."

They waited while she went to the front room and made the call. He strained to hear but couldn't catch what she said.

She bustled in a minute later. "I don't think she was expecting that call. When I asked her if she was happy with her purchase, there was a long pause. She just said 'yes, thank you' and hung up."

He nodded. Now they were getting somewhere. "Something's up between Miss Jessie and Mr. Buford Lowe, alias Winky-Blinky. Time for us to find out what."

Chapter 18

On the way to see Winky-Blinky, after they dropped Jasper off at his dormitory, they stopped at City Transfer. Mr. Manchester knew buggies as well as anybody in town, and Catfish wanted to show him Jasper's drawing of the one-seat buggy. Mr. Manchester said it looked like a Stanhope gig. He showed them a picture in a catalog: one two-person bench seat and a spindled back, just like a wide Windsor chair. Mr. Manchester said there weren't many in this part of the country, but they were popular back east for heavy harness showing.

Next stop was the town square to show the same drawing to Mr. Moon. He spent most of his days watching the goings-on around the square as he shined shoes. He didn't remember ever seeing a buggy like that but said he'd look out for it.

When they got to Buford Lowe's residence on Mary Street, Catfish looked around for a red buggy. Didn't see one. No place to keep one, either.

Winky-Blinky himself answered Harley's knock at the door. His jaw dropped, and his eyes started jumping. He began to push the front door shut but hesitated, glanced over his shoulder, and reluctantly stepped back toward them.

"What do you want?" he asked in a quiet voice.

"How do, Mr. Lowe," Catfish said more loudly than usual.

"You mind if we have a word with you?"

"Who is it, dear?" called a female voice from inside.

Three rapid blinks, one big wink. Then again. "I'm going out for a minute, Milly. I won't be long." Lowe stepped out, shut the door behind himself quickly, and hurried away from the house.

They followed, Catfish almost trotting to keep up.

"What do you want with me?" Lowe asked, his voice cracking.

"Just a word or two."

"About what? I don't know you."

"Name's Catfish Calloway. I believe you already met my son, Harley."

"Look, I'll pay it back. I swear. It wasn't much, and I'm good for it. Let's just work something out, and nobody has to know anything."

Lowe glanced back at his house. When he spotted a woman in the front window, he accelerated his pace around the corner. Finally out of sight, he slowed a little but didn't seem very relieved.

Catfish grabbed him by the sleeve and stopped him in the middle of the street. "Mr. Lowe, we're not interested in whatever you've got going on with Miss Jessie. Unless you lie to us."

"About what?"

"About what happened that night at Miss Jessie's sporting house."

"Which night?"

"The night of the killing."

His eyes went wild. "Are you police?"

"We're lawyers for a boy accused of a murder he didn't commit."

Lowe brightened. "So you're not here about me?"

"No, sir. But if you lie to us, we might just make you our business."

"I have no reason to lie. What do you want to know?"

"You went to Miss Jessie's that night, didn't you?"

Lowe's face reddened. "I did."

"Where'd you tell your wife you went?"

He swallowed hard. "Sunday night's my card night, and she goes to bed before I get home. The game ended early."

"What time you get to Jessie's?"

"I don't know, maybe about eleven. I don't carry a watch." He started walking again.

Catfish surged forward to catch up. "You remember a boy leaving as you went in?"

"Maybe."

"Your memory better improve, Mr. Lowe, unless you want to carry on this conversation at the sheriff's office."

Lowe's eyes took off. "No, no, I remember him, but I don't know who he was."

"What'd you do when you got inside?"

His pace quickened again. "I, ah, I visited with one of the ladies boarding there."

"Miss Sadie?"

He nodded.

"How long you visit with her?"

"I don't remember. Not long."

"Ever see Miss Georgia?"

"No, never."

"Did you see any other men customers?"

"No."

"Hear a gunshot?"

"No. That happened after I left. I read about it in the paper."

"What time did you leave?"

"I don't remember. Maybe close to midnight." His pace quickened again.

Catfish tugged on his sleeve. "Hold on, Mr. Lowe, you're wearing me out."

They stopped, and Catfish caught his breath. They had the man's attention, but there was more he knew.

"Now, how do you get about town?"

"I walk. Or take the trolley. Why?"

"Did you drive a red buggy of some kind to Miss Jessie's?"

"No, I walked. It's only about three or four blocks from my house."

"You see a red buggy there?"

His eyes jumped into action. "Maybe, I don't really remember."

He did. He saw it.

"Think hard, Mr. Lowe," Catfish said.

"All right, yes . . . I do remember a carriage of some kind. It was unusual . . . A racing rig, maybe."

"For trotters?"

"Maybe."

Catfish pulled Jasper's drawing from his pocket and gave it to Lowe. "Look like this?"

"Yes."

"You know whose it is?"

"No."

Catfish put the drawing back in his coat pocket. "You know Bud Orman?"

"No."

He didn't seem to. But Orman had to have been there that night.

"Did you see any other men at Miss Jessie's that night?"

"No," he answered too quickly.

"You sure?"

"I didn't see any other men except that boy you asked me about."

Catfish looked up toward Franklin Avenue and scratched his chin. "Mr. Lowe, you see that clock tower?"

"Yes."

The red brick clock tower rose over the nearer buildings. The sun reflected off the white clock face set into the gray slate mansard roof.

"That's the courthouse. You'll be answering questions there if you don't tell me the truth right now."

Four blinks, two winks. "Look, I can't be a witness in your case. I just can't. It would ruin me. My wife would leave me, and I'd lose my job."

"Maybe you should've thought about that before now."

He began to whimper. "Please don't get me involved in this." He wiped his eyes with a handkerchief and glanced around, then took off up the street again. "I'll tell you what you want to know, but please don't get me involved."

"What'd you see?" Catfish asked in his serious voice.

"There was a man. A young man. When I left the . . . boarding house, he was crossing the street from the Red Front and tossed something into that buggy you asked me about. Then he came back across the street, heading toward the boarding house."

"Miss Jessie's?"

He nodded.

"What'd he look like?"

"I don't remember, I really don't. I'm sorry. I wish I could help you, but I wasn't really paying attention to him."

"How young was he?"

"Older than the boy you asked me about. Maybe a little younger than you." He nodded at Harley.

"What was he wearing?"

"I told you, I don't know."

"Wearing a hat?"

"No."

"What color hair?"

"It wasn't dark, but I don't really know."

"So he had light-colored hair?"

"Maybe."

Catfish hooked his arm through Lowe's. "Mister, if you give me enough information to find that man, I won't have to tell anybody about you. You want to cheat on your wife and steal from your employer, that's your business. But if I don't have enough information to find that young man with the red buggy, I'll have no choice but to tell the sheriff you're a witness. Then everybody'll know what you been up to."

"But I'm not a witness," he said. "I didn't see anything. Please, please, I'm telling you the truth."

"What did he say to you when you passed him?"

"Nothing, I swear. I've told you everything I know." He broke down in tears and buried his eyes in his hands.

Catfish pulled out his calling card. "Mr. Lowe, you remember anything else later, you let me know."

"Oh yes, sir, I sure will." He stopped walking and faced Catfish. "You won't tell anybody about me, will you?"

"Tell anybody about what?" He gave him the card, turned his back on Lowe, and walked off. He glanced over his shoulder. "But you better hope I find that man with the light-colored hair and the red buggy."

Lowe scuttled toward home as Catfish and Harley walked on toward the surrey.

"Where we going, Papa?"

"To pay a call on Bud Orman."

"Do you think he was the fellow there that night?"

"I don't know anybody who'd say Bud was young, but then again it was dark. Let's talk to him. See if he has a red buggy."

Chapter 19

Papa had said Bud Orman was in his mid-forties, but that was overly generous. His face looked as though he'd been through at least another decade of hard living. His face seemed weighted by heavy wrinkles and hooded gray eyes.

His office was a repository of relics from his tinsmithing and saloon-keeping days, jumbled with sundry papers on every surface and rolled-up plats in the corners and on the floor. A county map stretched across his desk. The room reeked of kerosene from five lamps. A calendar hung crookedly on the wall beside his desk, and every day passed had been Xed off. On the opposite wall, a mounted fox head sported a miniature derby hat between his ears, a pipe protruding from his mouth, and a bow tie and winged collar under his long, pointed snout.

"How can I help you, gentlemen?" Orman asked, rocking back and propping his alligator skin shoes on the desk.

"I have a few questions about a sporting woman you might know."

Orman grinned, flashing yellow teeth. "Oh, y'all looking for a romp, eh?"

"No, sir. I'm too old and he's too busy."

A tarnished spittoon hid in the back corner near the dapper fox. Every now and then, Orman discharged a tobacco-brown projectile at it with practiced precision. *Ding!* Harley's chair, thankfully, was well outside the flight path, and Papa seemed unfazed by the barrages of spittle arcing over his shoulder. He'd be taking that suit to Hop Lee's laundry.

"This girl's involved in a case we're defending," Papa said matter-of-factly.

"Oh, I see. Who is she?"

"Miss Jessie Rose."

"Don't know her." He shook his head definitively.

His answer was surprising. Orman didn't act as if he was lying, but then again, a man like Bud Orman was probably as adept at his lying as he was at his spitting.

"Oh? I thought you might be acquainted somehow," Papa said, scratching his head until his hair flopped over his forehead. "Probably in her late twenties, black hair, came from New Orleans a couple of years back. Slight accent."

"Sorry. I know a few whores, but not that one." Orman broke into another big grin. "I can fix you up with a fine mulatto gal, if that's your taste."

Ding!

"Kind of you, but we'll pass on that," Papa said.

Orman rocked forward and searched his desk until he found whatever he was looking for beneath the map. "If you're having trouble, mister, try some of these." He held up a box of oriental sex pills. "Friends tell me they work. Don't know myself, of course." He cackled.

"No, sir. But thanks kindly for your offer."

Orman shrugged.

"You know a man named Buford Lowe?" Papa asked.

"Never heard of him." He seemed as sure of that as anything.

"Got a nervous eye twitch."

"Don't know him. Sorry."

Papa rubbed his hands along the thighs of his pants. "Well, sir, looks like we've troubled you for no good reason. We'll let you get back to your business."

He got up, and Harley did the same.

"Sure, always happy to help law."

Papa drove the surrey back to the office. They hadn't learned much from that cagey old man. Harley wondered what Papa thought but didn't ask. It would come once he'd digested it thoroughly.

He urged the horse into a trot up the long, straight stretch along Fourth Street, and his white hair flew back from beneath his black Stetson No. 1. He didn't even slow at the intersections, except when they approached the Katy Railroad tracks on Jackson.

Would he look toward the depot? Harley didn't stare, but he shot his father more than a glance. He knew how Papa felt.

When the Katy came in, they'd repainted the old Missouri Pacific terminal. It had been eight years, but it looked much the same. The carriage rattled over the tracks.

Harley looked down. *We could talk about that day. About Schoolcraft. About the trial.*

As soon as they were across the tracks, Papa lashed the horse into the final stretch. In no more than a minute, he parked outside the office on Fourth Street.

As Papa tied the reins, Harley finally asked, "Do you think Orman's lying about Miss Jessie?"

"Probably."

He followed Papa into the office.

"How do, Miss Peach." Papa swept by.

"Welcome back, sir." She eyed Harley knowingly.

He trailed behind Papa into their office. Papa headed for his desk, tossing his hat on the table in the center of the room, and Harley went to his own desk.

He glanced at Papa across the table. "Why didn't you ask him whether he owned the whorehouse?"

"Didn't want to scare him off." Papa put his satchel on the desk, then took off his coat and carried it back over to the coat hook by the door.

"Scare him off from what?"

"From lying, if he's got a mind to."

"Huh?"

Papa spoke over his shoulder as he removed papers from his satchel. "Lies hop off a killer like fleas off a coon dog. Give him a chance, and he'll lie. But if he thinks you're watching to see what hops when you get close, he'll shy away."

Maybe Papa noticed something he didn't. "He didn't act as if he was lying—to me, anyway."

"He's lying if we find he knows Jessie Rose."

"Yes, sir."

Papa sat and whirled his chair to face him. "Now, Harley, don't you think it's about time you go look at those deed records?"

It finally sunk in why a mortgage on furniture from Jessie Rose to Bud Orman might be important. Harley stood up again abruptly.

"Right, Papa. I'll go now."

***

Harley pored over the big clothbound deed books in the county clerk's office, looking for any legal instruments filed by Orman in 1893. He'd have filed a lien on the furniture if Miss Jessie had executed one to him, so he could enforce it by foreclosure if necessary. There were no liens in Orman's name in the grantee index. The grantor index under *R* showed nothing for Jessie Rose. Harley even checked Georgia Gamble and Sadie Wiggins. Nothing. He didn't know Big Joe's last name. Jessie had other girls working for her, but he didn't know their names either.

Just as he was ready to leave, he decided to check the grantor index under *O*. He couldn't conceive why there might be a conveyance *by* Orman rather than *to* him, but he could hear Papa's voice asking if he checked anyway.

And there it was.

The index entry jumped out at him: *William Robert Orman, Grantor, to J. R. Reneau, Grantee.* He pulled the proper deed book and flipped through it until he found the page. Orman had conveyed the whorehouse property after the fire to J. R. Reneau. Could Miss Jessie be Jessie Rose Reneau?

He made some notes and got up to leave. What would Papa expect him to do next? He'd probably ask if Harley had wired Orleans Parish to see if they had a record of Jessie Rose Reneau, so he might as well try to find that out first.

At Western Union, he wired his deputy sheriff friend: FOLLOWING UP PREVIOUS INQUIRY. DO YOU HAVE RECORD OF WHORE NAMED JESSIE ROSE RENEAU?

He checked back an hour later, and a reply had come. JESSIE ROSE RENEAU CONVICTED JUNE 1892 PROSTITUTION. FINED FIFTY DOLLARS. COULDN'T PAY. SERVED TWO MONTHS JAIL. RELEASED. NO RECORD SINCE.

He didn't have to hear Papa actually say it. *There's your query. How could she afford to buy a sporting house in Waco when she couldn't even pay a fifty-dollar fine in New Orleans?*

He stared at the deed book. Maybe Papa was on to

something. If Bud Orman wasn't Miss Jessie's boss, then who paid for that house? Or had there really been any payment at all? Maybe the sale was just a sham. Maybe Orman was at the bottom of it all somehow.

Chapter 20

After that, Papa remained convinced that Bud Orman was somehow involved in the killing of Georgia Gamble. He said it had to be him—there was nobody else who made sense. Orman must have been at the sporting house that night, and he must have arrived in a red gig. Lowe was mistaken that the man there had been young. Orman had lied about not knowing Miss Jessie. It was just a matter of finding proof, Papa said.

They spent the rest of May and into June searching for that evidence. Papa sent Harley to city and county offices. Next, it was the utility companies. But the answers were always the same. Jessie Rose paid the bills herself—county property taxes, bawdy house fees, telephone bills, water bills, electricity bills. No trace of Bud Orman anywhere.

Then Papa sent him back to look again. This time he wanted to know who paid those bills before Orman put title to the place in Miss Jessie's name. Was it Josie Bennett or was it Bud Orman? Harley came back with an answer Papa didn't like: Bud Orman had paid all the bills on the house before the fire. Josie Bennett never had.

Papa sent him back a third time to check the other whorehouses on Orman's Alley. The deed records, the tax records, the utility records—all in Bud Orman's name.

Still not satisfied, Papa went back to see Bud Orman, despite Harley's protests that the man obviously wasn't involved. This time Papa confronted him directly about ownership of the house. Orman said he sold it to J. R. Reneau, but he never met Reneau in person. His son had handled everything for him. He didn't even know Reneau was a woman. No, he insisted, he didn't know if J. R. was actually Jessie Rose.

He finally got testy when Papa just wouldn't take no for an answer. "I wouldn't know this Jessie Rose woman if she kissed me on the ass. Now get the hell out of my office."

Far from being satisfied, Papa became more suspicious than ever. He sent Harley back to the county clerk to see whether it was Orman himself or his son who'd brought the deed in to record, but the clerk refused to talk about it. He said instructions had come down that nobody in the office was to help the Calloways anymore. He wouldn't say who the directive came from or the reason for it.

Papa attributed it to Orman.

Harley crossed his arms and shook his head. "Why would the county employees help Orman? It doesn't make sense."

"Orman's a lying scallywag. He's lying to them, too."

"I'm sorry, Papa, but I think we're chasing up the wrong tree on this. The trial date is fast approaching, and we've got to either find another defense for Cicero or try to make a plea agreement."

Papa shot straight up from his chair and stabbed his finger at Harley. "We're not pleading that boy guilty to anything. Henry Sweet is counting on me, and I won't let him down. I'm not as willing as you to give up so easily."

That stung. Papa hadn't rebuked him like that since he was a boy.

Papa paced around the office, blowing cigar smoke like a

chimney. Finally he announced their next move. They'd try to link the red buggy to Orman. He told Harley to watch Orman's office during prime business hours before and after noon. How did Orman get lunch? How did he go to business meetings outside his office?

At midmorning, Harley parked the surrey on the next block of Fourth Street, where he had a good view of Orman's place. He watched Orman come and go. It was such a waste of time. Yes, he had a carriage, but it was a dark-green coal box buggy with a vermilion stripe and dark-green cloth trim—nothing like the one Jasper had described.

Papa still wasn't satisfied. If Harley had been that stubborn about something, Papa would have said *Son, don't be pigheaded.*

Mid-June came, and they still had no proof Bud Orman was involved with the killing. Trial was imminent, yet Papa became more insistent. He rented a second-floor room in a boarding house across the street from Orman's office, which was also his home. His instructions to Harley were simple: Sit by that window in the late afternoon and early evening and watch whoever came and went at the close of business. Just in case, Harley was to do the same in the morning hours when business opened for the day, and he should watch for Miss Jessie in particular. She must bring their earnings to Orman somehow—or maybe she'd just send Big Joe. And watch for that red gig.

Papa entrusted Harley with his old LeMaire binoculars from the war. "They've a good eye for the enemy." Then he said he wanted a photograph if Miss Jessie or the red gig showed up. Papa told him to see Miss Peach about using her new camera.

Harley was shocked his old-fashioned father would suggest the use of a modern contraption. Miss Peach's parents had given her an Eastman Kodak Number 2 pull-string camera, and she had been taking photographs of the colonel outside the office. She told Harley that Papa had laughed at the small black box and expressed grave doubts it could generate photographic images without glass plates, but when she gave him a snapshot of Colonel Terry, he'd been impressed.

So Harley spent one late afternoon at the window and again the next morning. He peered between the drapes at Orman's place, the lights out behind him, binoculars in his lap and Kodak by his side.

It was ridiculous.

The first two efforts were uneventful. The second afternoon of spying was particularly hot. There was no fan in the room, so he opened the window to let the warm summer breeze blow directly into his room. He rested the binoculars on the windowsill, folded his arms, and sat back to watch. At some point, despite his best efforts, he fell asleep in his chair.

He snapped awake to cackling laughter on the street below. The breeze had blown the drapes back, exposing both spy and spyglass to the street below, where Orman stood gawking.

"Your daddy still looking for a whore, sonny?" He bent over double, laughing. "I'd be happy to give him those Ozmanlis pills."

That was it. He'd had enough. He rushed back to the office.

Even after all this, Papa wasn't bending. Harley braced himself over the work table with both hands, glaring at his father.

"It doesn't make sense, Papa," he railed. "It's a waste of time. Orman just doesn't have anything to do with this case."

"Hold on there, young man—"

Harley shoved the binoculars across the table toward him. "I'm done spying on Orman."

"You've just got to trust my judgment on this," Papa replied.

"Look, sometimes things don't make sense. They just happen. Bud Orman's the very kind of fella who'd get mad at a sporting girl and shoot her because it suited him."

Papa stood up and pointed a shaking finger at Harley. "If Henry Sweet had given up on me, you wouldn't be here today."

He stormed out.

Harley felt pinned in place, unable to move. *I'm not a quitter. Please don't think that.*

Miss Peach appeared in the doorway and leaned against the door jamb. "Are you all right?"

"Sure." He wasn't.

"Why's he so stuck on Orman?"

Harley's stomach tightened. "I have no idea. It just doesn't make sense to me. We're just over two weeks away from trial, and we have no proof whatsoever that Bud Orman was involved in any way, much less that he was the killer."

"Yet he believes it more than ever," she said. "It's as though the weaker our defense gets, the more he digs in." She came closer and leaned against the edge of the table. Her voice was softer. "Mr. Harley, is there something else going on with him? Maybe something the two of you don't talk about?"

Harley dropped his head into his hands. There'd been talk at the courthouse that Papa had lost his touch—but that had been eight years ago. And Papa had tried the Lawson assault case just last year, and he'd been brilliant. He'd won the case.

"I don't know what to do," he finally answered, still staring down at the floor between his feet, "except pray that things don't get any worse before he comes around."

Chapter 21

It was June eighteenth. Two weeks from trial and, in Harley's view, they had no defense. Yet, Papa didn't seem worried. They were reviewing the week's upcoming appointments together when William Brann dropped by their office unexpectedly that Monday afternoon.

Other than their brief introduction at the McLelland Bar, Harley hadn't had much of a chance to get to know Brann, although Papa enjoyed his company. Brann wasn't yet forty, about ten years older than Harley. Even a few minutes of conversation revealed a man who was intolerant of intolerance, stalked hypocrites like prey, relished the persona of provocateur, and searched continuously for provocation. The *San Antonio Express* had sent him to Waco to cover the Sweet case, which was now scheduled to begin in a fortnight.

Brann candidly admitted this case made a better story than the usual whorehouse killing because upstanding citizens sanctioned the sin. On the other hand, he was uncomfortable at appearing to join forces with the likes of Preacher Jones. While the wages of sin might be death—spiritual death, according to Jones—Brann found worldly death a more compelling subject for his storytelling talents. It was clear that his narrative required a victim, not necessarily innocent, and a villain, not necessarily profligate, though a story embarrassing to public officials also suited him just fine.

It was no coincidence that a rival newspaper was interested in the case too. Today, apparently, they'd beaten Brann to the story.

Brann sat on the corner of the worktable. "Have you read the *Daily Times-Herald* today?"

Harley rocked back in his chair. "That's the new Dallas paper, isn't it?"

Brann nodded.

Papa looked disinterested. "I only read Dallas papers right before I get the dyspepsia."

"Well," Brann said, "you might go next door and stock up on Pleasant Pellets. You'll need them after you read this."

Papa sighed. "What is it?"

Brann produced a copy of the offending paper and read the headline aloud: "'The Sporting House Killing.'"

"Sounds more like the title of a potboiler," Harley said.

Brann continued reading. "'College Boy Slays Waco Whore in Legal Bordello.'"

Papa chuckled. "The mayor won't care much for that."

Nor his imps, Harley thought.

"Neither will Baylor," Brann replied.

"Who's the reporter?"

"Babcock Brown."

"Let me see." Papa reached for the paper. "Coffee's on the stove, Brann. Help yourself."

Brann poured a cup and settled at the head of the table. Papa adjusted his pince-nez and read the article aloud: "'Waco's legalized prostitution district, one of only two in the country, known by locals and indulgent city leaders as The Reservation, was recently the scene of a skin trade murder. The McLennan

County grand jury issued an indictment of a college boy for gunning down a whore who made the fatal mistake of laughing at his manhood, or lack of same. Eighteen-year-old Cicero Sweet, a freshman student at Baylor University, now cools his heels in the county calaboose, the district judge having denied bail. Locals report he is remorseless.'"

"What locals?" Papa peered up at Brann over his specs.

Brann shrugged.

Papa read on. "'A twenty-two-year-old soiled dove, known as Georgia Virginia Gamble, was found dead in her own bed, covered in her own blood, while her assailant lay prostrate on her boudoir floor, too drunk to flee. The smoking derringer was still in his hand.'"

Papa huffed and shook his head.

"Hyperbole, perhaps?" Brann said.

"Just dead wrong," Papa answered. "'The madam, Miss Jessie Rose, described Sweet as a fellow who couldn't hold his liquor and couldn't control his temper. According to witnesses, minutes before the blast resounded through the Reservation, the whore laughed at him, and that set him off.'" He lowered the paper, scowling. "Who are the witnesses to this nonsense that she laughed at him? Miss Jessie have a peanut gallery in that room?"

"Have you spoken with the madam herself?" Brann asked.

Papa snickered. "When I questioned her, she shut tighter than a virgin at a camp meeting, which I believe is generally contrary to her nature."

Brann pulled a White Owl from the box on the table.

"This public attention probably interrupts her otherwise lucrative trade," he said between puffs, "and she doesn't appreciate that. Washington Avenue, as far as I've been able to discern, is your city line between Gomorrah and Waco proper.

You have the sin sirens on one side and the sinners itching to backslide on the other. Miss Jessie straddles the best whoring real estate in the whole Reservation, and that makes it the best in the state."

Papa nodded.

"It must be one of the whores who'll say the girl laughed at him," Brann suggested.

Harley made a note of it. They'd need to be ready for whoever it is. "The madam didn't say anything about that at the inquest. They were all downstairs when it happened."

Papa continued reading. "'Reaction among Waco residents is indifferent. No one cares that this unfortunate child of legal licentiousness fell at the altar of public profit. The mayor refused to speak with this reporter. Baylor President Rufus Burleson was quick to disclaim the murderer and denounce the whore. Also refusing to discuss the case was Sweet's lawyer, the prominent Waco defense attorney William "Catfish" Calloway, whose courtroom skill as a cross-examiner is legendary. His sleight of hand has secured the acquittals of a notorious bank robber, a wealthy wife beater, and an impecunious pilferer of the public treasury.'"

Papa curled his mustache. "Has it occurred to him that just maybe they weren't guilty?"

"The reporter himself is guilty of awkwardly artless alliteration," Brann said.

"'Locals who know him contacted this reporter to inform him Sweet has a short temper and a taste for a long drink. Just months before this murder, he beat another Baylor student after drinking beer on campus'—that's a lie—'and he and his consort in debauchery, fellow college freshman Jasper Can—' God damn it!"

The colonel's head shot up.

Papa flung the paper into the trash bin. "That's the last straw."

Brann and Harley exchanged glances.

"Jasper's just an East Texas farm boy," Papa growled. "He didn't even know it was a sporting house. It's all goddamned lies. Sorry goddamned bastard's out to make six bits off two decent youngsters' bad luck. Even purgatory won't take reporters like him." Papa vented steam like a locomotive in a railyard. "And I'd like to know who's telling the goddamned reporter those goddamned lies. And why."

Harley hadn't seen him this worked up in years—since Houston's case. But he acted more concerned about the mention of Jasper than the fight with Peter DeGroote. If Captain Blair didn't know about the fight before the article, he sure did now. It would be harder than ever to get him to agree to a plea deal.

Papa pulled out his pocket watch, inserted the key, and began winding.

No one spoke.

After the clicking stopped, he tucked the watch back in his vest pocket.

"Gonna be a fight, boys."

He clasped his hands behind his back, strode away from them, then turned. "I'll not let those boys pay the price for other men's sins."

He spoke in a voice Harley knew well. It must be the same voice Papa's cavalry troopers had heard back during the war.

His steel-blue eyes met Harley's. "Come two weeks from today, Calloway & Calloway go to trial."

Papa had just issued the order to mount for the charge.

It was folly, but Harley didn't challenge him. Papa wasn't in the listening mood.

Harley's place was not to make reply. Not to reason why. Lord Tennyson had it right.

Forward, into the Valley of Death.

Chapter 22

Catfish ruminated over the newspaper article and underlined things to follow up on. Bud Orman must be feeding false information to that reporter, who didn't have the good sense to see it for what it was. Henry's son deserved a trial in court, where Catfish could cross-examine his accusers, not a trial by newspaper. It just galled him. He reached for the White Owl box he kept his trial gear in and removed the minié ball, fingering it so intently he didn't even notice Miss Peach come in.

"Mr. Calloway, here's the mail." Miss Peach placed a rectangular package on the table behind him. "Did you order something from Montgomery Ward & Company?"

He dropped the bullet back into his trial box and swung his chair around with delight. "Oh, that's the new Iver Johnson. Been waiting for that."

He tore into the package.

"What's an Iver Johnson?"

"Pistol. Brand new model, not even in the catalog yet."

"Oh," she said, betraying some disappointment. "It must be small."

"That's why I ordered it." He chuckled at the advertising slogan on the inside of the pasteboard box lid: HAMMER THE HAMMER! Then he stood up and pulled off his shoulder holster.

"This Smith & Wesson's getting too heavy for an old man to tote."

She shook her head. "Well, you shouldn't be toting anything. It's 1894."

"That's the second time you've reminded me of that lately." He removed the pistol from its box and examined it from every angle. Nice lines.

"And it's still 1894. Modern gentlemen don't carry pistols in town anymore."

"Thankful I'm not a modern man, then." He broke the top of the pistol open to inspect the cylinder and whirled it around before snapping it shut again. He held the small gun underneath his left armpit where a new shoulder holster would go, then pointed at the black handle. "Looky here. You'll like this."

She bent closer. The hard rubber grips had round medallions under the hammer on each side, and small owl faces peeked out from them. "Owls?"

"Aren't these little critters pretty? I'm naming this little beauty Iver"—he showed her the left owl, then flipped it over to show her the right—"and his twin's Johnson. You ever seen such bright-eyed hoot owls?"

She tapped the white owl on the top of his trial box. "Did you buy it because you like owls?"

"Owls are wiser than men."

She shook her head disapprovingly.

"Boys may grow up into men, but they're still just boys."

He put the pistol inside the trial box and shut the lid. "Perfect."

"You're not planning on taking that to court, are you?"

"Why not?"

"You really think you might need it there, of all places?"

"Might." He'd thought a lot about his cross-examination of Bud Orman, and Orman was just the kind of man not to take it well and do something foolish in court. "Remember Old Man Smiley's trial?"

"It must have been before my time."

"Maybe. Anyway, when Smiley's son—he was an ornery cuss—when he jumped on the prosecutor and beat him right there in court, I realized there's no place a man should go unarmed."

She looked unconvinced.

He shrugged. "Next time you go to the hardware store, pick up a box of thirty-two-caliber bullets for me."

"Yes, sir." She shot him her standard look of exasperation. Then her expression changed, and she pointed. "Mr. Calloway, I was just wondering, what's that metal object in your trial box?"

He picked up the minié ball. "Oh, that? Nothing. Just a jigger, a memento from the war." He dropped it back in his box and stuffed the box into his satchel. "How long you been with me now, Miss Peach?"

"This is my third year." Ever since graduating from Baylor. She fussed around the room, straightening books and papers.

"Have you heard from your mom and pop lately?"

"Yes, sir. I got a letter from my mother yesterday." She rolled up a big plat Harley had been examining that morning, evidence in a land dispute he was working on, and leaned it against the side of his desk. "They're doing fine. She sends her regards."

They were awful nice folks. Her pop was a reformed newspaper editor who decided to take another direction in life after his daughters graduated from college. Opened a little country store in Eulogy, a little country town in the northern tip of Bosque County.

"I know you haven't been up there in a month of Sundays."

He smiled. "After the trial, why don't you take a few days off and go see 'em?"

She smiled back. "Thank you, Mr. Calloway, I'll do that."

"Harley and I appreciate what you do for us, you know."

Her back was to him as she put a book in its place on the shelf of Harley's desk.

He went to the stove for a cup of coffee. "I don't suppose I ever getting around to letting you know that."

She turned to look at him. "No, sir, you don't. But I know it anyway. Thank you."

The talking-phone rang in the front room, and she went to get it. She spoke briefly and returned. "You'd better take this call yourself."

"Who is it?"

"Professor Perkins. He says it's important."

Catfish went to the talking-phone—the first time he'd ever used it himself, but this was important. Perkins sounded upset. Apparently, the Baylor president, Rufus Burleson, had gotten a visit from some high-and-mighty person—Perkins didn't know who—about that damned newspaper article and was now considering taking disciplinary action against the boys. Expulsion had been mentioned.

Damnation! If Baylor expelled those boys right before the trial, every man on that jury panel would know about it. If the state of Texas thought Cicero was guilty, and the newspapers all thought he did it, and Baylor believed it so strongly that they expelled him, then Cicero's goose was cooked. Jury'd be tainted before trial ever started. Damned if he'd let that happen.

"Perkins, do you think you can get Burleson to meet with us before he takes any action?"

"Probably. He's a fair man."

"Good. I want him to meet Henry and Jasper face to face before he punishes them. The president's got to know these aren't bad boys."

"I agree."

Catfish could still see the fear in their eyes. Innocent, pleading. Familiar.

He had to stop this. Those boys couldn't be expelled.

God give me the skill to save them. Don't make Henry Sweet endure what I did with Houston.

Chapter 23

The president was old as Methuselah and nary ever smiled. The very idea of going to see him in his office was scaryfying. It was like going to the schoolmaster's office back home, and he always got licks on them visits. Jasper figured licks would be better than what the president likely had in mind. Professor Perkins said the president might not let him come back for classes in the fall term. Jasper wouldn't be able to face his folks if that happened.

He took a big breath and let it out slow. He should just quit fretting. It wouldn't be so bad.

The president's office was in a big new three-story red brick building folks called the main building or just "Main" for short. It was the kind of place you expected smart folks to be, and it made Jasper downright edgy. It had them five tall spires like church steeples pointing straight up toward heaven. He didn't know if that was their purpose, but he wasn't sure he wanted God to take notice of what was fixing to happen there.

Him and Professor Perkins waited by the front steps. Just after that big bell struck, a surrey pulled up on Fifth Street. Mr. Calloway, Mr. Harley, and Mr. Sweet got out and come on up the sidewalk, talking and pointing here and there as they did. They all met up by the front steps of the main building.

Mr. Calloway said he wanted to visit a spell before they went in. "Jasper, do you understand that President Burleson is considering whether to expel you and Cicero?"

"Yes, sir."

"I don't know what he's gonna do, but you best mind your p's and q's."

"Yes, sir, I understand."

A clutch of girls come out of Main and swarmed around them. Mr. Calloway waited for them to move on. "He'll probably ask you what happened. Just tell him the truth."

"Yes, sir." Didn't Mr. Calloway think he would?

More students and one of the lecturers poured out of Main, chattering away about things that weren't exactly serious compared to the reason Jasper was there. Mr. Calloway stopped talking again until they got on by. The campus was pretty quiet because summer school was smaller. Jasper had laughed when he read the student catalog's explanation about the summer classes: "Life is too short and its opportunities too precious for earnest people to waste three of the most valuable months of the year." Maybe they didn't know July was the time earnest people harvested their cotton, and life would be even shorter if they couldn't make ends meet. A goodly number of his friends was back home helping with the harvest. He wished he was there, too.

George Truett come out among the students leaving Main. George was a little older but had always been real nice to Jasper. He did part-time pastoring at a Baptist church to pay for school.

"Hello, Jasper," George said.

Jasper gulped. Thank the Lord that George didn't know why he was there with the lawyers.

"Howdy," he choked out.

Mr. Calloway continued after Truett passed. "Have you been

in any other trouble while you've been here at Baylor?"

"No, sir. Not a lick."

"Never been to a sporting house before?"

"I ain't never been to no sporting house," Jasper stammered, "except that once."

Professor Perkins shook his head. "You *haven't ever* been to *any* bawdy house."

"That's what I said."

"Jasper, *ain't* isn't proper English."

"It ain't?"

"It isn't."

"But Mr. Calloway says *ain't* sometimes."

Mr. Calloway looked at Professor Perkins and then back at him. "Son, you came to college to be better than your elders, didn't you?"

"No, sir. I come because my mother wanted me to."

Mr. Calloway smiled. "Well, she wants you to use proper grammar."

"Yes, sir."

"President Burleson needs to see you're suited to college."

"Yes, sir."

Mr. Calloway and Mr. Harley started whispering to one another. They must be talking about his grammar. He clapped his eyes shut. *Don't say "ain't." Don't say "ain't." Don't say "ain't."*

"Professor Perkins," Mr. Sweet said, "I've never met President Burleson. Is there anything I should know?"

Perkins glanced up at the third-floor windows above them. "He's a good and decent man. I think he feels a heavy responsibility to see Baylor's reputation is maintained appropriately. He's very proud of this institution. He was president back before the war, when it was located in

Independence. Then he came here to be president of Waco University. When Waco University merged with Baylor in '86, he became president of Baylor again."

"Henry," Mr. Calloway said, "Dr. Burleson's a Baptist, of course, and so takes his religion seriously. He's not gonna be easy with the boys' going to a sporting house."

"Nor am I," Mr. Sweet said.

Jasper looked down at the sidewalk and stuffed his hands in his pockets.

"I think we just go in there and shoot straight with him," Mr. Calloway said. "I can't imagine he'd do anything that might contribute to one of his students being convicted of murder."

"Yes," Professor Perkins said, "I agree. He genuinely cares about students. And he needs to understand an acquittal is in Baylor's best interest too."

"All right," Mr. Calloway said, "let's go."

He patted Jasper on the back and smiled like Daddy did.

Jasper took a deep breath, hitched up his trousers, and spit-dabbed his cowlick down. *Lord, don't let me say "ain't."* He followed the others inside.

***

Catfish settled into a chair in front of the president's desk, next to Jasper. He'd never been in the president's office—met him once at a social occasion over at Walter Fort's house, spoke a minute or two.

He studied Burleson, hoping to infer his intentions. Stately gentleman about eight to ten years older than Catfish. Wispy white hair and beard edging his bald head. Had a chicken neck. Dressed in a black suit, white waistcoat, shirt with winged collars, and a white bow tie. Might as well have been presiding over some official event. His eyes looked sad.

"Thank you for meeting with me, gentlemen," the president said from behind his large partner desk. "I have asked my stenographer to take notes on what occurs here. First, let me say to all gathered how sorry I am for the wrong done to that young lady. Flawed as she might be, she was still God's child. Let me say as well that I am troubled by the notion that two of our students were involved in the sordid business of the Reservation. I should first like to hear they were unaware of the nature of the establishment, if that is the case."

"Afraid that's not the case, sir," Catfish offered deferentially.

"I see." The president looked disappointed. "Mr. Cantrell, perhaps you could explain yourself then?"

"Yes, sir," Jasper said. "We was just going there to drink beer."

The president's white eyebrows arched. "Indeed."

Catfish raked his fingers through his hair and shot a warning gaze at the boy. Drinking beer wasn't much lower than murder and fornication on Burleson's list of damnable sins.

"I'm terrible sorry for that, sir. We *hadn't ever* . . . been there before. I know I made a poor choice, and I'm settled to whatever you feel is the right thing to do with me."

That was better.

"And whose idea was it to go there to imbibe intoxicants?"

Jasper looked sheepish and hung his head before looking at Burleson directly. "I reckon both of us sort of decided about the same instant. We been at the revival over at the Tabernacle, and it took a warm turn."

Catfish squirmed. Jasper wasn't in pari delicto with Cicero on that decision.

"If I might, President Burleson," he said in the same respectful voice he used in court. "We all realize the difficult situation this has put Baylor in, and I know I speak for both boys when I say they'd never intentionally do anything to dishonor this university. They both feel privileged they were allowed to study here, and we can all understand your obligation to keep up the university's very fine reputation."

"Mr. Calloway," Burleson said, nodding in Sweet's direction, "when parents like Mr. Sweet send their children away from home to live and study with us, they do so with an expectation we will look after them. In that respect, we stand in loco parentis, and we take that responsibility very seriously. I can't have other parents believe we condone licentiousness or drunkenness, much less homicide."

"Of course not, sir."

"If a Christian institution cannot be counted upon to uphold Christian principles, then what would become of God's kingdom?"

Catfish nodded.

The president folded his hands on the desk. "I have no small degree of pride in what we do here. This is the oldest educational institution in Texas. We have matriculated more than eight thousand students since 1845. We were the first coeducational school in the south and only the second in all of America. We are owned by the Baptist General Convention of Texas. I'm proud that only a very small percentage of our students have left these halls unconverted. The overwhelming majority have gone forth from here not only thoroughly drilled intellectually but with hearts full of love for God and for humanity. Mr. Cicero Sweet and Mr. Jasper Cantrell are only freshmen, of course, but we have the same expectations of them that we do of all our students."

"I know they understand that, Dr. Burleson," Catfish said.

"We have strict rules of conduct." Burleson picked up two

booklets from his desk. "Mr. Cantrell, I assume you read and studied our student catalog?"

"Yes, sir."

Catfish had made Jasper reread the catalog in preparation for this meeting.

"As well as our book of university laws?" Burleson asked.

"Yes, sir."

"And Mr. Sweet, I assume you too are familiar with our catalog?"

"I am."

Burleson flipped through the pages of one of the booklets until he came to the passage he wanted. "Including, I trust, this admonition: 'All experience in colleges and universities demonstrates that the unrestrained use of money ruins the one guilty of the folly. Every dollar furnished to students beyond actual want, as seen in the published rates, or signed in writing to parents by the teacher is a positive injury to the student and university.'" He fixed his gaze squarely on Henry. "I assume no teacher gave you a written request for extra money for beer or . . . other vices?"

"No, sir."

"And Mr. Sweet, do you concede that your son was found in a compromising situation in a house of ill repute?"

"I'm sorry to say he was. He and I—"

"That being the case, and with Mr. Cantrell making a similar admission, I don't see we have much choice in how to deal with this." Burleson closed the catalog and placed it on his desk.

Audi alteram partem. Catfish edged forward in his chair. "Respectfully, sir, both Cicero and Jasper are children of God too, and I'm sure you'd wish no ill upon them by your own hand."

"Of course not, but this is their doing."

He nodded. "Yes, sir, you're right about that." He reached into his coat pocket, pulled out a small booklet that appeared identical to the one in Burleson's hand, and turned to a dog-eared page. "Had a chance to look at your student catalog too, and found something of interest there. It's in the section on discipline, and I admired it when I saw it. Mind if I read it to you?"

"Of course not," Burleson replied.

Catfish pinched on his pince-nez. "'The discipline of the university is intended to be a great literary family, bound together by love, mutual interest, and kind offices. Appeals will always be made first to the tenderest, noblest impulses of the heart. Severer remedies will be used only when these fail.'" He looked up at the president over his spectacles before continuing in his jury voice. "We think the noblest impulse of the Christian heart, as your handbook itself says, should be the first resort in this case. Like you said, if a Christian institution can't be counted on to uphold its own Christian principles, then what'll become of God's kingdom?"

Burleson narrowed his eyes thoughtfully. "Is it a noble impulse to turn a blind eye to admitted sin? Especially when another child of God suffers for it?"

"Well, sir, with all due respect, Cicero Sweet may have sinned, but he's not guilty of killing that girl."

"That is yet to be seen, Mr. Calloway." His tone of voice seemed neither tender nor born of noble impulse.

"That's really my point, sir. I promise you, I'll prove at trial someone else killed that girl. He's not guilty of killing until a jury says so. The law of this land—built on Christian principles, of course—is that a man's innocent until proven guilty." He paused to let that soak in. "My worry is if Baylor expels these boys right before Cicero's trial, it'll be all over the papers and it'll cause the jury to believe he must be guilty, because Dr. Burleson wouldn't have punished him otherwise."

"I'm neither judge nor jury of that charge."

"Exactly. I felt sure you'd agree. All we ask is that you hold off on your own decision until after the jury decides what the truth is. We feel as if that's the noblest and tenderest thing for you to do, in loco parentis, and it would bring greater honor on Baylor if no one here condemned a boy before his day in court. Even Jesus had his trial."

The defense rests.

Burleson eyed Jasper, then Henry. He pushed out from his desk and rose. "I hope your Sanhedrin is more open-minded. I will consider it, gentlemen, and you will know my decision soon."

Chapter 24

Sunday, the first day of July, was hot as blazes. The house was muggy, and Catfish had all the windows up and the ceiling fans going. The colonel wouldn't stay indoors at all and snoozed the hours away on the front porch, oblivious to passing traffic. Every now and then he'd wake up, slurp water from his bowl, and then go back to sleep.

Catfish was in his parlor in a wing chair by the open window, his waistcoat unbuttoned, his tie loose, and his sleeves rolled up. It was the day before Cicero's trial. He'd been getting ready for days on end, but he still didn't feel ready. Miss Peach had been there most of the day, helping him go over the list of veniremen and decide who to strike from the jury.

Harley joined them just after noon. "Papa, I ran into Captain Blair at church this morning. You didn't tell me he'd offered a plea deal Friday."

"Didn't think it was important."

"Really?" Harley said, as if he couldn't believe it.

Why couldn't he get over that? It was time for trial. "I turned it down, of course."

"What did he offer?"

"Fifteen years hard time. Henry Sweet agreed with me." Catfish went back to reading his notes.

"Did you make a counteroffer?"

"Nope."

"Why not?"

"Cicero didn't do it."

Harley got up from the sofa and went to the front door. He just stood in the open doorway, staring outside somewhere. "I think we should offer five years."

Miss Peach was in the adjoining dining room going over her notes. She looked up through the open French doors at Harley and then at him.

"We've been over this before, son," Catfish said. "We're gonna try the case. No deals."

There was silence. Miss Peach hunkered back over her papers.

"Yes, sir." He returned to the sofa and slumped back. "I'll do some legal research on the jury charge. We should get a manslaughter jury instruction that helps us if we can."

"Why do we want a manslaughter instruction?" Miss Peach asked.

"If the jury believes Cicero killed her, they can still reach a verdict he didn't do it with malice," Harley said.

"How does that help?"

"The punishment for manslaughter is prison, not death. The maximum is two to five years. A manslaughter verdict would be a victory, in my opinion."

Catfish took a breath. Only a not guilty verdict would be a victory. He pushed his chair back and lit the White Owl he'd been chewing on. "Well, that instruction will be in the jury charge because they indicted him on the lesser included offense of manslaughter, but I have no intention of arguing for the jury to find him guilty of manslaughter."

"But—"

"No buts, Harley. Our defense is he didn't kill her."

Harley's face was getting red. "Papa, I've researched similar cases, and I think we have manslaughter facts. I know Mr. Sweet is your friend, but that doesn't change the facts."

"I'll just have to note your exception, son."

Harley was slow to answer. "Yes, sir."

Miss Peach fanned herself with her notepad.

Catfish flicked ashes impatiently. "Either of you need a cold drink?"

He'd put some bottles in his icebox the night before, and they'd be refreshingly chilled by then. Maybe cool Harley down so he could do his job.

"That would be lovely," she said. "I'll get them."

"None for me," said Harley.

"Icebox in the kitchen, darlin'. Bring me a Dr. Pepper, and a Circle-A for Colonel Terry."

He cut a glance at Harley and put his cigar out. "Judge Clark offered us the use of his library. I'm sure he'd be happy for you to go there after we get finished here."

"Right," Harley said.

"Here's my plan," Catfish said, propping his feet on a stool and staring at the ceiling fan. "I've been holding off on a subpoena of Orman because I didn't want Tom to know our defense. Let's get one out first thing in the morning and get him there Tuesday afternoon, just in case they finish up early. I expect they got about two days of testimony."

"Are you sure we can prove Orman did it?"

"Of course. He'll break under cross-examination."

Harley stiffened. "I'm not so sure of that, Papa. I don't think he had anything to do with it."

Catfish exhaled and shook his head. They'd been over that

before too. He covered his annoyance by accepting his Dr. Pepper from Miss Peach, who headed to the front porch with a bowl of ginger ale for the colonel.

"You've just got to trust my judgment," he said to Harley. "I've been at this a lot longer than you have."

"Yes, sir."

He took a long swig of soda and stared up at the ceiling fan. Neither of them spoke further on the subject, and the silence got louder.

"Well, gentlemen," Miss Peach said, returning to the hush of the parlor, "we do have some good news, don't we?"

"What's that?" Catfish said.

"It's no news—there's nothing at all in the papers about Cicero." She handed Catfish the two newspapers he hadn't bothered to bring in.

The main headline in Saturday's *Evening News* was about a man named Debs leading a railway strike in Chicago. The headline of the *Artesia* reported Josephine Jenkins's wedding to George Truett. Whoops—he was supposed to have attended that. He'd have to make excuses to Judge Jenkins.

"The only court news of interest I saw was about Judge Goodrich getting hung in effigy in Gatesville for the case he just finished," Harley said.

"That'll put him in a sour disposition," Catfish said. "But nothing about Baylor expelling Cicero, then—that's good news. Professor Perkins told me we should expect to see Burleson in the courtroom watching some of the trial."

"Maybe the jury will think he's there to support Cicero," Miss Peach said.

"Maybe. Can't hurt, as long as he keeps his mouth shut in front of the jury."

"Papa, do you still intend to call Professor Perkins as a character witness?"

Catfish shrugged. "Depends on how things go. We'll make that decision after we see their case. He'll be expecting to hear from Miss Peach if we need him."

Colonel Terry ambled in, belched, and plopped down in front of Catfish. He was rewarded by an ear rub and promptly went back to sleep.

A tall man walked down the sidewalk past the front window. "There's Wade Morrison," Catfish said. "Harley, he's on the jury list."

"I didn't realize he lived around here."

"Across the street two blocks up. He walks Washington on weekends, though I'm surprised to see him out in this heat."

Miss Peach put her soda on the table. "He's Mr. Lazenby's partner in the bottling company, right?"

"And he owns the Old Corner Drug," Harley added. "Do you think he'll be friendly to us if he gets on the jury?"

Catfish nodded. "Probably. Tom'll probably strike him."

Miss Peach examined the city directory that lay open on the table. "That reminds me, Mr. Calloway, I found something on that other venireman we were discussing earlier."

"Which one?"

"Thomas C. Tibbs. He's the manager of a clothing manufacturer on Fourth Street, Blake Manufacturing Company. The directory shows he's also got a real estate company and is a first vice-president at Provident Bank."

"Think I've met him. Blake is Slayden's company. Tibbs should be fine. Pretty far down the jury list, anyway."

Harley spoke as if he'd been preoccupied with something else. "Papa, will I be taking some witnesses?"

Catfish shook his head. "I promised Henry I'd handle it myself."

"Yes, sir." His head sagged.

"What about the red buggy?" Catfish continued. "Find out anything new?"

"Mr. Moon hasn't seen it," Harley replied. "I've checked every livery stable in town, but I found only one that stabled a horse for a Stanhope gig. It belonged to a fellow who moved here from St. Louis, but his rig has been down with a broken spring since before the murder. It's over at Hopkins Brothers. They're still waiting on a new spring to come in from back east." He shrugged. "And it wasn't red, anyway."

He started to say something else, then stopped and stared dolefully at Catfish. He'd picked up that look from Martha. Something was still on his mind.

Spit it out, son.

Finally, Harley continued. "I know you believe in Cicero, but we can't prove anybody else shot her, and they have a circumstantial evidence case we can't explain away. We should reconsider that plea offer." He had that *please, Papa* look. "He's going to get convicted if we go to trial."

Well, Harley was young. His spirit was still brittle. Catfish had been that way once—he'd just started trying cases and lost three in a row. He was rattled with self-doubt. Judge Clark pulled him aside and counseled him that a trial lawyer had to be fearless. If he was afraid of losing, he was finished. Harley just needed reassurance.

"Cicero's not getting convicted," he said with his jury voice. "I don't try cases to lose. You can count on that."

Harley got quiet. His eyes retreated downward before rising to meet his. "He's not Houston, Papa. He's just not. This is different."

Catfish tensed. So it was weighing on him too.

He studied Harley's face. Houston's hair had been a little lighter, but the eyes were the same. Except eight years ago, there'd been terror in Houston's eyes.

"You're right," he said. "Houston's case was different, and I see the difference. Trust me, son."

"I do, but I feel as if I must speak up on this because I disagree with you. It's your call, though."

Catfish didn't respond.

"I better go on over to Judge Clark's now," Harley concluded.

"I'll help you if you like," Miss Peach said. She'd been watching.

"Thanks, that'd be helpful."

They got up to leave. Catfish stood too and wrapped his arms around Harley.

"I know how you feel, and I hear you," he said softly. "There's no bringing Houston back, but we can win *this* case." He pressed Harley's head tightly against his shoulder. "I love you, son."

"I love you too, Papa. No matter what."

Catfish stepped back, still holding his son by the shoulders. "No matter what."

***

Harley drove the carriage with Miss Peach to Judge Clark's house over at Ninth and Columbus. The judge was an old friend of Papa's. He'd served in various posts in government, been a judge on the court of appeals, and was now practicing law again in Waco. He'd written a wonderful treatise on Texas criminal law that Papa always carried with him to court. He had a large private law library at his office in the Provident Building. At his home, they got the key and some well wishes from the judge, then rode on to the judge's office.

Harley wasn't in the mood to talk.

Miss Peach broke the silence. "Your father's really good at cross-examination."

"Maybe he's got something planned I just don't know about. He sure is confident about something. I just don't understand why he's accepted Cicero's story without really questioning it. He only sees Cicero's side."

"Do you honestly think Cicero has a chance?"

He wished he were as strong as Papa. He was a rock. To Harley, it felt like Houston's case all over again. And even rocks would shatter from a hard blow.

He swiped at the sweat beading on his forehead. "I'm worried."

"It's probably none of my business," she asked, "but what did you mean when you said Cicero wasn't Houston?"

She was right about the first part, anyway. It just wasn't something he could talk about. He glanced over and then back at the road ahead.

"Looks as though we're about there."

***

Catfish shuffled into the Growlery, the name he used for his library based on a similar room in *Bleak House*. He used to retreat there to save the family from the bad humors evoked by his cases. Now it was a place of gathered memories. He collapsed into his favorite chair next to the lamp table with Martha's photograph, the only one.

He closed his eyes. So many images. Her joyous laugh. Her merry eyes. Her gentle heart—his, captured. A kiss. Their vow. Two babies. Two men. Her illness . . . The day she passed. Their bed upstairs. Her pale face. Her cold hand. Her brave, sweet smile. Her voice, so weak: *When we were first acquent . . . your locks, like the raven . . . now like snow.* She couldn't finish the verse.

"And hand in hand we'll go."

Colonel Terry nudged his dangling arm, and he opened his eyes and wiped away a tear. "We both miss her, don't we, old boy? You were just a pup." He reached down and stroked the colonel's head. "We miss them both."

He closed his eyes again. So tired. Ten years ago, trying cases had been exhilarating. Now it was exhausting.

I'm worn out, Martha.

He sank his head back and drifted from that chair, that room. A gentle wind through giant oaks. One grave. Too soon, another. Why?

A different place. A dark shape hanging from a pitiless scaffold, swinging in the breeze. Turning. A face coming around, not yet distinct.

The shape changes somehow. Nearby, another face— watching. A bowler hat, a horseshoe mustache, a blackthorn cane. The face contorts in laughter. *Old man, you just don't have what it takes anymore. Isn't one failure enough to convince you? Save yourself. Quit now.*

The face vanishes, but Catfish bolts upright, flooded with doubt. Could he be right?

I told Harley he had to be fearless. But Martha . . . I'm so scared it's happening again.

Chapter 25

Miss Peach got up from the bench and went to the open window overlooking Second Street. She fanned herself with her notepad. It was dreadfully hot and still. She leaned out the window. Below, Colonel Terry slumbered on the top step of the courthouse. That sweet old dog wasn't about to abandon his master.

She turned back toward the doorway into the Nineteenth District Court. Next to it on the right, Jasper fidgeted on the bench.

To the left, Miss Jessie and Big Joe waited. Memories of his intrusion into Sadie's bedroom flooded over her—his foul odor, his drooping eye. He watched her right now as she crossed the waiting area and peered through the window in the courtroom door. She pushed him out of her mind.

Courtrooms always took her breath away. Mr. Calloway said a courtroom was a sacred place in a secular sense. This one was imposing—about sixty feet square and two stories high, with over a dozen tall compass-head windows beneath a ceiling beautifully tinned in elaborate patterns. Judge Goodrich administered justice from a decorated oak bench against the wall. Behind the bench stood a large docket cabinet. The court reporter, Mr. Lord, was at his desk. Waiting empty nearby were the witness stand and the jury box against the far wall.

Mr. Calloway, Harley, and Cicero sat around the defense table. Her chair was just behind them next to the bar rail. At the far table, Captain Blair sat alone. Two naked electric lightbulbs dangled on long wires from the high ceiling, and three ceiling fans rotated over the bar. Outside the bar rail under three more ceiling fans, a throng of faces packed the spectator gallery—men in every row of the cast iron, wooden-backed seats. Those to the front were the veniremen.

Mrs. Sweet sat next to her husband, and a handful of other women dotted the back rows. When Miss Peach took her place in court, she would be the only woman inside the bar.

Judge Goodrich finished speaking to the venire. Though Miss Peach couldn't hear a word, she knew that jury selection was almost over. The three lawyers crowded the bench, and Harley motioned for her to come in.

She turned to Jasper. Sweat streamed down his face.

"Wait here," she told the poor boy. "It won't be long."

She hurried in and took her chair behind the defense table, where she would take down the testimony so that Mr. Calloway could quote it exactly in his closing argument. Her actual job was more than that, though. Mr. Calloway had given her his usual trial instructions: *Sit behind us so you can see everything. Be my eyes and ears. Don't let me miss a thing, no matter how small. If a juror blinks, I want to know how many times.*

It was thrilling.

A bead of sweat trickled down her forehead. Even inside the building, the July swelter was oppressive. The tall courtroom windows had been thrown open to admit air, but the ceiling fans kicked it around in a torrid breeze that seemed worse than no breeze at all. Spectators fanned themselves with whatever they had available; her notepad, in fact, was saving her from heat expiration.

The lawyers returned to their seats, and the judge addressed the veniremen. "I want the following men to come forward, right there through that gate, and find you a place in the jury box: Mr. Eugene Cammack, Mr. Albert Durie, Mr. Edgar Russell, Mr. Frank Mitchell, Mr. William Plunkett, Mr. Fauntley Johnson, Mr. Wade Morrison, Mr. Samuel Powell, Mr. Philip Owens, Mr. Morton Smith, Mr. Joseph Wickham, and Mr. William Neale. Gentlemen, step up quickly now, please."

She'd researched all twelve. She marked a check beside each juror on her venire list. How interesting: Captain Blair hadn't struck Mr. Morrison as they'd anticipated. Mr. Calloway would be pleased. The twelve rose from all around the gallery and made their way to the front. The bailiff held open the swinging gate in the bar rail as one by one, they found their places in the jury box. It was nice to finally associate faces with the names.

The judge addressed those whose names he hadn't called. "The rest of you men may go about your business now. You're excused. Thank you for your service."

The room filled with the bustle of people leaving.

She took that opportunity to observe the gentlemen of the jury. Some were young but most were older, dressed in business suits of black, gray, or brown. They seemed somber and attentive. They could as easily have been in their Sunday pews.

The judge finished his instructions, asked the jurors to stand and raise their right hands, and then administered the oath: "I will a true verdict render, according to the law and the evidence, so help me God."

"Your Honor," Mr. Calloway said, rising, "we invoke the rule."

He always did that. He'd explained to her it was based on the wisdom of an old Bible story. If witnesses weren't allowed to hear each other's testimony, they'd be less likely to change their stories to be consistent with what others said. Good way to catch a liar, Mr. Calloway explained.

"All right, the rule's been invoked, and I'll ask all those who're going to be witnesses to stand up so I can talk to you about a thing or two. If there are any witnesses in the hallway, go get 'em."

Cicero looked at Mr. Calloway, who shook his head. They would decide later if he would testify. Miss Peach drummed her notepad. Her two bosses would probably disagree about that.

The bailiff went to the door and motioned for those outside to come in.

"Come stand over there," the judge said, directing Jasper, Miss Jessie, and Big Joe to stand at the bar rail. Two police officers joined them. "All you who're standing will need to go and wait outside until you're called. You're not permitted to hear the testimony of other witnesses. You can talk to the lawyers in the case, but nobody else. Y'all understand?"

They all nodded and then departed.

"Mr. Blair, you may proceed with the indictment."

"Thank you, Your Honor. Gentlemen of the jury, I'll now read to you the true bill of indictment returned by the McLennan County grand jury: 'Be it remembered that on the sixteenth day of April, 1894, the defendant, Cicero Sweet, in the city of Waco and the county of McLennan, did then and there, willfully and with malice aforethought, murder Georgia Virginia Gamble, a single woman of this county, against the peace and dignity of the state of Texas …'"

No need to listen to the rest. She'd read it before. She drew daisies on her notepad.

"The defendant will rise," the judge said. "Mr. Sweet, you've heard the charges against you. How do you plead?"

"Not guilty."

He sounded confident. Good. The jurors watched him, except for Mr. Mitchell. She jotted a note.

"Mr. Blair, you may open."

"May it please the court." He nodded to the judge and strode to a spot directly in front of the jury. "Gentlemen of the jury, I'll be brief. This is a murder case, and it's tragically simple. A young man went to the Reservation for pleasure. He drank beer, and he lusted after one of the legal working girls, Miss Georgia Virginia Gamble. They went to her bedroom. She laughed at his manhood. He got mad and mean. She pulled out a small derringer that she kept for protection against rowdy customers. Somehow he wrestled the gun away from her and shot her in her own bed."

Blair turned and pointed straight at Cicero. "That man, gentlemen, is the defendant, Cicero Sweet." He calmly faced the jury again. "At that point, the beer must have overcome him, because he passed out on her floor. That is what the evidence will show, gentleman."

He eased over to the empty witness stand and placed his hand on its balustered rail. "I will prove it with the sworn testimony of the investigating police officer, the doctor who examined the body, the bawdy woman who owns the house, and even the companion of the defendant on his venture into the Reservation." He stepped up to the jury rail and spoke with quiet intensity. "Cicero Sweet murdered that girl, and murder's wrong, no matter who the victim is or where the crime occurs. Murder can't go unpunished, even in the Reservation, or we're all in danger. At the conclusion of our proof, I will ask you to convict him of murder in the first degree. Thank you."

On his way back to his seat, he turned back around and

gestured toward the witness stand. "I neglected to mention one other witness. I won't trouble you to know his name now, but I want you to know we might call one other witness, but only if it's necessary. If we do call this witness, he'll dispel any doubts and leave you with absolute certainty of the defendant's guilt. Thank you."

Mr. Calloway eyed Harley, who shook his head. It was Harley's job to make sure they were prepared for all the prosecution witnesses. He turned to her, and she shrugged. She had no idea who Captain Blair could be referring to. She made a note to remind Harley to follow up on it.

She sank back into her seat just as a whistle blast from a steamboat on the river sent a two-inch cockroach scampering along the bar rail toward her. When it reached the chasm at the swinging gate, it gave up and turned back. Nasty creature. She shuddered and drew her next daisy.

Chapter 26

"The state calls Sergeant Dennis Quinn."

The officer smiled at Catfish as he passed by, keystone hat in hand, and took the witness stand. Catfish had known Quinn a long time and cross-examined him many times. A good policeman.

Captain Blair began the interrogation. "Tell the folks on the jury who you are please, sir."

"I'm Sergeant Dennis Quinn, city police."

"How long have you been a copper in Waco?"

"Ten years, more or less."

"And before that?"

"United States Army."

"Sergeant, the business at hand is a killing that happened in April," he said, turning his back on the witness and retiring to the bar rail. He crossed his arms and leaned against the rail. "Were you on duty during the early morning hours of April sixteenth of this year?"

"I was."

"What happened about one o'clock?"

"The telephone rang, and a woman said there had been a shooting in the Reservation."

"Where exactly?"

"Miss Jessie's bawdy house at the corner of Washington Street and Orman's Alley."

"What'd you do after you got that call?"

"Another officer and I went to the bawdy house."

"Who did you see there when you first went in?"

"The madam, who was a woman by the name of Jessie Rose, and another bawdy woman by the name of Sadie Wiggins."

"Describe for the jury the demeanor of these two bawds."

Quinn faced the jury. "They were distraught. Looked as if they'd both been crying for some time."

Good actresses. Probably peeled a few onions.

"What did the madam tell you?"

Catfish flew to his feet. "Objection, hearsay."

"It's a spontaneous utterance, judge."

"Overruled," the judge ruled, shaking his head.

"She said one of her girls had been murdered upstairs by a customer."

Blair moved to the end of the jury box and faced the witness, arms crossed. "What did you do next?"

"She led me upstairs to a bedroom in the front of the house, overlooking Washington Avenue. I understood it to be the room of a bawdy woman by the name of Georgia Gamble."

"Who did you first see there?"

"A man named Joe. He worked for the madam. He was holding a pistol on the man on the floor."

Blair edged closer to the witness. "I'll come back to that man on the floor in a minute. But first, did you find Miss Georgia there?"

"I did. She was in her bed, shot dead."

"Describe her body for the benefit of our jury," Blair said, eying the jurors. "Take your time and be as complete as possible, Sergeant."

The policeman spoke in an unemotional manner as if

describing an ordinary scene. "Yes, sir. She was on her back, completely unclothed. Her head was on her pillow, her eyes open and staring at the ceiling. Her right arm was crooked beside her with the hand open and facing up. Her left arm was hanging over the side of the bed. There was blood all over her chest and on the sheets. I saw a bullet hole in her chest."

"What age did you judge her to be?"

"Probably in her early to middle twenties."

"Any doubt in your mind she was dead?"

"None."

Blair walked to the court reporter's desk. "Let's talk about how she got that way. Sergeant, did you see any weapons about?"

"I did. There was a derringer on the floor at the foot of the bed."

Blair retrieved a small pistol from the desk with a paper tag dangling from the handle by a string. He took it to the witness.

"Is State's Exhibit One that pistol?"

"It is."

"Look like the same condition it was in that day?"

"Yes."

"We offer State's One."

"No objection."

"State's One is admitted," the judge said.

"What model of firearm is this?" Blair asked, holding the pistol in front of the witness.

Quinn eyed the gun like a gunsmith. "It's a Remington Model 95 rimfire double-barrel derringer in forty-one caliber."

"What do you see on the right side of the top barrel?" he asked, presenting the gun to the officer.

Quinn examined it again. "A bloody mark. It appears to be the impression of a finger. You can see some wavy lines in the dried blood."

Out of the corner of his eye Catfish noticed Cicero rubbing his hands together. He touched the boy's arm: *None of this points at you, son.*

Blair paraded the pistol in front of the jury box, giving each juror a look. It was cold black with bright ivory grips, small enough to conceal in a waistcoat pocket. It had two short, stubby barrels stacked one on top the other.

"Now for the one who used it." With the gun in his left hand, Blair turned slowly and deliberately to face Cicero and extended his right arm, stabbing his finger at him as he spoke. "Did you see the defendant, Cicero Sweet, in Miss Georgia's room?"

Catfish cut another glance at Cicero: *Don't react.*

The boy squirmed.

"I saw him."

"Where?"

"On the floor at the foot of her bed. Unconscious and naked."

Blair marched to a spot directly in front of the jury box, derringer still in his left hand, and pulled off his coat and tossed it onto his chair. "I'm going to demonstrate how he was situated, as you describe it." He kneeled on the floor, and the jurors leaned forward to see. "Tell the gentleman of the jury how he looked."

"He was lying on his back with his arms extended to each side above his head"—Blair flopped onto his back, stretching his arms as described—"and his head closest to the door and his feet closest to the bed."

Catfish leaned back. Blair always had a penchant for drama. Some jurors rose in their chairs to better view his performance.

Blair scooted around so his feet were next to his table. "So if the table there represented the bed and the defendant was laying where I am, then the door would be over my shoulder toward the jury box?"

"Yes, sir."

Blair's left hand shot straight up, thrusting the derringer into the air, a veritable P. T. Barnum. Still on his back, head toward the jury and feet toward his table, he fired the next question. "Did you see this pistol anywhere?"

"I did. It was on the floor next to his right hand."

"His right hand? Are you sure about that?"

"Yes."

"Step down here, Sergeant Quinn, and take this derringer"— the witness did so—"and place it exactly where you found it when you saw the defendant laying there in Miss Georgia's room."

"Here." Quinn placed the weapon about a foot from Blair's extended right hand.

"Right there," Blair echoed. He crawled back to his feet, never taking his eyes off the gun. He bent over it, never looking up. "Did you place it exactly as you saw it?"

"I did."

Blair bent closer. "Is the blood side up or down?"

The jurors leaned forward to see.

"Up."

"On which side of the gun?"

"Right."

"By which of the defendant's hands?"

"Right."

Blair rose to his full height, as if filled with the outrage of an indignant people. He repaired to his table and spun slowly to face the jury.

Catfish yawned.

"Who lay lifeless on that bed?" he asked, gesturing as if the bed rather than a table were before him.

"Miss Georgia Gamble."

He let the name resound a moment.

"You may return to your seat, Sergeant," Blair said, doing the same. "Did you see anything else which might give a clue as to the cause of the defendant being unconscious?"

"Yes. There were empty beer bottles on the floor of the room."

"How many?"

"We collected six."

"Did you at some point arrest Mr. Sweet?"

"I did. We got him awake enough to move, and then I took him into custody."

"Did you also take the derringer into your possession?"

"No, sir. Detective Palmer arrived pretty soon, and he took charge of the investigation. I think he took the pistol and other evidence."

"Pass the witness." Captain Blair nodded in satisfaction and took his seat.

Catfish stood at his table. He glanced at Henry and his wife in the front row of the gallery, placed a hand on Cicero's shoulder, and smiled at the witness. "How do, Sergeant. You mind if I question you from my feet rather than my back?"

"Sure," Quinn replied, smiling back.

"I'm not as young as the captain and might have trouble getting back up," he said, grinning.

The jurors smiled too—Blair wasn't that much younger.

Catfish looked over at Blair. "You didn't get any blood on your papers there on that bed, did you?"

A juror laughed. Blair ignored the question.

Catfish turned to the witness for the first time. "I'd like to start with some things I wager you and I can agree on. It's important, isn't it, the killer of this young woman be brought to justice?"

"Yes, sir," Quinn said.

"Do you think, though, it's important to bring the right man to justice?"

"Of course."

"Can we agree that convicting the wrong man would be a terrible injustice?"

"Certainly."

"And letting a killer go free because an innocent man is convicted instead would endanger"—he extended his hands toward both spectators and jurors—"innocent folks?"

"It would."

Catfish glanced up at the judge, who was fanning himself with a cardboard folder. "Do you think Judge Goodrich might tell the jury in his charge that if they have any reasonable doubts about who did it, then they must acquit Mr. Sweet?"

"I've heard that before, but I don't know about this case."

"Well, sir, getting the right man into the courtroom is the job of your police department, true?"

"True."

"Would you agree also that doing a thorough investigation is the best way to do that job?"

"Yes."

"Leave no stone unturned?"

"We try not to let one lie."

He could build a wall with the stones they ignored.

"Very well, let's visit about those stones," he said with an easy smile.

He came around behind the prosecution table and stopped between it and the jury. "I noticed on direct examination you didn't mention something."

Quinn looked uncertain. "What are you referring to?"

"Sergeant Quinn, did you take the time to examine Mr. Sweet while he was lying on the floor?"

"I did. As I said, he was naked."

Catfish tilted his head upward toward the ceiling. "You said he was face up?"

"Yes."

"So you saw the large knot on his forehead above his left eye?" He turned to the jury and pointed to his own forehead.

"I don't recall seeing that."

"Are you denying he had a knot on his head?"

"No, I just didn't notice it if he did."

"I see. If he had a knot on his head, that might indicate somebody hit him?"

"Maybe. Or that he hit his head on the bedstead when he fell over drunk."

"Fair enough." Catfish nodded. "But you didn't ask the madam or any of the others what they knew about that knot?"

"No."

"Like whether he had a knot on his head before he went upstairs?"

"No."

"That stone never got flipped over to see what was under it?"

Catfish swiveled to face the jury and lifted both hands, palms up: *Who hit him, fellas?*

"I don't even know there was a knot, Mr. Calloway."

"Fair enough. We'll be proving that later. But you did at least look at Mr. Sweet while he was still lying on the floor?"

"I did."

"Didn't have any blood on him, did he?"

"I don't remember any."

Catfish extended his right hand and flipped it over and back, examining both sides. "None on his right hand?"

"I don't think so."

He left his hand in front of his face. "Well, Sergeant, after you saw the blood on the right side of the derringer, didn't you naturally think to look at Mr. Sweet's right hand?" He gazed at the jurors until they were all watching him, and then he wiggled his fingers. "Particularly his fingers?"

"I suppose."

"Well, sir"—he extended his right forefinger—"if he had a bloody trigger finger, that'd be a mighty big stone to kick over, wouldn't it?"

"Probably."

"Either way, whether you checked or you didn't, you're not here to swear he had blood on his fingers?"

"He could have wiped it off. There was blood on the bedclothes."

Catfish scratched his head thoughtfully. "Here's another thing I was wondering about. Did you learn about a buggy, a red Stanhope gig, parked on the street across from the sporting house at the time of the killing?"

"No, sir."

"Didn't find out about that?"

"No."

"Mighty big stone."

Catfish shrugged at the jury: *Whose buggy?*

"Objection to the sidebar comment," Blair shouted.

"Move along, Catfish," the judge said, fanning himself faster.

"Yes, sir." He nodded to the judge before his gaze went back to Quinn. "Did you talk to any other customers of Miss Jessie's from that night?"

"No."

"Or anyone who was at any of the places next door?"

"No."

"Or at the Red Front Saloon?"

"No, sir."

"Or any hack drivers?"

"No, sir."

Catfish waited before asking the next question. Nothing like silence to get a jury's attention. Then he'd lob the killer's name like a firecracker right into the middle of the jury box and watch the shock on their faces.

"Sergeant, you mentioned Orman's Alley a minute ago." Catfish eyed the jury. "You know Bud Orman, don't you?"

"Yes, sir."

Catfish spoke with all the incredulity he could muster. "But you didn't think to question him?"

"No."

None of the jurors reacted at all to Orman's name. Not even Wade Morrison. Didn't they remember he was a murderer? He glanced at Harley, who didn't meet his eyes. Or wouldn't.

Catfish cocked his head toward Quinn. "Didn't even turn over that stone?"

"It wasn't necessary."

Still no reaction from the jury.

Catfish took his seat. Well, no worries. They'd understand. Just needed time. "Pass the witness."

"Sergeant Quinn," Blair said from his chair, "why didn't you go tipping over all those stones Mr. Calloway mentioned?"

"Wasn't necessary," Quinn said. "We didn't speak with the members of the Philo Literary Club, either."

The jurors chuckled, and so did Catfish. Harley didn't.

Quinn continued. "We had the customer the victim was with at the time, according to the madam, and he was in the room with her when they heard the gunshot. We found him lying next to her and the murder weapon. A clear-cut case to me."

"To me too," Blair said with a nod.

A juror nodded too.

Chapter 27

Miss Peach, seated at her post just inside the bar rail behind the defense table, fanned herself while waiting for the next witness. Her blouse clung to her body. After the noon break, Judge Goodrich had permitted the gentlemen to shed their coats. Neither Captain Blair nor Mr. Calloway had taken advantage of the judge's kindness, and sweat stained their suits. Why had Mr. Calloway worn a black suit on a hot July day?

A noise at the rear of the courtroom caught her attention. A pigeon had flown onto the windowsill of one of the north windows, where it perched to view the proceedings. Probably bored with what he saw, the plump visitor entertained himself by throatily cooing, a charming distraction from the heat. She drew the bird's silhouette at the top of her notepad, then another and another until there was a flock.

Captain Blair called as his second witness Dr. Hardy C. Black, a medical man with the bearing of intelligence.

"Do you have any official positions?"

"I'm the city physician."

"Where's your office?"

"In the Provident Building, room 93."

Captain Blair rocked back in his chair, and it squeaked loudly. The pigeon launched into flight down the central aisle of the spectator gallery, flapping loudly over the defense table. Miss Peach flinched until it glided to a noisy landing in a window to the judge's left. The bailiff shooed him off, but not before it stained the windowsill in protest. A feather floated toward the bench and finally settled on the floor.

Captain Blair seemed unbothered. "Do you have any official duties regarding bawdy houses?"

"I do. By city ordinance, bawdy houses are licensed, and one of the licensing requirements is that all the girls must have a physical examination by the city physician twice a month. I perform those examinations. My job is to make sure the girls are healthy. That also protects their customers, of course. It's a salutary by-product of legalized prostitution."

Blair rose from his chair and stood beside the prosecution table near the jury. "Did you ever have occasion to go to Miss Jessie Rose's bawdy house?"

"Many times."

"Did you know a working girl there by the name of Georgia Virginia Gamble?"

"I did. I performed many physical examinations on her. The last one was April fourth of this year."

Blair took a document to the court reporter for marking and then handed it to the witness. "Is State's Exhibit Two your certificate concerning that examination?"

"Yes, sir. As you can see, I signed it."

"Is it part of your office records?"

"It is."

"I offer State's Two."

"No objection," Catfish said, half rising to his feet.

"Admitted," the judge said.

"Read it for the benefit of the jury, please," Blair said.

Dr. Black adjusted his spectacles. "'Waco, Texas, April 4, 1894. City physician's certificate of examination. This is to certify that I have carefully examined Miss Georgia Virginia Gamble and find her in a sound and healthy condition, and not infected with any contagious or infectious diseases. This certificate expires June 4, 1894. Fee paid, two dollars. H. C. Black, M. D., City Health Physician of Waco.'"

"Do your records show who paid that fee?"

"The madam of the house, Miss Jessie Rose."

Blair returned to his table, glancing at the jury. Miss Peach looked too. They still seemed awake and alert, but that might not last if the good doctor's testimony took a tedious turn through medical school on such a hot summer afternoon following lunch. The judge was already nodding off.

"I'd like to take a minute or two and have you talk about Miss Georgia, since the jury won't see her in court today."

"All right."

"How old was she on the date of her death?"

"I believe she was twenty-three."

"Do you remember her?"

He smiled. "I do. She was a delightful girl for one in her line of work. She had a sweet disposition. I enjoyed our visits immensely. I asked her once about her name, and she laughed. She said her mother was from Georgia and her father, whom she'd never known, was from Virginia. I believe she grew up in Georgia or Mississippi, maybe. I got the impression that Gamble was not her real surname."

"To your knowledge, did she have any family here?"

"I don't know of any. I think she came from elsewhere not long ago."

"Do you know where?"

"Fort Worth, maybe, but I'm not sure." Dr. Black turned toward the jury to explain. "These working girls move frequently from one town's bawdy district to another. It's illegal everywhere in Texas but Waco, of course, so they change names frequently."

"Do you know how long she'd been in the horizontal trade?"

"No, sir."

Judge Goodrich's eyes had shut and his head dipped. Miss Peach hid a smile.

Captain Blair eased next to the jury and lowered his voice while the witness narrated Miss Georgia's medical history. Then he glanced at the judge and said loudly, "All right, then."

"Overruled!" the judge erupted, even though no objection had been made.

The jurors smiled discreetly.

"Let's move along, Captain Blair," the judge said.

"Yes, Your Honor," Blair said without breaking stride. "Dr. Black, let's turn now to Monday, April sixteenth of this year. Did you have occasion to go to Miss Jessie's bawdy house?"

The witness first examined his notes. "I did. I received a telephone call from the house. Detective Palmer was there investigating a murder. He asked me to come examine the body."

"Describe what you found when you arrived."

Dr. Black recited facts now familiar to everyone in court, though he went into pathological detail concerning the body, the blood, the bullet wound, and the cause of death. Miss Peach stifled a yawn. How could murder become so dry?

Mr. Calloway scooted his swivel chair away from the table, turned his back on the witness and the prosecutor, and propped his booted feet up on his leather satchel not three feet in front of her, facing the jury. He lit a cigar. A cloud of smoke wafted up until it was captured by the swirling currents of the nearest fan, which dispersed it. She knew exactly what he was thinking—Miss Georgia was dead, and no cross-examination, no matter how lively, might revive her.

"Describe for the jury the appearance of the entrance wound."

"It was slightly irregular . . ."

Mr. Calloway dispatched a perfect smoke ring across the courtroom floor at the spittoon squatting in polished brass readiness just inside the bar. Despite the fan whopping continuously above, it maintained itself perfectly and landed upon the spittoon, as if that was where it properly resided when in court.

". . . no wound on the posterior of the body . . ."

Captain Blair remained intent on the testimony. The judge's eyes batted, then popped open again, then shut. Mr. Calloway hurled his rings with the precision of a cowhand lassoing a steer. Three more rings stacked perfectly onto the spittoon.

". . . cause of death was by gunshot wound to the heart . . ."

From inside the front corner chair of the jury box, there came an explosion of throat-huffing. Miss Peach flinched as if the pigeon were threatening to land again. A wad of spent tobacco arced over the jury rail and landed squarely in the brass receptacle.

Ding!

Neither judge nor prosecutor nor any other court official altered the faithful execution of their duties. Spittoons resided at the end of every spectator bench, and spitting and dinging were normal courtroom sounds. Normal, but certainly not couth.

". . . death was instantaneous . . ."

She glanced at the judge, still sleeping, and Captain Blair, still oblivious. But the gentlemen of the jury were more intent upon the spittoon than the witness. Might more marksmen be planning to join in a precision feat?

". . . no pain . . ."

The next of Mr. Calloway's rings took flight, the juror huffed in preparation, the ring floated, the brown stream arced. Bull's-eye.

Ding!

Mr. Calloway winked, and the juror nodded.

"Pass the witness," Blair concluded.

The sudden quiet awakened the judge. "Move along!"

Mr. Calloway whirled his chair around, rose, and extinguished his cigar in an ashtray.

"Dr. Black, that gunshot wound was"—Mr. Calloway stabbed the air with his forefinger—"right in the heart, true?"

"Yes."

"Best place to shoot folks if you intend to kill 'em?"

"Probably, although the head would also do it."

"When you examined the wound, you didn't see any signs of powder burns, did you?"

"No."

"Didn't find any unburned gunpowder lodged in the wound itself?"

"No."

"That tells you the shooter didn't hold the gun up against the lady's chest?" He touched his forefinger to his heart.

"Probably."

"So Doc, if I'm hearing you right, this shooter hit her dead center in the heart without pressing the gun up against her?"

"Maybe, but that's a little beyond my expertise."

Mr. Calloway walked over to the court reporter's desk near the witness stand. "Dr. Black, did Detective Palmer tell you the weapon they found was a derringer?"

"Yes."

He wrinkled his face. "Ever shot a derringer?"

"No, sir."

"Seen one?"

"Probably."

"Well, let me show you the very one they found in Miss Georgia's room." He retrieved the pistol and handed it to the witness. "Take a gander at State's Exhibit One. Look like a derringer to you?"

"Yes, sir."

"What would you say, that barrel's about what, three inches?" He indicated with his thumb and forefinger.

"Probably."

"Not very long to burn up all the gunpowder in the cartridge?"

"That's beyond my expertise."

"Fair enough." He took the pistol back and placed it on the desk. "Don't know much about guns?"

"No, sir."

"Fair enough," he said with a warm smile. He went back to the bar rail. The jurors turned toward him, listening. He liked to cross-examine witnesses from there so that all eyes were on him rather than the witness. He hooked both thumbs in his vest pockets. "Let me ask you something you do know about."

"Medicine, I hope."

"Yes, sir. The human body. That's your bailiwick, isn't it?"

"It is."

"All right, then." Mr. Calloway scratched his head. "You a drinking man, Doc?"

"No, sir."

"Never?"

"Never."

He nodded. "But when you studied medicine, didn't you learn about what alcohol does to a person's body?"

The doctor dipped his head in agreement and grinned at the jury. "Yes, sir. That's why I don't drink."

Mr. Calloway smiled back. "Well, sir, you're wiser than most folks—me included, I'm afraid."

A few jurors chuckled.

"Let me ask you this, though. Doesn't alcohol get in the way of a man's vision?" He squinted. "Make it blurry?"

"It can."

"Sometimes he just can't see straight?" He squinted more.

"Sometimes."

"Sometimes he gets shaky or wobbly?" He wobbled.

"It can."

"Hard to shoot straight if you can't see straight and you're shaky?" He squinted and wobbled.

"Unless you're so close you can't miss."

"Ah!" Mr. Calloway transformed his right hand into a gun, thumb for a hammer and index finger for a barrel, and pointed it at his own heart. "Like with the muzzle of the gun pressed up against the body?"

"Yes."

He dropped his finger gun and took a few steps along the jury rail. "But no powder burns on her body"—he glanced back to the witness—"right?"

"Right."

"Thank you, sir. That's all, judge."

Blair rose again and took the derringer over to the witness. "Dr. Black, did you see the blood on the barrel of the derringer?"

"I didn't really examine the gun. That's your field, not mine."

"If there was blood, you'd think the gun had to be close to the victim's body, wouldn't you?"

"Objection," Mr. Calloway called. "Leading and speculative."

"Sustained."

"Pass the witness."

"That's all, judge," Mr. Calloway said.

Mr. Calloway took his seat and winked at Harley, who nodded back.

Miss Peach wiped her pen. Just as he'd planned, Mr. Calloway had planted the idea that another man had been there that night. He'd even put a name to him: Bud Orman. With Dr. Black, he'd then cast doubt on Cicero's ability to fire the fatal shot. Mr. Calloway seemed quite pleased with how it had gone.

Harley gazed over his shoulder at her. She blinked encouragement. His face betrayed the worries he'd expressed to her outright, that. Mr. Calloway was building expectations among the jurors that he'd prove who the killer was. Harley didn't think they could do it.

They'd never disagreed so bitterly before.

She forced herself to draw a daisy.

Unless Mr. Calloway had something up his sleeve she didn't know about, Harley was right.

Chapter 28

Blair announced his next witness, Jasper Cantrell.

Catfish wiped his palms with a handkerchief while the boy made his way to the witness stand. Jasper had neatly parted and slicked down his hair and he wore a winged collar and necktie, but the sleeves on his coat were too short, as were his trousers. Jasper was a smart boy, and Catfish hadn't needed to explain to him that in a sense he was on trial today too. He wasn't facing prison or the scaffold like his friend, but the possibility of going home under the shame of expulsion from college for misconduct visibly weighed on him. Catfish, too.

Jasper straightened his tie three times as he followed the bailiff toward the witness stand. They passed President Burleson, who was on the front row of the spectator gallery. Jasper appeared startled to see him and nodded respectfully before settling into the witness chair. His eyes cut to Cicero, who nodded back. Jasper rubbed his hands down his trousers repeatedly.

Catfish tried to make eye contact with him—*Remember, Jasper, I'm your lawyer too*—but the boy's eyes flitted around the room.

"Jasper," Blair said, "were you and the defendant together on Sunday evening, April fifteenth?"

"Yes, sir."

"Where'd you go?"

"Professor Charlton took all the boys from the dorm to the revival at the Tabernacle."

"Did Brother Sam Jones preach about bawdy houses?"

"Yes, sir."

"And drinking?"

"Yes, sir."

"Did you and the defendant then go to a bawdy house and drink beer after that revival?"

"We went to a house, yes, sir, and there was some drinking going on. I never opened mine."

"Whose idea was it to go to the bawdy house?"

Jasper hesitated, eyeing Cicero, and finally spoke. "I reckon it must have been Cicero's."

Catfish caught his eye. *It's all right, son. Just tell the truth.*

Blair continued. "Did you or the defendant tell anyone you were going there?"

"No, sir."

"Why not?"

"We was supposed to be in our room. We was sneaking out, and ain't . . . wasn't . . . nobody at Baylor knew nothing about that." Jasper glanced toward Burleson. "I got some powerful regrets about breaking them rules. It was all our own doing and nobody else's."

"What time did you leave your room to go to the bawdy house?"

"Probably around ten thirty or so."

"Did you smuggle yourselves out?"

"Well, sir, we tried not to make no noise, if that's what you mean."

"After you got to the bawdy house, did the defendant drink beer?"

Jasper eyed Cicero. "Yes, sir."

"Did you see Miss Georgia Gamble at some point?"

"Yes, sir. Another lady introduced her by that name."

"Was the other lady Miss Jessie?"

"Yes, sir."

"Were they whores?"

Jasper gulped. "I reckon they was, sir."

"Did you see the defendant take an interest in Miss Georgia?"

"He danced with her, if that's what you mean."

"At some point that night, did Miss Georgia and the defendant go upstairs?"

"Yes, sir."

Blair glanced at his notes. "What'd you do at that point?"

"I left."

"Where'd you go?"

"Outside. I sat against a telephone pole to wait for Cicero."

"Did you fall asleep?"

"Yes, sir."

"What woke you up?"

"A loud noise."

"A gunshot?"

"A scream."

"Where'd it come from?"

"Sounded like from Miss Jessie's house."

"What'd you do then?"

"I ran."

"Why?"

"I was scaryfied."

Blair smiled at him. "That's all. Thank you, Jasper."

"Catfish?" the judge asked. "You got questions?"

"Yes, Your Honor."

Catfish rose, peering at Jasper. First thing they needed to deal with was President Burleson.

You can do this, son.

"Jasper, you a little nervous?"

"Yes, sir."

"Ever testified in a court before?"

"No, sir."

"All right, let's visit about you first." He sat again and rocked back, then flashed Jasper a big smile. "Where you from?"

"Fayette County."

"Live on a cotton farm?"

"Yes, sir. Outside of Flatonia."

"Tell us about your family."

"Well, sir, there's my momma and my daddy. Daddy's a farmer. I got some brothers and sisters, and they's younger than me."

"You the first one in your family to go to college?"

"Yes, sir."

"Tell the gentlemen of the jury how you felt about going off to college."

Blair started to rise and object, but then settled back in his chair.

Jasper took a deep breath. "I was happy to do it, in a way, and not so happy in another. I liked the idea of getting smarter and learning things. I like learning a lot, but honest truth is I just didn't want to leave home. I miss my folks and my brothers and sisters real bad. I miss the farm. Just everything about it. The big city's an awful nice place, and folks are real nice here"—he glanced at the jury—"but if I had my druthers, I'd be back home with my family." Tears burst from his eyes, and he quickly wiped them away with his sleeve and sniffled. "My mother wanted me to go to college and better myself. It was the most important thing in the whole world to her, and so it was real important to me." He broke up again. "It'd break her heart if I didn't get educated."

Catfish discreetly glanced at Burleson, whose expression remained unchanged, and then at the jury. Every single head was bent.

"Not much more, Jasper," he said, "but we got to talk about that night."

They had to help Cicero.

"Yes, sir. I'm fine."

"When you and Cicero were talking about going to a bawdy house, did he ever say he wanted to kill anybody?"

"Of course not, Mr. Calloway. He's not like that."

"Did he take a gun with him?"

Jasper shook his head. "They don't allow no guns in the dorm."

"Ever see him angry that night?"

"No, sir."

Catfish leaned forward, resting his elbows on the table and folding his hands under his chin. "Jasper, this is really important now." He touched his own forehead. "Did you ever see Cicero hit his head that night?"

"No."

"So when he went upstairs with Miss Georgia, did he have a knot on his head?"

"No, sir."

"All right, two more things and we'll be done." He rolled his chair back from the table and wheeled it around toward the jury. "When you were outside Miss Jessie's, did you see any other men?"

"Yes, sir. A bald man was fixing to come in as I was going out."

"And did you see any carriages outside?"

"Yes, sir. A two-wheeler rig was parked on the street all the time I was under that tree."

"Anybody there with it?"

"No, sir."

"Describe that carriage for the gentlemen of the jury."

"Like I said, it was a two-wheeler buggy. Just one horse, of course. It was red. The seat had a fancy back to it."

"Spindle-back?"

"I reckon."

"Was that red carriage still there when you heard the scream?"

"It sure was."

"Last question: You ever heard of a fella named Bud Orman?"

"No, sir."

"Thanks, Jasper. That's all."

Catfish felt as relieved as Jasper looked. Jasper's testimony proved to Burleson he wasn't a bad boy, and on top of that, he'd backed up Cicero's story. Now the jury had also heard about the red buggy and the presence of the other man.

Three witnesses done, and things couldn't be going better.

The judge gave the jury a midafternoon break before the next witness. Catfish, Harley, and Miss Peach lingered outside the courtroom in the waiting area while the judge dealt with some other matters.

Catfish put his hand on Harley's shoulder. "I'd say we're in mighty good shape, wouldn't you?"

Harley shot a glance at Miss Peach, who didn't react. "I think it'd be better if you stopped mentioning Bud Orman."

Catfish frowned. "Why?"

"The more they hear of him the more they'll expect us to prove he's the killer."

Catfish nodded. "We will."

Miss Peach cleared her throat. "Excuse me, but I think I'll wait inside." She returned to the courtroom.

"We're not changing our trial strategy this late," Catfish said. "And it's working. Jasper did a beautiful job. Burleson won't expel him after that."

Harley shook his head. "Jasper isn't the one on trial. But if Cicero gets convicted of murder, they'll both suffer the consequences." There was something new in his voice, not quite anger.

Catfish stiffened. Harley needed to get over it. They both had to have clear heads. "Our clients deserve lawyers who believe in what they're doing."

He expelled a breath. "I'm not sure I do."

This was no time for dissension. Two innocent boys and their parents were counting on him. "Then stay out of my way."

He threw the courtroom door open and left Harley standing outside.

Chapter 29

"I've got one more witness for today, Judge, and we should be able to finish up our case in the morning," Blair announced. "We call Miss Jessie Rose."

As the bailiff went to get her, Harley leaned over. "I'm sorry, Papa."

Catfish ignored him and watched the door. The bailiff sounded the hallway, and she sashayed in, her skirt sweeping the floor. Wore a wide-brimmed shade hat and a blouse of fine linen with a high collar and a black bow tie. How many faces did this gal have? This was the same girl who'd showed up at the inquest, but she was an entirely different genus and species from the madam they'd met at the sporting house. Maybe there was yet another face to peel back for the jury.

"State your name, please," Blair said from his seat at the table.

"Jessica Rose."

"Are you a licensed madam in the Reservation?"

She answered with an elegant elevation of her chin, as if she'd been anointed by a royal decree. "I am licensed by the city of Waco to operate a lady's boarding house."

"How long have you had the house?"

"A little over a year."

"Where is it?"

"Washington Street."

Blair stood just feet away from her, but the men on the jury paid him little mind. They gawked at the dark-haired madam. She had that effect on men.

"Let me take you back to the evening of April fifteenth at about eleven o'clock," Blair said, crossing his arms and shifting closer to the heedless jury. "Were you at the house?"

"I was."

"Who arrived about that time?"

"Two young men."

"Do you see one of them in this courtroom?"

"That young man there." She pointed a delicate finger, and the jurors gaze followed its direction to Cicero.

Cicero looked down.

"Your Honor, may the record show that Miss Jessie identified the defendant, Cicero Sweet?"

"The record will show that."

"Now, Miss Jessie, in your own words, tell the gentlemen of the jury what happened after they arrived." Blair sat on the corner of the table.

The rumbling, hissing, whistling noise of a locomotive swelled outside the south windows, drowning out every other sound and rattling the courtroom. Miss Jessie fanned herself with an oriental fan for several minutes until the train passed and quiet returned.

She faced the jury and spoke in an easy manner. "The young gentlemen were"—the clock tower above the courtroom struck four times, and she waited for that too—"the young gentlemen were quite excited to meet the ladies of my household. I invited them into the parlor, where we had polite conversation. They were both very charming. They desired beer, so I had some brought over from a nearby establishment. They began to drink,

223

and we were soon joined by Miss Georgia, who had been upstairs getting acquainted with another gentleman. Mr. Cicero was particularly attracted to her, and they danced to the music of my player piano. It wasn't long before he led her upstairs. The other young man left."

Catfish shifted in his chair. She was good at testifying. Must've spent more time in court than some lawyers.

Blair jotted a note. "What time was that?"

"I wasn't looking at the clock, but it was after eleven o'clock."

"What was the next you saw or heard of the defendant or Miss Georgia?"

"Just after midnight, I was reading in the parlor and I heard a scream. It sounded like Miss Georgia and it came from her room, which is just above the parlor. A gunshot exploded right above me— it startled me so. Big Joe came in, and I retrieved my pistol. We waited at the bottom of the stairs to see if anyone came down."

"Where was Miss Sadie?"

"I think she was in a back room. We all met at the stairs."

"What happened then?"

"Nothing. It was quiet."

"What did you do?"

"We went upstairs, outside Georgia's door, but didn't hear anything. I knocked and called her name, but she didn't answer."

"What happened then?"

"We opened the door."

"What'd you see?"

"She was on the bed, shot dead. There was blood everywhere."

"Describe how she appeared."

Catfish raised his eyebrows. It was coming—the *look of ineffable terror.*

"Her eyes were open. She had a look of ineffable terror."

The only two times he'd ever heard the word *ineffable* uttered in Waco were by that sporting woman in that courthouse.

Blair turned his back on the jury and crossed the room, stopping between the defense table and the judge's bench. Damn, Catfish should have warned Cicero about this. Blair always did this in murder cases.

Don't look down, son!

Slowly, deliberately, Blair faced Cicero, eye to eye. Cicero appeared unsettled and looked down.

"What else did you see?" Blair asked, without taking his eyes off Cicero.

"Mr. Cicero was passed out on the floor."

"Where was he exactly?"

"At the foot of the bed. Sprawled on the floor."

"Describe him," Blair said, still staring at Cicero.

"He was naked and unconscious. A derringer was on the floor near him."

Blair finally lifted his stare from Cicero, who looked up only when Blair sauntered back toward the court reporter's desk. Cicero shot a glance at his lawyer.

Catfish suppressed any reaction. The jury was still watching.

Blair retrieved the derringer from the desk. "Did it look like State's Exhibit One?"

"That's Miss Georgia's gun. She kept it in the nightstand by her bed in case of trouble."

"What else did you see?"

"Empty Lone Star beer bottles all over."

"What did you do?"

"Big Joe checked Miss Georgia, but she was dead. He held my gun on Mr. Cicero, and I went downstairs and telephoned the police."

"Was the defendant ever awake before the police arrived?"

"Just once, for only a minute or so." She eyed the jury and opened her mouth as though she intended to add something but decided against it. She peered at Catfish.

He stiffened. Something was up.

"Then he passed out again."

"I see," Blair said. "Between the time the defendant and Miss Georgia went upstairs and the time you heard the scream and the gunshot, did anyone else go to her room?"

She lifted her chin and nodded without hesitation. "No."

Catfish watched her closely. She thought she was as formidable as he.

"How can you be sure?" Blair asked.

"We had only one other gentleman visiting after that, and he went to a downstairs bedroom with Miss Sadie. Nobody else went upstairs."

"When did the police arrive?"

"Within minutes."

Blair nodded to her. "Thank you, Miss Rose. Pass the witness."

"Ma'am," Catfish said, rising to question her from his table, "this is not the first time we've met, is it?"

"I'm not sure. Are you one of my customers?" She gave a coy smile, causing some of the jurors to grin.

Yes'm, you are formidable.

He smiled back at her. "No, ma'am. Our meeting was strictly in daylight and on business. My son, Harley, and I visited you at your house not too long after this incident. You remember now?"

"I think so." She glanced at the jurors. "We have so many men visit us."

"Well, ma'am, we asked to talk with you about what happened when Miss Georgia was killed, didn't we?"

"Oh yes, I remember now."

"And you refused to discuss it with us, didn't you?"

"I recall it was a busy day."

"All right, well, I'm happy to discuss it now," he said in a genial way, "if that's fine with you."

"Suit yourself."

"Tell me, Miss Rose, you own that sporting house yourself?"

"I do, as I told the other gentleman earlier."

"Well, what causes me to ask is that an associate of mine talked to Miss Sadie about it," he said, scratching his head, "and Miss Sadie told her a man actually owned the place and that you called him the boss."

She seemed untroubled. "I doubt she said that, because it's not true."

The fleas were hopping. He glanced at Harley.

Catfish ambled back to the bar rail behind Blair.

"Well now, Miss Rose, you've got a mighty fancy sporting house, don't you?"

"I'm not sure what you mean. I'm proud that it's a very nice place to entertain guests."

"Yes, ma'am. It sure is. It's the only brick sporting house in the whole Reservation"—he made a sweeping gesture toward that part of town—"isn't it?"

"I believe that's correct."

"It's two stories and has electricity and a talking-phone?"

"You must mean a telephone."

"It's right there on Washington Avenue, not back on the other side of the creek?"

"That's true."

"Would you say you've got the best venue for a sporting house in the whole Reservation?"

"Probably."

He faced the jury with a dubious expression. "And you own it by yourself?"

"I do, as I said before."

His eyes narrowed. "Well, now, Miss Rose, you came to Waco in 1893, right?"

"Yes."

"So you bought this place pretty soon after getting here?"

"I suppose."

"Bought it from Bud Orman?" he asked, hurling the name into the jury box again.

Still no signs it hit.

"Yes."

"Let's see," he said, "that was after he got tried for murder, wasn't it?"

"I don't know anything about that. I don't know the man."

"So you moved here last year," he said, pacing along the rail, "and almost right away you bought the only brick sporting house around?"

"I believe I answered that earlier."

"Before you came here you lived in New Orleans?"

"I did."

"Did you go by the name of Jessica Rose Reneau when you lived there?"

"Sometimes."

"You were a sporting girl in New Orleans?"

"I was an actress. Reneau was my stage name."

"Oh, an actress." That just might have been the truth. "You haven't done any acting since you moved to Waco, have you?"

"No, I'm a business owner now."

"So you wouldn't have any reason to use the name Reneau here in Waco?"

"I might have, I don't recall."

"When Bud Orman deeded you that property, didn't you go by Jessica Rose Reneau?" He walked to the defense table and picked up a document. "In the legal papers?"

"I might have."

"You say you were an actress in New Orleans? You weren't a sporting girl?"

"No, I was an actress."

"So there wouldn't be any reason for the authorities to arrest you for being a prostitute?"

"No."

"Play acting's not against the law in New Orleans, is it?"

"Not the sort I did."

He picked up a different document and flipped through it. "Didn't you get convicted of vagrancy in New Or—"

"Judge, I have to object," Blair said. "That doesn't have anything to do with this murder."

"Goes to her credibility," Catfish answered quickly.

"Overruled."

"Weren't you convicted of vagrancy?"

"Yes, but that's not prostitution."

"Since you've moved to Waco, our city police have picked you up for vagrancy too, haven't they?"

"Yes, and I paid a small fine and was released," she answered dismissively.

"Cost of doing business?"

She didn't answer.

"Cost of doing business, ma'am?"

"I don't know what you mean."

"Running a sporting house must get mighty expensive, true?"

"Life's expensive."

"Well, in addition to occasional fines, you pay your bawdy house license fee every quarter, your electricity and talking-phone bills every month, and on top of that I expect you've got mortgage payments too?"

"Running a business is expensive."

"Sure is. I agree with you there, ma'am."

She shrugged.

"But you still say you own that building by yourself and nobody's helping you with expenses?"

"That's right."

"You don't have a boss?"

"Only myself."

"By the way, there's a gentleman visitor to your house who drives a red Stanhope gig buggy, isn't there?"

"I have no idea what kind of carriages my guests use."

"Have you ever seen a red two-wheel gig parked outside your house?"

"No."

"All right. Let me ask you about the night of the killing."

"It's about time."

Catfish smiled. Now she was cracking a little. "Yes, ma'am. My wife used to say sometimes I beat around the bush too much." He put a hand on Cicero's shoulder. "Anyway, you got a pretty good look at Mr. Sweet that night?"

"Mr. Cicero? Yes, I did."

"Before he went upstairs with Miss Georgia, did you ever see him hit his head anywhere?"

"No."

"Did you see a knot on his head that night?"

"No."

"Either before or after the shooting?"

"Not at any time."

This cross-examination couldn't be going better. The jurors all seemed less enchanted with the madam—she was beginning to show her true colors. Reasonable doubt was raising its head. One more point to cap it off.

"Final thing. You mentioned on direct that after the shooting, while Cicero was lying on the floor, he woke up briefly?"

"He did."

He picked up yet another document. "Now, if I remember right, that's something you didn't mention in your testimony at the inquest before Judge Gallagher, was it?"

"He didn't ask me."

"Oh, I see." He wrinkled his face. "You didn't think that was important enough to tell the justice of the peace at the inquest?"

"I would have told him if he'd asked. I didn't know I was permitted to volunteer information I wasn't asked about."

"Well, of course you are, ma'am. Didn't you realize you should have told him what you knew?"

"I suppose not. It's good to know now, though, because I know something else I haven't been asked about yet." A slight smile flashed across her face, then vanished. "Would you like me to tell you what your client said to me that night in Miss Georgia's room after he came to?"

Catfish curled his mustache. "He said something?"

She nodded, chin high.

"You didn't mention that on the direct examination by Mr. Blair."

"I wasn't asked."

He glanced at Blair, who studied the floor as if in deep thought. Was this a trap? Harley shook his head discreetly, but the jurors all stared at Catfish. Too late to turn back.

"All right, what did he say?"

"He said, 'I'm sorry I shot her.' And then he passed out again."

Chapter 30

Catfish reeled at Miss Jessie's answer. Should've seen that coming. How'd he let that vixen lure him into it? This was the mysterious confession Blair had mentioned months back. But now all eyes were on him. He fought to control any outward reactions that would betray his uncertainty about whether to ignore it or try to discredit her.

Cicero handed him a note: "I didn't say that!"

Maybe there was another way, but it was a long shot. He had to stay calm, concentrate, and carefully set it up.

"Any more questions?" the judge asked, impatiently.

Catfish glanced at Harley. "May I have a moment to consult with my son, judge?"

"Be quick."

He leaned down. "I need you to do some things."

"Of course."

Catfish took his seat and started writing frantically. The pencil lead broke, and he pulled from his waistcoat pocket the silver magic pencil on the end of his watch chain. He tugged one end until the lead point popped out the other, also exposing the inner barrel. He didn't use it often and had forgotten what Martha had engraved on that inner cylinder: *Houston & Harley*.

His chest tightened. Unable to control his thoughts, his mind rushed to another trial, the fear in Houston's eyes, then to Schoolcraft's recent taunts: *Old man, you just don't have what it takes anymore.* Was the scoundrel right?

He glanced at Harley and furiously scribbled names on a piece of paper and said in a low voice, "Get instanter subpoenas issued for these people. For one o'clock tomorrow afternoon."

"Are you all right?"

Catfish hissed. "Just do it."

He hurriedly scratched more instructions on the paper and pushed it into his son's hands. "Get to the sporting house before Jessie and Joe get back there. I'll stall them here as long as I can."

***

The door of the bawdy house closed behind him as Harley stepped into the entrance hall.

"Are you Miss Sadie?" he asked.

"No, sugar, I'm Miss Nora, but I'm just as pleasurable. Want to spend some time with me instead?"

"No, ma'am. Thank you kindly, but I'd like see Miss Sadie."

"In there," Nora said indifferently. She nodded toward the parlor and disappeared down the hall.

Harley went into the parlor. Maybe this would be easier than it was at Miss Josie's. A girl lounging on a love seat broke into a smile and tilted her head alluringly at him.

"Miss Sadie?" he asked.

"That's me."

"Could I speak with you?"

"Do you really want to talk?"

He pulled out his wallet. "Could we go to your room for some privacy?"

"Of course, honey, right this way."

She led him down the hallway to a bedroom in the back and closed the door behind them. It was still daylight, though. He had that part going for him.

"Three bucks."

Several coins clinked to the floor as he tugged his money clip from his pocket. "I have ten for you, and another ten for later."

"What you got in mind, mister?" she asked cautiously.

"Oh, not what you're thinking, ma'am. I have a friend who wants to buy you a beer at the Red Front. If you meet him there at eight o'clock tonight, you'll get a beer and the other ten bucks."

"Yeah?" She crossed her arms. "Well, why don't your friend come speak for hisself?"

"He's busy right now but can get there by eight." He flashed a ten-dollar bill. "Is that all right with you?"

She thought for a moment, eying the cash in his hand, then snatched it. "Sure thing, mister. I'll be there."

The sweaty scent of intimacy rose from her in waves. He averted his eyes, as if he would no longer smell it if he looked away.

"One more thing. Don't tell Miss Jessie or Big Joe."

"Huh?"

"It's a secret, all right?"

"Look, mister, I don't work for no other houses."

Harley shook his head. "It's not that. He just doesn't want other people to know you're meeting him. He's a prominent man in town."

"But he's willing to go to the Red Front?" She snickered. "That don't stack up. But you promise he'll give me fifteen bucks, and I won't even tell my own self."

"Deal."

***

The saloon was thick with smoke and the smell of dirty men and cheap beer. The colonel curled up to sleep at Catfish's feet anyway. Girls from Mary Doud's sporting house next door were working the customers, and he'd declined two by the time Sadie arrived a little after eight o'clock. He recognized her from Harley's description and waved her over.

She slinked up to his table. "You the gent wants to pay me twenty-five bucks?"

"Have a seat." After she settled, he added, "I thought it was fifteen bucks?"

"Nope, he promised twenty-five."

"That's fine." He got her a beer at the bar.

"You have my money?"

He reached into his pocket and pulled out a stack of bills, peeled off two tens and a five, and slid them across the table.

She stuffed them down her private place and took a swig of beer. "What do you want me to do for you, mister?"

He leaned back and puffed on his White Owl. "Just talk."

She smirked. "What talk's worth twenty-five bucks?"

"Information." He blew a smoke ring. "About the night Miss Georgia got shot."

She slammed her beer on the table. "Oh, you a copper?"

"Lawyer. I represent the boy accused of killing her."

She scraped back her chair and got up. "Well, Mr. Lawyer, thanks for the twenty-five bucks."

"Wait." He touched her arm gently. "I need your help, ma'am. Actually, my client needs it. His life may depend on it. Please listen to what I have to say, and if you want to leave after that, you just get up and go."

She settled back into the chair and took another drink. "Talk."

"Thanks." He leaned closer. "Look, I believe my client didn't do it, and I think you know that."

She huffed. "Every killer I ever seen says that."

"Yes, ma'am—well, this time it happens to be true. I know you know it is. I'd just like you to know something about the boy your employer is setting up. He's eighteen and foolish. He wanted some fun and it went bad, as fun sometimes does. Miss Sadie, if he gets convicted of murder, they're gonna hang him. He's got a family that loves him."

"Yeah? Well ain't that sweet?" She gulped her beer. "What's it to me?"

"Maybe nothing. But I think maybe you got hard talk and a soft heart. I think maybe you had bad luck yourself. Maybe things happened to you that you didn't have any say over."

"You don't know nothing about me, mister."

"No, but I know girls like you. I know why you do what you do. I understand that. Folks do what they gotta do to get by. You probably been in danger for your own life before, I expect, maybe more than once. You know what it's like to be afraid. Well, ma'am, Cicero's afraid. He's scared to death. All I ask is for you to answer one question."

She frowned. "Yeah, what's that?"

"After Miss Georgia got shot, when you and Miss Jessie were in her room, did Cicero ever say anything?"

"Are you joshing? That boy was cold, dead drunk. He didn't say nothing."

It was time. Catfish nodded to a man at a nearby table, who got up and approached.

"Miss Sadie Wiggins?"

"Yeah, what's it to you?"

"I'm a deputy sheriff, and this is a subpoena for you to appear in court tomorrow afternoon at one o'clock." He dropped the folded paper on the table in front of her.

Catfish gave a brief nod. "Thanks, deputy, you can leave."

Sadie guzzled her beer and slammed it down. "You son of a bitch."

"Please, ma'am. I only did it so you won't get in trouble with Miss Jessie. You can tell her you have to go to court or you'll get arrested."

"You going to pay me another twenty-five bucks to do that?"

"Sorry, ma'am. I'm not allowed to pay witnesses."

"I ain't no witness, and I ain't doing nothing for the likes of you." She shot out of her chair and hurried for the door.

He had to change her mind. If she told Miss Jessie, then lying in court would be just another of her job duties. He and the colonel followed her outside and down the street toward the sporting house.

"Wait, Sadie, please," he called after her. "A boy's life depends on it."

"I don't give a damn about that boy," she yelled over her shoulder.

A man appeared on the street ahead, walking toward them. A big man. Catfish recognized him as they drew closer.

"Miss Sadie," Big Joe called, "you all right?"

"This man's bothering me, Joe."

"Yes, ma'am." Joe pulled something dark from his belt. "I'll take care of that."

Colonel Terry uttered a low growl as the man advanced through the dark.

Chapter 31

Big Joe slapped the blackjack in his empty palm. The smack provoked another growl from Colonel Terry.

"Colonel, hush up!" Catfish said. "How do, Joe, nice to see you again."

"I don't like the idea of you bothering Miss Sadie," Joe said, still advancing. She watched from behind him, hands on her hips.

Catfish didn't budge. "Just talking to her."

"Well, mister, she don't wanna do no more talking." He stopped about five feet from Catfish and crossed his arms, the blackjack hanging from his right hand. "My advice to you is just to back way off Miss Sadie—and Miss Jessie too, if you knows what's good for you."

Catfish stiffened. "That sounds like a threat."

"Do it now?" The blackjack struck his left palm with a crack. "Well, just maybe it is."

"Stand down, Joe," Catfish said, widening his stance. "Just let me finish my conversation with Sadie."

"You or that mangy cur gonna make me stand down, old man?" He kicked at the colonel but missed.

Colonel Terry growled back.

"Hush up!" Catfish stepped in front of the dog. "Don't make me call my twin hoot owls."

"Hoot owls?" Joe snorted and glanced back at Sadie.

Catfish pulled the small black-handled pistol from under his coat and pointed it straight at Joe's head. "One's Iver, other's Johnson, and they don't much care for blackjacks."

Joe broke into an ugly grin. "Ain't you a little old to be drawing down on a man?"

Catfish cocked the hammer with a metallic double-click. "As for myself, I've got no tolerance at all for threats."

"It's fine, Joe. Let's get," Sadie said, turning her back and walking away.

Joe lowered the blackjack. "You best let it be, grandpa."

Catfish eased down the hammer and holstered his pistol. "I'll see you in court, Miss Sadie."

***

"Papa, I don't think Miss Sadie will even show up."

Harley and Henry Sweet had met Papa back in the office after his meeting at the Red Front.

Papa took off his coat and draped it over a chair. "We'll see. She's been around courthouses enough to know a judge can haul her down there whether she's willing to go or not."

"Even if she does come," Mr. Sweet said, "why would she be willing to testify Cicero didn't make the statement? Jessie would tell her what to say, wouldn't she?"

"Probably. But I'll give her a chance to tell the truth."

Harley drummed his fingers on the table. There's no way she'd get on that witness stand and swear her employer had committed perjury. Papa was wrong about this. It hadn't been that bad a day in court except for Miss Jessie's surprise at the end, but calling another witness who'd back her up was foolish.

"Why don't we call Professor Perkins instead?" Harley asked.

"I've decided not to call a character witness." Papa opened the White Owl box and offered one to Sweet.

"No, thanks," Sweet said. "Why not call a character witness? I thought you planned to?"

"I suspect Blair knows about that fight with Peter DeGroote," Papa said. "He can read the Dallas paper too. He can ask Perkins about it on cross."

"But Cicero didn't hit Peter," Sweet said.

"I know, but Peter says he did. That's all Blair needs." Papa blew smoke at the fan. "He can impeach a character witness like Perkins with Cicero's prior bad acts."

He was right about that. Papa was finally taking Peter's story seriously. They should just rest without calling any witnesses and argue to the jury there was reasonable doubt.

"I don't understand," Sweet said.

"If Perkins testifies Cicero's got a good reputation in the community for being peaceful—that's what a character witness does—then Tom can ask him on cross if he's heard about any bad things Cicero's done. Like punch Peter DeGroote."

"Even if they're untrue?"

"Doesn't matter. Judge will let him ask."

"I didn't realize that," Sweet said.

Harley remembered something Blair said at the end of his opening statement—something about another witness he might call. "Do you think Peter's the unnamed witness Captain Blair told the jury about this morning?"

Papa snickered. "The one who'll supposedly remove all doubt about Cicero's guilt? Probably. Tom said he didn't know if he'd call that witness. Probably thinking if we call a character witness, he'd call Peter in rebuttal."

"That makes sense. I'll tell Professor Perkins we're not calling him," Harley said.

"Good," Papa said. "After we call Sadie and Big Joe, it'll be time for Orman."

No Papa—we can't do that. It would just make a bad situation worse. They shouldn't call any of them.

"After Orman, we'll put Cicero on."

What could Cicero possibly say? He didn't remember anything that would help. They should rest without calling any witnesses.

Papa tapped his ashes into a tray. "Jury'll think he's hiding something if he doesn't testify."

Harley looked away. It would be worse if Captain Blair destroyed him on cross.

But Papa was set on his plan. His remark outside the courtroom earlier—*stay out of my way*—was all the proof Harley needed that Papa wasn't willing to hear disagreement.

He nodded. "If he doesn't call Peter, then all we'll have ready to go in the morning is your opening statement, since our witnesses won't arrive until after noon."

"But Blair told the judge he was going to finish his case in the morning," Sweet said. "Maybe he does have another witness. Maybe the unnamed witness is somebody else."

Harley leaned forward. "Papa, he might be right. Captain Blair told the judge he had one more witness today—that's Jessie—and then he'd finish in the morning. If Peter were to be a rebuttal witness, he'd have to testify after we call a character witness. Then who did he mean to call in the morning before he rests?"

Papa pondered that. "Another fella stood up this morning when the judge asked witnesses to come forward."

"Who was that?" Sweet asked.

"Another policeman, not in uniform but wearing a badge," Papa answered. "Didn't recognize him. Can't imagine what he'd say that'd warrant such a build-up by Tom in his opening."

Harley's eyes flitted from Papa to Mr. Sweet and back. "You're right, Papa. I'd forgotten him. He must be the mystery witness. I thought he'd probably just testify about the scene of the murder, but Quinn did that."

No good would come of this. Harley ran his hands through his hair as the others looked at him blankly.

"What could this man possibly have to say that would convince Captain Blair to make it the climax of his case?"

Chapter 32

The next morning Miss Peach found Mr. Calloway hunched over the defense table, his chin cradled in his hand, waiting for Blair's final witness. He looked exhausted. Poor man, he must not have slept at all. He did that every trial, but somehow he was always able to reach down deep and find the strength. This day would be no different.

"We call Harrison Palmer," Captain Blair announced.

Mr. Calloway and Harley exchanged looks.

She'd never heard of him. Mr. Calloway had asked Harley to interview all the witnesses, but Harley had never mentioned him. She flipped back to her notes of Blair's opening statement: *He'll dispel any doubts and leave you with absolute certainty of the defendant's guilt.*

Detective Harrison Palmer of the Waco Police was as serious and self-confident on the stand as any young gentleman might be. Blair established that Palmer had been a Waco police officer for only one year after learning his trade over three years on the Philadelphia police force.

Miss Peach sniffed. He was hardly more experienced as a policeman than she was as a stenographer.

She flipped back to a clean page in her notepad.

Captain Blair stood at his table. "Were you asked to

investigate a homicide involving a bawdy woman by the name of Georgia Virginia Gamble?"

"I was."

"When was your first involvement?"

"The same day her body was discovered. I went later that morning, after I got to work."

"What was your job at the scene of the murder?"

"To take statements from witnesses and collect the evidence. I interviewed the madam, Miss Jessie Rose, another whore by the name of Sadie Wiggins, and the madam's protection man, name of Joe."

"What did Miss Jessie Rose tell you?"

Mr. Calloway half rose. "Judge, that's hearsay, and the jury's already heard everything she had to say anyway."

The judge nodded. "Got anything new, Captain?"

"Well, Your Honor," Blair replied, "I'm just showing her story has been consistent all along."

Mr. Calloway folded his arms. "If he's gonna say she noted 'a look of ineffable terror' on Georgia's face"—he glanced at the jury—"I stipulate she did, judge. I bet she's used that line to everybody in the Reservation."

Several jurors chuckled.

The judge shot Blair a sour look. "Captain, move along to something new."

"I'm happy to, Judge. Detective Palmer, let's talk about the gun."

"Yes, sir."

"Had it been disturbed before you got there?"

Mr. Calloway lifted a finger. "Objection. He could only speculate about what happened before he arrived."

"Sustained."

"All right," Blair said with some exasperation. "Where did you find it when you arrived?"

"On the floor at the foot of the bed in Miss Georgia's bedroom."

"What did you do with it?"

"I examined it closely. Then I broke it open to see if it had been shot."

"Had it?"

"Yes, sir. One round was discharged."

"What did you notice about the barrel?"

"This firearm has two barrels, one over the other." He used his two index fingers to demonstrate the stacked barrels. "The right side of the top barrel had blood on it."

Blair took the derringer to the witness and showed it to him. "That it?"

"Yes." Palmer pointed to a red stain.

Then Blair slowly strode along the jury rail, displaying the pistol to the jury as he went. At the north end of the jury box, he turned back to face the detective. "What did you notice about that bloody spot?"

"It contained the impression of a finger," Palmer answered with a touch of drama.

Blair again walked the bloodstained pistol back along the jury rail. Each juror leaned close to examine the impression again.

"Detective Palmer," Blair continued, "based on your experience, especially the experience you gained while on the police force of the city of Philadelphia, what is the significance of that bloody finger impression?"

The detective addressed the jury with a sanguine expression. "It enabled me to determine who held the gun."

Mr. Calloway sprang out of his chair, almost knocking it

over. "Whoa now, Your Honor, I'm gonna object to that. He can't do that just by looking at a spot of dried blood."

"On the contrary," Blair replied, glaring at Mr. Calloway as if to challenge him, "that is exactly what he did. He'll be happy to explain his scientific methods."

"Scientific?" Mr. Calloway sneered.

Miss Peach's pen ran dry, and she quickly switched to another. Neither Mr. Calloway nor Harley had ever mentioned anything about this so-called science.

"Let's hear it," the judge said.

"Detective Palmer, explain to the court and jury how a trained professional like you can examine the impression of a finger left in blood and identify whose finger it was."

"Certainly."

With the bearing of a college professor, Palmer lectured the jury in the science of finger mark analysis. He was quite arrogant, Miss Peach thought, and he spoke quickly. She wrote furiously to capture his exact words.

"Every human being carries, from his cradle to his grave, certain physical marks that don't change character and by which he can always be identified without doubt," Palmer said. "These marks are his signature, his physiological autograph. They can't be counterfeited or disguised, and they don't wear off. There are no duplicates of a man's finger markings in all the swarming populations of the globe. This autograph consists of the marks on the hands and the feet. If you look at your fingers"—he held up his own—"you'll see clearly defined patterns such as arches, circles, long curves, and whorls."

Blair stood quietly, examining his own fingers as if to suggest that others do the same. Every curious person in the courtroom, including the judge and every juror, inspected his own hand, then his other, and then his neighbor's. Comparisons followed. Expressions of whispered wonder passed among them.

Miss Peach sketched her own whorls and arches on her notepad.

"Let's have order," the judge finally called.

Blair cleared his throat. "Detective, how did you employ this science to identify the murderer?"

"First, I made a careful drawing of the bloody print on a piece of cardboard. Then, using a pantograph"—he pulled the metal instrument from his pocket and expanded it—"I enlarged it ten times, so it would be more visible to the naked eye."

"What did you do then?"

"I got a drinking glass and filled it with water. Then I went to the jail and paid a call on the defendant."

"What did you do?"

"I said, 'Here, young man, I've brought you some water,' and then I handed it to him."

"Did he take it?"

"Yes."

"With which hand?"

Palmer held up his own. "His right."

"Which side of the gun was the bloody finger mark on?"

"The right."

"What did you do then?"

"I waited until he finished drinking, and then I took the glass back, careful to hold it by the bottom. I took it to my office whereupon I examined it under a magnifying glass."

"Were there finger markings on the glass?"

"There were." ⸮

"How many?"

"Several. Enough to make my comparison."

"What did you do then?"

"I took another piece of cardboard and carefully drew the markings as I examined them under the magnifying glass. Then just as I had done with the drawing of the bloody finger mark, I enlarged them ten times using a pantograph. Finally, I laid the drawing of the bloody impression side by side with each of the six impressions from the drinking glass."

Mr. Calloway began to rise.

"Detective Palmer," Captain Blair continued, "tell the jury the result of your scientific investigation."

Mr. Calloway's hand flew up in a stopping motion. "Objection! This is hocus-pocus, not science. I've been practicing law for almost thirty years, and I've never seen any court allow finger smudge evidence like this nonsense. It's not evidence at all. He might as well just pull a rabbit out of a hat and call it science."

He wiggled both sets of fingers in front of him as if he were performing a magic trick.

Blair looked cool as a cucumber. "I have law, Your Honor."

"Let's have it," the judge said.

Captain Blair took a law book to the bench and pointed to the relevant text.

Miss Peach exercised her cramping wrist. Finger marks. How interesting. Was this methodology a product of the progress of human knowledge, or was it no better than superstition?

While the judge read the case, Mr. Calloway spoke sarcastically. "I've never seen any case that permits a palm reader to testify, Judge. This is claptrap."

"Well, Detective Palmer is a man of science," countered Blair, his voice cracking, "and maybe you haven't opened a law book in a while, Catfish."

Mr. Calloway bowed up. "If our law books permit trial by soothsayer, then I haven't missed a thing."

"He can mock science if he wants—"

"Hang on, gentlemen," the judge said, sliding the book across the bench to Mr. Calloway. "Have you read Clark against State of Texas?"

Mr. Calloway quickly scanned the case, flipped to the next page, and shook his head. "This is a case about footprints in the dirt that matched a defendant's boot." He slammed the book shut and gave it to Blair. "Doesn't have anything to do with whorls and ridges on fingers."

Blair's back was to her but his arms waved with animation. "That opinion, and those cited in it, permitted comparisons of footprints, and fingerprints shouldn't be any different. Except a finger leaves better prints because it's got patterns on it, while a boot sole doesn't."

The judge was already nodding. "All right. I've never heard of such, but I can't see why a footprint would be admissible yet a fingerprint wouldn't. I'll allow it."

Mr. Calloway turned but shot a glare at the judge. "Note our exception."

"You have your exception, counselor. Now sit down, and let's get on with it."

"And a running objection?" Mr. Calloway added.

"That too," the judge said, scowling.

Blair resumed. "Detective Palmer, let me repeat my question to you. What was the result of your scientific investigation?"

Palmer fussed with his four-in-hand knotted tie so that it was perfectly aligned with the stripes in his silk vest. He lifted his chin toward the jury. "On the barrel of that gun stands the assassin's natal autograph, written in the blood of the helpless whore.

There is only one man in the whole earth whose hand can duplicate that crimson sign: the defendant, Cicero Sweet."

Cicero shook his head furiously.

Mr. Calloway sat stoically with his chin resting on steepled hands, lost in thought. He had to do something quickly, though. Blair was finished, and the judge and the jury were watching him expectantly. Detective Palmer had an infuriatingly smug expression.

Finally, Mr. Calloway rose. "Your Honor, this is the first we've heard of this finger smudge business. I request a recess."

"Very well, court will be in recess for fifteen minutes."

"Maybe until this afternoon, Judge?"

"No, sir. I'll give you an hour. Gentlemen of the jury, be back in the deliberation room in one hour sharp."

As soon as the judge and jury exited the courtroom, Mr. Calloway took off like a shot.

"Where are you going?" Harley shouted after him.

"To get something from the Growlery. Be back."

"Can I help?" Harley asked, but he was already out the door.

Miss Peach gathered her things, perplexed. Mr. Calloway's library was crammed with reading material. He was a voracious reader, even more so since Mrs. Calloway died, according to Harley. He had hundreds of books and stacks of magazines going back years. He read every issue of *Harper's*, *Munsey's*, and *The Century* cover to cover. He even subscribed to the British periodical *The Strand*. She'd enjoyed their discussions about that British detective Sherlock Holmes.

What could he possibly need from the Growlery?

She and Harley went next door to the Blackwell Hotel, where Harley brooded over a cup of coffee. Forty-five minutes later, they found Mr. Calloway already back in court at the counsel table, hunkered over some magazines.

"What are you reading?" Harley asked.

"Just fiddling." That meant *don't bother me now.*

A stack of magazines stood beside him: *The Century Illustrated Monthly Magazine*, five issues in addition to the one he was frantically reading. She pressed her lips together. A literary magazine?

Henry Sweet came over, but Mr. Calloway waved him off. Harley glanced at Miss Peach. She shrugged back. Harley took his seat and waited.

Something was brewing.

Chapter 33

Papa stood, arms crossed, at the defense table. "Detective Palmer, do you mind if I ask you a few questions?"

"Not at all."

"That's great. I just found your testimony fascinating." He nodded his head as if he was puzzled with something. "Maybe you can help me on some things I'm curious about."

"I'll try to help you understand."

Harley glanced at Papa, then back at the witness. There was arrogance in the policeman's voice. He was going to teach Papa a thing or two. Harley had no idea what Papa was going to do, but he was certain that Papa was the master, not the pupil. He eased back to watch.

Papa gave the officer an uncertain expression. "Do you think the blood on that derringer came from Miss Georgia?"

"Yes, sir."

"So when she got shot, blood sprayed out and some of it landed on the gun?"

"I presume so."

"And then the killer touched the barrel?"

"Yes."

"So it had to be the killer who touched it?"

"Yes."

"Couldn't be the mark of somebody else like Miss Jessie or Miss Sadie or Big Joe, or even you or Sergeant Quinn?"

"No, it matched the defendant."

"I see. Well, I'll come back to that matching business shortly." He paced back to the bar rail. "You do know Miss Jessie Rose, Miss Sadie Wiggins, and a man named Big Joe were also there at the sporting house at the time of the shooting, right?"

"That's my understanding."

He wrinkled his nose. "You didn't compare finger smudge marks from any of them?"

"No, nor of President Cleveland." The jury rewarded him with a chuckle, as did Papa. "The bloody print matched the defendant. There was no need to compare others."

"I'll come back to that. For now, though, that pistol somehow made its way from the sporting house to the courthouse and was brought to both the county courtroom for the inquest and the district courtroom for this trial. So other folks touched it somewhere along the line, right?"

"True. But your client matches the prints."

Palmer was putting everything on the match. Was Papa baiting him?

He grinned at the officer. "Yes, sir. I promise you I'll get to your science in a minute. But for now, somebody other than the shooter touched the gun?"

"True."

"All right. And I expect your science can't tell you when the person who laid that print actually touched it?"

"It had to have been before the blood dried."

"Sure, but you don't know at what point in time before it dried?"

"Not with certainty."

"What you do know for certain is that this impression was made after she got shot?"

"True."

"It's not proof this person who made the print was holding the gun at the time of the shooting, is it?"

"It proves your client touched it."

Papa scratched his head and swung his back to the jury. He winked at Harley and slowly turned toward Palmer. "Well, sir, you keep bringing me back to it, so I expect we better talk about this science of yours. Is it called finger smudge science?"

"Physiological autograph evidence."

"Physiological . . . autograph . . . evidence," he repeated. "Sounds awful smart. One thing I was wondering when I heard you talk about this—did you go to some school to learn about it?"

"Not specifically, no."

"So there's not a"—he gazed up at the whirling ceiling fan as if to find the words—"department of physiological autography at some college back east somewhere?"

"Not that I know of."

Papa nodded and ambled toward the jury, stopping right in front of them. "Not some laboratory where they do experiments to see how many times a smudge print comparison gets it wrong or gets it right?"

"Not to my knowledge. This field of scientific understanding is relatively new."

"New science, huh?" He cocked his head to one side as if it might look different viewed from another angle. "Well, where is it exactly you picked up this new finger smudge science?"

"I first learned of the use of physiological autograph evidence as a tool of criminal investigation when I was in the police department in Philadelphia."

"Oh, you did, eh?" Papa eyed the witness in amazement. "So back east, they did comparisons in court as you've done here today?"

"Not that I recall."

He gave Palmer a look of disappointment. "Philadelphia detectives didn't testify to juries about it?"

"I don't believe anyone has thought to do that yet."

Papa's eyes widened. "Oh, so you're the first one smart enough to figure it out?"

"I'm sure it's been done elsewhere, probably by Scotland Yard."

"Maybe that detective Sherlock Holmes? He's done it?"

"I don't know."

"Have you heard of anybody anywhere in Texas doing what you've done here?"

"Not testifying in court, but it's well-known science around the world. There was a scholarly article published in *Nature* magazine in 1880 about studies done by Dr. Henry Faulds, a Scottish physician, while he was in Japan. I believe he even worked with Charles Darwin on it. Other scholars have taken up the study in the last seven or eight years, particularly in Britain. Scotland Yard, as I said, has great interest in it. The technique is used by prisons and police departments in this country for identification purposes of many kinds. The army uses it to identify recruits."

"*Nature* magazine, eh? So you based your work on this scholarly magazine article?"

"In part."

"Got a copy of it I can look at?"

"No."

"You read it?"

"I've never actually seen a copy of that article, no. I've just heard about it."

"Did you check with the library here in town?"

"No, sir."

"Well," Papa said, thoughtfully, "I suppose you can't be expected to read an article you don't have, can you?"

"Certainly not."

"Read any other articles about finger smudge science?"

"No."

"Not a one?"

The detective had the sense to look uncomfortable by this point. "No."

"Well, I'll circle back to that in a minute. But first, you said something a few minutes ago I thought was so well put, I'd like to remind the jury of it."

Papa went back to Miss Peach and took her notepad. Since her notes were for him, she'd taught him to read her shorthand.

Back at the defense table, he pinched on his pince-nez, flipped through the pages, and placed the pad on top of an open magazine, leaning over it with both arms extended in support. "Miss Peach takes down the testimony for me word for word, and I wonder if she got this right."

Palmer sat upright, straining his neck, struggling to see what Papa was reading.

"You tell me if she didn't record it right. Here goes: 'Every human being carries with him from his cradle to his grave certain physical marks which do not change their character, and by which he can always be identified, and that without shade of doubt or question. These marks are his signature, his physiological autograph, so to speak'"—he peered at the jury as he said the words—"'and this autograph cannot be counterfeited, nor can he disguise it or hide it away, nor can it become illegible by the wear and the mutations of time.'"

He looked up over his spectacles straight at Palmer. "Does that sound like what you just testified to?"

Palmer's eyes darted to Blair then back to Papa. "Very close. I don't believe I discussed mutations."

"No, I don't think you did either. In fact, I'm afraid I might have misled you a bit, Detective. I wasn't actually reading Miss Peach's notes. I was reading from this magazine article."

He held up a magazine.

Blair jumped up. "Objection! Hearsay."

Papa shrugged. "Impeachment."

"Overruled."

Papa took the magazine over to the witness stand. "It's not *Nature* magazine. It's *The Century Illustrated Monthly Magazine.* Take a look at page 237 in the June 1894 issue." He pointed to the relevant passage and held it out toward Palmer. "Did I read that cradle-to-grave part exactly how it's written there?"

Palmer studied the magazine page, then flipped to the next and back again. He turned it over to see the front cover, then the back, and then returned to the page in question. He took so long the jurors began to glance at one another.

Finally, he spoke. "It appears so."

"Isn't that passage from *Century Magazine* identical to the testimony you gave on direct examination a few minutes ago?"

"I don't remember my words exactly, sir."

"Fair enough," Papa said.

Palmer should have just admitted it and saved himself some embarrassment.

"Miss Peach did take these notes of what else you said earlier," Papa said, putting down the magazine and picking up the notepad. "Let me quote you from her notes this time: 'There are no duplicates of a man's finger markings in all the swarming populations of the globe. This autograph consists of the marks on the hands and the feet. If you look at your fingers, you'll see clearly defined patterns, such as arches, circles, long curves, and whorls.' Was that your exact, word-for-word testimony?"

Palmer stared at him silently.

"Detective?"

"It sounds similar, but I'm not sure it's exact."

"Now, listen to this from the article in *Cent*—"

Blair exploded. "I object to this, Your Honor. This article's not evidence. It's hearsay."

"Goes to the man's credibility, judge. It may be hearsay, but it's hearsay he's spouting in court like it's his own."

"Overruled."

Harley crossed his arms and smiled discreetly.

"Listen to this passage from the magazine, detective: 'Whereas this signature is each man's very own, there is no duplicate of it among the swarming populations of the globe.' You and the author here both see folks swarming around the globe, huh?"

Silence.

Palmer swallowed hard. "The author and I are both speaking about a common truth, so I'm not surprised by similarity of expression."

"So you and this author both *coincidentally* chose the words 'swarming populations of the globe'?" Papa peered over his pince-nez.

"Apparently."

"All right." Papa nodded. "That author goes on, 'If you will look at the balls of your fingers, you that have very sharp eyesight, you will observe that these dainty curving lines lie close together, like those that indicate the borders of oceans in maps, and that they form various clearly defined patterns, such as arches, circles, long curves, whorls, etc., and that these patterns differ on the different fingers.' Sure sounds like what you said, doesn't it?"

"There are material differences, counselor."

"Sure, you're right. Let's try another then. Did you also say this on direct examination, as Miss Peach recorded it? 'On the barrel of that gun stands the assassin's natal autograph, written in the blood of the helpless whore. There is only one man in the whole earth whose hand can duplicate that crimson sign, the defendant, Cicero Sweet.' Did you say that to the jury under oath?"

There was another extended moment of silence before Palmer finally answered aloud, voice tight. "Something like that, I think."

"So the 'assassin's natal autograph,' that's the way you put it?"

"Yes."

"Well, sir, let me read to you one final passage from this article," he said, placing his finger on the bottom of the page. "'Upon this haft stands the assassin's natal autograph, written in the blood of that helpless and unoffending old man who loved you and whom you all loved.'" He paused and stared at the jury. "'There is but one man in the whole earth whose hand can duplicate that crimson sign.'"

Papa tossed the magazine back on the table and stroked his whiskers thoughtfully. "So you and this author both coincidentally came up with the phrase 'assassin's natal autograph'—and the 'crimson sign,' to boot?"

"It appears so," Palmer said quietly.

Papa nodded. "Well, sir, to be honest, you did read a magazine article after all now, didn't you?"

Palmer picked at a bit of skin on one finger. "It's possible I read it sometime back and forgot about it. Perhaps I adopted someone else's verbiage without realizing it. But the science is sound."

"Detective, I expect there's nothing really wrong with borrowing a few words here and there, is there?"

"Not at all, as long as they're correct."

"Right, and as long as you borrow 'em from someone writing the truth?"

Suspicion flickered across his face. "I suppose."

Poor fellow. He was right to feel the noose tightening.

Papa showed him the magazine again. "Look back here at the beginning of this article. It was published just last month. Do you see the author's name there?"

Silence.

"Detective?"

"I do."

"It's not Dr. Henry Faulds, is it?"

"No."

"You said he wrote the truth in *Nature* magazine?"

"He did."

"And this author's not Charles Darwin?"

"No."

Papa took a step backward and raised his voice. "If you don't mind, read the name of the learned man of science for our jury, please sir."

Palmer closed his eyes briefly and sighed.

"Mark Twain."

Chapter 34

The courtroom erupted in laughter.

"Mark Twain?" Papa asked Detective Palmer. "You mean the storyteller?"

Palmer remained silent.

"Isn't the article part six of a serial called 'The Tragedy of Pudd'nhead Wilson'?"

The witness was silent.

Papa flashed Harley a triumphant look as he turned toward the bench. "Judge, I'd sure like the jury to read all about Pudd'nhead Wilson's learned smudge science. So if Mr. Lord will mark these six magazines as defense exhibits, I offer them into evidence."

"No objection," Blair muttered, neither looking up nor rising.

"They're admitted," the judge ruled.

"That's all my questions, Judge," Papa said. He turned toward his adversary with a grin. "Say, Captain Blair, was that Huck Finn I saw in the waiting area? He your next witness?"

The courtroom broke into laughter again.

"Order!"

"The state rests," Blair said.

"We'll take our lunch break now, gentlemen. Be back at one o'clock."

The room exploded into motion and talk.

Harley watched his father mingle with the others with a mixture of pride and amazement. Only Catfish Calloway could get the entire courtroom to laugh at the state's expert witness right at the apex of the prosecution case. His cross-examination had left them with plenty of reasonable doubt. Papa had always told him to end on high note.

Harley pulled his files toward him, gathering his thoughts. "Are we going to rest now too?"

Papa rocked back in his chair, relishing the moment.

"We don't need to call any witnesses, do we?" he repeated.

"We got 'em on the run now," Papa said.

Surely he wouldn't call Orman and the others now; there was no reason to. It was done. They shouldn't give Blair a chance to recover. Papa knew that. Papa preached that. At least he always had in the past.

"So we rest, right?"

"No, son, we can't let 'em get away. It's time to sound the charge."

Harley blinked, struggling not to appear defiant. The burden of proof was on Blair, not the defense. Had Papa forgotten things that had always been gospel to him? Apparently he had something else in mind now.

When court reconvened at one o'clock, Papa announced he intended to call witnesses and make his opening statement.

"May it please the court," he said, nodding to the judge.

"Counsel," the judge replied.

"Gentlemen of the jury, it's time for you to hear the other side of this sorry business. What you'll see is a murder did occur in the sporting house, but the killer wasn't this young man." He placed his hand on Cicero's shoulder. "This boy was there to enjoy pleasures he had no business thinking about. Like the old proverb goes, you lie down with dogs, you get up with fleas. The Reservation is a place where deplorable things happen, and unfortunately, Cicero didn't realize that. He should have known better, but he's only eighteen. And now he finds himself here in court, accused of a terrible crime by a madam trying to protect somebody and a police department too willing to accept things at face value. They want you to convict this boy based on a young pup detective's fiction science. Well, gentlemen, if the state of Texas won't bring you the truth, I will. I'm gonna put Cicero in the witness chair and let you judge him for yourself. Unfortunately, he can't remember what happened that night, probably a combination of too much beer and a blow to the head delivered by somebody you haven't heard about. Yet. One thing you'll know for sure, though. If he was a killer, he wouldn't be saying he didn't remember. He'd have made up a story. Because killers lie, don't they? And other people sometimes lie to protect killers."

Harley shifted in his seat. Maybe this would go more smoothly than he feared.

"Last thing, gentlemen, I will also put the actual killer in that witness chair. Count on it. Thank you."

No, Papa! Why couldn't he see the folly of this?

"Call your witness," the judge said.

Harley glanced at Miss Peach. Her face was blank.

"We call Sadie Wiggins."

Several minutes passed as everyone waited for the bailiff to return from the waiting area.

Harley began writing Papa a note, but he scratched it out. It was too late. Papa was committed to this course.

"Is she here, Catfish?" the judge asked after a time.

"I don't know, Judge. She got served with an instanter subpoena last night."

The courtroom door finally creaked open, and the bailiff held it for Miss Sadie. Big Joe followed her in and plopped down on the front row just across the bar rail from the witness stand. He crossed his burly arms.

Harley slid forward in his chair. If there was any hope Sadie would tell the truth, it was without Joe staring at her. He leaned over to Papa and nodded toward Joe. "The rule."

Sadie went to the witness stand, where she was sworn.

"Your Honor," Papa said. "The rule's been invoked, and another witness just came in." He pointed at Joe. "That man, Judge."

The court sent Joe outside. Harley settled back.

"Are you Sadie Wiggins?" Papa asked.

"That's me."

"Where do you work?"

"Waco."

"Who employs you?"

"A lady."

"What's her name?"

"Jessie."

"Jessie Rose?"

"Yep."

"Let me get right to the point, ma'am. Were you present at Miss Jessie's sporting house in the early morning hours of April sixteenth?"

"I don't recall dates very well."

"Were you there when Miss Georgia Gamble was shot?"

"Yep, but I didn't see it."

"Did you go to her room after the gunshot with Miss Jessie and Big Joe?"

"Yep."

"Did you see this young man?" he said, placing a hand on his client's shoulder. "Cicero Sweet?"

"Yep."

"Where was he?"

"On the floor."

"In what state was he?"

"Drunk."

"So he was passed out?"

"Yep." She paused as if gathering her energy. "Except he came to for a minute."

Harley's fingers tightened around the arms of the chair. She was going to lie. He willed his father not to press her.

"Did he say anything?"

"Yep, to Miss Jessie," she replied, confidently. "He said, 'I shot her. I'm sorry.'"

"Are you sure about that, Miss Sadie?"

"Very sure."

"Now, we heard Miss Jessie testify about that yesterday." Papa seemed unaffected. He went back to Miss Peach, whispered to her, and waited while she flipped through her pad. He took the pad and pinched his pince-nez into place. "You sure Cicero didn't say, 'I'm sorry—I shot her,' rather than 'I shot her—I'm sorry?'"

Miss Sadie looked toward the window in the courtroom door. Joe was outside, looking in. She closed her eyes and mouthed something silently. "Yep, you're right, mister. He said, 'I'm sorry I shot her.'"

She stole another glance at Joe.

"Isn't the truth, as you told me last night, that he never came to and didn't say anything at all?"

She looked away. "That's a lie."

Papa returned the notepad to Miss Peach. "Miss Sadie, did you have an opportunity to see Miss Georgia after she'd been shot?"

"Yep."

"Would you describe her for the jury please, ma'am?"

"She had a look of ineffable terror on her face."

Papa looked at the jury and raised his eyebrows. "Ineffable terror?"

"Yep."

"You know what that word *ineffable* means?"

"I sure do, mister. It means she looked real sorry she'd been killed by your client there." She pointed at Cicero.

No help at all, really. Harley let out his breath as quietly as he could.

"Thank you, ma'am," Papa said after a pause. "You've been very helpful."

"No questions," Blair said.

"Call your next witness, Catfish."

"Your Honor, we call Joe Buckrum."

Sadie departed, and Joe took the stand. He gave Miss Peach his one good eye. What was that about? Flies buzzed around his face, but he ignored them.

"Folks call you Big Joe?"

"Some do."

"What's your job for Miss Jessie?"

"Working."

"Do you provide protection for Miss Jessie and the girls?"

"Objection," Blair called. "Leading."

"Sustained."

"Ever have to use your fists?"

"Yes, sir."

"What for?"

"Knocking on them doors when them customers' time's up."

The answer drew laughter from the jury box, and Papa just shook his head with a smile. "All right, let's try something else. Did you see me last night talking with Miss Sadie?"

"Objection, leading."

"Sustained."

"Where were you about eight o'clock last night?'

"I don't remember."

"Who'd you run into on the street?"

"I don't recollect being on the street."

"What did you hold in your hand last night when you and I spoke?"

"Objection, leading."

"Catfish, he's your witness. Don't lead him."

Papa glared at the witness intently. "Where's your blackjack now, Joe?"

He had a blank look. "What blackjack?"

"Ever met a hoot owl named Iver?"

What was Papa doing?

Joe chuckled. "Met an owl?"

"Your Honor, I'm done with Joe."

Papa slid back into his chair next to Harley and said under his breath, "Joe may look dumb as a stump, but he's not."

No more witnesses, thankfully. It was time to cut their losses.

As Joe exited the courtroom, Harley saw someone outside who made his heart sink. He nudged Papa and nodded toward the man, still visible through the window. It was Bud Orman.

"Papa, we don't need him. Let's rest our case."

"It's not his time yet, son."

Harley riffled the edges of the papers before him, trying to tamp down his rising panic. This whole case was spinning out of control. Did his father have any plan left at all, or had he been reduced to grabbing at straws? How could it get any worse?

Papa stood up and addressed the court. "We call Cicero Sweet."

Chapter 35

Catfish sniffed victory in the sultry courtroom air. He'd routed the haughty detective's frontal attack. All that remained was to march Cicero out in front of the jury, parade that characteristic Sweet family sincerity, and then deliver the coup de main—the cross-examination of Bud Orman—to expose his mendacity and leave the real killer for all to see.

"Do you swear to tell the truth so help you God?" the bailiff asked.

Cicero stood straight as an arrow, his youthful face innocent, earnest. "I do."

As Cicero mounted the witness chair, Catfish positioned himself in front of the jury. "Turn to these men over here. I want you to look them in the eye and tell them the honest truth. Did you shoot Miss Georgia Gamble?"

"I don't believe I did, sir, but honestly, I don't remember what happened."

"So you can't truthfully swear either you did or didn't?"

"No, sir."

Catfish held Miss Peach's notepad before him. "The two sporting girls swore, and this is word for word out of both their mouths, that you came to and said, 'I'm sorry I shot her.' Now tell the jury, did you say that?"

"I don't remember saying that, but I don't think I would have, since I don't believe I did shoot her. I had no reason to."

Catfish returned to his swivel chair, rocked back, and crossed his legs. He'd have preferred a stronger denial, but with the boy's memory loss, that's all they would get. Would have to do. He wheeled around so he could see the Sweets. Henry locked eyes with him.

Trust me.

He scanned the side of the courtroom where the Sweets were. There were fewer folks here than when the sporting girls testified. Brann sat in the back, as did Babcock Brown and some other reporters. Jasper perched next to Mrs. Sweet; the judge had excused him from the subpoena after he testified, and he was no longer required to remain outside the courtroom.

"Are your folks here in court?" Catfish asked.

"Yes, sir. They're back there on the front row." Cicero pointed.

It was at that moment that he spotted Thaddeus Schoolcraft on the other side of the gallery. The bastard's blackthorn cane stood upright in front of him, and he'd folded his hands over its head. Their eyes met, and Schoolcraft grinned.

He glanced at Henry Sweet, who looked back with an expression of hope. Catfish groped for his trial box and the spent minié ball, then made a show of studying his notes for almost a minute. He had to expel Schoolcraft and that other trial from his mind. Henry deserved his full attention.

"Catfish, you done?" the judge finally asked.

"No, Your Honor, I'm not." He shuffled through his papers. "Cicero, is your family here in court?"

Cicero shot a glance at Harley. "Like I just told you, my mother and father are over there." He pointed again.

"Right." Catfish squeezed the bullet tightly. "Got brothers and sisters?"

"Yes, sir. I'm the oldest. I have two brothers and one sister back home."

"Lived in Washington County all your life?"

"Yes, sir."

"Why're you in Waco now?"

"I attend Baylor University. I started last fall, and I'm in my second semester now—or I was until this happened."

Catfish glanced at Dr. Burleson, still on the front row.

"I've been in jail since April," Cicero finished.

"Let's talk about what led to that." He stood up and continued the questioning from the corner of the defense table. "Where'd you and Jasper go on the evening of April fifteenth?"

"To a revival at the Tabernacle. Mr. Greer took all us boys to see it."

"Now, Cicero," Catfish said in a fatherly tone, "did you go to Miss Jessie's sporting house after that sermon?"

"Yes, sir."

"Was it your idea or Jasper's idea to go there?"

"It was mine. Jasper just went along because I wanted him to. He didn't have anything to do with all this, Mr. Calloway. He was just there. I feel bad I got him in trouble."

Catfish hoped President Burleson was listening.

"You said you don't remember what happened that night. Is there anything you do remember?"

"I remember the revival, and going back to the dorm, and taking a hack to the Reservation. I remember going in and meeting the madam and the girls."

"You remember Miss Georgia?"

Cicero nodded. "I danced with her, and then we must have

gone upstairs, but I don't remember anything after that."

"How many beers you have?"

"I'm not sure, sir. Way more than one."

"Tell the gentlemen of the jury whether you felt the effects of that beer?"

Cicero smiled. "I sure did. As a matter of fact, I felt it well into the next day. I had a powerful bad headache."

Catfish paced behind the prosecution table toward the jury box. They were very attentive.

Keep it up, son.

"You remember receiving a blow to your head?"

"I sure don't. I do remember having a big goose egg on my head the next day, though, and it hurt awful bad."

"Show the jury where it was."

Cicero pointed to the right side of his forehead.

"Did you have that knot when you danced with Miss Georgia?"

"No, sir. I don't know how I got it."

"What's the next thing you remember after dancing with the sporting girl?"

"Being in the county jail."

Catfish blinked approval at Cicero. "Pass the witness."

As he strode back to his seat, he fought the urge to glance at Schoolcraft, but then looked anyway. The man's right hand moved deliberately from the head of his cane to his throat. He wrapped his fingers around his neck and tightened them so slightly that probably only Catfish noticed.

He answered with a cold, hard stare. *Go to hell.*

He slid into his chair, avoiding Harley's attempts to catch his eye. He was done being second-guessed by his own son. Henry was depending on him. His strategy was working.

Blair swaggered forward. "Mr. Sweet, my name's Tom Blair, and I'm the county attorney for McLennan County. I have a few questions for you."

"Yes, sir."

Blair picked up the derringer from the court reporter's desk and held it in front of Cicero. He turned it so that the bloody mark was visible to the jury.

"Have you ever seen this gun?"

"Only here in court."

"You see this dried blood on it?" he asked, turning the bloody mark toward Cicero.

"Yes, sir."

"And the finger mark in it?"

"I'm not sure what that is, sir."

"Have you ever held this gun?"

"Never."

"Did you ever touch it here on this spot where the dried blood is?"

"No, sir."

"So your sworn testimony is that's not your finger mark on the bloody derringer?"

"No, sir. It can't be."

"If you don't mind, Mr. Sweet, hold this derringer in your right hand," he said, handing over the pistol. "Now, extend your right trigger finger for me and hold it so the jury can see. Is that bloody mark right under the tip of your trigger finger?"

Cicero checked. "It looks like it."

"All right," Blair said, taking it back and laying it near the court reporter. He returned to his table. "You and your friend Jasper Cantrell went to the Tabernacle earlier that evening, you said?"

"Yes, sir."

"You heard Reverend Sam Jones deliver a sermon?"

"We sure did."

"In that sermon he preached on licentiousness and drinking?"

"And all the other sins too."

"Yes, he did. And condemned them too, didn't he?"

"Yes, sir."

"Let me read you what the newspaper said about that sermon and see if you remember it the same way. It says this: 'If you can block off a place, call it a Reservation, and license licentiousness, why don't you reserve a few blocks where a man can commit murder and go unpunished?' Do you recall him saying that?"

"Yes, sir."

"You remember the preacher's words pretty well, then?"

"I do."

"Did you consider the Reservation a lawless place where murder might go unpunished, Mr. Sweet?"

"No, sir. I never thought about it, really."

"Isn't it true you got the idea of going to the Reservation from listening to that sermon?"

Cicero shifted in his chair. "Probably."

Blair advanced toward him. "You went there intending to drink beer?"

"We were thirsty. It was a warm evening."

And closer. "And to lay with a bawdy girl?"

"Yes, sir."

Closer still. "Before you went upstairs you drank beer?"

"Like I said earlier, yes, sir."

Now he was face to face with the boy. "You had at least six Busch beers, didn't you?"

"No, sir. It was Lone Star."

Catfish tensed. *Steady, boy.*

Blair fired back: "You remember it was Lone Star?"

"Yes."

"You remember that well?"

"Yes, sir."

"You weren't drunk before you went upstairs?"

"No, sir."

"You got upstairs without falling?"

"Yes, sir."

"Took your clothes off?"

"I reckon."

"Well, they found you naked. You're not saying Miss Georgia undressed you, are you?"

"No, sir. She didn't do that for sure," he said, blushing. "She just tended to her own clothes. I took my own clothes off."

Catfish's fingers opened and closed around the minié ball. Cicero had claimed he didn't remember anything. *Careful, son.*

Blair paused as if surprised. "So you do remember it?"

"No, sir, I don't," Cicero stammered, "but I don't think she'd have to take my clothes off me."

Blair pressed him. "Well, do you remember it or not?"

"I don't, I—"

"So she could have undressed you?"

"I just don't know."

"You lay with her, right?"

"Yes, sir."

"You do remember it after all?"

"No, sir."

"Which is it—you do or you don't?"

Cicero clenched the witness rail. "You have me confused, Mr. Blair."

"Your Honor," Catfish said, jumping up, "I object, he's being unfair with the witness."

"Cross-examination," Blair replied, shaking his head.

"Overruled."

Catfish shot Cicero a cautionary look: *Listen carefully to the questions.*

"How could you be confused?" Blair asked without letup. "You were there. Either you remember or you don't, Mr. Sweet."

"I don't recall anything."

"Oh, so now you don't remember anything at all?"

"No, sir, I do remember some things."

Catfish's grasp of the minié ball tightened.

"You remember dancing?"

"Yes."

"Going upstairs?"

"Yes."

"Taking your clothes off?"

"Maybe."

"Laying with Miss Georgia?"

"I don't exactly recollect it."

"Didn't she make light of your manhoo—"

Cicero pounded the witness rail. "No!"

His response dissipated into the silence of the courtroom.

"You're saying now you do remember what happened?"

Cicero blinked rapidly. "Ah . . . no, sir."

"So she could have said that?"

"Maybe. I don't know. I don't remember."

"And you got mad?"

"Like I say, I don't rightly remember anything about that."

"And she got scared and pulled her derringer?"

The boy's voice dropped. "I sure didn't see anything like that."

"Are you saying you actually remember that she didn't pull her gun?"

He shook his head, slowly at first and then faster and faster. "No, sir."

"Then you took it away from her and shot her dead, didn't you?"

Cicero slammed both hands down on the rail and shouted, "No, sir, no, sir. I didn't shoot her."

A juror looked away. Another shook his head. Others stared down. Catfish willed the boy to meet his gaze, gain some composure.

"So you remember it now?" Blair asked.

Cicero returned his gaze from Catfish to Blair and drew a long, shaky breath. "No, sir, I don't. But I wouldn't have shot her. It's not my way."

Damn it! He'd warned Cicero about that. Catfish squeezed the minié ball until it hurt.

Blair let silence overtake the room, then spoke deliberately. "It's not your way."

There it was—Blair was on it. Too late to stop him from smearing the boy with the tale about Peter DeGroote.

"So you're not the kind of young man who'd murder somebody?"

Cicero folded his hands in his lap. "No, sir. I wouldn't hurt anybody."

"So you've never been in any fights before?"

Catfish sprang to his feet. "Objection! Character evidence, not admissible."

"He opened the door to the defendant's character when he said he wasn't the kind of man to hurt somebody," Blair replied mildly.

"Overruled."

"Back to my question. Are you saying you haven't been in any other fights?"

"No, sir. I haven't, not that I recall."

"If it's contrary to your nature to fight, wouldn't you remember whether you'd ever been in one?"

"Probably."

"And you don't remember any?"

"No, sir."

"So you're denying you've ever been in a fight?"

Catfish half rose again. "Judge, I object, this is getting repetitious."

"I'm just trying to get a straight answer."

"Overruled. Answer the question."

"No, sir," Cicero said. "I haven't been in any fights."

"Ever?"

"Never." He clutched the witness rail.

Blair paused, still intent. Still motionless.

Cicero stared back, wide-eyed.

"You remember having a debate last fall on campus with another Baylor student named Peter DeGroote?"

The boy's eyes cut rapidly from side to side, then settled again on the prosecutor. "Yes, sir. He whipped me good."

"And you got mad, didn't you?"

"No."

"Drank beer to get your courage up?" Blair's color was rising.

"No."

"Hunted him down?"

"I did run into him at the creek."

"You were angry?"

"No."

"You whipped *him* good, didn't you?"

"I didn't."

Blair was almost shouting.

"You punched him and knocked him to the ground, didn't you?"

"No, that just didn't happen."

Cicero lifted his chin and sat back.

"So." Blair spoke slowly and deliberately, surveying the jury. "You're just not the kind of young man who'd hurt anybody?"

"No, sir, I'm not."

"Well, we'll have to see what Peter has to say about that." Blair spun around and headed back to his table. "Nothing further, Judge."

***

The judge darted out the side door, leaving everyone in place.

"He's gotta answer the call of nature," Papa said to Harley. He motioned for everyone to gather close around the defense table. "Miss Peach, go out to the waiting area and make sure Orman's still there."

She left. Henry Sweet joined them and put his hands on Cicero's shoulders.

"Mr. Calloway, how'd I do?" Cicero asked.

"You did fine, son, just fine."

Harley glanced away. Papa was just reassuring him; Blair had turned him every way but loose.

Papa grasped Harley's elbow. "Let's get the killer in here next."

He blanched. "There's reasonable doubt in the evidence already. Is that really nec—"

"We need him now for sure. We've got to prove he's the killer before Blair can call Peter DeGroote in rebuttal to talk about that fight."

It was now or never.

Harley cleared his throat. "I feel strongly about this. We don't have anything at all on Bud Orman. He won't help us. Let's rest our case and just deal with Peter if they call him. They may not. All he can say is that he and Cicero got in a fight. He can't say anything about the killing of Miss Georgia. It's just a distraction."

He glanced at the anxious faces gathered around the table. Papa was at least listening now.

"But if we put Orman up there and it goes wrong," Harley continued, "the jury might decide Cicero's guilty just because we can't prove otherwise. It's not our burden of proof."

But Papa didn't look at him. He looked at Mr. Sweet.

"It's your call, Catfish," Sweet said. Mrs. Sweet gripped his arm.

Papa rocked back in his chair. He was about to speak when Miss Peach returned.

"Orman wasn't there," she said, "so I asked another man who was in the hall. He told me Orman went outside to get a smoke, and I saw him through the window. He's on the street talking to somebody. And I saw—"

"Good," Papa said. "Ask the bailiff to get him back in here."

Harley glanced back at the windows in the courtroom doors. A man was looking in.

Harley pointed at him. "Is that the man you talked to?"

She looked. "Yes, and—"

"That's Sterling DeGroote," Papa said.

A younger man appeared beside him.

"And Peter," Harley added. "Captain Blair must be calling him in rebuttal as soon as we finish."

Miss Peach took a step forward and discharged a big breath. "Mr. Calloway, please listen—I need to tell you something else important. The red buggy. It's parked on the street."

"What?" Papa asked. "Are you sure?"

"Yes. Near the front door."

"That decides it," Papa said. "I told you it's Orman's buggy."

Harley held up a hand. "Wait—Papa, we don't know whose buggy it is. It might be Orman's, but it might be DeGroote's. Peter told me his father let him use their buggy. It could belong to somebody else."

Papa chewed on that silently.

"Let's rest our case and let Blair call Peter," Harley said, trying to keep the pleading tone from his voice. "You'll have an easier time prying it out of him with leading questions on cross than if we call him ourselves."

Papa scratched his head. "I don't want to call him, son. I'm gonna call Orman."

"Then will you wait so we can see if Peter drives the red buggy? If he doesn't, you can still call Orman."

"I agree," Miss Peach said.

Papa chewed on that too. "All right."

The judge returned to the courtroom and reconvened.

"The defense rests," Papa said.

Finally, a positive development.

The judge then announced he was not feeling well and adjourned for the day—another helpful thing, at least for now.

Papa leaned over and issued his next orders before waving for Henry Sweet and heading out of the courtroom with him.

Harley sat down again next to Miss Peach. He was to get another instanter subpoena issued; Papa wanted Winky-Blinky in court the next morning to identify the owner of the red gig. Miss Peach filled out the subpoena form as he dictated the content.

She was writing the final details when a disturbance outside the courtroom drew their attention.

Through the door windows, two men squared up, face to face, one with his back to them. Papa shouted at that man before Mr. Sweet stepped in and dragged him away. They disappeared down the stairs.

The other man turned around, facing them. His horseshoe mustache framed a curling lip. He tipped a cane to his bowler hat and departed.

Chapter 36

Harley was in court early the next day. He couldn't get Papa's clash with Schoolcraft out of his head. He'd stopped by the house after leaving the courthouse but learned nothing. Papa said he was tired and going to bed. He'd looked awful.

When Papa arrived at the courtroom, Harley asked him about Schoolcraft.

"Not now, son."

Harley just stood there. He could help—if only Papa would let him. He looked to Miss Peach for reassurance.

She seemed worried.

Spectators dribbled in early to claim the best seats, Jasper among them. Was he worried too?

Buford Lowe bumbled up to Papa, winking and blinking uncontrollably. "You promised you wouldn't involve me in this."

Papa stood. "We think we might've found the fella with the red buggy, but we aren't sure. We have to see if you can identify him."

"That's all? You don't need me there?" He nodded toward the witness stand, visibly shaken by his surroundings. "And then I can leave?"

"I'll need you to wait outside the courtroom after you identify him. You likely won't have to testify, but it's a possibility."

Lowe trembled, then winked and blinked. "I can't. I'll be ruined. My wife will leave me, and I'll lose my job."

"It probably won't be necessary." Papa touched his arm. "I'll do my best to get what I need without calling you. Just sit in the gallery with Harley. When the man comes in, let him know whether he's the one you saw toss something in the red buggy and go into the sporting house. Then Harley'll take you outside." He paused, pressing closer. "I know this is hard on you, but an innocent boy's life depends on this."

Harley led Lowe to a seat on the west side where they'd be able to see Peter when he came in. And then they waited. Lowe fidgeted constantly.

Fifteen minutes later, Peter DeGroote arrived with his father. The bailiff led Peter to the jury box and placed him there to wait until court reconvened.

Harley leaned close to Lowe. "Is that him?"

"I'm not sure. I didn't see him very well, and it was quick."

"Let's get closer."

He led the reluctant Lowe to the bar rail, not fifteen feet from Peter DeGroote. Lowe took a long, hard look and nodded once. Harley signaled to Papa and took Lowe outside.

As they stepped into the hallway, they ran into Bud Orman, arriving under subpoena. He stank of hair oil. Neither he nor Lowe appeared to recognize one another. Another broken connection—what a relief. Harley instructed Lowe to wait there and went back inside.

"Orman's here too," he told Papa. "They don't know each other."

"All right." His expression was blank.

Harley waited, but Papa said nothing. "So we can release Orman now, right?"

Papa sagged back into his chair and stared off into space. "I expect we'll still call him."

Harley opened his mouth to reply, closed it again, and then just stared at him. *Why, Papa? Why can't you hear what Cicero Sweet doesn't have the guts to say?* Damn that boy for putting Papa through this.

Harley froze in place as his father penciled words into his notes for Orman's examination. He was going through with it. How could Harley stop him now?

Harley twisted away from his father. His eyes caught Miss Peach's, and he crouched beside her, pleading with hushed desperation. "Something's wrong with Papa. He's going to call Orman. He's just blindly charging on. Cicero is guilty, and the jury knows it."

"What about Peter? What if he was there that night?"

Harley shook his head. "We don't have any evidence connecting him to Miss Georgia. Nobody saw him with her. There may have been other men there too with other whores. We can't prove a murder connection to anybody else."

Miss Peach glanced at Papa. "He honestly thinks Orman's the killer."

"Orman has even less to do with it than Peter. He doesn't own the red buggy, doesn't own the bawdy house, wasn't there, has no motive. We can't prove anything."

Her eyes narrowed with concern. "Why's he so insistent?"

He'd been hoping she would have an explanation—other than that Catfish Calloway had lost his touch. "I don't know, I really don't. I've thought in the back of my mind that maybe he had some secret strategy he just wasn't sharing with me, but he doesn't. That's obvious now."

"Do you think it has something to do with his loyalty to Mr.

Sweet? He's worried for his friend?"

Harley shook his head. "I'm more worried about Papa than Mr. Sweet or even about Cicero. He'll get what he deserves. Papa doesn't deserve this."

"And if the jury convicts Cicero, Mr. Calloway will be devastated. There must be something we can do."

The bailiff opened the side door. "All rise."

***

"I call Peter DeGroote in rebuttal," Blair announced.

The boy's clothing was much less colorful than Harley had described before. Catfish glanced back to Sterling DeGroote, watching from the gallery as his son was sworn in. Catfish had no idea where this testimony would lead. Fatigue washed over him.

Blair nodded at the judge and began. "Peter, are you acquainted with the defendant who's sitting over there at that table?" He pointed. "Cicero Sweet?"

Peter didn't look at Cicero. "I am, though not well."

"How do you know him?"

"We were both in the literary society at Baylor."

"Did you have an encounter with him last fall after a debate?"

"Excuse me," Catfish said, rising, "may I reserve my exception to this testimony, judge?"

"Your exception is noted."

"To repeat," Blair said, "did you have an encounter with the defendant?"

"Yes, sir."

"Tell us about that."

"Well, I debated against him back in November. I won. Afterward, I was having a picnic on Waco Creek with a young lady named Chloe Malone. We spread a blanket on the bank and were having sandwiches and ginger ale."

"Tell the jury what happened."

"Yes, sir." He addressed the twelve men in the jury box. "While we were there, Cicero came up. He was drinking beer, acting like he was mad at me over losing. He was bothering Chloe, so I asked him to leave."

"Did he?"

"No, sir. He sat down and was rude to both of us. I asked him again to leave. He finished the beer and threw the bottle in the creek. Then he started another one. I got up and told him to leave."

"What'd he do?"

"He got up in my face and cursed me. I told Chloe we should leave, but Cicero pushed me down." For the first time, he glanced over at Cicero, who was shaking his head. "When I got back up, he punched me and knocked me into the creek. Then he tried to hold Chloe's hand."

"What happened?"

"We started fighting. Chloe told us to stop but we kept on. Then all the sudden, Cicero just got up and walked off."

"Did he hurt you?"

"Not seriously. I had bruises and a bloody nose."

"Did you tell anybody about that fight?"

"I didn't think there was any point."

"Pass the witness."

Catfish took a deep breath. He had to pull himself together, block out all distractions, concentrate on the issue: Could Peter be the murderer? If the red gig was his—but he'd been so sure it belonged to Orman. He would have to see where that led.

"Peter, did you come to the courthouse today in a buggy?"

"Yes, sir. It's my father's. He lets me use it until I can afford my own."

Catfish removed his pince-nez, rubbed his eyes, and stood. "Is it a one-horse rig?"

"Yes."

"Your horse about sixteen hands?"

"I'm not sure. He's a big horse."

"Buggy got a spindle-back seat?"

"It does."

"Is it a red Stanhope gig?"

"Yes, it is."

"You don't see many of those in this part of the country, do you?"

"We brought it from New York when we moved here."

"Folks use them up there to show heavy harness horses, don't they?"

"Yes, sir. Father did that some when we lived in New York."

Catfish eased out from behind the table to a spot near the corner of the jury box. "Peter, did you visit Miss Jessie's sporting house in that gig on the evening of April fifteenth?"

Peter's eyes darted to the gallery. "Ah, no. I didn't. I've never been in the Reservation."

Catfish's breathing quickened. The boy was lying. What was he hiding? "Didn't you park that gig on the street across from the sporting house some time before eleven o'clock?"

"No, I told you, I didn't."

A rush of energy swept over him. "Didn't you go first into the Red Front Saloon?"

"I've never been to the Red Front."

"Then you left the saloon and went back to your buggy?"

"No! How many times do I have to say it?"

"Then"—Catfish made a pitching motion—"you tossed something into it and went into Miss Jessie's place, didn't you?"

"I did not."

Catfish glanced at the window in the courtroom door to see if Lowe was looking in. He wasn't. "Don't you remember passing a bald man who was coming out at the same time?"

"I wasn't there, Mr. Calloway."

"So if the bald man says you were, he's lying?"

"Yes, sir. I wasn't there, I swear it."

"Didn't you see that man in the courtroom today?"

"No."

He paused. "So you're saying you didn't have anything to do with Miss Georgia's killing?"

"No, of course not, I wasn't even there."

"Right after this killing happened, you told your father about that fight you claim you had with Cicero, didn't you?"

"I mentioned it. Father asked me if I knew him after we heard what happened at the whorehouse."

Catfish leaned forward. "Your father mentioned it to me, and so a few days later, my son, Harley Calloway, went out to your house in Provident Heights to talk to you about that, didn't he?"

"Yes, sir."

"And you told him the same story you told the jury?"

"I did."

It was so clear now—it was Peter, not Orman. "Did you also talk to a newspaper reporter from the Dallas *Daily Times-Herald* by the name of Babcock Brown?"

"I'm not sure."

Catfish turned around to scan the gallery for Brown. He spotted him on the right side of the room taking notes. "That man back there in the striped vest?"

Brown awkwardly waved at Peter.

"No, sir. I don't believe I ever talked to him."

"I'm wondering then how that reporter got his story about Cicero and you?"

"I don't know. You'll have to ask him."

"Did you contact him, Peter?"

"I didn't even know him."

"Didn't you know he was in town writing a story about the killing?"

"No."

More lies.

He went back to counsel table and pulled a newspaper from his satchel. "Well, did you read a story in the paper in which Brown wrote this? 'Locals who know him contacted this reporter to inform him that Sweet has a short temper and a taste for a long drink. Just months before this murder, he beat another Baylor student after drinking beer on campus.' Did you see that story?"

"I don't read the Dallas paper."

"So you're not the local who contacted Brown about that fight after the debate?"

"No, I'm not. I don't know how he heard about the fight."

Catfish crossed his arms. "You said on direct examination you didn't tell anybody about it?"

"Nobody except my father. I didn't want to get Cicero in trouble, and I wasn't hurt that badly anyway."

"So other than your father, the only people who knew about it were Cicero and Chloe?"

"That's right."

Catfish nodded toward his client. "Now, Cicero testified before the jury yesterday, and he swore he didn't punch you."

"He's lying."

"I see." He smirked. "So you think Cicero—for some reason—while he was in jail, talked to the reporter and told him—for some reason—about a fight he had with you months earlier?"

"I don't know what Cicero did."

Catfish held his hands up. "Well, if it wasn't you and it wasn't Cicero, then the other person must've been Chloe?"

Peter rubbed the back of his neck. "I don't know. Why don't you go talk to her?"

Catfish lowered his voice. "She's not really local though, is she? Doesn't she live in Carolina?"

"I think so."

"You think she wrote to reporter Brown?"

"Maybe." His fingers drummed the rail. "Ask him."

"I wonder how that could have happened? How would the reporter know to contact her? Or how would she know to contact the reporter?"

"You'll have to ask her."

Catfish leaned forward, hands braced on the defense table. "Isn't the truth, Peter, you spread a false story about Cicero to shift the attention away from somebody else?"

Peter breathed heavily. "No, that's not true."

Killers lie. "Didn't you want the case against Cicero to be so clear he'd just plead guilty and folks would stop looking into the killing?"

"No, that's not true."

"Didn't your father ask me if we were going to plead him guilty?"

Peter shifted in his chair. "I don't know."

"Who are you trying to cover for?"

"No one," Peter shouted.

"Is it Bud Orman?"

Peter's eyes popped wide. "I barely know him."

He knew Orman? Maybe they were together in this. "Oh, so you know Bud Orman?"

"I've met him, but he doesn't have anything to do with this."

"Well, sir, if it's not Bud Orman you're protecting, it must be yourself?"

"No, I—"

"Weren't you at Miss Jessie's that night?"

"No!"

"Did you shoot Miss Georgia?"

"Of course not. I wasn't there, I tell you."

Killers lie.

Catfish went to the court reporter's desk, picked up the derringer, and turned it in his hand until the bloodstain was visible. Whether finger smudge science was valid or not, the killer wouldn't be willing to give his finger mark in evidence, just in case it was.

Harley was scowling at him, brow furrowed, shaking his head.

Yes, son, it's time to drive the charge home and finish this.

"Peter, are you willing to give the court a mark of your trigger finger to see if it matches the bloody finger mark on this derringer?"

"Of course I will."

What?

Catfish peered into the young man's face. He was bluffing. He looked worried.

Call the bluff.

He got a sheet of paper. With his magic pencil, he traced the outline of the derringer and placed it on the rail in front of Peter.

He pulled a handkerchief and got his pen knife from the trial box, then sliced across his left thumb, drawing gasps from the gallery. Two thick globs of blood dripped onto the paper where he'd drawn the barrel of the gun. He pressed his thumb into the handkerchief, folded the knife, and put it back in the trial box.

Peter's eyes were wide.

Exhilaration surged through Catfish. "Peter, touch the blood with your right trigger finger."

Admit it—you killed her.

The jury leaned forward as one.

Judge Goodrich craned his neck.

Blair looked uncertain but rose anyway. "I object."

Catfish wiped his forehead with the bloody handkerchief. "Judge, is the learned prosecutor objecting to his own finger smudge science?"

"Overruled."

Every eye in the courtroom turned toward Peter. He looked at the judge, glanced back to Catfish, and shot a last questioning look at his father.

Just as he reached for the paper, a commotion erupted in the gallery. Sterling DeGroote was on his feet, swatting with one hand at the woman next to him who was trying to tug him back into his seat.

"Stop this slander," he yelled as he pulled his sleeve free of her grasp. "It's me he's protecting. Leave him alone!"

Chapter 37

"Hold on just one minute, sir," Judge Goodrich called to Sterling DeGroote. "You need to take your seat."

Catfish's head was spinning.

"Question me, not my son," DeGroote yelled back.

"Well, sir, maybe they'll want to get to that in minute—but right now, you sit down and keep quiet or I'll have the bailiff take you outside."

DeGroote settled back into his chair.

The judge addressed the witness. "Peter, please touch the paper."

"Yes, sir." Peter sat forward and pressed the paper. "There."

Some jurors eyed the paper, but most went back to gawking at the intruder in the gallery. How was Sterling DeGroote involved in this mess? Catfish had no choice but to find out.

"I'll let that dry while I ask you some more questions," he said. Catfish tried to see the bloody mark, but he was too far away.

"So Peter, do you know what your father's talking about?"

"Yes, sir."

"Maybe you better tell us, then."

Peter looked silently from Catfish to his father.

"Peter, tell us," Catfish repeated.

The elder DeGroote slid to the edge of his seat. His wife clutched his arm. "It's all right, son. Tell him."

Hands on the witness rail, Peter took a slow, deep breath. "I did go to the Red Front and Miss Jessie's that night, and I'm not proud of it—but I didn't have anything to do with Georgia's death. I didn't want anyone at Baylor to know I was at a whorehouse. I was afraid they'd expel me right before my graduation."

Several members of the jury shifted uneasily in their seats.

"So I told my father. Later, after we heard about Cicero being arrested, Father said since Cicero had been caught red-handed, he'd plead guilty and nobody would have to know I was ever there."

Catfish swiped away a rivulet of sweat from his forehead. "So you told your father you were at the sporting house?"

"Yes, sir."

"And he said nobody would find out you were there if Cicero pleaded guilty?"

"Yes."

That didn't make sense. "Why did you assume Miss Jessie and her employees wouldn't tell the police you were there?"

"They just wouldn't."

"Why?"

Peter looked reluctant to speak. "Because they work for Father."

What? That couldn't be.

A murmur rustled through the gallery.

"They work for who?" Catfish asked.

"My father owns Miss Jessie's whorehouse. It's in her name, but he owns it."

"So Miss Jessie, Miss Sadie, and Big Joe all work for your father?"

296

"Yes."

Catfish pressed his temples. What did it mean? "They lied to protect you and your father?"

"I don't know."

"Because you shot Georgia Gamble?"

"No, sir, I did not." Peter glanced at the jury, then at the paper in front of him. "Compare the marks. You'll see."

Killers lie.

Catfish wiped away the sweat from his temples. Every person in the courtroom watched him intently, waiting to see if he would step forward to compare the marks. He glanced into the gallery at Henry Sweet. Henry nodded. Catfish resisted the urge to look to the left but did. Schoolcraft flashed him a grin.

He took a step back. Exhaustion drained every muscle.

"Catfish, are you finished?" the judge asked.

He had no choice.

"No, sir."

Catfish walked over to the witness stand. He laid the pistol on the paper side by side with the drawing, studied it a moment, turned the derringer to face the opposite way, and studied it again.

He stepped back. The boy was telling the truth.

"Pass the witness." He went back to his table, unable to meet his client's gaze, and sagged into his chair.

"Papa?" Harley whispered. "Does it match?"

Catfish rubbed his forehead with one hand. Who killed the whore? If it wasn't Peter—just as he thought all along: Orman was the killer.

"Papa?"

"It's Orman," he whispered back.

"What?"

"Captain Blair, do you have questions?" the judge asked.

"Yes, Your Honor, a few more." Blair walked to the witness stand and examined the finger marks for himself. He left the papers and gun there and went back to his table. "Peter, let's get to the truth of this. Tell us what happened when you went to the bawdy house."

"I went there about nine thirty or ten—maybe later, I don't remember. I went upstairs with Georgia. I liked her. She was nice to me, and we were . . . together. Then I left for the Red Front to get a beer. After that, I went back to Miss Jessie's and up to Georgia's room. I found her in bed with Cicero. I got mad and yelled at him to get out, and he yelled back. Georgia tried to get us to stop. I yelled at her for being with him, and she said he was no man compared to me. She laughed at his manhood, and that made him madder. He got up in my face."

The boy looked at Cicero this time, frank and forthright.

"That's when she pulled her derringer from the drawer and pointed it at us and told us both to get out."

Cicero gripped the table.

Peter's head shook ever so slightly. "I slugged him, and I left. I was mad. I just ran out."

"Where did you hit the defendant?"

Peter shifted his focus back to Blair, his face sober. "In the head."

"With your right or your left fist?"

"Right."

"Did you knock him to the floor?"

"He fell back on the bed."

The pieces were coming together more clearly now. The boy must be telling the truth; how else would he know about the blow to Cicero's head? But when had Orman arrived?

"Was Georgia alive when you left?" Blair continued.

"Yes, sir. I swear to God."

"Alone with the defendant?"

"Yes, sir."

"And she had the derringer?"

"Yes, sir."

"What happened then?"

"I went downstairs to leave. Just about the time I got to the downstairs hall, I heard the gunshot. Miss Jessie asked me what happened, and I told her. She got her gun and we all went back upstairs. We found Georgia dead and Cicero lying unconscious on the floor. Miss Jessie told me to leave, she'd take care of things. So I did."

. . . *Orman* . . .?

"Where did you go after you left Miss Jessie's?"

The words were tumbling from the boy like a creek after a gully washer. "I went to the Pacific Hotel. I was supposed to pick up my father, who was playing cards there. He was expecting me."

"Tell us what happened there."

"I went in and found Father in the bar with Mr. Orman, Mr. Schoolcraft, and Mr. Shaughnessy."

Catfish's head snapped up. Of course! Orman was in cahoots with Schoolcraft.

"So your father was playing cards with Bud Orman, Thaddeus Schoolcraft, and Cooter Shaughnessy."

"Yes, sir."

"Did you speak with them about what happened to Miss Georgia?"

"I did."

Catfish gazed at the dizzying rotation of the ceiling fan above. But Orman already knew what had happened, didn't he?

Blair rubbed his chin. "What did you say?"

299

Orman. Orman did it.

Harley leaped up. "Objection, hearsay."

What?

Blair shook his head. "Spontaneous utterance, Your Honor."

"Overruled. You may answer."

"I said Cicero Sweet killed a whore."

Blair had Mr. Lord mark the paper with the bloody fingerprint as an exhibit, and the court admitted it into evidence. "Peter, is that your finger mark on the derringer?"

It was Orman's.

"No, sir, it's not."

Blair took the derringer and the paper to the jury rail and laid them out side by side for the jurors to see. They all crowded around. Couldn't they see that it was Orman's print?

Catfish grabbed the minié ball from his trial box and clutched it tightly, looking back at Henry. *I won't let this happen. I couldn't save my own son, but I won't let this happen to yours.*

"Pass the witness," Blair said.

Everyone looked at Catfish.

Didn't they understand?

Harley touched his sleeve. "Papa?"

He gaped at his son.

Schoolcraft glared at him.

His head throbbed. Orman and ... Schoolcraft. They were mixed up together. Schoolcraft had caused all this, just like he had in Houston's case. He'd call Schoolcraft next, after Orman.

"Catfish?" Judge Goodrich asked.

"Papa, do something."

Catfish stared at the minié ball in his hand, a shot from another time.

Harley rose again. "Nothing further, Your Honor."

Chapter 38

Harley spent the recess begging his father not to call Orman, but he wouldn't budge. Papa said Orman was involved somehow—Peter proved that. If Peter hadn't touched that gun, he said, it must have been Orman.

It made no sense to Harley, but Papa was convinced.

Harley asked Miss Peach to sit with them at the defense table rather than behind. Maybe her presence would calm him. Calm them both.

"We call Bud Orman." Papa stared into the spectator gallery, his jaw pulsing.

Harley twisted around and followed his gaze to Thaddeus Schoolcraft. Why was he here, and why was he having such an effect on Papa?

Papa opened his clenched right hand and placed the spent minié ball on the table. "Your name is Bud Orman, isn't it?"

"William Orman, to be exact."

Papa leaned forward on his hands. "Mr. Orman, did you murder Georgia Gamble?"

"Of course not. Your client did, counselor."

Papa rose slowly. "You're not the sort who'd kill somebody?"

"No, I'm not."

"So you don't you find occasion to kill people from time to time?"

"Objection!" Blair jumped up. "He's impeaching his own witness."

"Catfish," the judge said sternly, "if you put him on the stand, you vouch for his credibility."

"Judge, respectfully, if I might?"

"Come up here, gentlemen," the judge said testily.

All three lawyers hurried to the bench.

Harley strained to hear as Papa spoke in a suppressed voice. "I don't believe that's the law anymore. I'm entitled to impeach any lying witness, including one I put on the stand. He's not free to lie just because I called him."

"Your Honor," Captain Blair said, "it's right here in the Code of Criminal Procedure, article six hundred sixty-eight: 'The rule that a party introducing a witness shall not attack his testimony is so far modified as that any party, when facts stated by the witness are injurious to his cause, may attack his testimony in any manner"—he looked up at the others—"except by proving the bad character of the witness.' That's what he's trying to do, Judge, prove bad character."

"If you have a prior inconsistent statement to impeach him with, Catfish, I'll consider it," the judge said, frowning at Papa, "but you can't just attack his character like that."

"Judge, I beg you, it's the heart of our defense. If I can't show he's a murderer, I can't prove he killed Miss Georgia."

"He just told the jury the killer was Peter DeGroote," Blair said. "Which is it?"

"I'll sustain the objection."

The lawyers returned to their places. Papa clutched his minié ball in his left hand. His right began to tremble.

"Papa," Harley whispered.

Papa didn't respond. His eyes remained fixed on Orman. His hand still shook.

He finally erupted, voice cracking and eyes blazing. "Did you shoot W. F. Houghston?"

Papa!

Blair leaped from his chair and pounded his fist on the table. "Judge!"

Papa turned on Blair.

"You defended him," he shouted.

Blair made a move toward Papa, but Judge Goodrich intervened. "Stop! Both of you. Mr. Calloway, I sustain the objection. You *will* move on to something else. Now!"

Harley sagged in horror.

Papa nodded and ran trembling fingers through his hair, causing it to straggle over his forehead. He took a deep breath and then let it out slowly. "You're a bartender and sporting house tycoon, aren't you?"

"Objection, leading."

"Sustained." The judge's face was still red.

Papa braced himself again on the table and took another deep breath. The intensity in his voice was so unlike him. "What—do—you—do for a—living?"

"I sell real estate."

"Do you—own—Miss Jessie's—sporting house?"

"I used to, but I sold it long before your boy there paid a call on her whores."

Papa shifted the minié ball to his right hand, then stared at it in the palm of his hand. Slowly, his eyes rose to meet Orman's. "Isn't the truth that you did own it on April fifteenth, that you shot Georgia Gamble because she wasn't working hard enough to suit you, and Miss Jessie and Peter DeGroote are lying to protect you?"

Harley looked away. Sterling DeGroote owned Miss Jessie's.

It was clear on the record.

Orman smiled and replied calmly. "As I already told you, I didn't shoot her, and I don't even know Jessie Rose."

Papa's jaw clinched, and he thrust a shaking finger at Orman. "You went there—in a—red—buggy?"

"No."

"The same red buggy—you came to court in today—with Peter DeGroote?"

Papa, stop.

"I came here on the trolley. One of the jurors sat near me." Orman pointed. "Mr. Morrison. Ask him."

Morrison seemed startled, glanced toward Papa, and quickly looked down.

"You rode here in DeGroote's red buggy, didn't you? You goddamned—liar ..."

Papa.

Blair shifted in his seat but didn't object.

Judge Goodrich intervened anyway. "Mr. Calloway—"

". . . you goddamned—murdering liar. Tell the truth."

Orman cackled. "Counselor, you're coming unhinged. Afraid you're losing this case too?"

A snicker sounded from the gallery. It was Schoolcraft.

Papa jerked toward him, then twisted back to the grinning Orman. Papa's eyes turned feral, and he lunged for the White Owl box on the defense table.

Harley's pen went clattering across the table as Miss Peach brushed past him and snatched the box away. Her face was as white as the owl on the lid.

"Damn you," Papa bellowed at Orman.

"All right, that's enough," the judge shouted. "Counsel, up here, right now!"

Blair hastened to the bench. Harley rose quickly and led Papa by his arm.

"Mr. Calloway," the judge said, the veins in his neck straining, "I will have you removed from the courtroom unless you control yourself."

Papa was motionless.

"Do you hear me, counselor?"

Papa gripped the edge of the bench so tightly his knuckles went white.

Harley raised his free hand in supplication. This was over. "Your Honor, he does hear you, and I promise it won't happen again. Perhaps we could have a short recess?"

The judge pointed at Harley, his finger shaking. "Get control of him, Harley." He looked up at the jurors. "Court is in recess for fifteen minutes. Bailiff, remove the jury." He stormed off the bench and disappeared through the side door.

What was happening?

"Papa, come over here and sit down," Harley said, steering him by the arm.

Miss Peach helped guide Papa back to his chair. A distant peal of thunder sounded through the windows behind the judge's bench. Harley shuddered.

Papa sat breathing heavily, staring straight ahead, clutching the arms of the chair. "Did you see—Orman—whispering— with Schoolcraft?"

"What?" Harley asked.

"When I called him to the stand—he was sitting back there"—he pointed to the spectator gallery—"whispering with Thaddeus Schoolcraft—did you see him?" His eyes were wide as if he'd seen a ghost.

He'd never seen his father like this, not even in Houston's

trial. "No, Papa, Orman was outside when you called him. He wasn't sitting with Schoolcraft."

"He was. I—saw them."

There was a sudden commotion behind them. Harley twisted to see Jasper trying to hold Mr. Sweet back. Mrs. Sweet gripped his arm.

Henry Sweet shook his fist at Papa and yelled, "What are you doing? You're going to get my son convicted."

Papa rose and lifted his hands toward his old friend. "Henry . . ."

"He's doing his best," Jasper said.

Harley got between them. "Please, Mr. Sweet, let me deal with this. It'll be fine."

"Is this the way you repay your debts?" Mr. Sweet shouted.

Mrs. Sweet seized one of his hands, begging him to stop. Her pleas finally prevailed, and with Jasper's help, she led him away.

Miss Peach pulled Harley away from Papa and breathed a horrified whisper into his ear. "Harley, his pistol is in that cigar box. He was going to shoot Orman."

"Get him back to the office. I'll take care of things here."

They left.

***

When court reconvened, Harley apologized again and advised the court he would take over while his father was indisposed. He wished Miss Peach was still there.

Cicero's eyes were wide, and he was breathing heavily. Harley gave him a reassuring look.

The next thunderclap was louder than the last. The dangling lightbulbs over the bar shivered as lightning flashed through the south windows. The bailiff went to close them.

The prosecutor approached Orman. "Where were you on the evening of April fifteenth of this year?"

"I was playing cards at the Pacific Hotel."

"Who with?"

"Thaddeus Schoolcraft, that man out there in the gallery," he said, pointing.

Schoolcraft nodded at Blair.

"Who is he?"

"He's a detective for the Katy Railroad."

"Who else was there?"

"Oh, let's see, it was Cooter Shaughnessy and Sterling DeGroote."

"Mr. Shaughnessy the city alderman?"

"Yes, sir. Mighty fine card player."

"When did you finish your game?"

"Late, about two o'clock in the morning, if I recall."

"Thank you, sir."

Harley half rose from his chair. "No questions. We rest our rebuttal case."

Harley sat silently at the defense table as Orman and the others left. DeGroote had bought the whorehouse from Orman, and he'd known all along that Peter was there at the time of the killing. Shaughnessy had tried to pressure Papa into pleading Cicero guilty, and Schoolcraft had been on the grand jury that indicted Cicero, then tormented Papa at every opportunity.

Harley bit his lip. So Peter hadn't shot Miss Georgia, but why had they protected him? Was it nothing more than to protect the good DeGroote name?

The courtroom finally emptied. Since Judge Goodrich had adjourned until two o'clock in the afternoon, Harley went back to the law office. Miss Peach was there alone. Jasper had escorted the Sweets back to their hotel room, she said, and Papa had taken off walking down Fourth Street. A thunderstorm was drenching downtown, but she'd been unable to stop him from going out in it.

"Harley, what's wrong with your father?" she asked as soon as he'd put down his things.

He sighed and shook his head.

"That was not the same Catfish Calloway who won Lawson's case last year with his brilliant cross-examination of the accusing witness." She stood with her hands on both hips. "His examinations of Peter and Orman were disastrous."

"That's unkind."

"It's not—it's troubling. Something is wrong with him. He became so emotional. He doesn't lose control of himself like that. That's not who he is." She sat in a chair next to him, her arm on the table. "Before this case, he never would've hurled unsupported accusations at a witness. Catfish Calloway is a master of cross-examination, but that Catfish Calloway didn't show up today. Something's wrong."

"He's just under pressure. And he's tired."

"It's more than that. He screamed at Orman. He cursed in court—the Catfish Calloway I know doesn't even curse in front of ladies, much less court. And he was going to shoot Bud Orman. He just was. Orman was right: Mr. Calloway was unhinged. Have you ever seen him act like that in court?"

It wasn't the time for this.

"Well, I haven't," she said.

He stared at the table.

"When I graduated from Baylor," she said, "I thought I was in love with a young gentleman. I was convinced we were a perfect match, and I'd already imagined our wedding day. My friends didn't think he was right for me, and I couldn't understand why. It was only after he left me for another girl, when I got some distance from the relationship, that I was able to see things more clearly. I think when you want something to be true badly enough, especially something very personal, then sometimes you ignore things that don't seem right to a more detached eye. I think Mr. Calloway wants to believe Cicero so much that he can't see the truth about him."

Maybe she was right. "Why he would become so emotional about it, though?"

"Do you think it's something to do with your brother? I've noticed you two never speak of him—except once, last Sunday when you said we should accept Blair's plea offer and you said Cicero wasn't Houston."

He met her eyes reluctantly.

"What does Houston have to do with this case, Harley?"

The world dropped out beneath him. Everything. It had everything to do with Houston. Why had he not realized that?

He stood on wobbly legs. "We've got to find Papa."

Chapter 39

Catfish charged through the downpour. He hadn't expected a thunderstorm when he set out from the office, but the rain didn't matter one bit. Nothing mattered. By the time he crossed Franklin Avenue, he was drenched. His frock coat was sodden, slapping his legs as he churned past the post office.

Colonel Terry trotted along beside him.

"Scat! Get on back, Colonel," he commanded, but the hound ignored him.

The Baptist church loomed ahead through the slanting rain. Henry's voice resounded in his head. *What are you doing?* Thunder cracked overhead. *You're going to get my son convicted.*

He broke into a trot down the alley beside the Blake building. *Is this the way you repay your debts?*

Lightning flashed in the western sky. He turned on Fifth Street, then crossed the tracks on Mary Street.

Orman cackled. *Counselor, you're coming unhinged.*

A tall spire barely visible ahead through the deluge. Turned right on Jackson. He ran. *Afraid you're losing this case too.* Stumbled in a pool of rainwater. Methodist Church on the left—got up. *You're losing.* Ran along the Katy tracks past Sixth Street—*losing*—across Seventh—*this case too*—the rain slackened—*this*—*case*—*too.*

He slowed. Almost out of breath. The colonel stopped ahead

of him and looked back, panting.

Catfish bent over double, wheezing for air. Water streamed down his face. He could barely make out landmarks ahead. Just beyond Eighth Street, the Brazos Compress smokestack rose into the mist beside near the Katy Hotel. In front of it, a locomotive; to the right, the green-and-yellow passenger depot. He fixed on that place and slogged toward it. Why did it draw him?

Bootblack Ben perched on a stool under the hotel awning, waiting for a customer. He waved. Catfish ignored him and stumbled toward the place. The train. The Katy depot.

He staggered to a stop. It was the first time in eight years he'd stood so near that spot.

It all looked so different. Back then it had been a MOPAC depot. There was the spot where—he couldn't go there. His legs wouldn't move, and he didn't want them to.

Was there someone standing on the spot? He squinted through the drizzle.

There was, yes. A bowler hat, a horseshoe mustache, a blackthorn cane. His hand like a noose around his neck, laughing: *This case, too.*

He dissolved in the mist.

Catfish slogged back the way he'd come, the colonel beside him, down Jackson to Seventh. Away from the depot— *Houston!*—away from the spot.

I'm so sorry.

Away.

***

Miss Peach touched Harley's arm. "I'm scared."

"I am too," he said.

She wished she could just hold him tightly.

311

He brought the surrey around, and she scrambled in.

Gentle rain pelted the fabric roof. He lashed the horse, and the carriage lurched forward. They went south down Fourth Street. Few people were out in that rain. Some waited under shop awnings for it to let up.

She glanced across the seat at him. Harley couldn't keep holding it in. She had to help him. "Have you ever seen your father like this?"

"Yes." He kept his eyes on the road, but she still saw the fear in his eyes. "Once."

"When?"

"Eight years ago. During Houston's trial."

"I didn't know he was a lawyer."

"He wasn't. He was the defendant."

"What?"

"He was on trial for murder."

Her hand flew to her mouth. "Oh, my." How could she not have known something so important about her employers' family?

Harley turned right onto Webster. There was no sign of Mr. Calloway. She twisted her hands in her lap during the awkward silence as they turned back toward town on Fifth.

"He was accused of murdering a man at the MOPAC Railroad depot."

Was she sure she wanted to hear more?

"Papa defended him—he was convinced it was self-defense. He couldn't accept that Houston would deliberately kill someone."

Goose bumps prickled her arms. "And did he?"

He shook his head. "I don't know. There were several eyewitnesses. They said the man got off the train and was walking toward the passenger terminal. Houston got off the train behind him and yelled at him to stop. Houston had a gun. When he turned around and saw Houston's gun, he reached for something, and Houston shot him."

That didn't make sense. "But why?"

Harley turned left on Franklin. "Houston was coming home from a trip. They said a carpetbagger from back east was sitting across the aisle. They struck up a conversation, and the carpetbagger asked Houston about his family. He told the man about Papa, about his service in the war, but the man took offense and called Papa a traitor to his country. They got into a shoving match, and a railroad detective on the train had to separate them."

"So Houston shot the man because he insulted your father?"

"That's what the railroad detective testified. Papa cross-examined him, trying to shake his story about Houston's animus toward the man, but Papa got so upset—like he was today—that all he could do by the end was curse at the witness."

"Oh, my."

They passed the Hotel Palmo. Still no signs of her boss. Her hand was shaking.

"That detective was in court today," Harley said unexpectedly.

"What? Why?"

"I don't know. His name is Thaddeus Schoolcraft."

"The one who played cards with Orman? Mr. Calloway said he was whispering with Orman in court."

He nodded grimly. "I think seeing him today is what upset Papa so. Schoolcraft took on Houston's case almost as a crusade and saw to it he was prosecuted aggressively. Schoolcraft and Papa hate each other."

Dampness appeared around his eyes. This must be so hard on

Harley—and on top of that, to watch his father fall apart. Poor dear.

She touched his sleeve lightly. "Were you and Houston close?"

"We were the only children in the family to survive into adulthood. He was born before Papa went off to war, and I was born after he got back. He was my big brother, and ... Yes. We were very close."

She leaned out into the mist as if searching down the cross street, trying to give him a moment of privacy. "I'm so sorry."

"The jury convicted him. They gave him the death penalty."

She snuck a glance at his face. "So he was hanged?"

Harley reined the horse left onto Eighth Street and nodded. "Papa blamed Schoolcraft."

Miss Peach frowned. Maybe not just Schoolcraft. Houston's trial had obviously been very personal to Mr. Calloway. He'd gotten too emotionally involved in the defense—just as he had now with his war buddy's son.

That was it.

She clutched Harley's sleeve again. "Don't you see what's happening now, Harley? He blamed himself for Houston's death because he couldn't save him in the trial. His emotions got in the way. He thinks Houston died because of his failure as a lawyer—and now it's happening all over again with Henry Sweet's son. He must be terrified."

Harley's eyes grew large. "Not Papa."

"Yes, don't you see? Cicero's case is very personal too—Mr. Sweet saved Mr. Calloway's life in the war. Did you see the way your father was fingering that bullet?"

Harley was silent. He lashed the horse.

Miss Peach twisted to look every direction as the buggy

rattled up Mary Street and crossed the Cotton Belt tracks. Where was Mr. Calloway? When they reached the Jackson Street crossing near the Katy Hotel, Bootblack Ben waved and beckoned them over.

"Haw!" Harley barked, pulling the surrey around the parked locomotive and toward the hotel.

"Mr. Harley," Ben called, "I done seen your father out running in this rain. Something was awful wrong."

Miss Peach's stomach clenched.

"Where was he headed?" Harley asked.

"That away." He thumbed south over his shoulder. "Had Colonel Terry with him."

Harley raised a hand. "Thanks, Mr. Moon."

She gripped the side of the surrey as he lashed the horse into a trot and they surged into the downpour.

"Hold on," he said. "I know where he's headed."

***

Catfish slumped back against a live oak tree, his legs splayed before him. Rain fell from the overhanging limbs in steady drips, as it did from every oak and pecan in Oakwood Cemetery. The colonel's head nestled on his thigh. Both of them were soaked to the bone.

"It doesn't matter, Colonel." He rubbed the hound's ear until his eyes closed.

Eight feet away was a tombstone: MARTHA CALLOWAY. BELOVED WIFE & MOTHER. 1836–1885. REST IN PEACE.

Numbness washed over him. "Martha, I need your guidance. I feel so helpless. No matter what I do, it turns out wrong. Henry Sweet's boy is going to hang unless I find a way. Henry's counting on me, as I counted on him in Kentucky." He wiped his eyes with the back of his hand. "I acted the fool in court today, honey. I embarrassed Harley. I failed Cicero. I let Henry down, and Jasper too. What do I do now?"

A gust of wind blew a small branch loose from the tree to his right. It fell in front the other marker, the one that was harder to look at. HOUSTON CALLOWAY. *AUDI ALTERAM PARTEM.*

The other side.

He never could make them hear Houston's side.

"I'm so sorry, son. It's my fault."

Now it was happening again. Why couldn't he make people see the truth anymore? Was he the only one who saw it clearly, or was he the one who could no longer see?

He was bone-weary—hadn't slept during the trial. He turned back to his wife's headstone and closed his eyes. So tired.

Miss Jessie's garishly painted face taunted him from behind his eyelids: *Would you like me to tell you what your client said?* She couldn't be telling the truth. He turned his head. *I'm sorry I shot her*—Cicero couldn't have said that. *On the barrel of that gun stands the assassin's natal autograph, written in the blood of the helpless whore. There is only one man in the whole earth whose hand can duplicate that crimson sign, the defendant, Cicero Sweet.*

"Martha, there's nothing to this finger smudge science," he murmured.

I'm gonna put Cicero in the witness chair and let you judge him for yourself.

When I called Cicero, he did tell them the truth as he remembered it—*I danced with her, and then we must have gone upstairs, but I don't remember anything after that.* Because of the beer, or a blow to the head? *You're not saying Miss Georgia undressed you, are you? No, sir. She didn't do that for sure.* Cicero was just confused. *She just tended to her own clothes.*

He flung an arm over his closed eyes as a shield against the rain. "He was confused."

I took my own clothes off. Confused, right? Wasn't he? He said he didn't remember. *I don't recall anything.* That had to be the truth. *And she got scared and pulled her derringer? I sure didn't see anything like that.* He meant he didn't remember, didn't he? *I'm not the kind to hurt anybody . . . I haven't been in any fights . . . You're just not the kind of young man who'd hurt anybody? No, sir, I'm not.*

"He's not, Martha. Is he? Henry's boy couldn't be."

Cicero pushed me down. When I got back up, he punched me and knocked me into the creek. That didn't have anything to do with Georgia's death. *She laughed at his manhood, and that made him madder.* Peter was lying? *Just about the time I got to the downstairs hall, I heard the gunshot . . . We found Georgia dead and Cicero lying unconscious on the floor.*

His arm fell away from his eyes, and he straightened, hands sinking into the mud as he pushed away from the tree. The rain was stopping. He had to share the truth with his truest partner.

"I told the jury myself: Killers lie, don't they? Killers do lie. And I told them I would put the actual killer in that witness chair."

A glint of sun streaking through the parting clouds bounced off of her tombstone.

"God help me, Martha, I did. I did put the killer on."

He pressed his muddy hands over his face, hoping not to see any more, but he did. The tighter he shut his eyes, the clearer it became. The same courtroom. The same witness chair. Thaddeus Schoolcraft's grinning face, blurring into Bud Orman—*you're losing this case too.*

The jail yard. A young man hanging from the scaffold, swinging in the breeze, turning toward his father . . . *Houston!* . . . turning away . . . turning . . . coming around

317

again—no, a different face. This face was not his son. This face was someone else's son.

Cicero.

The killer was Cicero.

The colonel nuzzled him. He wiped the mud from his face and scrambled up.

What had he done? He'd put Cicero on the stand, and the boy had lied. He did kill her. He'd lied to save his own skin, and now he was going to hang.

Catfish was the one who couldn't see the truth.

He staggered to the tombstone and touched her name; saw her sweet smile and stumbled down the cemetery road.

God, help me. Let it not be too late to save his life.

The colonel trotted beside him. They came to a tall monument shooting up through the tree branches. IN MEMORY OF THE BRAVE MEN AND DEVOTED WOMEN OF THE SOUTH. He was standing among departed comrades, gone one by one over the years since the war. He strode down the street. There it was; the marker was small. J. C. JENKINS. Judson Cicero Jenkins. He fell to his knees beside his old friend, his old law partner. Judge Warwick Jenkins's brother. Cicero Sweet's namesake. The three had ridden together—Catfish and Henry Sweet and Cicero Jenkins, the daring captain of Company K. Cicero's commanding voice still rang in his ears: *Fear not death, men. The day goes to the bold. Forward!* They'd done bold things in those days—terrible things, in order to survive. The three of them had survived.

And that was the answer, wasn't it? After all this time, it came from the voice of his friend: *The day will go to the bold.*

He knew how to save Cicero.

***

Miss Peach gripped the seat as the surrey rattled through the gate into Oakwood Cemetery. They turned right down the first lane. The rain had stopped, and the air was steamy.

She held tightly as Harley put the horse into a gallop. "The family plot's up ahead on the right."

She scanned the cemetery. Mr. Calloway and the colonel were walking up the road. "Look, there he is."

Harley turned left in front of the Confederate Memorial and met him in the street. He leaped out, and they embraced. Mr. Calloway's eyes were shut tight over his son's shoulder.

Miss Peach turned her face away as her eyes filled.

Harley spoke first. "Are you all right?"

Mr. Calloway broke the embrace and grinned as if he'd seen something amazing. "Of course I am."

He and the colonel both looked like drowned rats, but it was the old Mr. Calloway. He was standing in a puddle of rainwater, but his bright blue eyes sparkled. "When God got around to making Texas, the only weather he had left was floods and droughts."

She managed a laugh through the tears she couldn't hold back.

He jumped into the back seat of the surrey behind her and squeezed her shoulders.

"Colonel, up." The hound joined him. "Go to my house, son, and be quick about it. I need some dry clothes. Miss Peach, we'll drop you off at Sam Kee's first. Get me a plate of fried rice and a pot of ginger tea." He peeled off some soggy bills from his money clip and handed them over her shoulder. "Take it to the courthouse. Get yourself something too."

"Are you sure you can eat?" she asked.

"Darlin', I'm starved. Can't argue to a jury on an empty

stomach. Harley, while I'm changing clothes, I need you to do two things."

"Yes, sir?"

She snuck a peek at Harley. He felt it too. She could just hug them both until they burst.

Mr. Calloway leaned between them. "Take the jury list with you and stop by the Pat Cleburne Camp office. Check their membership records for which jurors were in the war."

Miss Peach broke into a big smile and twisted around. "Mr. Calloway, he could just use the *talking*-phone at the courthouse."

Mr. Calloway roared with laughter. She beamed back.

Harley glanced at them both, smiling. "I better go in person."

"And one more thing. Go tell the jailer to bring Cicero to the county courtroom. And get Henry Sweet there too. We'll talk there over lunch."

She knew that voice.

Harley nodded. "Yes, sir." He eyed her.

She just couldn't hold back the tears. She shrugged and shook her head.

He snapped the reins. "Get up there!"

Chapter 40

"We need to have a very frank conversation."

Cicero and his parents sat on the other side of the table from Catfish, watching him with anxious eyes as he gulped a heaping plate of fried rice. The county court deliberation room where they met was small, stuffy, and smelly. No fan, only one window. No one else had an appetite.

He looked straight at Cicero. "Be honest, whether what you have to say is good or bad for your case. Now's the time to tell it straight. My question's this: Do you actually remember what happened or not?"

Cicero shook his head immediately.

"You see, I've got some doubts about your story after hearing you testify."

Cicero opened his mouth to answer, but Catfish held up a hand. "Wait. Before you answer, let me just tell you a few things. I'm sorry to say this, but I believe the jury's gonna convict you based on the testimony they've heard, especially today. Peter DeGroote was honest once he finally decided to be, but you were inconsistent and confused. I never should have asked him to give a finger mark, but I did—and even to my eye, it was completely different from the one on the derringer."

Catfish took a sip of ginger tea and wiped his mouth with a

handkerchief. "I've defended you based on what you told me the truth was, but I think other witnesses have disproved your story. I've tried to prove someone else shot Georgia Gamble, but the evidence always comes back to you."

Henry shook his head. "You're wro—"

Catfish thrust a hand toward him. "Wait! You'll have your say when I'm done."

Cicero started breathing rapidly. "I—"

"Hear me out," Catfish commanded. "When court reconvenes, Judge Goodrich will charge the jury. He'll tell 'em that if they believe beyond a reasonable doubt you're guilty of first-degree murder, they should convict you. He'll tell 'em if you're guilty of first-degree murder, they may punish you by death."

He paused to let that sink in. Cicero stiffened, then began to tremble. His mother sobbed into her handkerchief, and Henry patted her back gently.

Catfish spoke with all the authority he could muster. "After the judge reads that charge to the jury, we'll argue your case to the jury. Captain Blair will argue for first-degree murder, and I believe the jury will agree with him. Captain Blair will ask for death."

He pushed his plate away and sat back. "What shall I argue, Cicero? I can't tell 'em someone else killed her. The evidence foreclosed that defense. I could argue in good faith that the state failed to prove your guilt beyond a reasonable doubt—there's still no eyewitness to the actual shooting, so the case is circumstantial—but I can't in good faith argue that you're innocent because I don't believe that anymore. So what should I argue?"

"I don't know, sir." Cicero's voice cracked.

"I believe there's a way to save your life, but it'll require you to take the witness stand again—and tell the truth."

Cicero's eyebrows shot up, and he nodded enthusiastically. "I did, Mr. Calloway, I did."

He lit a cigar, leaned back on two legs of the chair, and blew smoke to the ceiling.

"I'm speaking as your lawyer, and in my opinion, the jury thinks you lied to them. I believe correcting the lie is the only way to save your life."

Cicero's facade dissolved, and he buried his face in his hands. His father put an arm around him, but he pushed it away.

Henry folded his arms and glared at Catfish. "Now look here, you can't just abandon Cicero like this. Catfish, you owe me."

He'd known this would be a bitter pill to swallow. "I'm sorry you feel that way, Henry, but I don't have any choice. I've made some mistakes in this case, and I regret them. I should have pushed for a plea bargain in the beginning. Harley tried to get me to do that, but I was pigheaded. I think we could've gotten an agreement for a reasonable number of years in pri—"

"No, no prison," Henry said.

"Yes, prison—but it's too late for a deal now. Our only chance now is giving the jury the option to choose prison over death."

Mrs. Sweet's sobs intensified.

Henry leaned forward, sliding both palms forward on the table toward Catfish. "I haven't testified. I could take the stand and say I overheard Peter admit he shot her. Put me up there, Catfish, and I'll say that. You owe me, dam—"

Catfish shook his head and held up both hands. "No, sir, I'm not putting anybody on that witness stand to lie. Done that already, and that's why we're here. There are only two options. Either I argue to my best ability that there's reasonable doubt and ask for an acquittal, or I argue that he's guilty of manslaughter and try to save his life. Those are the only two options—and frankly, Henry, in my opinion there's only one."

Henry pulled back indignantly. "They can't convict a decent boy for killing a whore. Tell them she was just a whore."

"They'll give him death if I say that. I know you're scared, Henry. Believe me, I understand how helpless you feel right now. I've been in your shoes. As much as you want to do something to protect Cicero, there's nothing you can do. But there is a way he can save his own life. It's risky, but it's his only chance."

Henry's face crumpled. He tried to touch his son again, but Cicero wouldn't let him.

"The choice is yours, Cicero," Catfish said, "nobody else's. So I'll ask you the question again. Do you actually remember what happened?"

Cicero threw himself forward onto the table, arms over his head, and sobbed uncontrollably. After a minute or so, he answered in a barely audible voice. "Yes."

"You willing to testify to the truth?"

"Yes." He sat up, red-faced. "I don't want to die. I'll do whatever I need to."

Catfish finished his ginger tea and slid the cup out of the way. "I just want you to tell the truth. Let's talk about what we'll do."

***

Not a single juror more than glanced at Cicero when he took the stand. Wade Morrison bent his head and crossed his arms; he'd even avoided eye contact with Catfish when the jury came in. Only a single juror watched Cicero now.

"Cicero, is there something you want to say to the court and the jury?" Catfish asked.

"Yes, sir."

"Go ahead."

Cicero turned in the witness chair to face the jury. His eyes were red, but he didn't cry. "I haven't been exactly honest with you about what happened. I do remember some other things."

Catfish peeked at the jury. Half were now more attentive. That's progress.

"I remember being in bed with Miss Georgia. I don't remember Peter DeGroote being there, but maybe he was at some point. Anyway, I was on the bed. I felt real dizzy and everything was blurry. She was poking me and yelling at me. She had that pistol and was pointing it at me. I tried to knock it away and it went off. I saw blood on my hand, and I wiped it on the sheet. I remember trying to get off the bed. I reached for the doorknob, but the door swung closed and I fell. The next thing I knew, the police were carrying me away."

A sob burst from his throat. "I didn't mean to shoot her. I'm so sorry."

Catfish eased closer to the jury box. Some of the jurors were still eying Cicero; most didn't. He faced Cicero and crossed his arms. "Did you lie to these men earlier?"

"Yes, sir."

"Why?"

"I was scared. I don't want to die."

"Did you intend to kill her?"

"No, sir. I had no reason."

"Do you regret what you did?"

"I do."

"Anything else you want to say?"

"No, sir. Just, I'm so sorry."

Catfish nodded. "Pass the witness."

"All right." The judge rubbed the back of his neck. "Captain Blair?"

Blair rose stiffly. He wasn't likely to let Cicero off easily.

"So, Mr. Sweet, your new story is you do remember what happened?"

"Yes, sir."

"That you shot her but didn't mean to?"

"That's the truth."

Blair scowled at the boy. "So when you told us before you didn't remember anything that happened after the two of you danced, that was a lie?"

"Yes, sir."

"You were lying then, but you aren't lying now?"

"That right."

Blair shook his head. "You want us to believe your new story, but not your old story?"

"Yes, sir." He cast an imploring look at Catfish.

Catfish rolled the minié ball in his hand. He'd done all he could do; justice would take its course.

"I think I understand." Blair shot a knowing look at the jury. "Nothing further, Judge."

Chapter 41

The clock tower struck four. Catfish scanned the spectator gallery as the judge concluded his charge to the jury. Almost every seat in the courtroom was occupied. Watchers fanned themselves against the sultry heat left behind by the afternoon thunderstorm. They were all there—Schoolcraft, Orman, Shaughnessy. Three other aldermen, the mayor's imps, sat in different spots. Brann, Brown, and the other reporters were scattered through the gallery, hunched over their notes. Even Miss Jessie had made a public appearance, tastefully attired at the end of the last row, fanning herself with her oriental fan. The seat next to her remained empty—the last empty seat in the whole courtroom. The Sweets clutched hands tightly in their front row seats. Jasper watched from two rows behind President Burleson. Miss Peach smiled encouragement.

Harley nodded toward Catfish's right hand. He hadn't noticed he was drumming his fingers. They both knew this was the biggest risk he'd ever taken in any case, but they agreed it was Cicero's only chance.

Prison or death.

Captain Blair opened calmly. "Reverend Sam Jones preached here back in April, and everybody went. He said one thing that caused folks to think him a prophet: 'If you can block off a place, call it a Reservation, and license licentiousness, why don't you reserve a few blocks where a man can commit murder and go unpunished?' Well, gentlemen, not six hours later, Miss Georgia Virginia Gamble fell victim to a murderer's hand—in the Reservation. There's no way to change it, but is the rest of what he said prophesy? That a man can murder in the Reservation and go unpunished?"

He moved closer to them. "I say to you, gentlemen, that's where prophesy fails. Because that's in your hands, and I'm confident you won't tolerate murder, whether it's in the Reservation or in the Baptist church, whether it's a poor working girl in a bawdy house on the wrong side of town or a banker's wife in the finest house in the best neighborhood."

The jury was hanging on his every word. Tom Blair was good. He knew how to connect with folks.

"I say that's what will happen because I agree with something else Reverend Jones said in that sermon: 'You can hang a few anarchists in Chicago every few years and think you've killed out anarchy, but if you have a law on the books that you don't enforce, you've got anarchy right here in Waco, Texas.' You remember the striking coal miners in Indiana and what they did last month? The authorities had to call out the militia, didn't they? Even closer to home, in the Indian Territory, they called out federal troops to protect folks from the miners. When laws aren't enforced, innocent people get hurt."

Trying to scare them into a death sentence.

Blair paced in front of the jury box, eyeing each juror as he passed. "If you let murderers go free this time just because the victim's a bawdy woman, next time it'll be a decent woman. Or her child. No, gentlemen, Reverend Jones got that one right. 'The juror who does not bring such offenders to justice is a particeps criminis to their damnable rascality.'"

He stopped at the end of the jury box and turned back to face them. "Do you remember what I asked the defendant?" He sauntered back along the bar and stared at Cicero. "I said, 'Mr. Sweet, did you consider the Reservation a lawless place where murder might go unpunished?' He said, 'I never thought about it.'"

Blair snorted. "Well, gentlemen, he sure did a lot of thinking about that sermon, didn't he? The preacher preached against drinking, and Mr. Sweet decided he wanted beer. The preacher preached against laying with a bawdy woman, and Mr. Sweet put that sin on his list too. The preacher preached against lawless places like the Reservation where sins go unpunished, and Cicero Sweet felt free to sin as he pleased there. That poor working girl made the mistake of insulting his manhood, and he killed her for it—with malice aforethought. He didn't think he'd be punished for killing a whore."

He stood with his hands on his hips. "For most of the trial, the defense claimed some other man somehow shot her while the defendant was passed out on the floor." He pointed left and spoke in a mocking voice: "It was Bud Orman!" Then he pointed right: "No, no, wait, it was Peter DeGroote!"

He raised both hands to the ceiling and shook his head. "Then they ran out of other men to blame. It was only at the very end of this trial, after failing to put the murder off on somebody else, desperate for a way to survive, that the defendant finally admitted he killed her. He came up with a brand new story, and now he wants you to believe he didn't mean to kill her."

Blair cocked his head in puzzlement. "Now how is it Sweet can shoot a girl dead in the heart and not intend to kill her? For the life of me, I don't see it. No, gentlemen, the defendant acted with malice aforethought. Judge Goodrich instructed you that if he acted deliberately it was first-degree murder. Well, take the defendant's own words on that. He said to Miss Jessie, 'I'm sorry I shot her.' Miss Sadie heard that too."

He ambled back to his table, glancing toward Catfish. "Here's something Catfish and I happen to agree on. In his opening statement to you, he said, 'Killers lie, don't they?' They sure do, gentlemen, especially when their lives depend on it. This young man would do anything to save his own skin. Cicero Sweet lied when he swore he didn't remember what happened. He thought you'd take him at his word. When he decided you didn't, he tried something else. He admitted that he lied but told a new lie: He shot her, but he didn't mean to. Can you trust his new story?"

A juror shook his head.

Blair went to the court reporter's desk and lifted the gun. "He lied about some other things too. I handed him this derringer and asked him if he'd ever touched that gun before. At first he swore to you he didn't, but I brought you scientific proof he did." He showed them the bloody print. "So finally, he admitted he did touch it, but he came up with a new story: He tried to knock it away and it went off. His new story—it was an accident."

He shook his head slowly. "The defendant lied under oath about something else. After he said he wasn't the kind of man who'd hurt a working girl, I asked him if he'd ever been in any fights before, and he said no, he hadn't—swore to it right there in that witness chair. I brought Peter DeGroote in here, and he sat in the same chair and told you all about the day the defendant got mad about a college debate and beat him for it, knocked him into the creek. Sweet had been drinking that day, too. The defendant didn't want you to know he's the kind of man who'd do that, so he lied about it."

He looked from juror to juror. "Just as his own lawyer told you, killers lie. And just like his own lawyer told you, he did put the killer in the witness chair."

And Cicero fessed up to it.

"Gentlemen, the evidence is overwhelming. Cicero Sweet is guilty of first-degree murder. Don't let a murderer go unpunished just because the victim was a working girl in the Reservation. It's still murder. Thank you."

Catfish nodded at Blair as he returned to his seat: *Very eloquent, my friend.*

He shut his yes. *Lord, may I find my voice. Words are my only weapons now. If they can't save this boy's life, what use are they? What use am I?*

"Mr. Calloway," the judge said, "you may proceed."

He was the only man in the muggy courtroom who hadn't shed his coat at the judge's invitation. The buttermilk suit he'd changed into after the rain showed sweat stains already. A bead trickled down his forehead.

He approached the jury, nodding to the bench. "May it please the court."

"Counsel," the judge replied.

"Gentlemen of the jury." He rolled the witness chair over in front of them. "One thing before I begin."

He sat in the chair and leaned forward, arms resting on his knees, right in front of the jury. He stared down briefly, then looked up at each juror. Every eye was fixed upon him.

"I owe you fellas an apology and an explanation. This morning, I said some things I'm ashamed of now. I acted poorly. I used vulgar language. I was disrespectful of the judge and of Captain Blair and of you, and none of you deserved that. My old teacher, Professor Sayles, would be disappointed in me because I dishonored our profession, and I pray forgiveness. But whether you can forgive me or not, I hope you won't hold my failing against my client. I don't really have much of an explanation for my behavior. You see, Cicero's father, Henry Sweet"—he nodded toward his pal—"he's an old friend. We rode together in the war. I owe him my life, and so I'm afraid I let my emotions get the best of me. I'm truly sorry."

Would they forgive him?

He stood.

"But this trial isn't about Catfish Calloway or Henry Sweet. It's about Henry's boy, a young man perched precariously on the edge of life. He's a young man who should be eagerly anticipating a happy future, but instead fears the hangman's noose. We don't ask you to set him free. Respectfully, Captain Blair, we don't think the killing of any person should go unpunished. No, gentlemen, we ask you to punish him fairly and wisely. We ask you to render your verdict from the noblest impulse of the Christian heart."

He glanced at President Burleson in the second row. "A very wise man reminded me recently how important that is. It's what gives us humanity in a world of wicked impulses."

He stood behind the chair, resting his hands atop its back. "Cicero takes responsibility for what he did and stands ready to pay the price, whatever you see fit. He was weak, and he knows it. He had a weakness for strong drink, and he gave in to it. He had a weakness of the flesh, and he indulged it. He had a weakness of courage, too. He hid the truth from you at first. In the end, though, he was man enough to sit again in that chair, under the same oath before God and law which he had by human frailty transgressed, and found courage to admit he lied. To admit his guilt. To face you and invite your punishment."

He faced Blair. "Captain Blair says this young man would do anything to save his own skin. Well, sir, I agree that Cicero Sweet lied to save himself. To survive. He lied to save himself. It's not very admirable. No virtue in that lie." He deliberately paced the breadth of the jury box. "But I ask you, gentlemen, where has virtue been in this trial? Where did you see a noble heart? Was it Miss Jessie when she lied to protect Peter and Sterling DeGroote? Did a noble impulse emanate from Peter or from Miss Sadie or Big Joe, who told the same lies? Where in the prosecution case did we see nobility?"

He searched the spectator gallery. "Was there a noble impulse from Detective Palmer? Was he forthright with you when he led you to believe he got his science from scientists when in truth he got it from Mark Twain's yarn?" He picked up the magazine. "A storybook lawyer named Pudd'nhead Wilson told a storybook jury this: 'Upon this haft stands the assassin's natal autograph, written in blood. . . . There is but one man in the whole earth whose hand can duplicate that crimson sign.' No, there's no nobility in Palmer's deceit. Gentlemen, there was little true character displayed in this case on either side, I'm afraid. Had he watched this trial, Preacher Jones might well have said, 'Let him among you who is without sin cast the first stone.'"

Catfish walked behind Cicero and put his hands on the boy's shoulders. "This boy sinned. He caused Georgia Gamble's death. But does he deserve to die for it? Judge Goodrich instructed you that he must be guilty of first-degree murder before you may condemn him to death. The question for you is this: What crime is he guilty of? Is it murder in the first degree, or is it manslaughter?"

He patted Cicero's shoulder and moved on. "Judge Goodrich instructed you that first-degree murder requires you to believe, beyond reasonable doubt, he acted with malice aforethought. What's that? The judge told you. Cicero must have formed a decision to take the life of Georgia Gamble with a sedate and deliberate design. His mind must have been cool in forming this purpose. You heard Peter's testimony, and Cicero's too. Those two boys exchanged heated words. It happened suddenly and unexpectedly. Peter slugged him, and Cicero fell back on the bed, dazed. He wasn't thinking clearly. He opened his eyes and saw her pointing a gun at him, and he knocked it away. It went off. It hit Miss Georgia."

He wasn't sure any of them believed it.

"Does that sound cool and deliberate? Sedate? Or was what he did something different? Was it manslaughter?" He retrieved the judge's jury charge from the bench and read it: "'Manslaughter is voluntary homicide, committed under the immediate influence of sudden passion, arising from an adequate cause, but neither justified nor excused by law.' Remember what Judge Goodrich told you about sudden passion. It could be anger, rage, sudden resentment or terror, rendering him incapable of cool reflection." He returned the charge to the judge. "Cicero Sweet, in sudden terror at facing a gun, reacted instantly. He might have caused the gun to go off, but he didn't intend it. It was hardly cool reflection."

He passed the prosecution table and paused. "Captain Blair is one of the very finest lawyers I know. I'm sure he'll say Cicero acted deliberately because Miss Georgia laughed at him— 'insulted his manhood' is how he put it. Peter DeGroote told you that story, and Cicero swears it never happened. Who's telling you the truth? Both told you lies about that night. Who do you believe? Does it make sense that Georgia and Cicero had been together in that bed since just after eleven, but it was only hours later after Peter arrived that she insulted Cicero's manhood? Where had his manhood been before Peter arrived?"

One juror smiled.

He rubbed his hands together. "Why do people lie, gentlemen? Peter lied for the most dissolute of reasons, to protect the DeGroote family from the shame of their indiscretions. They were willing to send a boy to the scaffold to save themselves from public embarrassment. What a sorry thing to do."

He faced Cicero. "Why did Cicero lie? I don't aim to excuse him. There's no excuse. All I ask is you understand it. He told you why. He lied to save himself. To survive."

It was time.

Fear not death, men. The day goes to the bold.

He picked out the five jurors who were on the veteran's list from the Cleburne Camp office and made eye contact with each, one by one, as he spoke. "I've thought a lot about survival lately. Earlier today I was in the cemetery among the graves of men who served in the war. Today is July fourth. Thirty-one years ago, thousands of young men were worried about their survival—at Gettysburg, at Vicksburg. Henry Sweet and I rode behind Captain Cicero Jenkins, this young man's namesake. We were in middle Tennessee about then, all Cicero's age. Some of you worried about survival three decades ago, too."

He locked eyes with juror Sam Powell. *I know you remember the Red River swamps. And the bloody ground at Mansfield.*

"In war, we did terrible things in the name of survival, didn't we? We killed other boys. We did it before they could kill us. That's the way it was in those terrible days, in that terrible war. What are men willing to do when their survival is threatened? Captain Blair condemns Cicero for lying to survive, and I say men do terrible things to survive. Condemn him to death because he lied, if you choose—but you must live with that decision."

One of the five looked down.

"It will soon be your responsibility to deliver the most solemn decision that any human is ever obligated to make. I know you don't take that duty lightly. Cicero Sweet will leave this courtroom today living or dying by your choice. You hold his life in your hands. After you make your decision, each of you will go back to your lives—to your loved ones, to the farm or the drugstore or the railyard or wherever you live or work. You'll go about life as before. But every night when you lie in bed, as your loved ones slumber, you'll ask yourself—did I do right?"

More looked down. Others watched Cicero. One glanced at his parents. Another fanned himself and stared off into the air. Wade Morrison listened, arms crossed.

"Each of you must make that choice for yourself. You must decide in your own heart what's right, and you must live with your choice all the rest of your days. You are each strong men; that's why you were selected. You're not the kind of men who'll let someone else overbear your own convictions about right and wrong. You're not the kind of men who'll surrender your beliefs just so deliberations will end and you can go home."

He let that sink in. If a hung jury was all that was possible, so be it. Was he reaching them at all?

"What is the right thing to do? What punishment is just? Judge Goodrich instructed you that you may punish manslaughter by a verdict of two to five years in prison."

He rolled the witness chair back across to the stand. All eyes followed him. He felt old and tired.

The bell in the clock tower above struck five times. Outside, Colonel Terry bayed at it from the courthouse steps.

Catfish stared upward, waiting. When bell and hound fell silent, he took from the court reporter's desk the Bible used to swear witnesses and placed it on the witness rail. He braced himself on the rail and went to his knees, straining as he did. His knees popped loudly.

"I've been fortunate in my lifetime never to have to beg anyone for anything"—his voice cracked—"but gentlemen, I'm not proud. If I can save a boy by begging, I will beg, and I do so now. Please, with God's grace, spare Cicero's life. I beseech you: Hear the other side. There's been too much killing in our time. When we were young, foolish old men sent us to war to kill other young men. Now we're the old men. Have we learned any better? Did we not see enough dead boys on the bloody battlefields of our youth? Is making another mother and father grieve really the right answer today? As we near the end of the bloodiest century in human history, is more killing still the answer to wrongdoing? A jury has the right to deliver its verdict with a mighty hand of retribution."

He raised his right hand above his head and clinched his fist. "But might doesn't always make right." He released the fist and placed his hand over his heart. "Is retribution the best impulse of the Christian heart?"

He pinched his spectacles onto his nose and opened the Bible, turning pages until he found what he wanted. "'He hath shewed thee, O man, what is good; and what doth the Lord require of thee, but to do justly, and to love mercy, and to walk humbly with thy God?'"

Not even human breath made a sound. He shut the book, removed his spectacles with a trembling hand, and struggled to his feet. *Lord, help this old warrior rise one more time.*

He returned the Bible to its place and brushed himself off. "If we kill one more boy, will folks be any kinder to one another? Will the world be any better? Any safer? Must young men of this modern age still die so that fearful, foolish old men feel righteous? Will we all be at peace then?"

He walked slowly back to his table, beads of sweat streaming down his face. His soggy white hair clung to his forehead. His eyes were moist. He placed his hands on Cicero's shoulders.

"The question is not so much what kind of young man Cicero is; it's what kind of men are we. Walk humbly, gentlemen."

He sat.

Blair's rebuttal came swiftly. "Cicero Sweet wasn't a soldier in war. He didn't shoot Georgia Gamble in self-defense. He murdered her because it suited him. If you don't condemn this killer, you send a message by your verdict to other men who think they can murder at their will in the Reservation. You'd condemn to death other people—whores or innocent people, anyone who angers them. Gentlemen, stand up for the law. Against anarchy. Stand up for decency. Save lives by your verdict. The defendant, Cicero Sweet, is guilty of murder in the first degree. And the penalty for death is death."

The courtroom remained subdued as the twelve jurors filed out for deliberation. Catfish stood as they went, a trickle of sweat stinging one eye closed.

Blessed are the merciful.

Chapter 42

At seven forty-two, the jury knocked.

Catfish tightened his tie.

The courtroom refilled—Cicero, Harley, and Miss Peach joined him at the defense table. Captain Blair was at his. In the gallery, the Sweets bent in prayer with Jasper beside them, head bowed, all three with hands clasped.

At eight, the clock tower bell pealed.

"All rise!"

Solemn silence settled upon the courtroom. First judge, then jury took their seats.

"Mr. Morrison, I understand you've been elected foreman?" the judge asked.

He rose. "Yes, Your Honor."

"Has the jury reached a verdict?"

"Yes, we have."

"Very well, I'll now read through it."

Catfish prompted Cicero to rise. They stood side by side, facing the court as the judge leafed through the pages. Cicero's fingers clenched the edge of the table. Catfish folded his hands behind his back, eyes fixed on Judge Goodrich. It always ended thus—this moment, this inward breathlessness, this outward calmness. This quiet crest of disquiet.

Judge Goodrich finally spoke. "It appears you've found the defendant, Cicero Sweet, guilty"—a mother's gasp—"of manslaughter."

A rippling murmur passed across the room.

"Is that correct?"

"Yes, Your Honor."

Blessed are the peacemakers.

"And you've assessed punishment at the maximum?"

"Yes, sir, that's our verdict."

"Cicero Sweet, I pronounce you guilty of manslaughter and sentence you to five years confinement in the state prison."

Chapter 43

It was a fine day to rock on his front porch, smoking a cigar and reading a newspaper. The colonel's head popped up when a hack rolled up on the street.

"Afternoon, Mr. Calloway," called a familiar voice. "Mind if I stop by?"

Catfish waved. "How do, Jasper. You're always welcome. Come on up here."

Jasper paid the driver and hopped down, pulling his bag after him. He sat in the other rocking chair and rubbed Colonel Terry's ear. "Catching up on the news?"

"Story in the Dallas paper about the trial." He laughed. "Comes out the same way, but it sure sounds different the way Brown tells it."

Jasper nodded. "Cicero's really going off to prison?"

"He is. He's decided not to appeal."

"I'm downright sorrowful for him, but I reckon that's better than hanging."

"Cicero thinks so."

Jasper looked pensive. "So he really shot that girl, Mr. Calloway? Is that the truth?"

"That's what the jury says. They said Cicero killed her but didn't do it with malice in his heart."

"Were they right?"

"Juries don't often get one wrong. They're generally better than that."

"I ain't never thought about that."

He'd thought about juries a great deal. "See that live oak over yonder?" He pointed. "It's been there for hundreds of years. A jury's like an old oak tree. It's a beautiful thing to watch, but its true value isn't so obvious. It has deep roots extending way under the surface that keep the soil from washing away. It may be tossed and turned by a strong wind, but it's too strong to blow over. It always rights itself. The only thing that'll set over an old oak is a man who cuts it down for his own reasons." He appreciatively inhaled the fresh air. "I'd lost faith in that old tree, Jasper. I'd always stood up to folks who tried to cut it down, but I lost faith in juries for a time. Not anymore. They did the right thing by your friend Cicero."

"I'm sure sorry for that girl."

"Me too." He tossed the newspaper on the porch and crossed his arms. "What about you? Looks like you're headed out of town with a packed bag. President Burleson didn't expel you, did he?"

He couldn't help but grin—he already knew Burleson hadn't.

Jasper's eyes widened. "Oh no, sir. He give me a strong talking-to, lectured me about this lesson and that lesson, and I reckon I've learned most all of 'em. He told me I'd be welcome back in school come fall, and as long as I walked a straight and narrow path, I'd graduate someday."

"That's mighty fine, Jasper. I know you will." And when the boy got home soon, he'd find a letter from Baylor advising him that an anonymous gift had been made to pay his tuition. A sound investment.

"One thing's for sure," Jasper said. "I ain't inclined to go near no whorehouse. So anyways, I'm fixing to head home for the rest of the summer. There's cotton to pick. Got a train later for Flatonia. I figure I best tell my folks about all this before they hear about it from somebody else. I'd told 'em I was staying here to finish some schoolwork, which is the way I've thought of it."

"If you need me to write them a letter for you, I'd be happy to."

"Thank you, sir. That's real nice of you, but I think I best do my own talking now."

Catfish smiled. "Good for you, son."

Colonel Terry rolled onto his back, extending his paws toward the ceiling. Time for a belly rub.

"I sure am gonna miss the colonel," Jasper said, reaching down to fulfill the request.

"When you come back to college next fall, he'll still be here. Hound dogs always are. That's what makes 'em God's perfect creation."

The colonel moaned softly from the rubbing.

"How's that?" Jasper asked.

"God made us men to be loyal to one another, but sometimes that causes us grief. Two-legged critters will let you down or cripple themselves trying not to. Sometimes friends betray you. Even family can disappoint you, or you them. But a good ol' hound dog is always there for you, whether you deserve it or not. That's the noblest impulse of the canine heart."

Jasper bent over and let the colonel take a last lick. "Well, sir, I reckon I better go. I just wanted to say thanks for taking my side with Baylor."

"You're quite welcome. That's why I'm here."

***

It was a fine day to sit across a corner table from Tom Blair in the Bismark Saloon. After every trial in which they battled like mortal enemies, they met there over a drink to remind themselves they weren't. Miss Peach said it was like Shakespeare wrote: *Do as adversaries do in law. Strive mightily, but eat and drink as friends.* They smoked White Owls, and the loser bought the drinks.

This night, each of them treated the other. And for the first time, Catfish brought Harley.

"Catfish, I want you to know," Blair began, "it wasn't my idea to ask for death."

"I know, you don't have to—"

"Yes, I do. I want you to understand. Shaughnessy and DeGroote and others insisted on it. I thought it was just because that preacher was stirring everybody up. I didn't know DeGroote had his own horse in the race."

"I know you didn't." Catfish tapped ashes into the brass spittoon. "I didn't, either."

"I feel a little dirty now."

"You shouldn't, my friend. You were just doing your job."

"Thanks."

Catfish dipped his head. "It's me who should apologize. I let it get personal, even with you, and I'm sorry for that."

"I didn't take it that way." Blair blew smoke at the wall. "Are you going to appeal the punishment?"

"Cicero's happy to escape hanging. He's young. He can make a new life somewhere else after prison."

"Just so you know," Blair said, "I had two other people tell me Cicero drank too much and attacked them. He beat one pretty bad. Neither would testify, though."

"Where'd you find them?"

"Schoolcraft came to see me."

Harley huffed. "Why does he care?"

Catfish shook his head. His son was too defensive sometimes. "Leave it be. We're done with Schoolcraft for good."

"I hope you're right about Cicero making a new life," Blair said, "but I'm not so sure."

Catfish nodded and blew smoke at the air. "I'm sorry for his folks."

"How are they?"

"Henry's bitter." He ran his fingers through his hair, causing it to flop over his forehead. "Still says Cicero didn't do it, and he's not very happy with me."

"He should be grateful you saved the boy's life," Blair said.

"He'll figure that out some day." He exchanged glances with Harley. "Things like that take time."

Blair finished his drink, and after a warm goodbye he left.

Catfish loosened his tie.

Harley took a sip of the new Scotch whisky the proprietor had brought. "Papa, he was right about Mr. Sweet. You saved Cicero's life."

Catfish's cigar left a haze over the table. "The jury did that."

"But your speech moved them to it. I watched them, especially the veterans. It was when you said 'no more killing.'" His eyes gleamed in the lamplight.

A fleeting whiff of kerosene from the lamp pierced the smoke. The war. Catfish shut out the smell of death. That war did not measure his life.

The law. It was peaceful and civilized. In war or peace, killers sorted out their differences by violence. If lawful folks were going to be better than killers, nobody should die as the result of a trial.

He poured himself some of the new Scotch. "Like I told the jury, it's more about who we are."

345

"Maybe the legislature will figure that out someday."

He snorted. "Maybe even in your lifetime."

Harley tilted his head. "By the way, I happened to pick up your trial box today. It seemed lighter."

"Lighter?"

"Like maybe you'd taken something out."

"Oh?"

"Your new pistol."

Catfish scoffed. "I don't stow that in my trial box."

He took off his coat, revealing the pistol snug in his shoulder holster.

Harley's eyes dropped. "Wasn't it in the box during the trial?"

"Of course not. Why on earth would you think such a thing?"

Harley reddened. "No reason—I mean, I must've thought you did. Maybe something Miss Peach said. But I also noticed you holding that minié ball during the trial. Wasn't that in your trial box?"

"Sure, although it had no business there. Took it and my saber home to the Growlery, where they should've been all along."

They both sipped their whiskys.

Catfish pulled off the shoulder holster and placed it under the table.

"Speaking of Miss Peach," he said, "did you get her off to Eulogy?"

Harley nodded. "She was grateful for the time off you gave her."

"She deserves it."

"I told her that. We couldn't have done it without her."

Catfish settled back in his chair, then lofted smiling eyes at his son. "Awful sweet girl."

Harley flushed again.

Catfish persisted. Sometimes a young man needed a nudge. "Apparently doesn't have a beau."

Harley shifted in his chair. "She's our employee."

"She's more than that."

"Regardless, she and I," he said, gulping the whisky, "we were talking about that bullet you took to trial. Will you tell me about it?"

Catfish raised an eyebrow. He didn't already know?

He leaned out to catch the proprietor's attention as he passed by. "Mr. Kophal, I like that new Scotch whisky."

He squinted to read the label.

"Strathisla, 1888," Kophal said. It didn't come easily to his Germanic tongue.

Catfish winked. "Another, please."

Harley leaned forward. "You were going to tell me about the bullet?"

"We were on a raid behind enemy lines in Kentucky, and I was in a dire situation. My horse got shot out from under me. The regiment retreated, and I was all alone in the middle of a crossroads, hunkered down behind my horse. That bullet hit my carbine, not six inches from my head. I dug it out of the carbine stock later and kept it as a reminder of what Henry did next."

Harley's face was tight. "What?"

"He galloped back and rescued me. Took one in the leg himself when he did."

"I didn't know."

Henry, too, must have thought of that day whenever he limped while others walked. Because of their friendship. "My loyalty to Henry blinded me, just like you said. Just couldn't accept that any boy of Henry's might be guilty." He rocked back in his chair and smiled. "You're a fine lawyer. I'm proud of the way you took over for me when I was out of my mind."

Harley smiled back. "Proud of you, too."

"I should have trusted your judgment more. You saw through Cicero right away and knew exactly how we should represent him, long before I did." Had he only listened.

Harley tilted his head. "I may have jumped to the right conclusion, but it was without any tangible basis. I didn't even know the truth about Peter or his father at that point. I believed them. I should have had the patience to make sure of my theories before I pushed them."

"Calloway & Calloway," Catfish said. "There's a reason it's a partnership."

Harley nodded. Then his expression changed. "Papa, you didn't cause Houston's death. You know that, don't you?"

Catfish looked down at his drink.

"I've wanted to talk about this before," Harley continued, "but the time never seemed right."

"I expect we couldn't do it till now. I was wrong about Cicero … Maybe I was wrong about Houston, too."

"So you think he was guilty?"

For so long, Catfish had fretted over what happened to Houston, bouncing from anger to guilt to hopelessness and back again. Never doubted Houston's story, though. Maybe should have. A lawyer who wasn't so close to him probably would have. Probably should have. He'd simply accepted Houston's story because he loved him.

Harley looked so much like Houston. He couldn't protect either of them from life's perils. All he could do was trust them.

He wiped a tear.

It was a fine day to lay the past to rest and get on with living.

He'd borne the weight of Houston's death long enough. Sometimes it's easier to forgive others than yourself. Too late to change the past, but other clients still needed him, and he felt the fire in his belly for the first time in a very long time.

He sipped the Strathisla. The water of life tasted sweet again. It was such a fine day.

"Papa?"

"You know, son, maybe Brann has the last word for Houston, too. Did you read his piece in the San Antonio paper?"

Harley shook his head.

Catfish shoved the folded newspaper across the table. "Last page."

He sat back and nursed his cigar as he watched Harley read to himself by the light of the lamp.

Thus ended the case of THE SPORTING HOUSE KILLING. Cicero Sweet was bound for the state penitentiary in Huntsville to serve his time. Thanks to Catfish Calloway, he cheated the hangman. *Audi alteram partem.* One side shouted TRUTH, the other MERCY, but God demanded both. "Mercy and truth shall go before thy face."

But what is the truth about Cicero Sweet and Georgia Virginia Gamble?

Truth and only truth is eternal. It was not born, and it cannot die. It may be obscured by the clouds of falsehood, or buried in the debris of brutish ignorance, but it can never be destroyed. It's all that is, or was, or can ever be. It exists in every atom, lives in every flower, and flames in every star. When the heavens and the earth shall pass away and the universe returns to its cosmic dust, divine truth will stand unscathed amid the crash of matter and the wreck of worlds.

Falsehood is an amorphous monster, conceived in the brain of knaves and brought forth by the breath of fools. It's a moral pestilence, a miasmic vapor that passes like a blast from Hell over the face of the world. It may leave death in its wake and disaster dire. It may place on the brow of purity the brand of the courtesan and cover the hero with the stigma of the coward. It may degrade the patriot and exalt the demagogue, enslave a Horatio and crown a Humbug. It may cause blood to flow and hearts to break. It may pollute the altar and disgrace the home, corrupt the courts and curse the land, but the lie cannot live forever.

But what of us who cannot wait until the lie is dead and damned, who must move forward in its backwash? For us, there is only one truth which matters. It is the truth declared by twelve citizens, good and true, for it is their truth which dictates the further progress of human affairs. We must accept that truth and go about our lives accordingly; otherwise, there is no peace.

For the slayer and the slain, only divine truth matters. Whether it is known or unknown to the rest of mankind is of little consequence.

—William Cowper Brann
The San Antonio Express
July 8, 1894

Author's Notes

Some may doubt whether Catfish Calloway ever existed, since there's no mention of him in historical records. Likewise, some may dismiss other characters as pure fiction for the same reason: Harley and Miss Peach; Cicero Sweet and his father; Jasper Cantrell and Bootblack Ben; Miss Jessie, Miss Sadie, and Big Joe; Sterling and Peter DeGroote; Cooter Shaughnessy and Thaddeus Schoolcraft.

None may doubt, however, that Judge Levi Goodrich presided over the Nineteenth District Court in 1894, that Tom Black was the County Attorney, that Warwick Jenkins was the county judge or that he and his brother, Cicero Jenkins, were both veterans of Terry's Texas Rangers in the Civil War.

The historical record proves without doubt that Champe McCulloch was the mayor of Waco; that Bud Orman was convicted twice of killing Bud Houghston; and that Bob Lazenby owned the company that made Dr. Pepper famous. No student of late 19th century America would doubt that William Cowper Brann penned eloquent essays exposing human weakness and became quite well known for it across America, his circulation mounting to 100,000 before publication ceased. Indeed, his concluding commentary about truth chronicled in the last chapter may be found—mostly verbatim—among the pages of *The Iconoclast*.

Likewise, none may question the existence of the places inhabited by Catfish and his contemporaries. Sanborn insurance maps, photographs, and extant newspapers remove all doubt about those places. While the wonderful, noisy old McLennan County Courthouse at Second and Franklin designed by Wesley Dodson was torn down long ago, as was the city hall, the historic suspension bridge still spans the Brazos River. Bronze longhorns now scramble toward it, reminding us of Harley's reminiscence of Chisolm Trail herds crossing that bridge when he was a boy. Catfish's home remains intact on Washington Avenue, though title records for some reason don't reflect his ownership. Also standing today are Harley's boarding house, Wade Morrison's home, and Mayor McCulloch's home. A terrible tornado devastated downtown Waco in 1953 and took Sam Kee's Chinese Restaurant and Bismarck's Saloon, as well as many other places well-known to Catfish, though photos of them remain. Photographic evidence also confirms the existence of the Law Offices of Calloway & Calloway, though the name on the door isn't quite visible. Photographs show the famous Old Corner Drug Store, operated by Wade Morrison, where a pharmacist named Charles Alderton invented Dr. Pepper, and soda jerks sold eager customers a "Waco."

The Reservation, on both sides of Barron's Creek, operated as only one of two such legal districts in the entire country until just before America entered World War I, when the city decided it wanted the 45,000 soldiers of the proposed Camp Macarthur more than it wanted the whores. The madams of the Reservation believed both would get along nicely side-by-side, but Uncle Sam insisted otherwise. Women like Miss Josie Bennet and Miss Ada Davenport had plied their trade in the Reservation for almost twenty years. All that remains today are a few grand old oak trees which stood silent witness to what transpired in Satan's stronghold.

What about Miss Jessie's sporting house? The historical record confirms that Miss Josie Bennet operated her sporting house, a three story brick structure, at the corner of Washington and Orman's Alley until it burned in 1893, just as Harley discovered. While it was rebuilt and served as a female boarding house thereafter, Miss Jessie Rose's name is missing from any record of its operation. Curiously, the Bawdy House Register for 1894, now in the archives of the Texas Collection at Baylor University, fails to record her thriving business. Photographs taken in the early 1900's provide conclusive proof to doubting readers that such a place as Miss Jessie's existed.

The *Waco Evening News* of April 16, 1894 proves that Georgia evangelist Sam Jones preached a powerful sermon to the five-thousand in attendance at the Tabernacle and uttered most of the words attributed to him by Catfish and Brann, including these: "If you can block off a place, call it a Reservation, and license licentiousness, why don't you reserve a few blocks where a man can commit murder and go unpunished?"

Baylor University still proudly graduates thousands of young men and women. The campus building known in 1894 as the main building, where President Rufus Burleson met Catfish, Jasper, and Henry Sweet, is now known as Old Main, and Burleson's statue still stands out front. Baylor's law school, the first in Texas, counts among its graduates Cicero Jenkins (Class of 1860) as well as such notables as Charles E. Travis (Class of 1860), son of William Barret Travis; Temple Houston (Class of 1878), son of Sam Houston; and Watergate special prosecutor Leon Jaworksi (Class of 1925). It counts among its professors John Sayles, who taught Cicero Jenkins. Though this student's name is somehow missing from Baylor records, Sayles also taught

Catfish how to try cases. About one-hundred sixty years later at this writing, Catfish's chronicler still teaches law students there to try cases as Baylor lawyers.

Oakwood Cemetery guards the memory of scores of the people mentioned in this book. Some tombstones, especially Brann's, bear witness to their stories. One may still find the Confederate memorial and Cicero Jenkins' grave, where Catfish gathered the inspiration for his closing argument. The markers for the Calloway family, all seven who died in Waco, have sadly vanished.

In the new courthouse, erected in 1901 on Washington Avenue to replace the old, noisy one, Catfish, Harley, and Miss Peach represented clients. There, in the Justice of the Peace Court, Catfish's chronicler tried his first jury case. Today one may still hear lawyers beseech judges or juries to hear the other side. *Audi alteram partem.* As long as it is so, the rule of law is safe.

75365957R00208